LOUVRE ESCAPE

AN ARCHAEOLOGICAL THRILLER

DARWIN LACROIX ADVENTURE SERIES
BOOK 7

DAVE BARTELL

ISBN: 978-1-957269-04-7

To my mom, Gussie, whose sense of aesthetic inspires me to seek it everyday.

PREFACE

On 13 July 2023, France adopted a bill to fast-track the return of artworks looted during World War II.

"I hope it will be a year of decisive progress for restitutions."

Rima Abdul Malak, Minister of Culture

PROLOGUE

March 1945
Alsace-Lorraine, German-Occupied France

Ted Archer seized a handhold as the bomber jerked violently. The B-17's massive wings flexed in the storm's gathering fury. Lightning ripped the sky. Ted's eyes pinched closed as the blinding flash faded.

"Hang on, boys." The captain's voice in their headsets stated the obvious. Art Spencer, at twenty-seven, was the old man on the crew.

Sally Mae's ten men had been together since their first mission in mid-November. Thirty-five times, they'd joined hundreds of B-17s into enemy territory—delivering tons of high-energy explosives to crush German manufacturing. Fighters swarmed to protect their homeland, but each four-engine Flying Fortress bristled with thirteen Browning M2 machine guns. Getting close was like trying to grab a porcupine.

Today was their final mission. Last night in the pub, they'd drunk a pint to the toast "Home." Afterward, Ted lay in his bunk, hoping for a milk run—hitting a coastal city where the Luftwaffe had been exterminated.

This morning's briefing had been a bitter pill: strike a factory in Stuttgart, deep in the German homeland.

Ted focused on his instruments as the plane banked right. He cleaned the optics on the Norden bombsight for the third time since leaving England. *Be ready*. His stomach dropped as a wind sheer thrust them upward.

"Dang. This is like riding ol' Nightmare back home," said Tex, the nineteen-year-old waist gunner from Oklahoma. No one knew how he'd come by the nickname, but he'd bragged about being a rodeo cowboy so often that it had stuck.

"Where'd this weather come from?" asked Art.

"Don't know, sir," said the co-pilot. "Reconnaissance reported storms over central France but clear skies eastward."

"George, what's our position?"

"Checking, sir," said George, the navigator, sitting just behind Ted.

Both sat below the flight deck with the pilot, copilot, and engineer, Nick. Behind them was the bomb bay and then the rest of the crew: Harry, the radio operator, and Sean, a diminutive Irishman who fit in the belly turret. Two waist gunners, Tex and Carter, aimed out to the sides, and the tail gunner was Bob. Each man wore long underwear beneath heated jumpsuits, coats, and, for the gunners, flak jackets. They all plugged into their stations for electrical power, communications, and, most importantly, oxygen. Flying in an unpressurized B-17 was like standing atop Mount Everest—humans did not live long in the death zone without proper equipment.

The men chattered using their throat microphones about what they'd do first when back home. Ted tuned them out. While he welcomed the banter, his role as bombardier was vital to the mission's success. Today's flight path had them heading south towards Paris and then turning east to Reims and passing over the Vosges Mountains north of Strasbourg. Once across the Rhine River, they'd swing wide and come at Stuttgart from the south before hightailing it back to England.

And home. Ted thought of his parents in California and his girlfriend, Clara, working at the Douglas plant in Long Beach. They wrote to each other, joking about both spending their days inside a B-17—her riveting the airframe, him directing its payload. When they'd parted last year, he hadn't been ready to pop the question, but her letters had convinced him. *She's the one.*

Thinking of her had kept him sane these last few weeks. The war was winding down, but the enemy wouldn't quit even as civilian casualties mounted. Ted shook the thought off and focused on the job. He just wanted to go home.

Broken clouds gave glimpses of the farmland far below. Patches of green fit like puzzle pieces among fallow fields. Darker woodlands grew where the rolling hills were too steep to plow. A river snaked through it all, mercurial in the muted sunlight.

George announced, "We're passing Strasbourg and will cross the Rhine in three minutes."

Art's voice crackled in their headsets: "Roger that."

Ted's plexiglass dome in the B-17's nose gave him a 180-degree view—a front-row seat suspended thirty thousand feet above the earth. Only the bombsight was farther forward than him. Ted reflected on his crewmates. He'd grown close to *Sallie Mae's* crew. They'd trained as a group back in the States and spent virtually every moment together since arriving in England. They played hard when not on a mission, as life on a bomber had worse survival odds than being in the infantry.

Today, *Sallie Mae* flew on point in group one of the twelve-plane combat box—a diamond shape that reduced the group's attack surface. But enemy fighters weren't their concern at the moment.

Massive thunderheads darkened the sky. Another wind sheer swatted them. Ted braced himself against the bulkhead. *Jesus.* The plane leveled, and he frowned. Given this weather, his on-target rate would be zilch.

A perfectionist, Ted hated shoddy work. He was about to comment but then stopped. *It doesn't matter. Just finish the mission. We're going home.*

He focused on the bombing run. In sixty miles, *Sallie Mae* would turn hard right to approach Stuttgart from the south. He looked at the photographs of the Bosch factories, imagining his lineup again.

Releasing the bombs was his only job. As he polished the Norden's optics once more, all hell broke loose.

His body slammed into the instruments on the left wall, and a horrendous screeching came from aft. A boom rocked the plane. *Sallie Mae's* nose dropped. Ted watched the ground rotate ninety degrees. Another concussive wave punched them. Voices yelled over the intercom:

"We're hit!"

"What was it?"

"Did you see it?"

A blood-curdling scream.

Then, silence as the view outside the plexiglass rotated above the Rhine River.

Ted tapped his headset and turned the switch on the jack box. Nothing. *What the hell?* He looked at George, who shouted, "Art cut the comms!""

Ted observed the mayhem. B-17s scattered across the heavens as Art straightened their flight path. A long moment later, the headset comms came back on, and confused voices filled Ted's ears.

"Quiet!" yelled Art. When the chatter stopped, he asked, "Ted? Are you okay?"

"Yeah. What—"

"Get back to Bob," Art cut in. "I need a damage check."

"Roger that, sir."

Ted grabbed a portable oxygen bottle, connected his breathing hose, and noted the time. He'd have about eight minutes before needing the central oxygen.

"I need eyes, people," Art barked. "Sean, Nick, what's our formation? George, get me a position. Harry, find out what the hell just happened."

Ted yanked his comms cable and moved around George and Nick. He squeezed through the bomb bay catwalk, struggling aft as severe turbulence buffeted them. He nodded to the radioman, Harry, in midship before finding the left waist gunner, Carter, passed out, blood streaming from his forehead.

Ted whipped around, looking for Tex, the starboard waist gunner.

Must have gone aft. Then he saw it—a hole where the rear gun turret should be.

Past the waist gun openings, air tore through the cabin like a class five hurricane. Ted grasped the railing for dear life. *Where the hell's Tex?* He looked around but couldn't find him.

A few more steps, and he saw Bob. His body hung by his safety strap, buffeted by the wind, and his breathing mask had been ripped off. There was no way to reach him.

Damn! Ted offered a silent prayer and then focused on the damage. Nothing critical had been cut. He stooped and peered through the opening. Art had leveled the plane, and Ted could see five other B-17s in no particular formation. But one trailed smoke. Badly.

Three parachutes opened as the plane lost altitude. *C'mon. C'mon,* he thought, willing the others to safety. When all ten had deployed, he noted the time.

He fought his way back to midship, shivering in the frigid air. He patched into Tex's jack box, then moved across the fuselage. "Bob's dead. Carter's got a head injury. But seems stable."

"What about Tex?" asked the co-pilot.

"He's gone."

"Dead?"

"No. Tex is gone. I can't find him. Must have been sucked out."

"Jesus," said the co-pilot.

Ted bandaged Carter's forehead, ensured his air and heated suit were connected, and buckled him against the bulkhead. "Hang in there, kid," he said to the unconscious man.

Art's voice came over the comm. "Ted, what's the damage back there? The tail feels loose."

"Rear turret's destroyed, sir, but I didn't see any other damage from the inside."

"Thanks. Stand by."

Ted unplugged and moved forward to report when the parachutes had opened. Harry put a finger on a map east of Müllen. Ted plugged in to hear Art respond to the update.

"Roger that, Harry. George, plot the safest course back home. I've never seen anything like this. That wind sheer drove our tail into

Loaded Dice's cockpit. They plunged into group four below. Sean says we lost six planes, one of them the *Jolly Roger*."

Ted's heart sank. His childhood buddy, Sid Ipsen, was the *Jolly Roger's* co-pilot.

"I'm sorry, Ted," Art said gently.

"Thank you, sir." Ted unplugged from the jack box and trudged forward, where a whistling sound grew louder.

Holy Mother of God! Ted froze, his heart hammering. As daylight flooded through a partially open door, wind blasted into the bomb bay. A bomb on the starboard rack sagged against the door, pressing it open. Its arming wire had been yanked free, and its nose fuse pinwheeled in the rushing air.

Ted plugged in the jack box. "Art, we've got another problem!"

"Can it wait, son? I'm—"

"No, sir. We got a loose bomb."

Art flew from the cockpit, piling into Nick at the flight engineer's station. Both squeezed into the bomb bay door. Ted lay on the floor, his gloved fingers holding the fuse vane from rotating.

"How long did it spin?" Art yelled over the howling wind.

"I don't know, sir," said Ted. With all the commotion back here, I missed it on my way to check on Bob. Sorry, sir."

"Not your fault."

Turbulence rattled the bombs. As Art connected to an oxygen bottle, Nick said, "No way we can land with that thing. We're three hours from London.

"Where are we?" asked Art. "I'm not dropping these on Strasbourg."

"I'll check." Nick turned. Another wind shear slammed them, bashing Art's head into the bulkhead. His body crushed Ted's ribs. The kid yelped, pulling back his hand.

The plane bucked, ramming the bomb against the door. As Ted gasped for breath, the vane flew off.

Ted's eyes bugged out as he stared down a live five-hundred-pound bomb. Another bounce. He jumped up, heaved Art onto the flight deck, and ran to the bombardier station. He opened the bay doors and yanked the bomb release. The port-side rack emptied, but the starboard side froze. *Shit!*

He shoved past George at the navigator's station and grabbed the rope rail on the catwalk. The air roared in the wide-open bay. Clouds blasted past. While the dark green forest scrolled by, Ted murmured, "Please, God. Please. Let me see Clara again."

He ripped a screwdriver from where he'd taped it to the fuselage and worked himself flat on the catwalk. Ted repeated the prayer, *Please, God,* as he wrapped an arm around the narrow catwalk. He pressed close to the cylinder—death hanging by a wire—and reached out with the screwdriver.

The plane bounced, and his body flew up. He pulled at the catwalk with all his might and then slammed down.

"Oomph." Air burst from his lungs, but he hung on—his face mashed into the metal catwalk. He breathed and then reached for the shackle holding the bomb. Inserting the screwdriver into the mechanism, he pulled.

It jammed.

Shit! He slumped. Wind howled. His fingers were numb. *Please, God. I don't want to die.* Clara's smile filled his vision. Her hand reached for his. "Come on," she said from a memory last summer. He'd been afraid to jump into a water-filled quarry. Clara took his hand, giving him the courage to leap.

Ted concentrated and maneuvered the screwdriver inside the shackle. The plane bounced again. He pulled. The screwdriver snapped. The second bomb clanged into the first, knocking it free.

The third and fourth bombs fell, but one whacked his hand on the way out. He screamed and pulled himself out of the bomb bay.

"Ted?" Art had regained consciousness, but he still lay on the bomb deck.

Ted knelt, holding his fractured wrist. "I did it. They're away, sir."

"You saved our lives, son. And you're hurt."

"I'm just happy to be alive, sir."

"We all are, son. I'll see you get a silver star for this." Art got to his feet and yelled to the navigator, "George, where did we drop that load?"

"In the Vosges Mountains southwest of Strasbourg. Nothing besides farms."

That night, they drank to the memory of their lost crew member, Tex, and the men in the planes that had gone down. Ted made a silent toast to his friend Sid, co-pilot of the *Jolly Roger*. He sighed and looked at the bar, where a new squad with pressed uniforms and devil-may-care attitudes laughed and drank. They were heading on their first mission tomorrow.

Ted's melancholy soon passed, and a hand grasped his shoulder.

"Hey, everyone!" Art called out to the bar. The reverie paused, and he described Ted's heroic effort to loosen the bomb, saving *Sallie Mae's* crew.

Whoops and cheers erupted. Someone shoved a pint in Ted's good hand, and everyone there, including the publican, signed the cast on his left arm.

As the celebrations simmered down, George gathered Art and Ted close. "I have some news. When I filed the mission report, British intelligence confirmed there was a German prisoner camp where we dropped the bombs."

"Oh, no." Ted hung his head.

"They said 'was there,' Ted. The Germans abandoned it. We're winning the war, boys."

They clinked their pint glasses and drank.

"I'm glad we're going home, sir," said Ted.

"So am I, son. So am I," said Art, draining his glass. "Another round?"

"As long as you're buying," said Ted.

PART I

Present Day

France

1

Île Saint-Louis, Paris

Darwin Lacroix and Eyrún Stefansdottír held hands as they strolled the main street on Île Saint-Louis, the smaller of the two islands in the Seine River. The sun's angle left the narrow lane in shadow, but its rays cast warmth off the stone buildings. They'd finished a late lunch at Le Saint-Regis, one of their favorite cafes between the busy Latin Quarter and Le Marais.

After passing a few storefronts, they paused at an art gallery. Nothing captivated Darwin, but now that lunch was over, his busy brain reignited an internal debate. His focus zoomed out from the paintings and settled on their reflection in the window.

Eyrún stood a fraction taller in her boots. Her long, dark-brown hair glowed in the backlighting, and he could make out a few auburn strands. The pattern in her dress highlighted her glacier-blue eyes and offset her pale Nordic complexion. She smiled, focusing on a couple pushing a pram behind them.

Darwin sighed. His reflection belied his indecision. Intense green eyes squinted beneath knitted brows. Disheveled brown hair hung low over his left eye. He swept it back, reminding himself that he needed to visit a barber. *A shave, too.* He stroked his four-day beard. *Posture's better, though.*

The tension stemmed from his mental gymnastics during lunch, where he'd wrestled over how to begin a discussion with Eyrún. *Why can't I just say it?*

He'd toured the École du Louvre all morning, meeting department heads and professors. Last night's dinner with Eyrún and Vivienne de Poitiers, the dean, had convinced him. His insides hummed. To teach at the Louvre, the premier art and archaeology school in Europe. Unfettered access to the collections. Collaboration with teachers at the pinnacles of their careers. Students who were the crème de la crème.

But he'd be apart from Eyrún. She ran their foundation in Corsica—the Agrippa Centre for Archaeology, or ACA. Commuting on weekends didn't appeal to him, especially after their harrowing experience in Siberia. And they didn't need the money. *But École du Louvre...*

Eyrún squeezed his hand. "Where'd you go?"

"Erm." He focused on her smile.

Her eyes locked onto his. "C'mon. There's something I want to show you."

"Where?"

"Close by. Let's get an ice cream first." They held hands as she led him toward the island's middle.

Despite a substantial lunch, Darwin's stomach growled at the prospect of Berthillon ice cream. A minute later, they reached the legendary shop. He scanned the menu. "What are you having today?" he asked.

"I don't know. It's all so good. What about you?"

"Rose petal and chocolate lava."

Eyrún settled on lavender with a hint of Earl Grey tea and New Zealand kiwi.

"Oh, God. This is so good," she said, wiping a drip from her chin.

They tried each other's flavors and agreed the rose petal was unique. "Pairs well with the kiwi," said Darwin. "I could come here every day."

"Hold that thought."

His eyes widened.

Eyrún took a bite of the lavender and motioned for Darwin to follow her along Rue des Deux Ponts. Sunlight glinted off the River Seine as they approached the Tournelle bridge.

"Where are we going?" Darwin asked as they turned on Quai d'Orléans toward Notre-Dame.

The trees on the riverside walkway rustled in the breeze, casting dappled shade on the sidewalk. Eyrún crossed the street at 20 Quai d'Orléans and rapped a large iron ring on a pair of stout oak doors. Moments later, a well-dressed older man opened it. "Bonjour, Madame Stefansdottír," he said in a mellifluous voice.

"Bonjour, Kamal. This is my husband, Darwin." She leaned closer and whispered, "I haven't told him yet."

Kamal smiled and nodded with a conspiratory twinkle in his eyes. He shook Darwin's hand, and they exchanged greetings. Then Kamal turned toward the lift.

Darwin cocked his head, watching her.

She smiled coyly and entered the lift across the elegant marble foyer. The same marble covered its floor, and the brass cage gleamed. When they were inside, Kamal pressed five.

At first, Darwin thought Kamal was a concierge, but then he decided the man was far too well dressed. His bespoke navy blue suit fit like a glove, and a gold ring inlaid with emerald marked him as an affluent man.

The lift opened into a hallway with a single door. Kamal motioned Darwin out first, using the ruse to hand Eyrún a key. Darwin waited for her to exit, and then the two men followed her as she walked to the flat. She unlocked it. "Close your eyes."

Darwin did, and she took his hand. A breeze from the Seine swept through the open door as she pulled him inside.

"Keep them closed. And stay close."

The room smelled of beeswax, and each footfall emitted a soft squeak. He envisioned oak parquet flooring as their path meandered. Seconds later, he felt the sun on his face. She slipped behind him and covered his eyes with her hands.

"You asked what I was doing while you were in all the meetings at the Louvre. I know you haven't said yes to the job, but if you do, I'll have to visit Paris."

"Really?" His heart leaped.

"Really." Her hands moved away. "Now, open your eyes."

He gasped. The left bank spread before them, its low rooftops marching toward the horizon. The Pantheon's dome rose on the right, and in the other direction, a tower block mixed in with the Sorbonne and National Museum of Natural History. He glanced around the expansive outdoor patio. Potted plants stood among an arrangement of teak furniture, including a dining table, a sitting area, and two chaise lounges. Behind him, three large sliding doors created a glass wall.

The inside was divided into sitting and dining areas, with a large kitchen and island bar. A familiar hiss drew his attention. Kamal poured champagne into two flutes. He set down the bottle and placed a small box with a red bow between the glasses before retreating again.

"Eyrún?" Darwin looked between her and the box.

"I'll need a place to work. That is, if you take the job."

"My only hesitation has been all the time we'd be apart."

She swept a hand over the living area. "So…now you don't have to choose."

"It's decided, then. I'll tell them now." He grabbed his phone and thumbed a text.

Eyrún nodded to Kamal, who bowed and then left. When the front door clicked shut, she handed Darwin the box. He untied its bow and lifted the cover. A key on a silver ring lay in cotton.

"Mine?"

"Technically, it belongs to the Paris branch of the ACA. Its offices are downstairs."

"Does this Paris branch include bedrooms?"

Eyrún clinked his champagne flute. "Would you like a personal tour?" she asked with a mischievous smile.

2

Jardin des Tuileries

Christian Roche took a deep breath to slow his pounding heart. He'd not intended to break the news with such venom.

He sat next to his friend and colleague, Lionel, on a bench in Jardin des Tuileries . They'd got baguettes from the employee cafeteria in the Louvre and walked outside to give Christian room to vent. Sunshine from a cloudless sky bathed the garden, where the last of summer's flowers soaked up its warmth. Fewer tourists meant more open seats, but a significant number still meandered the Grand Allée between the Louvre and Place de la Concorde.

"I don't understand. That was supposed to be your promotion," said Lionel, sitting next to him on the bench.

Christian left his sandwich half-eaten and turned toward his friend. "So did I," he said, forcing down his anger. "The department head said the guest lecturer decision was made 'at the highest levels.'"

"That's bullshit," said Lionel. "Protest. The union will support you."

"I did, but she warned me to be patient. She says the guest appointment is only for a year. She still favors me for the role next."

"What if she's overruled again?"

Christian heaved a sigh. He'd been wondering the same thing. The senior lecturer position had been all but guaranteed to go to him when he'd left in June to lead a dig in Macedonia. When he'd returned to Paris two days ago, he'd still been high on a relationship with a doctoral candidate from Rome. He'd expected to get the new job, and the woman had promised to visit during the autumn break.

"I don't know," he said, poking through his lunch. As he half-listened to Lionel ramble about the politics in the Louvre's restoration department, he soon regretted bringing his cynical friend. Christian needed to vent, not be dragged down further.

Promotions were few. Art history and archaeology were not growing businesses. Despite France elevating cultural heritage as its superpower, job opportunities remained insufficient. The current boom restoring Notre-Dame would end in a bust. In three years, the hundreds rebuilding the lightning rod of Paris tourism would find themselves waiting tables. Medieval artisans had few options in the modern world.

They paid the bill, crossed Rue de Rivoli, and passed through the arch into the Cour Carrée, where they parted. Lionel entered a door to the basement labs, and Christian turned left toward the school.

As he reached the door, his phone rang. The caller ID showed Fernand-Widal Hospital.

"Hello?"

"Monsieur Roche?"

"Oui."

"I'm sorry, Mr. Roche. I have sad news about your mother."

Two days later, Christian entered his mother's house in the tenth arrondissement. Her death, while sudden, had not been unexpected. Her congenital heart condition had been deteriorating. He dropped the keys on the entry table and fingered a sweater and overcoat hanging on hooks. Her perfume had melded into the fabric.

He'd not been inside for over a year, as she'd kept to herself and preferred restaurants for their occasional meals. The sitting room's two leather recliners faced a carved marble mantle over an unused fireplace. The threadbare rug had seen better days. Tall windows looked onto the street, and books filled the opposite wall.

It was just as his grandfather had left it. He swiped a finger through the generous dust. *Why'd she keep it this way?*

His mother hated her father. Growing up, Christian heard the rants about her mother's alcoholism and her father's ceaseless traveling. She left home at sixteen and ended up in a commune in Provençe, where she gave birth to Christian at twenty-seven. They moved to Paris when he was a toddler, and there, she took her parents' money for rent and food, complaining about them all the while.

When Christian's grandmother died from her addiction, he grew closer to his grandfather, a conservator at the Carnavalet Museum in Paris. During his days off, they collected coins together. Christian loved sorting the coins while listening to daring tales about how their ancestors, the Teutons and Celts, overthrew mighty Romans. His grandfather's favorite story mentioned a battle between great armies and a treasure lost in the Alsace forest.

He snorted at the memory of the tall tale and moved to the kitchen —his mother's domain. Jars of herbal teas lined the shelves. Floral cups hung on hooks, and a vine sprawled around the room before eventually rooting in a pot near the sink. *That's going.* He tallied the changes he'd need to make before moving in, and then he headed upstairs.

In his grandfather's dying moments, he'd waved Christian close and rasped in his frail voice, "There are maps and photos…the treasure." His head lolled.

"Where, grandfather?"

"In—" A violent cough seized him, and his eyes rolled upward.

"Grandfather." Christian put a hand on his shoulder, rocking it gently. "The maps. Tell me where."

"House," his grandfather gasped and then was gone.

The house had gone to his daughter, who had prevented Christian from searching, saying she didn't want him to become like her father. He had looked for evidence when his mother had gone out, but eventually, he'd given up searching when his university curriculum demanded attention.

Christian smirked as he opened his grandfather's office. *It's mine now.*

3

Louvre

A month after inheriting the house, Christian had lunch with Lionel in the employee cafeteria, where his friend swiped through photos of his three-week holiday in Albania. Clear Mediterranean water lapped onto white sand as paddleboarders circled.

"Did you try one?"

Lionel snorted. "No. I prefer nighttime activities." He set his phone on the table. "So, have you found anything in your grandfather's place?"

"No," said Christian, taking a bite of food. He'd been through the downstairs library and his grandfather's upstairs office. Both places had only contained books on art and art history, especially on looting during the war—nothing unusual for a conservator. "My mother remodeled the basement into a sculpting studio. She papered the walls with a hideous floral pattern. The sculptures are no less dreadful."

"Sounds like you're the only one in the family with talent."

Christian's abilities as a restorer got him on the most valuable projects. Another colleague had commented that if Christian ever lost his job in the Louvre, he could make a killing as a forger. He'd considered it fleetingly, but he hoped to teach. He'd only been given one class per semester, however—not enough to live on, so he'd kept his conservator role.

"Maybe you're too good at what you do," said Lionel. "Only people lacking genuine talent get promoted."

Christian shook his head.

"You doubt me? Look what happened to your job. How's that guy doing, anyway?"

"I sat in on a lecture. The students like him."

"Keep after your mentor. Don't let him off the hook."

Christian kept thinking of Lionel's advice as they walked back from lunch. He'd looked up the guest lecturer and found his education was no better than his own. They'd both graduated from top schools. But the new man had one thing that he lacked: high-profile discoveries.

If only Grand-père's stories had a shred of truth.

Once in his basement office, Christian thought back to the times he'd spent with his grandfather. As a child, Christian suffered from severe allergies. This meant a life indoors with few friends and an overprotective mother. Coin collecting was an escape. As Christian's immune system strengthened and medical technology improved, his grandfather introduced him to metal detecting. They explored rural areas around Paris. He explained that amateur detecting was illegal in France, but in his job as a curator, he could lawfully investigate potential archaeology sites.

His grandfather told stories of lost treasures and how the Nazis used tunnels to hide stolen art. During Christian's first year at university, he asked about their family history. His grandfather explained growing up in Strasbourg and the family's complicated history. The Alsace-Lorraine border shifted multiple times. He related the story of a doctor who, was born in France, then following the Franco-Prussian war, attended school in Germany, and, after the Great War, went to medical college and then opened a private practice in France—all without leaving his hometown.

"What about relatives?" asked Christian.

"All gone. There was nothing for me." His grandfather was vague about his war record. He said that after Germany seized the Alsace-Lorraine territory, all the men were recruited to fight, including those who identified as French. He spoke of joining the resistance, but after the war, everyone claimed to be on the winning side. To avoid rampant persecution, his grandfather moved to Paris, where his ability to speak and read German landed him a job helping the Monuments Men—the group recovering looted art. He leveraged that experience into a curator position at the Carnavalet Museum. That gave him the influence to get Christian matriculated into the École du Louvre.

His grandfather loved hearing about Christian's progress, and Christian endured the retelling of stories, but during his grandfather's last months, especially when warped by chemotherapy, his tales became more outlandish. He talked about missing paintings and a tunnel. One day, in a semi-conscious state, he spoke about secret Nazi art dealings and how he'd gotten access to records at the Jeu du Paume Museum, the clearing house for looted art. But Christian was skeptical. His grandfather only held a mid-level position.

10th Arrondissement

Back at the house that night, Christian checked his email. The builder's quote to modernize the basement had arrived. After clearing out his mother's studio, he wanted to make an apartment he could rent on Airbnb.

"*Putain!*" He tossed the phone onto a chair. He couldn't afford €10,000—much less triple that amount. He opened a beer and, when tossing its cap in the bin, realized tomorrow was collection day. Downstairs, he greeted his next-door neighbor, Pascal, with garbage bags in hand.

"*Bonsoir,* Christian. *Ça va*?" After small talk, Pascal asked about the basement remodel.

"The builder said there's barely room for a studio. It will take too long to recover the investment."

"That doesn't sound right. Come, look at our basement."

Christian followed Pascal, saying hello to his wife in the kitchen before they went downstairs. Hand-hewn beams had been refinished, and rough stone walls painted white gave the space a contemporary feel while keeping the building's character. A long sofa ran along one wall of the rectangular space, opposite an entertainment center with a flat-mounted TV. A rolling partition separated an office area in the basement's rear.

"You should come for a movie some night," Pascal said while describing how he'd remodeled the space.

Christian's brows furrowed. Something was off. His space was half this size. He went to the room's street-facing side and counted the steps toward the back. "My basement ends here," he said, touching the wall.

"Are you sure?" asked Pascal.

"Oui." Christian measured the rest of the distance, knowing four of his shoe lengths were just over a meter. He counted twelve steps to a built-in desk and estimated two more steps to the back wall. He stood for a moment, looking at the desk. Then his eyes drifted to the far wall —stone like the other walls. *But...* He closed his eyes. His basement's back wall was smooth. *Did she plaster it? What if...* He held that thought as he thanked Pascal for the tour.

Back at his house, Christian ran his hands over the papered wall. He rapped on it. *Hollow!* After grabbing a stout knife from the kitchen, he slashed the paper. It stuck fast, but he scraped enough away to find a straight crevice filled with plaster. He worked the knife down and then up. The crevice angled right and then again downward. *A door?*

Ten minutes later, he'd cleared the wallpaper around a door. Plaster filled its keyhole. He dug some of it out with the knife and then sat on a nearby chair arm. He needed something more heftier. A glance at his watch told him the shops were closed. He blew out in frustration and then remembered his mother's sculpture tools. He'd put them in a box to give away.

Grabbing a small chisel, he cleared plaster from the keyhole before realizing he had no key. He swore, tossed aside the chisel, and grabbed a heavy hammer. As he pounded the lock with it, plaster flew, stinging his face. He drove a larger chisel between the door and frame, blasting away wood chunks.

The door moved. He dropped the chisel and, with two hands, swung the hammer against the lock. On the fifth swing, the door cracked. Christian tossed the hammer onto the chair. Plaster crumbled around the door as he shouldered it inward. He flipped a light switch on the inside wall. Nothing. He tapped his phone light.

A square table dominated the room's center. The broad ceiling light was dead, and the walls were covered with maps. Closer inspection revealed they were of eastern France—the Vosges forest northwest of Strasbourg. Photographs, some black and white, others in faded color, were pinned to the maps. Two of them were in German. He studied their legends: "1937" and "1944." *Strange.*

He moved to a bookshelf with titles on art looting, similar to the upstairs library, but the crucial difference was the language—German. A larger map of Europe was fixed to the opposite wall. Several lines of yarn had been pinned from areas around London and Stuttgart. His grandfather's deathbed words came back to him: "There are maps and photos. The treasure."

Christian fetched a lamp from the studio, plugged it into the nearest outlet, and brought it into the room. Everything had been left in order, like his grandfather knew he was dying. *Why didn't mother come in here? Maybe she didn't know?* He concluded that his lazy mother hadn't been able to find the key and had sealed it over.

He went back to the 1944 map. His grandfather had circled a dot labeled "Natzweiler-Struthof." He Googled it and recoiled at the result. *Concentration camp. That's not treasure.* He surveyed the room. *What the hell is this place?*

A poster of a Cezanne still life hung over the desk. *That makes no sense.* He looked at the maps again. *Unless...* He moved to the painting and lifted it from the wall, revealing a combination safe.

4

Île Saint-Louis

Darwin and Eyrún sat on the patio of their apartment, enjoying a bottle of Grand Cru Chablis. The afternoon sun radiated from the teak decking as they enjoyed wine and cheese to close out a busy week. Darwin had kicked off his shoes and rolled his sleeves past his elbows after bubbling about his success and kudos at the post-lecture champagne reception.

Eyrún smiled beneath her large, floppy hat, which covered her exposed shoulders in her cotton dress. She'd helped with his presentation. "You seem happier," she said, reaching for a slice of cheese.

He leaned back in the chaise lounge and crossed his bare feet. "I am." As he studied the wine's light honey color through the sunlight, he sipped some and then sighed. "It feels right. And I like the people. How did your meetings go?"

She filled him in. As managing director, Eyrún oversaw the entire Agrippa Centre for Archaeology, including the scientific work at the center in Ajaccio, Corsica, the archaeological digs it sponsored, and fundraising. Darwin served as chief archaeologist but left the day-to-day supervision of projects to a friend and former professor.

They let the day slide towards sunset, comfortable in the silence, except for the hum of traffic along the Seine's far bank. Darwin pointed at a wooden roof truss hovering over Notre-Dame. "We should get together with Aya," he said.

"That would be fun," said Eyrún, pulling a shawl around her shoulders as the sun set. "What should we do for dinner? I see Mom on Sunday."

They opted for a neighborhood restaurant. Then they watched a movie at home. They'd been invited to a birthday party the next afternoon. Saturday night would be quiet, as Eyrún was piloting their plane from Paris to Reykjavík.

5

10th Arrondissement

Christian willed the locksmith to go faster, shuffling from foot to foot as the man filled out an invoice. He tore it from the book and handed it over.

Finally! Christian paid the man in cash, locked the front door behind him, and sprinted downstairs.

Drilling through the safe's combination mechanism had taken a half-hour. The locksmith had made sure it had opened but had not looked inside. He'd left the door ajar, and they'd settled the payment.

Christian had exhausted all possible combinations he could imagine, but reality did not match the movies. No compilation of known birthdays or anniversaries had opened the lock.

He swept the metal spirals into a bin and used a handheld vacuum to pick up the tiny bits. He followed this with a damp cloth. Years of working as a conservator had taught him patience. Finally, he focused a bright light on the half-meter square safe and opened its door. The hinges groaned.

"That can't be." Christian deflated like a balloon. His mind raced.

Had his mother found the safe and opened it? *No. She couldn't have. She…* He spun around. *She would've remodeled this entire space.* He returned to the safe.

A single white envelope lay inside. It bore an inscription written by a blue fountain pen and bulged from its contents. *A key?* He couldn't tell. The envelope read:

For Christian

He slit it open, and a flat key with teeth on both sides tumbled out. Christian set it on the desk and sat down as he unfolded the letter.

Dear Christian,
I hope this note finds you well. I tried my best to give you a firm foundation for life. Your graduation with honors and acceptance into the master's program brought me great joy. Unfortunately, I know I'll be gone before you complete it.

I apologize for leaving the house to your mother. She is a lost soul. But my trust stipulates that she cannot sell it without your permission.

What follows is a confession. You may not like it. Your mother most certainly will not. Do with it what you wish.

The bottom third of the page was blank.
The blood drained from his face when he turned it over.

The treasure is real.

This key unlocks the clues.

He picked up the key. *What the hell?* One side of its bow was stamped with five digits, and the other was blank.

This makes no sense. Why would he need such a large safe for a deposit box key?

Christian stood and shined his light inside the safe. Nothing. He felt around for a hidden compartment and then sank back into the chair. After rubbing his face in disbelief, he checked his watch: 13:42. His grandfather's bank was still open.

By the time he reached the bank two blocks over, a thundershower was pouring down, soaking his pant legs. Christian identified himself and showed the manager a copy of his grandfather's death certificate. Unfortunately, the manager assured him the key was not for one of their boxes.

"Do you know which bank it might be?" Christian asked.

"No. Mr. Roche. I've not seen a key like that. Good luck with your search."

The storm still raged, and Christian ducked into a Starbucks to wait it out. From the different languages being spoken around him, it seemed that half the tourist population had done the same. He got a plain black coffee and stood at the wooden bar along the front window.

On a whim, he searched the internet using a picture of the key. A safe deposit box was the most common answer. He scrolled down and was about to swipe to another app when a colleague came to mind: Julia Anderson, a relocated Brit in the Louvre's art recovery and restitution department. *I should have thought of her before.*

He hesitated for a moment at the bin, confused by the slots for recycling, compost, and landfill. *Oh, screw it.* He dropped the coffee cup in "landfill" and headed to the closest Metro. The rain pelted his umbrella and chased him down the station's steps, where he elbowed around people waiting for a break in the storm before venturing out.

He'd have to change trains, but it meant he could enter the museum without getting wetter. The passengers looked as miserable as drenched rats. Puddles formed as umbrellas drained, and the air smelled of wet socks. He disembarked at Châtelet and found his way to line seven and a two-stop connection to Palais Royal Musée du Louvre. The underground Carrousel entrance was practically empty.

After badging through the employee entrance, he went down a level to a service corridor connecting the Louvre's wings and, minutes later, reached Julia's office.

"*Bonjour*, Christian," she said.

"Bonjour."

They kissed cheeks, and after small talk, he said, "I need your help on a personal matter."

"Oh?"

"I was going through my mother's house—"

"That's right. I'm so sorry, Christian. Are you okay?"

"I'm getting through it. She had a long life," he said, playing the sympathy card with more emotion than he felt.

"Still…"

"Thanks. I found a safe deposit key, but I can't find any bank records. Could your database point me in the right direction?"

"Dunno. Let's see what you've got."

He held the key out. She read the numbers on the bow and then typed on her keyboard. A moment later, she frowned and pointed to her screen. "As I thought. It's not a bank safe deposit box key."

As he moved around to look, she said, "It opens a vault in the Geneva Freeport. This was your mother's key?" Her tone conveyed suspicion.

Christian felt a chill. The Geneva Freeport glowed like a warning beacon in the art world. The massive warehouses stored goods in transit to minimize taxes on items just passing through. Hundreds of them existed, dating back to Roman times. However, it also contained the world's largest and most secretive art warehouse.

He nonchalantly picked up the key. "Yeah. She collected all kinds of odd bits for her projects. I wonder where she found it?" He examined it, hoping the lie sounded natural. While on the Metro, he'd debated bringing it to Julia. France had passed more aggressive restitution laws in the last five years. Art dealers now had a legal responsibility to alert authorities to items with shady provenance.

"What will you do with it?" she asked.

"I don't know. Probably nothing. My mother never owned anything more valuable than a purse."

Julia looked at him askance, and his heart skipped a beat.

"Well," she said, smiling, "You still owe me that drink you've been promising."

He thanked her and headed toward his office. But before getting there, he exited the building. He'd taken the afternoon off to let in the locksmith. Walking to the Metro, he pulled up a rail app and booked a seat on the last train to Geneva. He'd call his boss en route and tell him something else had come up.

6

Île de la Cité

Notre-Dame cast long shadows across its forecourt as Darwin approached the temporary offices of the restoration crews. From this angle, she almost looked normal until he got a clear view between the towers. Sun glinted off the scaffolding shrouding the cathedral's main body. It rose in an inverted cone over the space where the new spire was being installed.

Darwin had not been this close since visiting a few months after the fire. Today, he'd been invited back by the same archaeologist, Aya Raiss, head of the *Crypte Archéologique*.

"*Bonjour*, Aya," he said as she walked from a tent containing pieces of the collapsed vaults and other statuary.

"*Bonjour*, Darwin."

After their greeting, she answered his questions about the repairs. The tents held significantly fewer objects than on his first visit. "We should go," she said, handing him a hard hat.

She led him to a construction lift, and a minute later, they rose through the scaffolding. As the breeze increased, Darwin glanced at

Aya. Her long black hair flowed from beneath her hard hat, adding height to her petite form, but she was still a head shorter than him.

"Are you okay?" she asked.

Darwin had a white-knuckle grip on the cage, and his eyes were fixed on the cathedral's stone exterior. "I'm fine. It just feels..." He glanced at the thin mesh surrounding them. "Too open."

"Well, don't look down when we get up top."

Darwin took a deep breath, steeling himself as his desire to explore overcame his trepidation about being a hundred meters above the city. He studied Aya. Her brown eyes glowed with a fierce determination he remembered from their discovery of a tunnel running beneath Notre-Dame soon after the fire. They'd been working to find out how a man had run into the burning structure and stolen a relic before seeming to vanish in the flames. No human remains had been found, and Darwin was convinced the man had gotten out through a secret exit.

Aya shared a rumor she'd heard from a dead colleague who'd been on the 1960s dig that had discovered the crypt. Late one night, she and Darwin broke down an exhibit wall to find a doorway. This opened into an unknown tunnel beneath Notre-Dame, leading to a tomb the thief had used to get underground from inside the cathedral.

But they were betrayed, and police entered the tunnel behind them. That's when Darwin learned of Aya's secret identity: *La Chauve Souris,* the bat, a notorious urban underground explorer. She led them on a wild chase beneath the Seine River and into the Paris catacombs, where they escaped into the Metro.

Fortunately, Aya remained undiscovered. Like Darwin, she was an above-board archaeologist most of the time, but acting as *La Chauve Souris* allowed her to use frowned-upon methods to access sites.

As they reached the top, the lift rattled, and they stepped onto a wooden walkway atop the stone walls. The dense tubular scaffolding gave Darwin a sense of security as curiosity won over fear. The buttresses were reinforced with wood and iron fasteners. He looked up as a man he recognized walked toward them.

"*Bonjour*, Pierre," said Aya, bumping fists with the tall, well-built man. "You remember Darwin Lacroix?"

Pierre smiled. "*Mais, oui. Ça va,* Darwin?"

"*Bien, Pierre. Et tu?*" said Darwin, shaking Pierre's hand as both men grinned slyly. Pierre had been in the police detail that had chased them through the tunnels.

"Pierre is now a fire inspector and agreed to show us around today," said Aya.

"Cool," said Darwin.

Pierre explained his role in checking the installation of fire-suppression systems in the new forest—the trusses that formed Notre-Dame's roof. He pointed toward the bell towers. "We've been installing six per day." He motioned them to follow. About halfway to the riverside tower, they squeezed between the tree-sized beam onto a platform above the vaults.

Darwin placed a palm on the hand-hewn beam. What looked smooth-cut from a distance had imperfections left from the axes. He recalled a YouTube video in which a carpenter stood on a log and swung a wide-blade ax to trim it square. Manual saws were used to fell the trees and build the trusses. However, despite the cultural significance of repairing the cathedral using original technologies, the construction teams opted for modern cranes to lift the structural supports.

Pierre pointed to the transept vault. "That is where the guy took the relic."

Darwin had to imagine the tiled floor far below and the ceiling in reverse. From here, on the vault's upper side, the cathedral's beauty was in the joining of raw stone and gravity to hold them in place.

"They're placing another truss. Let's go look."

Aya followed Pierre, with Darwin after her. Darwin looked toward the river where a wooden triangle hung from a wire dangling from a crane one and a half times the cathedral's height.

Pierre led them to a point where the walkway wrapped around the chevet. The buttresses spread outward like spokes in a wheel. The western sun radiated off the stone, and Darwin imagined days when exposure to the elements made working unpleasant. They stopped near a group of a dozen or so people, some well-dressed. "Who are they?" he asked.

"Donors and dignitaries," said Aya, hair whipping around in the breeze channeled up the stone walls. "Our funding comes from many private sources. Giving tours is one way to keep it flowing."

Pierre stepped away to perform his job while Darwin gaped. The triangle—tiny from below—was now massive, with five twenty-meter-tall trees cut and fit together. Workers grabbed ropes hanging from the truss's corners to prevent it from rotating.

Darwin held his breath as the crane lowered the truss. It paused a meter from the roof and then moved at a snail's pace until a worker on one side shouted. His opposite yelled a moment later, and another talked to the crane operator by radio. Time froze. The observers hushed.

Workers waved flags. The line holding the truss went slack, and a worker emerged at the peak. She detached the rope and swung it free. Darwin blew out the breath he'd been holding and joined the gallery's spontaneous cheers and claps. "That was amazing."

"I still get chills every time I see it," said Aya. "When you first visited, there was still a serious debate about whether she could be saved. We've come a long way. Let's go down. There's one more thing I want to show you."

They said goodbye to Pierre and waited for their turn in the lift. Darwin looked across the canal between the two islands at his apartment. He'd talked with a neighbor who'd described her horror while watching the cathedral burn. He imagined a history book a couple of centuries in the future describing the fire and reconstruction in one paragraph before moving on. *If that much,* he snorted.

A quarter-hour later, he and Aya stood over an opening on the cathedral floor. Tiles had been stacked around a pit ten meters square. A grid marked the locations of tombs in the floor. Aya explained the unknown burials. "We've identified high-ranking church leaders and filled gaps in the record. Good thing you visited today. We're closing it up next week."

Darwin had seen online photos, and while the sight was more interesting in person, it was less so compared to the action he'd witnessed above. As if answering his unasked question, Aya said, "You're probably wondering why I showed you this."

"Erm."

"Come." She nodded toward the tomb that led to the tunnel they'd found. She looked around to determine they were alone and then said, "Remember when you asked if it extended to Saint Chappelle?"

"You said it was blocked off in the 1970s car park construction."

"Correct. But our adventure got my exploration bug going again. My colleague. You know, the other one."

Darwin smirked with a secretive expression. "*La Chauve Souris*?"

She returned the smile. "She worked out the directions and found the tunnel to Saint Chappelle."

His eyes went wide.

"No, no," she said. "I haven't gone public with it yet. I'm saving it for after Notre-Dame reopens."

Darwin's eyes darted from side to side as he worked out the direction. An idea formed. He calculated the distance, knowing the tunnel under Notre-Dame exited on the Left Bank of the Seine.

"I've seen that look, Darwin. What are you thinking?"

"Any chance there's a tunnel from Saint Chappelle to the palaces at the Louvre?"

"Interesting that you ask." She chuckled. "Are you up for another adventure?"

7

Geneva

Christian woke at eight, having reached the hotel after midnight. He showered, dressed, and went to a cafe on Quai du Mont-Blanc, between the Beau-Rivage and Grand Fairmont hotels. The storm had blown through during the night, but the wetness and trailing winds drove a damp chill through the streets. Thankfully, the cafe was only a few minutes' walking distance.

He ordered coffee and croissants. Outside, runners traversed Lake Geneva's *quai*-side. He contemplated exercise but then shook his head and opened the morning newspaper.

Forty-five minutes later, he walked to a taxi queue and, a quarter-hour after that, was approaching the Geneva Freeport. The elegance of the lakeside hotels had given way to bland utility where opportunistic weeds sprouted through gaps in the concrete. The number of trucks increased, as did fences and razor wire.

He exited the cab at a drab, 1960s-looking building. The freeport looked nothing like a high-end art storage facility. The lobby, however, had been remodeled more recently. He walked up to a thick plexiglass partition. "*Bonjour*," he said to the clerk.

"*Bonjour, monsieur*. How may I help you?"

"My grandfather left me this key in his will," said Christian, holding it to the glass. "Is this the right place?"

"May I see it?"

Christian passed the key through the slot, and the clerk entered its number on her keyboard. She leaned forward to read the text and then said, "Just a moment. I'll get someone to help you."

Minutes later, a woman in a dark blue suit came in from a side door. "Mr. Roche?"

"Yes."

"I'm Stephanie Grey. Please come with me."

Christian followed her to a well-appointed office and accepted her offer of coffee.

"Please have a seat." They sat, and she said, "You say this is your grandfather's key?"

"*Oui*."

"I'll need to see your passport and documents to confirm your access."

He placed his passport on the table and removed a folio from his bag. She examined the death certificate and his grandfather's trust and will. "Why did you wait sixteen years?"

"My grandfather left the key in a hidden safe. I only just found it during a remodel. How long has he had the box?"

"Let's see," she said, using a finger to authenticate at a computer. She tapped the keyboard and read from the screen, "Nineteen forty-seven."

Christian straightened in his chair. He hadn't known what to expect. The 1960s or 70s, maybe, but not eighty years. His brain swirled with possibilities as Stephanie said, "Let me confirm these documents, and then we'll go up."

His hands shook, and he set the coffee cup on the desk. *What would Grand-père need to store here? Why not a bank deposit box in Paris?*

The questions came faster than the answers. Fortunately, she handed back the documents moments later. "All is in order. Please follow me."

After they passed through a metal detector and his bag was

scanned, Christian followed Stephanie into a secure area. They took a lift two floors up and reached another door. This time, she placed a hand on a scanner, and the double door unlatched. Cameras left no blind spots for whoever was watching.

They entered a long hallway with flush doors every five meters—each stenciled with a number. "Here we are," she said, stopping at eleven. She used another hand scanner beside the door, and bright lights snapped on as she swung it open.

"Here's your locker, Mr. Roche." She pointed to a waist-tall door stamped with the number matching the key.

"I didn't expect something so large."

"This is one of our smaller units. If you'd like, I can stand in the hallway while you open it."

He had no idea what his grandfather might have stored that required privacy, but he nodded. She retreated but left the hallway door open. Christian inserted the key. It turned smoothly as it released the interior mechanism. He paused. Questions returned with more vigor. He'd envisioned a typical safe deposit box no bigger than a kitchen drawer. *But this? I could park my bike in it.*

He wiped a sweaty palm on his pants and grasped the handle. It required more effort to turn than the key. He felt the mechanism withdraw substantial latches, and then he opened it.

Wooden boxes of various sizes filled the space. Three stood the full height of the vault but were only a hand's width. He peered in. A faint antique-shop odor wafted from within. A fat manila envelope lay atop the boxes. He snapped a photo and asked Stephanie, "Is there a place where I can examine the contents?"

Christian sat at a table in a room devoid of windows or security cameras. The wooden boxes lay on a utility cart, and he stared at the manila envelope. A smaller white one labeled "Open First" was taped to it. His heart pounded as he slit the paper and removed a letter. His grandfather's blue handwriting flowed across its surface.

Dear Christian,

I apologize for the vague revelation in the letter I left at home. I needed you to be motivated to find this vault, but too much is at stake to leave a direct reference to the freeport.

When I learned my cancer would be fatal, I moved the last valuables here. Your mother would have sold everything but discarded the most valuable—how to find the lost treasure.

But let me begin with a confession:

My real name is Karl Meyer. I was born in Metz, Germany, in 1914. My birth certificate and passport are in the manila envelope.

Christian's vision closed in. He clutched the table and sucked in deep breaths. He'd speculated on many possibilities since reading his grandfather's first letter in the basement safe, but even in his wildest fantasies, this revelation was not among them.

A long minute later, he opened the larger envelope, spilled its contents on the table, and picked up the birth certificate. He couldn't read German, but all the documents had the same data.

Handwritten cursive listed Karl Meyer, born on 12 October 1914, to Franz and Gertrude Meyer.

Christian examined the passport, a worn gray booklet embossed with the German eagle coat of arms and labeled:

DEUTSCHES REICH REISE-PASS

Inside, a photo of his grandfather in his twenties was riveted to the page. All the relevant data, such as name, dates, and family status, had also been written by hand. Its pages were stamped with consulate visas and stamps from most European art cities, including Rome and Paris. In 1938, he had visited London and New York. The entries stopped in 1939.

Christian shuddered while examining a booklet labeled

"*KENNKARTE*," which Google translated as "Identification Card." The embossed eagle's wreath contained a swastika.

Christian's throat tightened. He forced a swallow against a hardening lump. *Everything he told me was a lie.* He slammed his palms on the table, shoved the chair back, and stood.

"Is everything all right?" Stephanie asked from the hallway.

"Yes. Sorry." Christian walked around the table to regain composure. He stopped at the cart and ran a hand over the pine boxes, yellowed from years in storage. His world reeled chaotically. His grandfather wasn't who he said he was. *Is this why Mother hated him? Did she know?*

No, he decided. *She would've told me.*

He stared at the document pile and sighed, wondering what else was coming.

8

École du Louvre

Darwin taught his first class, while Eyrún was still in Iceland. The day dawned gloomy from an overnight thunderstorm but was clearing when he started toward the École du Louvre. He pedaled his bike across Pont Marie and along the riverside path. The mid-morning traffic was light, and he crossed the boulevard at the lion's gate in the Louvre's long river-facing arm. He parked the bike and entered the main marble lobby.

Butterflies in his gut added to his nervous energy, and fifteen minutes into his first lecture, he paused. *Slow down. You've got all semester.* Faces looked up from laptops and tablets. "Just wanted to see I wasn't losing you," he said, covering the awkward moment. The remaining lecture felt more natural as he eased into the course syllabus.

Later that afternoon, he finished meetings with three doctoral candidates and was about to leave when he got a text from the dean, Vivienne de Poitiers:

Please come by my office. Some people would like to meet you.

Darwin: 2 minutes, then I'll head over.

Five minutes later, he reached Vivienne's office—a corner suite in the Pavillon de Flore overlooking the Carrousel and Tuileries gardens. Darwin loved the spectacular view and imagined the office was just another room before the 1871 insurrection and fire that destroyed the Tuileries Palace connecting the Louvre's two wings. Tourists saw today's Paris with curated landscapes, not its bloody past.

Vivienne turned from her guests and greeted him with an infectious smile. Today, she wore an impeccable houndstooth dress—Channel, he guessed from its crossed-Cs buckle. Clear-framed glasses complimented her black hair, cut in a bob with straight bangs. Elegant and scholarly, he thought.

"Darwin," she said, extending her hand. "Thank you for coming at a moment's notice. How was your first day?"

"I thought it went well. A little bumpy to start."

"Well, I'm sure you'll do great. Come. I'd like you to meet some people." She led him to a corner table where two individuals stood up.

"This is Fleur Legrand. She heads up the *OCBC*."

Darwin swallowed, his throat suddenly dry, and shook Fleur's hand, trying to maintain a neutral expression. He'd had dealings with the *Office Central de Lutte Contre le Trafic des Biens Culturels Federal,* better known as the art crimes unit of the National Police or OCBC, for short. Officers under Fleur's command had assisted Darwin in recovering church relics stolen by a doomsday cult.

Vivienne's voice rescued him from the uneasy moment. "And this is Lucien Marsan, *ministère de l'Action et des Comptes publics*."

Darwin shook the finance minister's hand, deciding the man's expression was so dour he must use Botox to freeze it in place. His cold eyes and matching gunmetal gray suit shouted bean counter.

"Now," Vivienne continued, directing them to chairs, "I'll bet you're wondering what this meeting is about?"

"It's about...erm..." Darwin smiled, looking at Lucien. "My contributions to the president's election campaign?"

"No," said Lucien, "I'm sure he's grateful. But he asked us to meet with you about a different matter."

Darwin's eyebrows raised. "I was joking."

"I am not."

Okay, then. Darwin had met the president of the republic on multiple occasions when his discoveries created significant positive news for France and the ACA extended the country's soft power across the Mediterranean. In addition, his role as special director of archaeology at the Vatican allowed for behind-the-scenes diplomacy.

Vivienne jumped in. "Darwin, we're thrilled to have you at the École du Louvre. I apologize for this sounding like some conspiracy, but I assure you it's not."

"Perhaps I can best explain," said Fleur. Not waiting for approval, she added, "When the president learned of your guest lecturing, he suggested you might be in a position to help us."

"That depends," said Darwin.

"Of course. It's not a demand. Hear us out."

Darwin nodded, and Fleur continued. "My team prosecuted the antiquities ring in Marseilles that you helped uncover. But as you know, a good many in that organization are still unknown to us. We suspect they have a group that's been operating inside the Louvre for decades."

"If not longer," Lucien cut in and laid a thick folio on the table. "Since the war, paperwork filing has been poor."

Darwin eyed the folio.

"These are objects we can no longer find in the collections," said Lucien, tapping the pile.

"We've had agents inside for years," said Fleur, "but they can't seem to get close enough to see all who are involved."

"I'm not sure I like where I think this is going." Darwin sat back, crossing his arms.

"We're not forcing you to do anything," said Vivienne. "But—"

"The president would be pleased if I looked around," Darwin interjected. "Assist France in protecting its cultural patrimony, so to speak."

"Not exactly in those words, but yes," said Fleur.

"Why me?" he asked.

"You are an outsider here, and few people know you," said Lucien, nodding to Fleur. She withdrew a sealed evidence bag from her valise and handed it to Darwin. He glanced at a handwritten letter in English.

"It's from an American who served with the Monuments Men recovery operation. He claimed there were unaccounted-for artworks. That insiders secreted away select pieces for their own purposes. We found the letter in a closed-case folio from 1947. There were too many egregious crimes that took priority over hearsay."

"That's a long time ago," said Darwin. "Not in an archaeological sense, but you know what I mean."

"You're right, but..." Fleur handed him printouts from eBay auction pages. "These objects are from the Louvre collection."

He flipped through them—three objects: a Minoan figurine, an Egyptian statuette, and a gold necklace listed as Roman. None of the object's descriptions contained any provenance. He looked up. "How do you know these came from the Louvre?"

Lucien took this question. "My department manages the inventory, as all its contents belong to the state. The pre-war and post-war inventories yielded a list of missing objects."

"What about the collections in storage? There must be hundreds of thousands."

"Correct. This is one of our problems. We have been digitizing the collection, especially the paintings. Our new storage facility in Liévin helps with this, but—"

"With insiders embedded in the system, you fear valuable objects can disappear in transit," Darwin finished for him.

"Precisely!"

Darwin stood and crossed to the window. He thought better while in motion. Below, people milled about in the Jardin de Tuileries. His gaze drifted across its tree tops to the Luxor Obelisk and then to the office towers of La Defense, a modern contrast to the old palaces.

Antiquities theft angered him. He believed the ancient past belonged to everyone. That was why he and Eyrún had founded the

ACA—to safeguard through awareness and education. He pivoted to face the Arc de Triomphe du Carrousel. The Louvre Pyramid was just visible at the window's edge.

Darwin wanted to help, but he was also a realist. *I can't fight it all.*

He thought of Eyrún. She'd messaged him from Reykjavík an hour ago. They'd promised each other they would spend a year in Paris, enjoying the city life and taking a break from adventure. He focused on the window's inside reflection. Fleur was leaning toward Vivienne, whispering in her ear. His brow furrowed as a theory emerged. *Was this job a lure to get me here?* Darwin refocused on the garden outside.

He hated being manipulated and pushed into a corner, especially when the task was vague. He knew enough about the antiquities underworld to know that outsiders didn't just walk in. *If their insiders can't get close, it's not likely I will.*

He was about to suggest he needed time to think about their request when he remembered advice from his best friend, Zac. "Say no, especially if you don't want to do something. Be clear. Later on, you can change to yes but on your own terms."

Darwin retook his seat. "No. This is not a project I can help with."

"Will you at least think about it?" Fleur pleaded.

"I have," said Darwin. A long moment of silence passed where he pressed his feet to the floor, holding his position.

Vivienne brought the topic to closure. "I think we have Darwin's answer. Perhaps he may reconsider after he's spent more time here."

Fleur and Lucien thanked Darwin for hearing their request and said their goodbyes. But as Darwin retrieved his bike and headed to his apartment, he couldn't help but think this was only their opening round.

9

Geneva

Christian continued reading his grandfather's tiny script.

I studied art history and became a professor at Staatliche Kunstschule in Berlin. Life in the arts became complicated as the National Socialists rose to power. Like a tsunami, by the time we saw the danger, it was too late.

I was 25 when war broke out. When France surrendered in 1940, I was sent to Paris to assist with inventorying artwork and supervising its removal to Germany.

In the war's closing months, I was reassigned back to Germany. When the certainty of our defeat emerged, I made preparations for life beyond the conflict.
During the Nazi's scramble for safety, my colleagues and I stole three box cars of looted art. We hid it in a workshop near the Natzweiler-Struthof camp, and planned to recover it after the war.

After the war, I escaped persecution by working with the Monuments Men to recover looted art. In exchange, the Americans gave me a new identity: Louis Roche, and I was given my curator role at the Carnavalet Museum. I met your grandmother there. She's French but worked in the Vichy government. Like me, she had a complicated past. We had each done things during the war. We stayed together by never talking about our past. I suspect that is why she succumbed to drink.

Sadly, we never gave your mother the love she needed. I was obsessed with finding the treasure. And your grandmother never wanted children.

Christian set down the pages again. The story they told explained much of the confusion he'd had growing up. His mother had lamented more than once, "They never wanted me." While that may have been true, his grandparents had provided financial care throughout their lives. Unfortunately, what his mother needed—their love—they'd never given.

He shifted his attention to the boxes. Before finishing the letter, he wanted to see what his grandfather considered so valuable that it needed to be stored in a no-questions-asked Swiss vault. Stephanie had provided a battery-powered screw gun, and Christian opened the largest box first. He set the meter-square crate on the table and backed out the screws.

He lifted its lid to reveal an oil painting of an outdoor winter scene with people dressed in seventeenth-century clothing. Some were skating, and others were trading goods. The buildings suggested northern Europe, and the muted brown shades hinted at the Dutch style. He didn't recognize the artist Hendrick Avercamp, but a quick search showed works exhibited at the Rijksmuseum in Amsterdam. The painting had no provenance documentation, which didn't surprise him.

The other large crates contained similar minor artists. Christian recognized the quality and guessed these might get low six figures at auction.

The small boxes held clocks. One was a wall-mounted design

featuring cherubs entwined in vines. He guessed it was from the Louis XV period, based on a similar clock he'd restored. The other two clocks were tabletop versions: one had a globe that rotated with the hours, and the other had a blue porcelain mantel with elaborate gold leafing. These, he knew, might sell at similar prices.

Sadly, even though he knew how to work around provenance, these had been looted—stolen as war booty. He needed space to think. He screwed the covers onto the crates and moved them back into the vault. The envelope, he kept. The letter had another couple of pages, but he wanted to finish it in a more private location.

He thanked Stephanie and asked how the vault was being paid for. She informed him it had a prepaid fifty-year lease and had been renewed in 1997.

10

École du Louvre

Darwin killed time between lectures by exploring Aya's theory that the Capetian kings used secret tunnels. He laid a handful of color prints on the desk. Philip II constructed the medieval Louvre fortress during his reign to protect Paris against the more powerful Dutchy of Normandy.

The original Louvre had defensive towers arrayed above moats and a massive round keep at its center. A hundred years later, they laid the foundations of Notre-Dame on Île de la Cité. Its construction went on for almost two centuries, and in between, Philip's grandson, Louis IX, built Sainte-Chapelle to house his collection of holy relics.

It's plausible, Darwin thought while sketching the layout on paper. He added dashed lines between the structures to represent tunnels. He would have scoffed at the idea had he not previously explored an unknown tunnel beneath Notre-Dame. The more he considered it, the clearer the logic grew.

If my enemies controlled the roads to the east and north, I'd want an escape route. Any crossing of Pont Neuf would be too easy to attack. A barge crossing would be equally perilous.

A tunnel, though, was perfect. He ended a dashed line just across the Seine, but he knew a tunnel could extend into the Left Bank quarries. He snapped a photo of the drawing and shifted to his other query—antiquities looting from Louvre collections.

The storage areas in major museums bulged with items. Over the centuries, people had bequeathed millions of objects from personal collections when grandad's cabinet of curiosities didn't fit modern decorating tastes. The vast majority of them lay uncatalogued.

He still had no intention of taking on Fleur's request, but curiosity's gravity well tugged him closer. He'd seen the British Museum's vast underground storage. The Pitt Rivers Museum in Oxford showed off row upon row of glass cabinets full of crockery, weapons, tattooing kit, and shrunken heads.

During the Western Enlightenment, scientific and technological gains matched philosophical and mathematical leaps. Few distinctions existed between amateurs and professionals as explorers ventured from Europe to understand and catalog the natural world.

For the time being, Darwin ignored the problematic issue of restitution as he considered the untold millions of uncatalogued objects. Digitizing them for study would be a decades-long process, with no funding in sight. On top of that, senior curators' incomes paled compared to other big-city jobs requiring similar education and experience levels.

Darwin had been lucky. His earliest discovery had netted millions. Eyrún's shares in her company's stock had shot skyward, as it could use the lava tube they'd discovered connecting Iceland and Scotland. They used their windfall to fund the Agrippa Centre for Archaeology.

A blog he'd printed out caught his attention. A trader of medieval cloisonne jewelry had written about purchasing items on eBay from sellers who did not recognize their value. He resold them to discerning collectors but suspected some pieces had come from the Louvre. He put two photos in the blog: one showing a Louvre exhibit case with precious ornaments from the Frankish period and another a piece bought online. They were almost identical, and the author surmised they were from the same find.

Darwin studied the photos. He wasn't an expert, but he could tell that the colors and workmanship were similar. He tapped out an email on his iPad to the collector using Proton Mail's encrypted service.

```
Would you be willing to talk about your
suspicions?
```

He signed it with his ACA credentials and then returned to his research. In less than five minutes, the iPad chimed with a reply.

```
Yes. But not over email.
Minh Tường
```

They corresponded in real-time until Minh agreed to meet and suggested tea at MyuMyu on Rue Philibert Lucot in the thirteenth arrondissement.

11

Geneva

Fatigue engulfed Christian as his train departed from Geneva and headed back to Paris, in part from traveling and sleeping in an unfamiliar bed but chiefly from what he'd discovered in the vault. His biological grandfather had lived a lie.

Does this mean I'm German? No, he decided. Both his parents and grandmother were French. *Mom must have known something. Why else would she hate him?*

He gazed out the window, looking at nothing in particular. The train rocked as it traversed the switches onto the main tracks. Christian searched his memories for clues. But aside from his mother's disdain for her parents and grandmother's disease, he found nothing. They'd loved him even through their own problems.

His stomach clenched at another thought. *What if my coworkers find out my grandfather's a Nazi art thief?*

Christian recalled visiting museums with his grandfather and collecting coins together. His grandfather had praised his curiosity and eye for discovery. Later, when choosing a field of study, his grandfather had all but held his hand, guiding him to the École du Louvre.

He'd not objected, but neither had he expressed desire. He hadn't known what he wanted and had followed the path of least resistance. In adulthood, he'd moved along his current career path, still following his grandfather's advice.

Son of a bitch. Grand-père was grooming me to find his loot!

Christian rubbed his temples against a blossoming headache and reclined his seat back. The train's swaying lulled him into a daydream. Minutes later, another TGV blasted by in the opposite direction. Now awake, he wriggled upright in the seat and pulled the letter from his shoulder bag. After skimming the first pages in case he'd missed anything, he read about his grandfather's wartime experience.

The war brought about a complicated history for me. I followed the news but had no interest in politics. When war erupted in Poland, we believed its purpose was to reclaim ancient German lands. But then it expanded, as you know. While the professional military fought, they assigned all other young Germans, including me, a job. Mine involved cataloging art.

But the greed escalated. I was assigned to the Einsatzstab Reichsleiter Rosenberg task force and sent to Paris. I worked first in the Louvre, then the Jeu de Paume, which we used as a clearing house. High-ranking officers visited and selected paintings for their private homes. I did not condone the looting but protesting meant execution. What mattered to me was the art and keeping it safe. I sought to preserve our collective past. My God, how foolish we were.

We produced catalogs of the art and sent them to Berlin, where Hitler himself could select. The bastards treated all of France like a flea market. The worst was Göring, whose greed knew no boundaries.

But in 1943, the war was going disastrously for Germany. They withdrew me to Berlin to manage the looted art, and with the increasing Allied bombing, I supervised the relocation of collections away from target cities.

I thought about the end and how I would survive. Talking about it posed a danger, yet I found three colleagues. One of us knew of an abandoned bunker near the Natzweiler-Struthof concentration camp.

Our plan was to recover and sell the art after the war, but a fluke ruined it. Allied bombs obliterated the surrounding landscape. The explosions caused a landslide and rendered the hills unrecognizable. I never heard from my colleagues again and suspect they were in the tunnel. This was in late March 1945.

After Germany's surrender, I survived by giving evidence at the Nuremberg trials against the ERR leadership. Then, they remanded me to the Monuments Men in Paris, where I helped with the restitution efforts. As I mentioned earlier, they gave me a new identity in 1947, and I continued life as a Frenchman.

I thought of the lost treasure but laid low as persecution of collaborators was high. But in the 1950s, people wanted to forget the war and move on. Your grandmother and I met, and she became pregnant with your mother in 1955. We married, and I started looking for the tunnel.

As the service cart arrived, the attendant placed a snack tray on Christian's seatback table. When they moved up the aisle, he returned to reading.

I visited the Struthof camp many times to locate the tunnel, but the landscape had undergone too much alteration. In those days, GPS was unavailable, and my colleague's compass directions lacked precision. In addition, I could find no records of the bunker.

The maps in the basement document my past searches. My colleague said the bunker went deep into the hillside, so the artwork must be safe. In total, we transferred the contents of three box cars from southern Bavaria.

In closing, know that, despite what your mother said, your grandmother and I always loved you.

Love,
Grand-père

P.S. The following page contains a list of paintings in the boxcars.

Christian flipped the page and read the list. He recognized many of the names, but the last line caused him to bolt upright, fingers tingling like he'd touched a live wire.

Raphael — Portrait of a Young Man

Raphael's missing masterpiece was the poster child of the Nazi loot. He'd read somewhere that it would fetch over a hundred million at auction. He sat back and smiled.

Finding it would be the discovery of a lifetime. I could write my own career ticket.

He bathed in the fantasy for a while, imagining a book and a speaking tour. But the bubble soon burst, leaving him in the reality of his current circumstances. He put the letter back into his folio and stared out the window at the farmland scrolling past. Just before dozing, he decided to visit Struthof and determine if there was even a shred of truth in his grandfather's claim.

12

5th Arrondissement

Darwin stepped out of his ride-share. Inside the pâtisserie, Minh stood to greet him. He appeared about Darwin's father's age. His smile and posture displayed a serene confidence.

"Please, choose," said Minh, pointing to the glass case after they shook hands.

Darwin paid for a palmier and a black coffee. The server said she would bring them to him. He returned to the table, where Minh sipped his tea after biting into his pastry.

"Looks good. What is it?" asked Darwin.

"*Bánh cáy.* A sticky rice cake with sesame, carrots, and gardenias. Try it."

Darwin took the offered piece and popped it into his mouth. An explosion of sugary sweetness gave way to savory sesame and a whisper of citrus. "Orange peel?" he asked.

"Yes. You have a discerning palate."

As they shared backgrounds, Darwin's coffee and pastry arrived. Minh was born in Ho Chi Minh City and immigrated with his parents to Paris in the early 1960s. He studied archaeology at École du Louvre and held a master's degree.

He laughed when he heard Darwin was a guest lecturer. "I tried teaching and field jobs, but the money's difficult. I started buying and selling in the Paris antique markets. Found I had a talent for it and now do it full-time." Mihn paused, studying Darwin. Then he asked, "What interested you in my blog?"

Darwin answered with a deeper description of his background, including his work as director of special archaeological investigations for the Apostolic Archive in Vatican City. That got a wide-eyed look from Minh, and he added, "It's a role the pope created after I found previously unknown documents. He wants the Church to be more transparent about its dealings. Realistically, I lead a small team to assess the impact of old records before making them public. It's more administrative than exciting."

"Isn't it all?" Minh mused. "I'm sorry for interrupting. Please continue."

"No worries." Darwin used the break to drink his coffee. "How sure are you that the pieces are the same as those on display in the Louvre?"

"Pretty sure."

Darwin finished his coffee. Minh's sudden, short answer tickled his finder sense. *What's he not saying?* Darwin wiped the pastry crumbs from his plate with a finger, licked it, and asked, "How do you know?"

"I have an eidetic memory."

"I'm jealous."

"Don't be. I never watch the news or horror movies."

Darwin nodded. "Hadn't thought about it that way."

Minh grinned. "You never answered why you're interested in my blog."

Darwin's wicker chair creaked as he leaned back and looked out the window. A dog walker and her pack passed by on the street's opposite side. He didn't have a crisp answer. *At least, not yet.*

But his instinct had been thrumming since he'd read the blog. Regardless of his statement to Fleur Legrand that insider theft at the Louvre wasn't his concern, he had an undeniable conviction that it was. He and Eyrún had founded the ACA, in part, to assist with anti-trafficking and restitution. It's image as an institution going after museum looting was only its public face—most of the struggle involved private parties.

Overall, societal awareness of looting and trafficking was leading to more legal action. Justice departments, backed by national laws, were cracking down on dealers. Internationally, nation-states made increasing restitution demands.

Darwin turned back to Minh. "I want to stop the thefts. Are you open to helping?"

"I might be."

13

Strasbourg

Three days after visiting Geneva, Christian took a late train to Strasbourg. The next morning he at a hearty breakfast at his hotel, tucked between residential buildings. His weather app showed a sunny but chilly day in Strasbourg, and he suspected it would be colder in the mountains. He went to his room and organized himself for the day. He wasn't an outdoors enthusiast but knew enough about proper clothes and boots from archaeological digs.

After paying the bill, he hired a car for the hour-long drive to Struthof. The metropolitan area transitioned to farmland, and the road soon ascended into the Vosges Mountains, where he entered the Heiligenberg Valley. The town names Urmatt, Lutzelhouse, and Wisches read like he was in Germany. A half-hour later, the map app alerted him to an upcoming left turn out of a traffic circle in Rothau. Five hundred meters farther, he navigated onto Rue des Déportés, where the houses thinned as the route climbed.

He took another left turn onto D530, where a small sign pointed to Camp du Struthof. The road narrowed and climbed through thick forest. He passed a marker showing four kilometers to Struthof and then rounded a hard switchback. He'd seen no cyclists today, but block letters painted on the road listed riders from some past race.

In fifteen minutes, he reached the car park and pulled in. Four tour buses and a dozen cars occupied a third of the spaces. He grabbed his pack and followed a group toward the camp. When they turned onto a path leading to a fortified gate, Christian saw rough logs forming double gates that towered to the height of six people. Barbed wire ran everywhere.

Putain. He shuddered. From studying ancient structures, he knew they'd built this for effect. Arriving prisoners would feel they'd reached the gates of hell.

He shook it off and continued along the road until he reached a memorial to the deported resistance fighters. From the side, the monument resembled a massive vertical pipe cut on the diagonal, its sharp end pointing skyward.

The camp overlooked a wide valley. On its far side, mountains rose in the haze. The terraced hillside camp, an open wound in the countryside, served as a reminder of the vicious past.

Christian stepped down the hillside to study the memorial. The interior curve of the monument had a grizzled human shape carved into it. The artist had captured the horror of a human starved to death. Nausea surged. He looked away, breathing in the cool air.

After a long moment, he dug a map from his pack and oriented it to the camp's layout. The pink granite quarry was on the hill above the camp. Prisoners marched a kilometer uphill daily to blast granite from the open seam. He'd studied various old maps and websites.

Google Maps showed a surprising number of dirt roads through the surrounding hills, but thick tree cover obscured them at ground level. His grandfather's map differed in the details of the ravine on the camp's right side. It showed a workshop constructed using quarried granite. The Junker aircraft company had sent engines there for refurbishing. The shop had a storage tunnel cut into the hillside at the back. Circumnavigating the perimeter fence, Christian found a trailhead that led to one of the dirt tracks.

He saw the road he needed to reach and cut across a section of sloping forest to save time. The crunching of leaves was the only sound as his feet sank ankle-deep in the detritus. He consulted his grandfather's notebook when he got to the lower track.

My colleague who knew about a tunnel built when the Nazis got paranoid from the Allied bombing. The workshop would be safe from anything other than a direct hit, protected by the deep tunnel.

Christian zipped up his jacket against the damp chill as he followed the hillside contour. Unfortunately, after backtracking and rechecking the map, he could not find the buried workshop. Another fifty years of growth had made it even harder to locate. *But,* he thought, *Grand-père didn't have modern LiDAR and satellite technologies.*

The roadbed was loamy earth compacted with ground granite, evidence that someone had made this track sturdier. He climbed a few meters up the hillside and dug away the dead leaves to reach the dirt. Even with modern technologies, archaeologists still confirmed human activity through soil disturbances, but a landslide would have overturned the layers. When he'd cleared a large square, he retrieved a trowel and began scraping.

A gunshot echoed. Bark blasted off a nearby tree, peppering his face. He dove, covering his head, and waited. The insect noises returned and then stopped again as footfalls crunched close.

"Get up," a male voice barked.

"Don't shoot me," said Christian, dropping the trowel and rolling over. The man, dressed in jeans and a camo coat, aimed his rifle at Christian's chest.

"What are you doing?"

"I, er…" said Christian, fumbling to come up with a story.

"Looting?"

"No. No. I'm an archaeologist. F-f-from Paris. The Louvre." Christian pointed to his pack.

"Bullshit. We see enough of your kind around here. Show me your bag." The man nodded for him to open it. Christian did and showed off its contents: a change of clothes, a toilet kit, and his Louvre employee ID.

The man compared its picture to Christian and then asked, "Why would an archaeologist from Paris be digging in this ravine?"

Christian decided the truth was best and said he'd come across a memoir describing the Junker workshop at the Struthof camp. He paused, assessing the man's reaction.

The man's face gave nothing away, but he lowered the rifle. "Go on."

Now Christian needed a plausible story, but eyeing the rifle, he kept a thread of truth in it. "I'm curating an exhibit on resistance fighters forced to work for German manufacturers. The memoir I found describes a workshop. Look, I have a map," he said, slowly reaching for his shirt pocket.

The man studied it and the surrounding landscape. "I've hunted in these woods since I could walk. There was never anything in this ravine."

"Is there anyone from that generation still alive? Or, perhaps, who left a memoir?"

"No. My grandparents are long gone. My dad says most folks never talked about the war and the camp. Wanted to forget it."

Christian had expected this. If his grandfather had searched this area for decades, he'd most likely interviewed the locals.

"What do you expect to find?" The man motioned with his head at the dirt square.

"Changes in the soil. It should show normal decay in the top layers and then be undisturbed beneath. It's a method we use to determine human activity. I wanted to find the extent of the camp and its outbuildings."

"This is my land. The Germans occupied it during my grandparents' time, but it was returned to my family. Well, all but the camp up there." The man pointed the rifle's barrel in that direction. "We don't want it. Bad memories."

This was good news to Christian as it meant not having to deal with getting permits to explore a state-owned site. Amateur archaeology was illegal in France, but on private land, he could stretch the truth. He was an archaeologist surveying to determine potential. He asked the man, "Would you mind if I explored the area? I'll let you know if I find anything valuable."

"Knock yourself out. My farm's at the bottom of this ravine." With that, the man turned and walked downhill.

Christian waited for the man to move out of sight before gathering his things and returning to where he was digging. He'd been itching to confirm something he'd seen when the bullet had smashed into the tree. Running the trowel's edge over the surface dirt, he isolated the objects—lighter bits of rock. He picked one up and used his phone's light to see it better.

There were bits of pink granite where there shouldn't be. *Sometimes, fortune goes your way*, he thought, bagging the fragment.

14

Paris

Christian went to lunch with Lionel the day after returning from Strasbourg He'd told his friend he had something important to talk about. After ordering, Lionel gave Christian a knowing grin and said, "I know that look. You're getting some. C'mon, spill."

Christian forced a smile and shook his head at his friend's lurid assumption. "It's a long story," he said.

Lionel shrugged and sipped his wine. "Where did you meet her?"

"It's not a woman," said Christian, and then he described the Geneva Freeport vault and his grandfather's revelation.

"No shit!"

"My thoughts exactly." Christian showed Lionel photos of the documents and then swiped to the letter. "Read this," he said as their lunch plates arrived.

A long minute later, Lionel sat up. "Raphael? This can't be real. How would your grandfather..." He trailed off, his eyes darting around like he was searching. "He—"

"Was a liar, Lionel. The son of a bitch was German. He was part of the machine that raped France." Christian's fist banged the table, rattling the utensils. Other diners looked up.

Lionel motioned for calm. "I'm sorry, Christian. Did your mother know?"

"No, only my grandmother, and she had her own secrets to bury. Christ, my family members are collaborators and Nazis. If anyone found out." The color drained from Christian's face.

"Relax. No one will find out. And even if they do, you're not running for election.

Christian sighed and took a bite of his cassoulet.

"So, what's in Strasbourg?" asked Lionel.

"Nothing. I followed the directions in my grandfather's notebook to a farm about sixty kilometers west." Christian shared details about the quarry and workshop. Then he added, "I was in the ravine, looking for it, when a guy took a shot at me."

"What?" Lionel's eyes bugged out.

"It was a warning shot. He seemed like a decent guy once we talked. Said it was his land and I could look around."

"Sure. Just ignore that he shot at your head."

Christian waved it off and told Lionel about finding the granite bits. "Here." He handed over the sample bag and described the contents as Lionel opened it. "I took the larger piece from the quarry. Pretty sure it's the same."

Daylight from their table-side window brought out the granules' pink tinge. Lionel studied them and said, "Looks like it, but you need to confirm."

"I'm taking them to our geology lab this afternoon," said Christian, reaching for the bag.

"But it's not convincing evidence of a landslide. I'm sure the quarry used dynamite to blow open the seam. Those pieces could have flown that distance."

"A kilometer?"

Lionel shrugged and bit into his sandwich. "You need more than this," he said through a mouthful.

"I know. I know. This is why I need the LiDAR."

"So, check out one unit at the school."

"They're reserved for months, and I have to list what I'm doing and where."

"Lie." Lionel licked his fingers and dried them on a napkin.

Christian admired his friend's direct approach, but then he considered the consequences. "I could, but INRAP's hardcore. If they figure out what I'm doing, I'm fired. Reputation ruined as well."

"True." Lionel nodded.

The *Institut National de Recherches Archéologiques Préventives* ruled with an iron fist. By law, everything in the soil was the property of the state. Unlike the UK and other European countries, France had no provisions for amateur archaeologists.

"You could buy a unit," Lionel said.

Christian snorted. "I looked. The cheapest high-quality unit is €30,000. And I need a drone."

Lionel smiled. "Sell the stuff in your vault."

"I can't. It's looted property. Someone will figure it out."

"There are ways."

"I'm not risking prison, Lionel."

"Let's say I know a guy who knows how to offload sensitive art."

Christian looked askance at his friend.

"What if it leads to you finding that Raphael?"

15

Île de la Cité

Darwin and Eyrún entered the *Crypte Archéologique* under Notre-Dame's forecourt as it closed for the day.

"*Bonjour*, Eyrún, how are you?" asked Aya, who met them at the ticket counter. They hadn't seen each other since their run-in with the catacombs police three years earlier. Darwin followed them down a short corridor as they exchanged news.

Aya badged into a staff-only area and led them to an office where a current map of Paris lay on a table beside prints of three older maps. She spread them out. "These came from the Carnavalet Museum, and this one is from the Louvre. Fortunately, the above ground in this part of the city has changed little in five hundred years. They paved the streets, but that only affects the surface layer."

"What about sewers?" asked Darwin.

"The construction may have destroyed some tunnels," said Aya. "Here's my theory—the medieval kings built a series of tunnels between their palaces and churches. The Hundred Years' War with England and ruling family divisions created a constant danger for kings. But you need some foundational history."

Aya pulled a simple map from a stack of papers. "This is a modern estimate of Paris in the ninth century. A wall built in Gallo-Roman times protected Île de la Cité, but the Seine was a navigable highway from Le Havre. For example, we know the Vikings laid siege in the eight hundreds.

"The Franks used Paris as a capital city, but it was mainly provincial until the Capetian dynasty. Between the tenth and fourteenth centuries, they developed Paris into the seat of royal administration, and it became a commercial and religious center.

"France has the richest farmland in Europe, and the Seine moved that food toward the Duchy of Normandy—"

"The Norman Conquest," said Darwin.

"Yes. That takeover set up centuries of fighting between England and France, which leads to my tunnel theory. The Crusades were the catalyst for massive fortifications. Philippe-August constructed a wall around the city's east bank in eleven-ninety and built the Louvre fort just outside to protect his kingdom from the Normans while he was away crusading.

"Over the next three hundred years, Paris experienced a massive build-out, including Notre-Dame and Sainte-Chapelle, that morphed the Louvre into a palace." Aya looked at each of them to confirm they'd followed her so far. Then she refocused on the maps.

"This is where the tunnels come in. I think Philippe-August dug an escape tunnel here." She pointed to the Louvre's main gate on a map from the twelve hundreds. "It went under the ditch and wall that enclosed the city."

"They built the Louvre outside the wall?" asked Eyrún.

"Yes. It was the main defensive fortification protecting the city from the Normans. Attacking armies would have to go through it. The surrounding wall also had a moat." Aya opened a modern map of Paris. "But as the city expanded and another outer wall was added, the Louvre became a palace."

Darwin knew this history from his school days, but he had daydreamed through much of it. Now, as a professional archaeologist, the complexity of Paris fascinated him. He studied the stratigraphy in the crypt exhibit. His ancestors had built the floor they stood on, constructing it on top of a Roman foundation, which had been built on a five-thousand-year-old Parisii settlement.

"Here's my theory," said Aya. "During the early Middle Ages, Saint-Germain l'Auxerrois was transformed into the Gothic cathedral we see today. Given the tunneling we discovered under Notre-Dame, I think it's plausible that a tunnel connects the Louvre to l'Auxerrois."

Darwin leaned over the map. "Let me guess," he said. "When the Capetian kings moved their palace to Île de la Cité and Louis the Ninth built Sainte-Chapelle, they extended the tunnel from l'Auxerrois to Notre-Dame."

"That's what I'm hoping," said Aya. "If we can confirm a tunnel to Sainte-Chapelle, then we have a proof point."

"Well, let's check it out," said Eyrún.

16

10th Arrondissement

Back at home that night, Christian's mind churned through the ethics of selling versus his personal ambitions. He paused on Lionel's comment. *How does he know people who can offload sensitive art? He's a restorer. He...* Christian had a sudden realization. Lionel liked expensive holidays. He'd looked up the resort from Lionel's last trip and found its cheapest rooms would eat up four months' salary. And then there were the escorts. Lionel always had photos of himself with gorgeous women.

Christian tried to rationalize it. His friend could be wealthy, or perhaps women found him appealing. But his thoughts kept returning to Lionel's boast about knowing a guy and his ambition.

He logged into a research database and entered "portrait of a young man." The screen filled with links. He clicked the first and read.

The painting by Raffaello Sanzio da Urbino was oil on a panel done in 1514. A confident, well-dressed man, perhaps in his thirties, stared from the canvas at the viewer. Scholars considered it a self-portrait.

The laptop screen showed a black-and-white photo of the painting, the only one ever taken, next to a colorized version. They'd added brown tones to the man's hair and sable coat, consistent with neoclassical works from the period.

The ruling Czartoryski family had gifted it to a museum in Kraków. In 1939, as the Nazis invaded Poland, curators removed it, along with a Rembrandt and a Da Vinci, and hid them in a house in Sieniawa. But the Gestapo discovered all three and gave them to the German-appointed governor, Hans Frank.

The artwork went to Berlin, destined for the Führer's museum at Linz, Austria. In January 1945, as Allies bombs rained on German cities, Hans Frank took the paintings back to Poland. But he fled within a month to avoid the advancing Soviets, taking as much of the artwork as he could to his villa south of Munich.

When the Allies arrested Frank in May 1945, they recovered many of the works he'd stolen, except for the Raphael. The sheer volume of looted art and the intervening Cold War complicated recovery. However, the Czartoryski family maintained that the *Portrait of a Young Man* was not missing but stolen.

Christian stretched and rubbed his lower back while pacing the small office. He shut the door and returned to his desk, where he removed his grandfather's notebook from his pack.

In March 1945, we arrived in Neuhaus after a harrowing journey. The train traveled only at night and parked in tunnels during the day. Allied bombers circled like vultures. We knew the war was over, and every man schemed to save himself. Two days out from Neuhaus, my colleague Heinrich suggested a plan. Steal some of the loot and hide it in a bunker near a deserted camp at Struthof.

The next day, we shifted the most valuable pieces into the train's last car as it sheltered in a tunnel outside Munich. That night, it would traverse the city and reach Tegernsee in the early morning. Before departure, Heinrich and I uncoupled it, and an hour later, Johann and Dieter arrived with two trucks. We loaded the treasures and headed toward Strasbourg.

We journeyed on back roads, but in the chaos, no one was stopping vehicles heading into the fight. We reached the camp on 13th March. The Germans had fled after transferring most prisoners elsewhere. We offloaded the cargo deep in the bunker behind the Junkers workshop, then split up. Regrettably, I went to Strasbourg where the Americans arrested me. Someone in Paris had put my name on the list of Germans involved in looting. I escaped harsh sentencing by giving evidence against Hans Frank and agreeing to repatriate stolen art. I never learned what became of Heinrich, Johann, and Dieter.

Christian laid the notebook on his desk. *It fits.* The painting's known history and his grandfather's testimonial made a contiguous provenance. He put a hand on the open pages. *If this is accurate, it's still in that bunker.*

He visualized the ravine near the Struthof camp. Its soil showed signs of disturbance, and the trees were consistent with eighty years of growth. He needed topographic maps from before 1940 to see where steep slopes could cover buildings. But that would only take him so far as the forest would obscure the ground.

Christian thought of recent discoveries in the Central American rainforests. Then he closed his eyes and sighed. *I need that drone LiDAR.*

Opening his eyes, he stared at his grandfather's notes and mentally crossed a line.

"I want this," he said aloud. Grabbing his phone, he messaged Lionel:

Contact your guy

17

Île de la Cité

Darwin and Eyrún put on polyamide jumpsuits against the cold, damp conditions. Black patches reinforced the arms, lower legs, and butts of the cardinal red fabric. As Eyrún pulled up her zipper, she glanced at Aya's royal purple suit with a black bat patch on its back. "Where did you get that?"

Aya smiled. "You like it?" She turned and touched a smaller, bat-shaped applique on her chest with "*La Chauve Souris*" stenciled on it. "The manufacturer did a custom job for a cataphile article it sponsored —no photos of my face. Can't risk my reputation."

"It's definitely you," said Darwin as he checked his redundant light sources.

"Let's go," said Aya, gathering her wavy black hair into a ponytail and pulling on her helmet.

Eyrún and Darwin followed her to a door marked "No Entry." Aya keyed in a code, held the door open, and followed them inside. A few steps in, she stopped them. "This section was full when I found it last year. I cleared it in my spare time. I had a lot of energy to burn from a failed relationship." She paused and swiped to a photo on her phone showing a solid block wall with two polished and stenciled stones nearer the ceiling. The smaller one listed "169," and the larger one "RUE DE LA CITE." "These blockage walls are all over the mines, most put in before the Revolution."

Eyrún ran her fingers over the Lutetian limestone. Its coarse blocks were darker than those used in the street-level buildings.

"The stone in here matches those in the crypt exhibits," said Aya. "They recycled it from earlier Roman structures."

They followed her through a wide, arched tunnel. Their strong LED headlamps turned the pale limestone a ghastly white, not the warm sunny glow that made Paris the city of light—more like Paris under a full moon.

"Does this follow any streets?" asked Eyrún.

"No. We dated the tunnel from soot left on the ceiling. It's about twelve-fifty, just after Sainte-Chapelle's completion and when Notre-Dame was largely done. The area outside the Palais de la Cité was gardens. The royals would have had to walk in the wide open to reach Notre-Dame. Assassinations were a common route to the throne, so all the more reason for a secret passage."

The tunnel ran straight for the length of a football field before another wall loomed. Aya stopped. "Here's where I need your help."

Darwin dropped the duffel he'd been carrying. Metal clanged from inside.

"Let's start with yours, Eyrún." Aya took her duffel and removed what looked like a toy truck but with a joystick handle and a color tablet. "Ground-penetrating radar," she said. It emitted a high-pitched squeak when she switched it on. Both Eyrún and Darwin were familiar with its use. Archaeology employed non-destructive methods to distinguish shapes invisible to the human eye. LiDAR recognized patterns in landscape or through dense growth, but GPR sent signals through the ground and mapped reflections from subsurface objects.

Aya held the scanner by its joystick and rolled it over the wall. "It's hollow," said Eyrún, looking at the tablet's image.

"As I thought," said Aya, "but I wanted to be sure. Now it's your turn, Darwin. I think these blocks might be best." She pointed at two fist-sized stones, filling a gap between the larger ones.

They put in earplugs as Darwin began chiseling the mortar. He pulled out the stones in less than five minutes, and Aya inserted a camera scope through the gap. They examined the video feed on her phone—a wide, dimly lit space opened on the wall's opposite side.

"Looks like steps," said Eyrún.

Darwin agreed, and Aya pulled the scope from the hole, saying, "Let's work an opening here. We can take turns."

"What about the blocks?" asked Darwin, grabbing a larger hammer and chisel.

"Pile them along the sides," said Aya.

They worked for the better part of an hour until, during Eyrún's turn with the hammer, they'd opened a large enough hole. "I need water," she said, wiping her sweaty brow.

Aya tested the blocks above the hole, and when they agreed they were solid enough, they went through to the chamber.

Fitted blocks marched up to stout oak beams in the ceiling. Darwin climbed two steps and knocked on the wood. "Solid. What do you think is up there?"

"I mapped the above-ground location of that wall to the sidewalk of the Boulevard du Palais, roughly adjacent to Sainte-Chapelle," said Aya, looking back at the hole in the wall. She paused as if calculating and added, "So, another six meters would put us under the chapel's apse."

"Maybe a tomb like Notre-Dame?" asked Eyrún.

"Perhaps. Let's drill a hole." Aya opened the duffel with the chisels and took out an arm-length drill bit. She fitted it to a drill and tested it.

"I'd say between these two beams," said Darwin. "Assuming they're square, it's about this deep." He spread his thumb and forefinger. He took the drill, worked it in about that distance, and pulled it out. Wood shaving spilled off the bit. He went in again. "Hit something." He backed the bit out.

Aya shined a handheld light on its tip. "Stone." She rubbed some of the material between her fingers. "Marble?"

Eyrún climbed up next to them and felt the dust. "Probably not. It's too yellow. I'll guess it's a better-quality limestone. Do you have another bit?"

Aya got a diamond-tipped bit from the bag, and they took turns drilling until Darwin broke through. "Lights out," he said as he lowered the drill.

"It's dark," said Aya, looking up the hole. "I'll get the camera." A moment later, she returned and snaked the camera through it while Eyrún held the phone. The black screen captured a faint light as Aya said, "It's through."

"Can't tell what's up there," said Eyrún. "But that light. Wait. Move back."

Aya worked the cable until a green glow centered on the screen. "It's not focused very well," she said and added, "Is it letters?"

"Sortie?" asked Darwin.

"Yes. That's it. An exit sign."

"I agree," Eyrún added. "But what are the faint lines?" She pointed to curves on the screen.

"Dunno," said Darwin. "Can we risk some light?"

Aya shrugged and tapped the phone screen. It flashed white and then resolved into focus as the low-light camera adjusted.

"Oh, my God!" said Eyrún. "It's beautiful."

"*Mon Dieu* is right," Aya squealed in delight. "It's—"

"Sainte-Chapelle's lower chapel," said Darwin.

They stared in wonder at the gold-leafed arches holding up the vaulted ceiling.

18

3rd Arrondissement

Two days later, after his lectures at École du Louvre, Darwin went to the Musée Carnavalet in Le Marais district to study construction records. He showed his credentials to a docent, who led him to the basement storage.

He'd not been in the museum since its 2021 renovation, and he paused at a Neolithic pirogue, a five-thousand-year-old dugout found during a dig in the 1990s. That reminded him of a more recent find in the fifteenth arrondissement: a hunter-gatherer settlement from the Mesolithic period. *Walking in our ancestor's footsteps,* he thought as the docent let him into the research room.

Darwin thanked her and found his way to the section with maps and drawings from the twelfth and thirteenth centuries. He didn't expect to find anything explicitly referring to tunnels, but he could infer where an underground space could and could not exist. In particular, deep foundations, defensive ditches, and moats would suggest where a tunnel would have to go deeper.

Yesterday, they'd visited Sainte-Chapelle to locate the hole they'd drilled through its floor. No one had been at that end of the lower chapel, and they'd kicked away the tiny chips the drill bit had pushed out. Darwin had covered it with the base of an electric fan used for ventilating. He, Eyrún, and Aya had debated where another passage would enter from the Louvre's direction but had found nothing.

So far, the biggest challenge was the time gaps. He focused on the likeliest points of entry: a crypt in Saint-Germain l'Auxerrois and Sainte-Chapelle. Working from the descriptions and other drawings, he sketched in Philipp Auguste's original 1190 wall, the locations of the gates and drawbridges, and the long-lost Rue d'Autriche. Massive renovations had turned the military keep into a palace, beginning with Louis IX in 1230.

Then, in the thirteen hundreds, Charles had created another wall around Paris, enclosing the Louvre. As the former keep became a royal palace, it ran out of space. In the fifteen hundreds, the Bourbon family built Hôtel du Petit-Bourbon next to Saint-Germain l'Auxerrois to entertain courtiers.

Darwin figured a tunnel to the cathedral was plausible, but it would have to descend ten meters below the basement level to clear the moats. He'd just started a list of questions when his phone chimed with a message.

Minh: You need to see this

He included a photo of a "Rare Antique French Clock." Darwin tapped the link to an auction page that described a tabletop clock created by Balthazar Martinot, valet de chambre to Louis XIV. The exquisite piece displayed the time on a rotating ormolu globe supported by two cherubs sitting on a bleu turquin marble base. The page listed the minimum bid as €23,000, along with a contact email.

Darwin: Beautiful

Minh: It disappeared from the Louvre in WW2

5th Arrondissement

An hour later, Darwin sat with Minh at a coffee bar near the Cardinal Lemoine Metro stop. He looked around. The only other customer sat three tables away and wore headphones as she typed on a laptop. "How did you find this?" he asked, nodding toward the auction site on his phone.

"I use an algorithm that searches underground auction sites and compares it to several databases of missing art."

"Won't others find it?"

"The site took down the auction after just three hours," Minh said.

"Meaning it sold?"

"Probably."

Darwin ran a hand through his hair and sipped his coffee. "Would they have other pieces? I mean, other pieces also stolen during the war?"

"They might, but these people usually wait months or years between selling pieces. It's a long game for them. They probably only answered emails from known collectors."

Darwin considered this. He and Eyrún had dealt with the antiquities black market at the ACA. They'd shut down an unscrupulous dealer and his network, including a notorious forger. The dealer was dead, his daughter was in an Italian prison, and the forger had disappeared back into the wind.

"What are you thinking?" asked Minh.

Darwin explained how they'd stopped insider thefts in the Vatican Museums. "I've always thought the cartel had other connections. Some of the people's confessions seemed too convenient. And the sentences were light."

"Art crime isn't murder," said Minh. "It's white collar—unfenced prisons and early parole. No one is harmed."

"That's bullshit." Darwin banged his cup on the table, and the barista looked up. He apologized and said in a lower voice, "Plenty of people are hurt. The past belongs to all of us, not just billionaires who bury our history in their private galleries."

"You don't have to convince me." Minh smiled, turning his palms up in surrender.

Darwin gulped down his remaining coffee. "What if you email the seller? Tell them you want the clock. If it's sold, tell them you're interested in similar pieces."

"Why me? You could do it."

"They'd ghost me. You said it yourself. They only respond to known collectors. I'll put up the money for purchase. We need this to prove the objects came from the Louvre."

Minh agreed, but he said his name had to stay out of any investigation.

19

Struthof Camp

Christian parked his rented caravan away from the farm's barn and workshop, where he had a clear view of the ravine leading up to the Struthof camp. The farmer had allowed him to stay but told him to share anything he found on his land. With the day growing late, he opted to open a bottle of wine after setting up camp.

Propping his feet on a small table, he leaned back and sipped from his glass. He savored the scent of mown hay. Long shadows stretched from the bales as the day's warmth faded. He drank again, sighed, and soon felt more at ease than he had in weeks.

They'd found a buyer almost immediately after posting the clock. The sale had netted €27,000, and Christian sensed it could have brought more in a public auction. He gave Lionel €5,000 as thanks for handling the transaction, but he also wondered how his friend seemed so adept at it.

Over the following week, he kept looking over his shoulder, expecting the authorities at any moment. Once, while he was learning to fly the new drone, a police officer approached. She stopped and talked on her radio for several minutes. He'd crashed the drone twice while paying too much attention to her. Finally, she walked over to say they'd gotten a complaint about the noise and for him to go somewhere else.

Lionel kept telling him to relax. "These kinds of auctions happen all the time. Nobody's looking for you."

That night, after dinner, he stepped outside the caravan. Lights glowed from the farmhouse in an otherwise black landscape. The sky glittered with stars, not quite as intensely as he'd seen on remote digs, but orders of magnitude greater than Paris. Their glow highlighted the forest canopy's dark outline.

A branch snapped. Insect chatter stopped. The bushes on his left rustled. Christian's heart thudded as he whipped around, remembering the farmer's warning about wild boars. He moved toward the caravan. Something shot out of the brush. He ran, slamming the door behind him.

He switched off the light and peered out the window above the tiny kitchen sink. Then he snorted, and his shoulders sank at the sight of a bobcat and two kittens.

The next morning, a heavy mist lay in the valley. The drone's LiDAR could see through cloud cover, but Christian needed to see the drone, especially if he lost control. He used the time to plot a grid on a topological map of the hill. Working from where he found the pink granite bits, he mapped a hundred-meter square in each direction.

He determined the GPS coordinates of the farthest corner and plotted the ten passes needed to cover the area. The drone's cellular chip would transmit the LiDAR data to a cloud server. He could get a real-time feed, but it would be difficult to assess and pilot the drone.

By late morning, the mist cleared, and he set out for the ravine. Far across the valley, a dust cloud rose from the farmer's hay baler. When Christian reached the road above the camp, sweat poured from his face. The day was turning hot. He found a shade tree where he could stay cool and also see the tablet screen better in the bright daylight.

Five minutes later, he hovered the drone over the spot where he'd found the granite chips. Then he flew it to the grid's starting point. Once there, he tapped "record" to send scan data to the cloud. The breeze and thermal currents from the warming forest buffeted the drone as Christian concentrated on keeping it level and on course.

He could just see it out about a half-kilometer downslope, its white body and rotors shrouded by the haze. Ten minutes later, it began its ascent on the third path. Christian's arms ached from holding the controller. This was harder than he thought. He forced himself to ignore a pebble under his ass. *Keep going.* His inner thighs began cramping from balancing the iPad as the drone moved downhill on the fourth pass.

Halfway up the fifth pass, the tablet sounded a warning, and a red circle showed five minutes of battery. *Shit!* He maneuvered the drone back towards him as the circle began a countdown to zero. He calculated he could finish the pass and safely landed it in the dirt next to him.

He stood and shook his numb hands. Then he looked at the drone. Its specs showed it could fly for forty-six minutes. Christian had thought he could fly the test grid in a half-hour, but he'd had to run at a higher power to counter the turbulence. It would take two hours to recharge. He looked downhill at the caravan and calculated—fifteen minutes down, recharge, thirty minutes back up.

He was ready to hike when a dark blue Renault pulled up. The passenger door with "GENDARMERIE" stenciled on it opened, and an officer stepped out. The driver joined him and said, "You can't fly that here."

20

École du Louvre

Darwin looked up at a knock. "Come in."

An interoffice courier entered the room and handed him an envelope. "I need a signature," she said, adding, "Thanks," when he returned it.

Darwin broke the seal. He'd requested two books on the restitution efforts after the war. This was not that. He slid out a folio. Someone had crossed out a "TOP SECRET" stamp and added another, declaring the contents "DECLASSIFIED" on 11 April 1984.

He peered into the envelope, looking for a note explaining the contents or who sent it. Nothing. He opened the folio and removed a copied SDECE form dated 12 October 1947. A quick search told him the *Service de documentation extérieure et de contre-espionnage* was the intelligence organization created in the war's closing years.

Merde. He shook his head at Fleur's attempt to lure him.

The form summarized an attached report, handwritten in English, by a US Army captain who worked in the Monuments, Fine Arts, and Archives Section Unit. He claimed a German official stole from the Nazis, who, themselves, had looted Paris.

"ALLÉGATIONS NON FONDÉES" was typed at the bottom, above the signature of the Louvre director. Darwin wrinkled his forehead. *If it's unfounded, why send it?*

He turned his attention to the monument's main report. Despite his English fluency, it took a few moments to adjust to the cursive writing.

The French authorities in Le Louvre are overlooking a severe breach. I have submitted four reports about a German insider stealing looted art for his purposes.

Karl Meyer, a mid-level functionary in the ERR, has been working with the MFAA to recover artworks looted by the Nazi regime. While cooperating with us, I have seen him destroy at least two documents. I raised this matter with the Louvre's assistant director, but he dismissed it.

I traced Karl's history. He taught at Staatliche Kunstschule in Berlin. The Nazis sent him to Paris in 1940 to catalog the art for removal. Rose Valland remembers him but said he was always in the background. She thinks they assigned him to remove private Jewish collections.

I went through his work. Gaps and claims of "lost in transport" are inconsistent with other curators' activities. I have documents and research to support my assertions.

After my last report in January 1947, I was told Karl Meyer had returned to Berlin and no longer a concern.
But something is not correct. I saw him at a cafe in Le Marais last week. When I approached him, he said his name was Dieter von Stein, and I was mistaken.

I urge you to investigate before too much time passes and people forget the details.

James Wilkerson

Captain, US Army MFAA

A magazine article from 1997 lay beneath the letter and SDECE form. Authorities had arrested a Louvre janitor in 1962 for smuggling pieces from the museum's underground storage and selling them at auction. A museum curator at an auction recognized an Egyptian necklace as a piece she'd unearthed in Armana, Egypt, in 1937.

The thief served his full fifteen-year sentence despite being offered reduced charges if he named the others involved. The prosecutor claimed the janitor could not have accessed the pieces without insider help. Years later, before dying, the thief confessed in an interview that "Le Louvre's curators have no idea what's in their storage areas. I was just a courier."

Last in the stack was a BBC article on massive corruption at the British Museum. After over two thousand treasures went missing, the museum sacked the director and security head.

Darwin had been in the British Museum's deep basement storage area where millions of items lay in drawers and boxes—much of it haphazardly cataloged. He recalled how easy it had been to swap a fake Egyptian stele for the real one.

He set down the BBC article, examined the SDECE report again, and then Googled James Wilkerson. Seventh on the list was a professor emeritus of art history at the University of Washington who served with the Monuments Men. The Seattle Art Museum honored his legacy by naming a new wing after him—the James Wilkerson Pavillon—where the museum also housed his extensive writings on art history, recovery, and restitution.

Darwin reread the former captain's letter, pausing on:

I have documents and research to support my assertions.

"Huh," he said, laying down the letter. He'd studied wartime looting and restoration in an art history elective course. The Germans had applied an industrial process to removing works they considered most valuable from the countries they invaded. They'd had experts cataloging art in the 1930s to prepare for their cultural appropriation.

Darwin's curiosity barometer blossomed.

Is it possible some underground network still exists?

He thought of Minh.

Could there be a connection between these new thefts?

Then, another thought trotted out: *Correlation does not imply causation.*

But one theme kept repeating:

No individual could pull off systematic theft.

His phone and watch both buzzed, ending his speculation. It was time to head to the airport for his flight to Rome. He replaced the documents in the envelope and stuffed them in his laptop case. The OCBC request had piqued his curiosity, but his other role in Vatican City also needed his attention.

21

The Farm below Struthof Camp

Christian studied a topographical map in the caravan while the drone charged. He'd also brought a ground-penetrating radar unit, but he calculated scanning over a hundred hectares on steep slopes would take weeks. "Shit," he said, massaging his face. He stretched his arms wide, popping a few vertebrae in the process and releasing the tension from gripping the drone's remote.

Feeling more energized, he went outside, where a lazy warmth had settled in the valley. The smell of sweet grass filled the air as a column of insects danced in the sun. He sensed the pace of life here differed little from day to day, except in the seasonal changeovers—spring planting and autumn harvesting. A far-off chainsaw broke the tranquility saw, and he refocused on his purpose.

The Struthof camp was to his right, elevated three hundred meters from his location. About thirty degrees left, a mountain peaked at a thousand meters. The ravine lay in between. He visualized the gap and decided the slope on the Struthof side was too steep for a structure. *It would be up there*. He studied the shallower slope up to the peak. *Wait!*

A thought struck. He ran back inside the caravan, looked at the topo map, and then brought up Google Maps on his iPad.

He aligned the map's orientations and zoomed out. *I thought so.* Struthof was on a line about twenty kilometers south of the direct flight path from London to Stuttgart. *What if the bombers flew an indirect route over France for safety reasons?*

He knew the Germans had occupied France, but had they retreated from this part *in early 1945?* He wasn't sure, but then he wondered, *Why would they drop the bombs here?* They wouldn't bomb a prison camp holding their allies. That made no sense.

He set aside the questions and considered the flight pattern. On a whim, he dashed outside and set up the drone. It had reached a ninety percent charge. *Good enough.* It took off, flying over the farmer's house and across the fields at the base of the slope.

No breeze meant it could hold a straight course. He flew a pattern over the field and watched the real-time data on his iPad. The LiDAR showed the dirt track near the field's edge and then two dark circles almost touching each other. His heart leaped as he flew the drone over the spot. *That's it.* He'd seen enough LiDAR images to recognize a soil disturbance.

He looked up, scanning the far tree line until he could make out the drone's hovering shape. *Got it.* He glanced back at the iPad and moved the drone toward the slope. Three more circles appeared under the adjacent trees just over the track. These showed depressions with raised rings. If he'd guessed right, the farmer's family had filled in the craters in their field.

Christian flew the drone back to the caravan, plugged it in the charger, and then gathered his pack. If the bombs continued in a straight line, his work with the GPR would become much more manageable—or, at least, more focused.

As he passed the farmhouse, he poked his head into the workshop. The farmer was welding a piece of equipment.

"*Bonjour*. Got a minute?" Christian asked when the farmer turned off the flame.

"Sure. Did you find anything yet?"

Christian explained that the police had disallowed the drone flights.

"Pfft." The farmer rolled his eyes. "Goddamned flics. Should spend their time on the corrupt corporations driving me out of business."

Christian let that pass. "Did your family, maybe grandparents, ever mention bombs hitting the hillside?"

"*Oui*. My grand-père said a load of bombs got dumped on the camp near the war's end. But the Germans had abandoned it two months prior."

"Did any hit your property?"

"Some. Grand-père filled them in."

Christian showed him the LiDAR results and said he was going to explore the forest opposite the field. The farmer sparked the welding torch and turned back to his work.

A quarter-hour later, Christian found the first of the depressions thirty meters into the tree cover. If he hadn't been looking for a crater shape, he would have missed it. Decades of leaves and brush filled the meter-deep bowl. He located the other two and looked back at the farm. The five craters might form a line, but they could have been from two planes flying in formation.

Christian turned around. The steep slope and leaves, mid-calf deep in places, would make for arduous hiking. He studied the iPad map. Another track began at the farm and went across the face of the hill a hundred meters higher. He backtracked and found the road as the field narrowed, and then he followed the track upwards to the right.

A few hundred meters in, the road looked like no one had driven on it for a long time. A densely wooded section brought a welcome coolness. Waist-high weeds swished around him, and the only other sound was gravel crunching underfoot. While following the road as it rounded to the southwest, Christian stubbed his toe on a rock.

He cursed and then stopped dead in his tracks. The road dead-ended ten meters ahead. His pulse quickened as he picked his way across the soil that had buried the road. The undergrowth scratched his arms, and his boots slid on the steep slope.

There!

The track emerged on the other side of the collapsed hillside. He looked back. The two tracks were level, separated by the massive slide.

I found it. Grand-père was right.

Once again, he imagined the accolades he would receive for finding the lost Raphael, but his elation faded as he stared at the massive landslide between him and the other end. He'd need heavy equipment to move that much soil.

22

Roissy

Darwin sat in the co-pilot's chair beside Eyrún in their Avanti EVO as she dialed in the flight plan from Le Bourget to Rome's Ciampino Airfield. She'd bought the plane a year ago to reduce the transfer times from Ajaccio to her family home in Reykjavík. While they loved living in Corsica, commercial flying meant two or three hops to get anywhere.

She'd fallen in love with the Avanti the first time she'd gotten it airborne. Its reverse-mounted engines, whale tail, and nose winglet made it faster than similar-sized jets. She liked its sophisticated auto-piloting capabilities but relished flying it manually. Its deft touch, akin to her racing cars, combined with its fuel efficiency, had made the purchase decision effortless.

Darwin liked the visibility from the wraparound cockpit and its spacious cabin. He had no interest in becoming a pilot but had completed training to assist in case of emergencies. As he read out the preflight checklist from the iPad, she responded, "Check," to each item.

A minute later, his job complete, he became a passenger, and Eyrún spooled up the engines and began a dialogue with air traffic control. Within five minutes, they'd lined up for takeoff, and she pushed the throttles. The thousand-horsepower turboprops pressed them into their seatbacks as the Avanti gained speed.

"V1," the automated cockpit voice called, followed seconds later by, "Rotate." Eyrún pulled back on the yoke, lifting the craft's nose off the runway, and in a moment, they were airborne.

"Gear up," she said.

Darwin flipped the switch, responding, "Gear up." He looked out his window as they banked in the normal climb-out pattern. Paris shrank, and sunlight glinted off the Seine.

They reached cruising altitude in ten minutes, and Eyrún engaged the autopilot. She checked the course settings and set a timer on her watch for a turn toward Rome. "Now's a good time to talk about what the OCBC wants," she said, studying the thick clouds blanketing the Alps.

"Sure," said Darwin, and then he summarized his initial meeting in Vivienne's office at the École du Louvre and the research that had led him to Minh.

"Do you trust them?"

"Not sure. I like Vivienne, but she's in a political role. Fleur and the finance minister, Lucien? No, I don't trust them. I mean, why do they need me to do their dirty work?" Darwin paused, watching Lake Geneva come into view.

"And Minh?"

"No reason not to, but I hardly know him."

"He was quick to find that clandestine auction," Eyrún said in a tone that conveyed suspicion. She focused on air traffic chatter as the Avanti's twelve-thousand-meter flight ceiling meant they were flying in busy commercial aviation corridors. Then she added, "Who do you think sent the letter from the American Monuments guy?"

"Had to be Fleur," said Darwin. "But she doesn't need me to pursue it."

"Maybe she does. If people are deeply embedded, she can't investigate without tipping them off."

They sat in silence for a while. At this altitude, the vast blue sky turned a deeper shade. The fuselage hummed from the powerful Pratt and Whitney turboprops, pushing them toward Rome. Their plane was like their mountain house, a place where they could escape their busy lives.

Their plan called for dropping off Darwin in Rome and Eyrún continuing across the Tyrrhenian Sea to Corsica, where she had a meeting at the ACA headquarters. She studied her husband's profile as he looked at Mont Blanc. His dark brown hair flopped over his forehead, covering his green eyes, but she knew his brooding meant Fleur's request had piqued his curiosity.

Nicknamed the Great Finder, Darwin was driven by discovery. The trick was getting him to choose. He didn't like to be told what to do, but once he decided, he was like a Labrador retriever on a squeak toy.

Antiquities theft also annoyed her. She'd almost lost everything at the ACA and still seethed about it. So, she planted a seed. "You could go to Seattle, see if there's anything in the American's memoirs."

Darwin started out the windscreen a little longer before answering, "Dunno."

"Well, talk to Richard. He's always a good sounding board."

"Maybe. We're going to lunch today."

"Tell him I said hi."

Italian air traffic control squawked over their headsets, and she focused on their approach.

After landing in Rome, Darwin disembarked at the terminal. He waved, and she blew him a kiss from the cockpit and then taxied back to the runway. Darwin would join her in Corsica in two days, and she was looking forward to a relaxing weekend together.

23

Vatican City

Darwin's ride share entered Vatican City through Saint Anne's Gate and dropped him off at the Belvedere Palace. The imposing Renaissance structure wrapped around a beautiful courtyard and a car park. Unfortunately, his office in the Apostolic Archive did not overlook the manicured gardens.

After meeting with his assistant, Charles, he went to his office to read the reports prepared by his team. In an hour, he'd sit through the monthly review where they cleared documents for release into the public archive. Most involved clarifying historical context written by long-dead people. Embarrassing secrets from past centuries rarely mattered in the modern world.

Two cups of coffee later, he felt alert enough for the mind-numbing debates that would ensue. While the documents were of minor historical value, differing department heads would circle, throwing their weight around like sumo wrestlers. An hour into the meeting, Darwin's stomach growled as he thought of lunch.

He'd been looking forward to discussing the OCBC problem with

Richard Ndembele, chief of staff to a cardinal and Darwin's liaison to the pope. It had been several months since they'd caught up. They'd developed a close friendship since the first meeting when Darwin broke into Richard's cathedral in Clermont-Ferrand.

Finally, the staff meeting ended, and Darwin trotted down the stairs to the gardens behind the palace. Richard was early for a change, standing at their preferred meeting place behind Saint Peter's Basilica.

"How are you, my friend?" His substantial cassock billowed as he bear-hugged Darwin.

"Good. And you?"

"Fine. Fine."

"And Eyrún, how is she?"

"She's wonderful and says hi."

"I love that woman. She's the best thing that ever happened to you." Richard laughed and wrapped an arm around Darwin's shoulder as they walked.

Darwin beamed and fell into step, crushed by the larger man's grip. He felt at ease in his friend's presence as if defended from the world's troubles. They caught up on the news while walking to their favorite restaurant, blocks from the basilica. Once they'd ordered lunch, Darwin laid out Fleur's request.

"Hmmm." Richard considered Darwin's current problem as he forked a piece of coppa from the antipasti plate. After a moment, he asked, "What are you afraid of?"

Darwin paused eating and dabbed his mouth. "I'm not afraid of anything. It's just…" He looked out the restaurant's front window. A knot of tourists studied their phones as one of them gestured towards the basilica. Darwin blinked. In the past few months, he'd thought a lot about his near-death experience in Siberia.

A month-long trip to San Francisco and a Yosemite road trip had helped heal the lingering horror—deliberate infection with the black death plague. And the offer to teach at the École du Louvre had diverted his attention.

He turned back to Richard. "I…"

Eyrún's labored breathing burst into his memory, ICU alarms shrieking as she passed out. *Putain*! He shook off the vision.

"Eyrún again?" asked Richard.

Darwin nodded.

"Look at me." Richard's low voice rumbled.

Darwin did, blinking to clear his eyes.

"The trauma is still fresh. Give it time to pass. Your relationship with Eyrún is strong. Talk with her."

"We do."

"Good. And consider your traditional faith. There are greater depths to draw upon."

Darwin held Richard's gaze, recalling his friend's stories from the Soweto slums, where violence had consumed him. Only Richard's discovery of a wider purpose had turned him from self-destruction.

"I know," said Darwin. "I'm just…dunno…"

"Perhaps you also need a fresh perspective."

"Sure. That's why I'm asking."

"Your mission at the ACA and your role here at the Vatican are after the same goal, no?"

"More or less."

"It sounds like the request to look around the Louvre is similar. I know you. You're curious. You get restless without a challenge. By the semester break, you'll be bored."

Darwin shrugged.

"Your job here is on autopilot unless your department finds something controversial," Richard said. "Step back from the responsibility. Poke around the Louvre. Lord knows what mysteries you can find in its basements." He took a bite of his lunch.

Darwin hadn't mentioned looking for the tunnels that connected the royal palaces. He shoveled in three bites before answering through a mouthful, "Maybe you're right."

"Of course I'm right. It's only a year. Take Eyrún's beautiful hand and run wild in Paris. If only I were a young man again…" Richard beamed.

"And not a priest."

"Yes. Well, you get my point."

They finished lunch, paid the bill, and returned to Vatican City. Darwin felt lighter on the return journey, grateful for his friend's insight and company. A warm afternoon settled in, and as they reached the steps to the Belvedere Palace, Richard stopped him.

"You might not like what's coming. You know His Holiness and your president have been collaborating."

Darwin winced and then groaned. "I should have known."

24

Paris

After a weekend in Struthof, Christian showed Lionel pictures of the progress being made in removing the landslide above the farm.

"Won't this arouse suspicion?" asked Lionel before taking a bite of his lunch.

"Not likely. The area has a lot of trees, and people at the camp are focused on tourism. If anyone asks, the farmer will say he's clearing a road on his land."

"What about the farmer? Do you trust him?"

"Enough. I'm paying more than his farm is earning and told him he'll get a cut of the finder's fees, which brings me to money. I need to sell the paintings."

Lionel sucked in through his teeth and glanced furtively at the other diners. "Remember what I told you. Too much too quickly can alert the authorities. We're not the only ones on the dark web."

"I know, but the job's bigger than I thought. It's only the farmer and a rented skip loader. He's telling me it'll take at least three weeks to clear the road, let alone dig out a bunker."

"How much do you need?"

Christian opened a document with line items and costs. His plan called for hand excavation once they found the factory building. "I'll need to take leave to do the work. I don't trust anyone, including the farmer if I'm not there."

Lionel wiped crumbs from his mouth while swiping the list with his other hand. "Okay." He looked up. "But let me handle this sale. You've used your ID enough. They're probably already watching you."

Blood drained from Christian's face. "But I thought you said—"

"You're fine. We used VPNs and encrypted browsers. At best, anyone tracking you would only trace it to the internet cafe we sat in. Don't worry about it."

"Fine," said Christian, regaining his composure. "You handle the details. Just let me know when the money comes in."

When they'd finished their lunch, Lionel told Christian to head back without him. "I need a few minutes to post the sale."

Christian put €15 on the table to cover lunch.

Lionel watched him cross the street, then sent a message:

He agreed.

A minute later came a reply

Good.

25

Vatican Apostolic Archives

Instead of departing as usual, Richard continued with Darwin, and they swung by the staff kitchen in the Belevedere building to get espresso. Darwin said he needed the bump to face what was coming, which turned out to be Max Keller, head of Vatican security, waiting in Darwin's office. After greetings, Max handed Darwin a large envelope with French diplomatic seals and an "eyes only" security label.

"What's in it?" Darwin asked.

"I don't know," said Max, "but the woman who delivered it is a known DGSE courier."

Darwin's face screwed up at the mention of the French equivalent of British MI6. He took the envelope with the enthusiasm of being handed a used tissue.

He was about to open it when Richard interrupted. "It's probably best to read that when you are alone."

Darwin laid the envelope on the desk. "What's going on?"

Max excused himself, saying he'd no idea and had completed his role as courier.

Richard waited for the office door to close. "Do you remember the pope's meeting with your president during his trip to Marseilles last month?"

Darwin nodded.

"Art and antiquities repatriation was on their agenda. I heard the topic expanded to include the restitution of wartime looting. During a meeting with Cardinal Santos last week, His Holiness asked me if you'd made a decision about working with the OCBC. I honestly had no idea the French government had asked for your help."

Merde. Darwin took a long, deep breath and then let it out while massaging his forehead.

"I'm sorry, Darwin. I know you hate this kind of manipulation."

"What's in there?" Darwin nodded at the envelope.

"I don't know, but His Holiness asked me to deliver this and read it prior to opening the envelope." Richard reached beneath his cassock and handed Darwin a white envelope embossed with the cross-key seal of the Holy See.

Darwin snorted as he took it. After breaking the seal, he withdrew a folded note. The thick white paper was longer than the previous ones he'd received from the pope. Dense cursive from a fountain pen filled the page.

Greetings Darwin,

I trust you are well and that you and Eyrún have found peace after the trauma of your last ordeal.

My museums have a problem that requires your exceptional skills. We fear that the art and antiquities looting ring, which you broke up, has resumed and is now woven into the fabric of the global museums that display cultural treasures.

Your president raised the topic of protecting our heritage during our last meeting. In particular, works looted during the Second World War are appearing on the market again. Most disturbing are rumors that some of our most trusted institutions are complicit in covering up restitution.

Please look into this. We agree you are well-positioned to investigate our suspicions. We must expunge this stain on our history. None of us can ignore it, including you. I hope the truth will lay to rest the questions your family has carried for decades.

Report, as usual, through Richard. And be careful. Unfortunately, I cannot tell you who to trust.

Yours in Christ,

Darwin laid the note on the desk.

"It's a long one this time," said Richard. Darwin pushed the paper across, and the big man read it. He looked up when finished. "Questions your family has carried for decades? What's that about?"

"Dunno," said Darwin.

"Maybe that's what the courier pack is about. I have a meeting in twenty minutes. I'll call you later."

"Sure," said Darwin. They hugged, and Richard left.

Darwin retook his seat behind the desk, rolled his head back, and stared at the ceiling. He'd lied to Richard just now. He knew the long unanswered questions. In 1940, just before Germany invaded France, his great-grandparents had fled Paris with his toddler grandfather. Beyond that, he knew few details. His grandfather, Emelio, always diverted queries.

Darwin had learned that, after arriving in Corsica, Emelio and his mother had spent months hiding in the mountain house's secret room. Emelio had said his mother's family was Jewish and that none who stayed in France survived the war.

Darwin had always been curious, but wanting to know and having the answers at your literal fingertips were not the same. He sat up.

Let's get this over with.

He opened the pack and withdrew a letter bearing the Great Seal of

France and a folio stamped "*ENFERME*" in red ink. Its yellowed typewritten label read:

Soutine Family
13 February 1951

The letter came from the president.

Dear Mr. Darwin Lacroix,

I hope you and Eyrún are well and enjoying all Paris offers. When you settle in, my wife and I wish to host you for dinner. Please get in touch with my assistant to schedule an evening.
My ministers tell me you are reluctant to investigate the misappropriations at the Louvre. I understand your misgivings, but I appreciate your unique talent for uncovering long-buried secrets.

The task is challenging. But when I met with the pope last month, we agreed you are the best person to investigate. France's war legacy haunts too many of us.
The enclosed folio documents your maternal grandmother's family during the war. Your grandfather declined the file. Having met him, I know he is a proud man. Not everyone wants to confront the ugliness that happened during that horrific period.

The French state has two paintings that belong to your family. Authorities recovered them after the war, but they remain unclaimed. One hangs in the Clermont-Ferrand Museum, and the other in Périgueux. We have informed the directors should you wish to take them.

You have my sincerest sympathy and apology for the violations committed by France and its people. I hope that exposing the transgressions will promote restitution and forgiveness.

Kindest regards,

Darwin pictured his grandfather, fiercely proud of his Corsican heritage. He would carry on for hours about his ancestors: ship captains, pirates, and freedom fighters. But Darwin had never understood his grandfather's reluctance to talk about his mother's family. Darwin had only learned what his grandmother had shared, but it appeared she knew little.

His heart leaped and then raced as questions piled up. *How did the paintings end up in museums? Why didn't Grand-père want them back?*

He envisioned the pictures he'd seen of wartime France and breathed deeply. *Everything's fine. It's all in the past. You'll be okay.*

He broke the folio's seal.

A half-hour later, tears streamed down Darwin's cheeks. Pages with twenty-three photographs lay across the desk. He'd studied the war in school, but seeing your own family's faces as victims was a gut punch.

His phone rang, showing Eyrún's caller ID. He accepted it and croaked, "Hi."

"What's wrong, Love?"

"I just..." He swallowed hard and gathered himself to explain the folio's contents.

"Oh, my God. I'm so sorry. This is what Emelio never told you?"

"He never knew. Never wanted to know."

"Are you okay?"

Darwin sniffed and reached for a tissue. "Yeah." He wiped his nose. "Yeah. I'm good. You called in the middle of it. That's all."

"The Nazis did horrible things."

"It wasn't them," he said, his voice hollow.

"What do you mean?"

"It wasn't the Germans." He settled a lump in his throat before continuing. "My great-grand-mère's family, the Soutines, owned a prosperous art gallery. The German invasion allowed the anti-Semitic fervor to overrun Paris. Neighbors, jealous of their success, betrayed them to the Vichy government."

Eyrún gasped.

"It's worse," he continued. "The authorities arrested them and revoked their citizenship. The government confiscated their property and deported..."

He sniffed, trying to hold back the tears that had returned, but then he exploded.

"*Putain!* They sent my family to death camps. The French murdered their own people!"

26

Bocagnano, Corsica

Darwin flew to Corsica earlier than planned and spent a quiet evening with Eyrún at their mountain house. She cleared her calendar, and they slept late the next morning. Darwin brewed a triple-shot cappuccino and drank it on the patio overlooking the gorge. The vast open space and silence helped him process the folio's revelations. Far below, autumn's colors had infiltrated the deciduous trees mixed in with the maquis, but at this elevation, pines dominated.

"Morning, Love," said Eyrún. Fresh from the shower and her hair in a towel, she padded barefoot across the flagstones and sat.

"Good morning. Did you sleep well?"

"Yes. I always do up here. You?" she asked, sipping from a teacup, her favorite French blue from a Paris shop.

"Surprisingly well, considering."

After breakfast, they hiked the trails on Mount Oro. The dusty heat on the southern slope had them work up a sweat. Lunch was rustic Corsican fare—figatellu dried sausage and smoky Sartène cheese—enjoyed by a stream. They tore pieces from a crusty sourdough baguette and washed it down with the clear, sweet water rushing beside them.

After the hike, Eyrún let the tub fill as they showered off the day's grime. The ensuite bath's floor-to-ceiling windows gave the feeling of floating above the canyon. When the bubbles peaked in the mineral bath, Eyrún got into the hot water. Darwin slid in behind her and massaged a sore spot.

Ajaccio, Corsica

After a lengthy afternoon nap, Eyrún drove them down the mountain to visit Darwin's grandfather, Emelio. The setting sun glowed over Ajaccio harbor as they turned onto Rue des Oranges, where Emelio lived in the twenty-room Lacroix family chateau. Their forebears had built it in the eighteenth century when the Lacroix shipping empire was at its zenith.

His grandfather, now in his mid-eighties, had lived here since 1940. Like Darwin, he held a doctorate in archaeology and had worked worldwide. Unfortunately, his grand theory that Romans had used lava tubes to navigate under Europe ruined his academic reputation until five years ago, when Darwin proved him right.

Eyrún took Darwin's hand as they entered the porte-cochère. He smiled and gently squeezed.

"Grand-père! We're here." Darwin called out. Rich smells wafted from the kitchen as his grandfather emerged, wiping his hands on a towel.

"Darwin!" Emelio said, wrapping his grandson in a hug. "And, Eyrún. You look more lovely every time I see you."

"Thanks, Emelio. And you, too. You're no longer limping."

"My physio says I'm fully fit. My ankle is perfect."

"And, hopefully, staying off ladders," she said.

They chatted while Darwin carried the folio he'd brought into the dining room, and then Emelio whispered, "How is he?"

"He's getting over it. You know how he takes things too personally."

"Pfft." Emelio blew out and rolled his eyes. "He doesn't get it from me. Thankfully, he has you to get him out of his doldrums. Come. I have a wonderful champagne ready."

Over dinner, Emelio filled them in on local gossip. Eyrún shared their goings on in Paris and Iceland. Darwin talked about the École du Louvre as Emelio peppered him with questions. It had been one of his dreams to teach there.

Darwin dredged the serving dish with his baguette as their meal wrapped up. The sumptuous veal pot-au-feu had spurred his prodigious appetite.

"I made Tarte Tatin," said Emelio as they carried the plates to the kitchen. "Leave the rest." He nodded toward the table.

Eyrún carried a tray with dessert into the library while Emelio poured cognac. When each dish was served, they sat back in leather armchairs. Darwin swirled the amber liquid in the crystal glass that Napoleon had given to Henri Lacroix, Darwin's five-times great-grandfather. They had been childhood friends on Corsica and business partners later in life as Lacroix Shipping ferried Napoleon's troops and supplies throughout the Mediterranean.

During Darwin's youth, the glasses stayed in a locked glass cabinet, but after a brush with death a couple of years back, Emelio had decided they were meant to be enjoyed, not saved for special occasions. Darwin scanned the library. So much Corsican history had happened here. He imagined the party hosted in this house during Napoleon's stopover from Egypt to Paris.

But shadows overtook him—not all the memories were happy. His eyes went to the folio next to the dessert tray. "Why didn't you want to know, Grand-père?"

"Because I lived it and because I don't remember them. I was only four when I arrived here, and being locked in the safe room was terrible." Emelio swirled his glass, staring into the cognac as if it had conjured bad memories.

"Did your mother know what happened?" asked Darwin.

Emelio shrugged. "People didn't talk about it. I remember her breaking down once when I was eleven. The post returned a letter she'd sent to her sister. It was stamped 'deceased.' She'd written to all her family, but this was the only one that came back. I think she grasped in that moment they were all gone."

"Did you know about the paintings?"

"No. I never opened the government's letters. I had no interest in something that would remind me of the unspeakable."

"I'm sorry, Grand-père," said Eyrún.

"It's fine, my dear. It was all so long ago," said Emelio. "When my generation goes, the war will become a distant nightmare shelved in libraries."

They sat silently for a time. Fatigue from the long hike tugged at Darwin, and his eyelids drooped.

"I have a photo album," Emelio said, bursting the quiet. "My mother brought it with her. I have pictures of the family and the house in Paris."

Eyrún and Darwin followed Emelio into the basement, where he rummaged through boxes until he found the one with the album. "Here it is." He sneezed from the dust.

Back upstairs, they paged through the album as Emelio narrated. "I vaguely remember the house. My grandfather played viola. I sometimes sat on his lap and held the bow. Grand-mère played piano."

He flipped to pages with photos of paintings in a large room. "Here," he said, pointing to two on the left wall. "These would be the ones the government recovered, now in the museums."

The walls of the room were densely packed, and Darwin estimated there were almost two dozen works of art.

"I never counted them," said Emelio. "There are individual photos of some of the larger paintings. My mother went to art school and wanted to take over the family gallery. But..."

Eyrún patted his arm.

"Like I said," he said with a shrug, "these are faded memories."

"Even so, Emelio, it must be painful," she said.

"I feel my mother's sense of loss more than any direct experience."

"Wait," said Darwin.

They turned at his sudden outburst. He continued: "There's a sheet in the folio from Fleur. It's..." He flipped through the pages. "Here." He laid a yellowed sheet of paper on the table. The letterhead for the *Einsatzstab Reichsleiter Rosenberg* bore the German eagle grasping a swastika. A typewritten list began with:

```
Inventory of 19 Rue des Tournesol
```

"That's my grandparent's address," said Emelio.

They compared the list of paintings to those in the photo album. Gooseflesh prickled as the connection between the album and the Nazi looting apparatus solidified.

"*Putain!* It's him." Darwin pointed to a signature.

"Who?" Emelio and Eyrún asked simultaneously.

"Karl Meyer. He's the ERR lackey who cataloged private collections for the Nazis. He's also mentioned in the declassified OCBC file."

Their blank stares caused him to take a mental step back and recap from the original request from Fleur to the OCBC file with James Wilkerson's allegation that Karl Meyer was involved in insider looting. "Remember," he said, looking at Eyrún. "I talked about this on the flight from Paris?"

"The guy in Seattle?"

Darwin nodded and ran a hand through his hair. His pulse quickened. He stood, walked to the bookshelf, and then spun and began pacing.

"What is it, Darwin?" asked Emelio.

"Don't you see? I get it now. The Nazis stole our family's art, and then, after the war, the bastard who did it collaborated with corrupt museum people. The American Monuments Man uncovered the corruption, but they ghosted him."

He stopped, leaned on the bookshelf for a moment, and then faced them. "But it's not just our family. It's thousands of families."

Darwin's fog of indifference lifted. *Grand-père's right. When his generation is gone, memories will only exist in stories. That's what the thieves hope—that we forget.*

Clarity of purpose precipitated from his confusion. This wasn't the ancient past he usually investigated. It was history within living memory.

"I'm going to help them," he said.

"What changed your mind, Love?" asked Eyrún.

"Because it's slipping away. Because we can make restitution while people still remember and we can all benefit from closure."

27

Paris

Two days later, Darwin met Minh for coffee and showed him the photos of the Hendrick Avercamp paintings.

"These are very nice," said Minh. "Black and white does not do them justice, but the detail is lovely. If I remember my art, he painted during the Dutch Golden Age. Vermeer would have been a contemporary."

"Spot on," said Darwin. He was here to enlist Minh's help in finding paintings stolen from the Soutines.He showed Minh color photos of several Avercamp paintings from the Rijksmuseum in Amsterdam and from the Périgueux and Clermont-Ferrand museums.

"These last two were taken from my family," he said, setting prints beside the photos.

Minh closed his eyes for a long moment. Then he said, "I've not seen them before, but I'll run a search. What will you do now?"

Darwin gathered the photos. "My wife and I are going to look at the paintings today. I'm not sure yet where that will lead us."

Orleans

Eyrún and Darwin played cards as the countryside rushed by outside. The sat facing each other across a small table in a high-speed TGV enroute to Bordeaux. Three hours ago, they'd visited the house where the Soutine family had lived in Paris. The neighborhood now looked vastly different than it had in the 1940s. The buildings were the same, but the storefronts and traffic had changed. Today's shops had wide awnings with roll-up metal doors covered in graffiti.

One of the photos in the album Emelio had given Darwin showed the house from the opposite side of Rue des Tournesol. Paintings could be seen behind large windows beside a door with a brass handle in its center. A simple sign, "Gallery Soutine," was mounted over the lintel. The adjacent building featured another gallery.

Tall windows filled the upper three floors, appearing exactly like today. Shutters folded back against the building's exterior, and plants grew in pots behind wrought-iron grating—a typical Parisian house. The formally dressed people gave away the photo's age: men in suits and women in dresses pushing prams with enormous wheels. The cars, fewer than today, had the bulbous curves popular in the early half of the last century.

Darwin had been grumbling that he'd learned nothing from the visit to his forebears house.

"What did you expect?" asked Eyrún, picking up a card after laying down a set of three.

"Dunno," said Darwin, studying his cards.

Darwin played a card. "Closure, mostly. Life moves on. The people living there now probably have no idea what happened to the original owners."

"True," said Eyrún. "I felt a little sad. We could have had relatives to visit."

"Yeah," Darwin acknowledged.

"Gin!" said Eyrún, picking up Darwin's discard and setting her cards on the table.

"That's three in a row!"

"What can I say? You suck at cards."

He stood and stretched. "I'm going to get a coffee. You want anything?"

Bordeaux

Ninety minutes later, the train pulled into Gare Saint Jean in Bordeaux and they disembarked into a cool breeze from the Atlantic Ocean, some thirty miles west. Sunshine poked through patchy clouds. Darwin had a bounce in his step, anticipating the first of two surprises Eyrún had mentioned as their train had slowed during approach.

"What is it?" he asked as they approached the taxi stand.

"You're the worst. Here." She let go of her case and pointed for him to load them in the taxi's boot while she gave the driver an address.

The driver followed the Garonne River as it elbowed toward its headlands. Open spaces lined its banks, a mixture of park and former warehouses that had turned into restaurants and co-ops. They passed a cruise ship meandering to a berth—its stark-white hull stood out like a marshmallow in the mocha water.

They crossed the river over the modern Pont Jacques Chaban Delmas bridge. Four massive concrete and glass towers dominated the mid-span and functioned to lift the roadway for passing ships. The taxi driver reversed course and, minutes later, stopped at a series of old brick buildings adorned with street art.

"Huh?" Darwin looked around, confused as he got their cases.

Eyrún joined him a moment later once the taxi had driven off. She grinned widely as a delivery truck blocking the street pulled away.

Darwin's jaw dropped in surprise. Then he burst out laughing.

"Welcome to the Darwin Ecosystem," said Eyrún.

The walkway between the building complex had a patch of grass with his name in giant gold block letters. He went to the signage and stood beside the chest-high D and smiled as Eyrún snapped his picture.

A security guard arrived and told Darwin he couldn't stand in the planted area.

"*Desole*," said Darwin, stepping out.

He and Eyrún toured the former military barracks—now the trendy Right Bank of Bordeaux. Its shops, co-op workspaces, and sustainable development projects had become the go-to place for the anti-corporate crowd. They picked a restaurant Eyrún had read about. Poco Pepe boasted a menu of ingredients grown in the Darwin Ecosystem's experimental farms—on the property.

They chose a pizza cooked in the restaurant's solar-fired oven. Their server explained the concentrated sunlight that augmented ancient techniques with modern materials. "We add small pieces of fragrant wood to enhance the flavor without having to consume large amounts of trees and minimize the pollution in the city."

A minute later, their wine arrived, chosen by the restaurant's shop, which specialized in small producers. Eyrún swirled her glass as Darwin studied the bottle—its label portrayed the vintner leading a plow horse through the vineyard. The biodynamic methods included innovative carbon dioxide capture using baking soda.

An hour later, sated from a lovely meal, they meandered through the shops on their way to the taxi stand. Darwin yawned. The afternoon's warmth, combined with the wine's lingering effect, had him thinking about a nap on the train to Perigord. Then, the unmistakable aroma of coffee wafted into his path, drawing him like a moth to a flame.

He passed up his usual triple cappuccino as too rich and chose a simple Ethiopian peaberry filter coffee. Eyrún ordered her favorite blue tea, and they sat at a cafe table where the building's shadow crept across the open space.

"This is nice," said Darwin. "It's how I envisioned our time in Paris."

"Me, too." Eyrún smiled, and her right cheek dimpled.

Darwin returned her smile, imagining them later in their boutique hotel in Périgueux. He forced himself back to the present moment. "What's the other surprise?"

She answered with her own question. "Are you done?"

Darwin nodded, and they headed toward the taxi stand. His insides hummed like a kid eyeing his birthday presents.

When the taxi passed the train station, he said, "I thought we were taking the three-fifteen?"

"We were," said Eyrún.

The driver turned a corner and stopped in front of a curved building bearing the unmistakable red signage for Porsche.

Darwin looked at Eyrún, who grinned like the Chesire Cat. "I miss my Macan," she said and paid the driver.

He laughed as they walked into the dealership. His wife loved fast toys. Her need for speed both thrilled and scared the daylights out of him. While his hobbies tended toward bookish exploits, Eyrún had grown up racing ice rallies in her native Iceland and had participated on an amateur team in the Dakar rally each of the last five years.

Her race-modified Porsche Macan was garaged at the ACA in Corsica. Darwin had gotten used to the white-knuckled rides up to their mountain house, but Paris was a more pedestrian experience. He loved it, but now he knew Eyrún had missed driving.

A half-hour later, he wedged into the passenger seat of a sleek gray and black glass Taycan GTS. The instrument panel looked like their plane—all touch displays. The only physical buttons were on the doors.

Eyrún tapped the drive button, and they rolled off the lot. The onboard navigation guided them out of metropolitan Bordeaux, and when they reached an open stretch, she tested the car's 590 horsepower.

Darwin mashed into his seat like he'd been thrust off a launchpad.

Eyrún whooped in delight and then let off the accelerator when the dashboard popped two hundred kilometers per hour. The kinetic energy recovery system slowed them. She continued at the legal limit for the rest of the journey but tested the Taycan's prodigious handling in the hilly sections.

28

The Farm

Christian woke to footsteps crunching on dry leaves. He opened an eye to see boots stop about two meters' distance.

"Wake up sleeping beauty. It's going to be another hot one," said the farmer.

Christian grunted. His body protested at the violation of the early wake-up. Every part of him ached from digging and hauling. Despite having a backhoe and dumper, they had to clear brush and remove trees.

He looked up at the farmer and said, "Give me a minute."

"I'll get the truck," said the farmer.

Christian tensed and released his muscles, which relieved the pain somewhat. Then he said, "You do that," as he studied the farmer looming over him. Deep-set eyes stared dully from beneath a forehead that overhung like a cliff. His dark brown beard blended into his shirt-less overalls where equally hairy arms and chest protruded.

"If I'm beauty, then he's the beast," Christian muttered to himself while watching the farmer trudge away. He rolled over, and after a long minute, threw off the sheet and sat up. The air, while cooler this morning, still held the stickiness that had driven him from the caravan last night. The heatwave that had settled on eastern France was forecast for another three days.

He entered the caravan to wash his face and inspect some itchy bumps on his cheek. "What the...," he said into the mirror while running finger tips along a half dozen bug bites. At least the gash in his right forearm looked better today.

After washing up with tepid water, he gulped from a cold bottle he kept in the mini fridge. The icy liquid somewhat revived him and improved his outlook. They'd been at it for a week with little to show for it. He figured the money he got from selling his grandfather's loot could sustain them for four weeks. His boss at the Louvre had already asked how long Christian needed to be away.

Fortunately, yesterday they'd seen a change in the soil where the slumped hillside had flowed across gravel laid on a roadbed. Unfortunately, they could not tell if that meant digging a few meters or fifty.

Five minutes later, the rumbling diesel from the dumper pulled up near the caravan. Christian shoved in another bite of ham before grabbing a bag of almonds. He steeled himself for another long day of digging and heading for the truck.

29

Périgueux

The next day at breakfast, Darwin got shaved truffles atop his eggs. It had been a decade since he'd visited the Périgord region to hunt for lava tubes used by the Romans. Like most cities in southern France, Périgueux's name was Latinized from its Celtic original—Petrocorii.

Eyrún drove them across town to the former cloister, which had been recycled as a prison before settling as a museum in the early eighteen hundreds. It had the same light-colored stone façade as the buildings in Paris. They arrived an hour earlier than their appointment with its director so Darwin could wander the first-floor archaeological collection.

"It's the fourth-most-important pre-historical collection in France," he said.

"There's a competition?" asked Eyrún, following him past display cases of bone carvings.

"Dunno. I just wanted to see the Neanderthal skeleton."

The museum had few visitors on this weekday morning, and the gallery covering the four-hundred-thousand-year human habitation of the Périgord region was as silent as the caves from which the objects had come.

They headed back to the entrance shortly before eleven, where the director was waiting for them. A woman in a fashionable pantsuit introduced herself as Delphine.

"Pleased to meet you. I'm Eyrún Stefansdottír." She shook Delphine's hand and added, "This is my husband, Darwin Lacroix."

"Nice to meet you both," said Delphine, shaking Darwin's hand. She asked about their journey, and they made small talk as they walked to the fine arts collection in the west wing.

She slowed when they reached a series of still-life paintings and then paused before the Avercamp. "It's one of our finer examples from the Dutch school," she said before retreating a short distance.

The canvas captured dozens of skaters on a frozen river. The action looked like any other street scene where people socialized and shopped, except they all wore blades strapped to their shoes. Darwin read its description, which mentioned that Avercamp had painted it during one of the coldest periods of the Little Ice Age that had gripped the Northern Hemisphere.

Darwin swiped to the photo on his phone and held it up. Eyrún looked over his shoulder at it and said, "It's definitely the same. How long have you had it?" he asked Delphine, who rejoined them.

"Since 1967. May I?" She gestured to his phone and took it when he offered.

"You're right. It is your family's painting. I'm so sorry."

"Thank you," said Darwin. "I appreciate how well you've taken care of it."

Eyrún leaned in to read its description and then asked, "The provenance says property of the *Musées nationaux récupération* pending restitution to its rightful owners. How does it work?"

Delphine explained, "It's the MNR database or nicknamed the Rose Valland database because much of the data came from her heroic efforts. But it's complicated now. The MNR currently has sixteen thousand items with no owner. Some two thousand are displayed in museums around France. Standard provenance states that a holder can claim ownership for up to thirty years."

Darwin knew this meant the painting was held in trust by the state, but he had also learned restitution efforts had ground to a halt decades ago. "It's a bloody legal shell game," he spat.

The women looked at him.

"Sorry." He shrugged and said in a more measured voice, "French Jews were stripped of their citizenship and property. The ERR 'recovered' the 'abandoned' art and transferred it to new ownership—members of the Nazi Party. After the war, the Germans or collaborators stashed the paintings in freeports like Geneva. In the mid-seventies, a bunch of art showed up on the market with the owners claiming thirty-year provenance."

"That sucks," said Eyrún.

"It's worse. The previous owners, if they weren't killed, have to prove their art was taken unlawfully. It's ludicrous."

"I'm sorry, Darwin," said Delphine.

"No, no, it's okay," he said, placing a hand on her arm. "You had no part in its arrival here. And you have displayed it in a lovely collection."

"Thank you." She smiled and then asked, "What would you like to do? You are the rightful heir."

"I don't know yet," he said. "We have no place to put it. May I think about it?"

"Yes, please. Take as long as you like. You know how to reach me."

They shook hands again, and Delphine departed.

Eyrún and Darwin spent another hour in the museum before heading outside. They strolled, hand in hand, toward the L'Isle River to look for a lunch spot.

Darwin walked with an easy step. The night before, he'd brooded, imagining the confrontation with his family's dark chapter. But the experience had been one of solace. Avercamp's depiction of daily life conveyed light, color, and gayety, and the museum had treated the painting and its provenance truthfully.

"What are you thinking?" Eyrún asked as they approached the river bank.

"I thought I'd feel more."

"Maybe there isn't more to experience. Like Emelio said, it was so long ago." She pointed to a restaurant on a river barge. "How about this place?"

"Looks great."

They boarded and were seated at a table on the stern where an umbrella mitigated the midday sun. Their lunchtime conversation turned to planning a summer holiday over a salad with roasted duck in homage to the regional delicacy.

After lunch, they walked off the rich food along the river path. When they approached the car, Eyrún grinned mischievously, saying, "Clermont-Ferrand is less than three hours' drive."

"True," Darwin acknowledged, "but we'd have to go through the Massif Central—"

"In a car made perfectly for such a journey—"

"With the woman I love—"

"And an expert driver," said Eyrún, opening her door.

Darwin got in the passenger side. "I'm game."

Eyrún touched "Drive," and the Taycan rolled away, silent as a golf cart.

30

Clermont-Ferrand

Three hours later, Eyrún slalomed through a tight series of bends leading into Clermont-Ferrand. Darwin looked out his window for Puy du Dome, the extinct volcano, but the wooded area obstructed his view. Unfortunately, they came up behind a regional bus, which forced Eyrún to go at a maddeningly glacial pace.

Darwin shifted in his seat, his ass numb from sitting too long. Their original thought of zooming through the mountains had succumbed to the reality of small towns choked with local traffic.

"Pull in here," he said, pointing to a vista point.

Eyrún did, and they got out. Darwin rubbed his backside, and Eyrún shook her arms. The vast plain of the Auvergne region stretched before them. Clermont-Ferrand lay below, and blue sky spread to the horizon, where the hills resumed their march toward the Alps. Amid the pale buildings and terracotta roofs, the black cathedral stood like a beacon, drawing attention to itself.

"It's beautiful," said Eyrún. "I forgot how unique it is."

The Notre-Dame-de-l'Assomption cathedral was constructed using basalt blocks in a Gothic style. Its twin towers soared a hundred meters above the city. Darwin had a special relationship with the Clermont-Ferrand. He'd made his first significant discovery deep below the cathedral's crypt. He'd also met his friend Richard Ndembele there.

Darwin's watch vibrated. He tapped its message.

"Putain!"

Eyrún jumped out of a stretch. "What is it?"

"One of our paintings showed up at auction." Darwin got his phone from the car and returned to Eyrún at the vista point railing. "You remember that guy I mentioned with the eidetic memory?"

"Yeah. Minh?"

"That's him. I showed him the photos of the paintings—"

"Right, you said he'd never seen them."

"He has now. They showed up in a dark web auction." Darwin held out his phone.

Eyrún looked at the screenshot of the auction site. Then Darwin swiped to a photo from the painting from the Soutine's album. "They're the same," she said.

"No doubt about it."

"What are you doing?" she asked as he thumbed a message.

When did it show up?

Minh: Earlier today. I created a profile. Said I was looking for Dutch masters from the Golden Age.

Darwin: Any replies

Minh: I didn't contact them. Told you first.

Darwin: Thanks. Don't do anything yet. I'm going to bid.

Minh: Okay

"Sorry, that was Minh," Darwin explained as he used a VPN to log onto the auction site.

"Are you buying it?"

"Hell, yes," he growled.

"Okay, then what?"

"Then what?" He looked up, his face flushed. "This is war. These people are no better than the thieves who stole from my family."

"Hold on, Love." Eyrún wrapped her hands around his.

Darwin tended to leap first and plan later. The warmth from her soft hands eased the tension in his arms. She smiled in that way he knew meant patience—let's work this out together.

"You're right." He sighed, his shoulders dropping as the fight-or-flight tension sloughed off.

"I get your desire to do what's right, but let's think this through. Earlier today, you sounded like you'd let it go. But it clearly runs deeper. How can I help?"

"I…" Darwin started, but then he paused. The anger that had gnawed on him while he'd anticipated what lay ahead in Périgueux had returned with a vengeance. He looked out over the valley while gathering his thoughts. The painting in the Périgueux was a peaceful end to a tragic history. But now, he had a target. "Someone's trafficking with my family's legacy. I have to stop it."

He held Eyrún's gaze.

"If I buy the painting, I can get to their IP address. Zac showed me how to set it up," he said, referring to his friend Zac's digital forensic skills.

"Good start," she said. "But we know these people operate in layers. The ones pulling the strings won't be on the other end of those IP addresses. We need a more covert approach—work our own back channels."

"Like?"

"Nahla, for one," said Eyrún, referring to an antiquities dealer in Alexandria. "She operates in that space between the law."

"That's a great idea." His busy brain whipped into a tornado of planning.

Eyrún laid out the first steps. "Let's go into town. Contact Nahla while I'm driving. We'll have a nice dinner. Tomorrow, we head back to Paris."

"You're brilliant." He beamed as he pocketed the phone.

"I know." She laughed.

The traffic sucked going into the city. Eyrún set the car's adaptive cruise control, and they discussed a strategy to get back the paintings and expose the Louvre thieves.

31

École du Louvre

Two days later, Darwin met Fleur Legrand in Vivienne's office. Lucien was away at a European Union finance conference, which suited Darwin. He needed action. Accountability would come later.

Vivienne's assistant served coffee, and after social conversation, Darwin shifted the discussion toward his agenda. He described his investigation and told them about visiting the Avercamp painting in Périgueux.

"*Mon Dieu!* Darwin, I'm so sorry," said Vivienne.

"Thank you," he said, "but while researching Hendrick Avercamp, I found another of his paintings at auction." He sipped his coffee before continuing. "We've developed sophisticated antitrafficking capabilities at my foundation in Corsica, and my staff tells me this auction site is known to carry stolen art, particularly from public collections."

Fleur raised her eyebrows at his assertion while Vivienne smiled attentively, a consummate politician.

While probing the site, we found two *ancien régime* clocks for sale that are registered among the Louvre's missing objects. Unfortunately, those priceless pieces had already been sold. But…" He paused for emphasis. "The same people sold the Avercamp."

"It's awful," said Vivienne.

But Fleur had paid closer attention to Darwin's words. "You said 'sold,' past tense."

"Yes." He smiled. "I bought it. Or I should say, I had someone in my network buy it."

"Who?" asked Fleur.

"That, I won't disclose, but I can tell you the Avercamp is in the MNR database marked as looted from a private collection. But that's not the most troubling part. The seller said they could get other pieces from the Louvre collections. If that's true, it confirms we have a serious problem."

"Sounds like you've had a change of heart about helping." Vivienne leaned forward in her chair and set her cup on the low table between them.

Darwin shook his head. She didn't get it—the depth of the hurt left by the Vichy government that had profited from the spoliation of its own people's property. His eyes burned at the hate-fueled antisemitism that had crafted laws dispossessing people of their citizenship, their goods, and their lives.

Above all, Darwin despised the greed that fueled antiquities and art theft—plundering the world's collective past. He locked eyes with Fleur. "I need access to your data. We don't know who's involved, so the fewer eyes, the better."

"Agreed. Can you come to my office? I'll get you connected with our experts."

Vivienne spoke up. "Wouldn't it make more sense to have them meet Darwin here? I mean, if there are insiders, as you say, they would notice him going to the OCBC, right?"

"Makes sense," said Darwin.

Fleur agreed and promised to schedule a meeting as soon as she could align her people. They wrapped up their meeting, and Vivienne asked Darwin to stay a few minutes after Fleur departed.

Darwin stood at the window and gazed at people passing through the carrousel to and from the Tuileries garden. Behind him, Vivienne said goodbye to Fleur and then walked across the parquet floor and stopped beside him. "I never tire of this view," she said.

"I could get used to it. Funny how tourists from all over the world come to sightsee, and for us, it's the backdrop of daily life."

"I hadn't thought about it like that."

"An archaeology professor once told me to never take your surroundings for granted. Discovery depends on noticing the tiniest bit in a sea of ordinary."

"Huh," said Vivienne.

On a wide, grassy section below, a trainer worked with her pack. Each dog stayed in its place as she moved backward. Nearby, on the broad path between the arch and garden, a man cast giant soap bubbles skyward. Children leaped, trying to reach the wobbly shapes.

"I see what you mean," she added.

"What was it you wanted to talk about?" Darwin asked.

"Well, for one, I'm so glad you decided to help us, but…" Her eyes darted around the office like she suspected someone was listening. Then she added, "I'm not sure I trust Fleur. Definitely not Lucien from the Finance Ministry."

Darwin remained impassive. On the drive back to Paris, Eyrún had quizzed him on who was involved. As they'd discussed their motivations, she'd suggested caution while determining who could be trusted.

Vivienne must have noticed his hesitation because she lightly touched his arm and said, "I don't distrust Fleur. It's just that, erm, the OCBC thinks the Louvre systematically colluded to block restitution efforts of private art stolen during the war."

"But that was long ago," he said, knowing the old accusations of museum competition for unclaimed art and the legal decisions claiming French patrimony—that is, the French people's collective heritage as owned by the state.

"Precisely. Anyone involved, if such a thing took place, is long gone. Look, it's probably nothing, but until we know their true motives, can you keep me updated with what you find?"

"Sure. I'll meet with Fleur here." He gestured toward her conference table. "You'll know what she knows."

"Thanks, Darwin. That's a relief. I knew you'd understand," Vivienne said, and then she changed the subject. "How was your minibreak with Eyrún?"

"Fun." He described the surprise lunch at the Darwin Ecosystem, and Vivienne laughed. They chatted a few minutes longer about an upcoming lecture, and then Vivienne's phone chimed.

"Forgive me," she said, glancing at the message. "I need to run to a meeting across campus. It was lovely chatting. And thanks. I know I can trust you."

Darwin checked his watch outside her office—twenty minutes to his afternoon lecture. *Time to follow my own advice,* he thought and exited the Louvre into the world-renowned garden.

32

1st Arrondissement

Lionel wrapped up his weekly lunch with Christian and exited the restaurant onto Rue Saint-Honoré. "I need to run an errand," he said, heading in opposite the direction. In a half block, he crossed the street, entered the Palais Royal Musée du Louvre Metro Station, and made his way to the Line One platform toward Château de Vincennes.

The signage above the tracks showed the next train was due in a minute, followed by another in three minutes. He walked to the far end of the platform and waited as the inbound train rolled to a stop. He stood back against the station's curved ceiling as the glass partitions opened.

A moderate midday crowd disembarked, followed by an ingress of those on the platform. Lionel did not board but looked at his phone for cover while watching everyone exit. After the train rolled away, he hurried to the small service door where the partition met the tunnel. He opened it using a stolen key and glanced at the station sign—two minutes before the next train.

Ample time, Lionel noted as he jumped onto the tracks and moved into the dark tunnel. He focused on avoiding the high-voltage rail. Fifty meters in, light reflected off the opposite tracks. His heart rate ticked up a notch as he scanned the right wall. *There!* He reached a door, fished a different key ring from his pocket, and slipped inside as the oncoming train rounded the bend.

Pitch blackness enveloped him as the door shut. He waited a moment to adjust and then switched on an ultraviolet light attached to the keychain. The rapid transit police had been installing cameras throughout the system. He didn't know if they'd put any in this tunnel yet, but he'd marked the floor several years ago.

The luminescent arrows guided him along the center of the service tunnel to a grate. He lifted it and descended a short distance before closing it and continuing down. Five rungs later, his feet hit concrete. Dripping water echoed in the darkness, and a dank smell permeated the air.

Lionel turned on an LED headlamp. Its stark white light illuminated stone walls slick with moisture. He stood on one side of a fetid river in the Paris sewer. Its opposite bank featured a similar concrete walkway. This main drainage beneath Rue de Rivoli carried the brown and black water to treatment plants outside the city.

At this point, he was parallel with the Louvre's pyramid. He went left, stepping over inlets from smaller sewers running under Rue de Rivoli side streets until he reached a chain stretching wall to wall. He used it to leap the two-meter river and continue another thirty meters until reaching a door with "*ETANCHE*" stenciled on it.

Lionel grasped the wheel-like handle at its center and turned it anti-clockwise to release the mechanisms holding its watertight seal. He braced one foot on the sewer wall and pulled. The door's massive hinges groaned, and when it had opened wide enough, he entered and resealed it.

"You could have come the easier way," a voice said from the darkness.

"*Putain!*" Lionel jumped. He pressed against the tunnel wall, protecting himself, his heart hammering as he aimed his torch at the speaker.

Vivienne de Poitiers laughed.

A minute later, he sat on a nearby crate. "What was so important we meet right away?" he asked.

Vivienne's impeccable attire was out of place in the grimy tunnel beneath the Louvre. It had been constructed during the interwar years as a fallout shelter and secret exit. To protect against flooding from the Seine River, waterproof doors had been installed. But it hadn't been used since the war and was inaccessible to the Louvre personnel. Years ago, the museum had contracted to fill the tunnels, but it never happened for lack of funding.

"You've been found out," she said.

"I doubt it," he replied with a snort. "What makes you say that?"

Vivienne paced as she recounted her meeting with Darwin. She finished with, "The paintings belonged to his relatives in Paris."

"So what?"

"He said he bought one of the Avercamps."

"Not likely," said Lionel. "I sold all three to someone I've dealt with before. We don't know each other beyond our online IDs. The money goes into our numbered account. We deliver the paintings to the Geneva Freeport. No personal contact."

"Let me see them," she said.

He showed her the photos of the three Hendrick Avercamp paintings. She zoomed into each one, studying the details. "These are excellent. And the provenance?"

"My colleague says his father owned them since 1945 after purchasing them at an auction."

"That's the other thing. What's happening with your colleague?" asked Vivienne.

"He's making progress. Said it will take another six weeks to move the dirt. That's why he needs the cash."

"But he hasn't told you where it is yet?"

"No, but I trust him. I know it's somewhere near Strasbourg, but right now, he doesn't know if there's anything but a collapsed hillside. He and the farmer are digging discretely."

"I thought you said—"

"Relax, Vivienne," Lionel said, knowing her sense of urgency sometimes bordered on panic. "We've got plenty of time."

"But the OCBC is poking around, and Darwin's making it his mission to find out who sold the paintings. He told them it proves insider theft." She froze, her fingers tugging at her sleeve. Then she added, "What if he traces you?"

"Not likely. But if you're that worried, then we go to ground. That's the procedure—stay quiet. Play the long game."

"No!" she said, balling her hands into tight fists. "I want that Raphael. Accelerate the process. Get your colleague to dig faster. Dig at night. Put more people on it. Hold back on the money until he shows you the location."

Lionel folded his arms, waiting out her tirade.

"You need to stay on Christian," she continued. "He's our only connection. Find where they're digging. And another thing, keep an eye on Darwin. He has a way of disrupting things."

Lionel jumped down from the crate. "I can't do everything at once."

"Find a way," she said. Then, looking at her watch, she added, "I have a meeting."

She spun and headed back inside the Louvre.

Lionel shook his head. *She's a nutcase. First one thing, then another.*

When he heard the watertight door close, he turned to another exit he doubted she was aware of. The organization was designed purposefully to separate knowledge. While she navigated its upper levels, he knew the inner workings—how art moved undetected.

He smirked at her name—Vivienne Clotilde de Poitiers. It reeked of *noblesse ancienne*. She was desperate to recoup lost respect and money. She'd inserted herself into a leadership vacuum following the death of the previous leader.

Lionel spat as he traversed a tunnel running below the Louvre's east-facing colonnade. *She's nothing but an administrator. A schmoozer.*

He pictured the former leader, Thierry Panchon, an archaeologist with deep field experience and a vast network—*a real pro.*

Lionel reached the exit point. He listened carefully for noises on the other side and, just before pushing through the opening, thought of his mentor again.

Thierry also got himself killed.

33

Île Saint-Louis

Aya Raiss joined Eyrún and Darwin at their apartment for dinner two nights later to discuss their next tunnel exploration beyond Sainte-Chapelle. She showed them how to make her grand-mère's lentil soup. Soon, caramelizing onions and fragrant spices filled the flat. Darwin poured them a Josmeyer Gewurztraminer from the Alsace region and sliced a saucisson and baguette to stave off his growling stomach.

An hour later, the soup was ready, and they took their bowls to the dining table. Outside on the Seine, Saturday night was in full swing as a *bateau-mouche* plied its way upriver. People danced on its upper deck, and the party lights and thumping bass reverberated between the buildings lining the river.

"This is yummy, Aya," said Eyrún, dabbing her mouth with a napkin after a spoonful of the lentil soup.

"It's my favorite," Aya replied. "This is a quick version. Grand-mère would simmer it for hours."

Darwin, already halfway through his bowl, grunted in agreement as he ripped a hunk of baguette and dipped it in the golden-brown soup. They ate in silence for a few minutes before Aya shifted the conversation to the tunnels.

"I spent days in the Bibliotheque Nationale, delving into architectural plans and construction on the Louvre. I've read volumes of correspondence. It's a *méli-mélo...*" She glanced at Darwin for a translation.

"A hodgepodge or jumble, no particular plan."

"I got it. But I like *méli-mélo,*" said Eyrún. "I'll have to use it."

Aya smiled. "As Darwin said, the Louvre we see today is a jumble of construction and remodeling. It looks like a contiguous project to anyone without a background in architecture or history."

She produced a drawing of the Louvre's original keep outside the wall erected by Philippe August in the twelfth century and ran a finger through its eastern gate into the city. "A tunnel would likely run under here to the l'Auxerrois chapel, also built around the same time. There were churches on the site going back to Clovis."

Eyrún's face screwed up. "Clovis?"

"Sorry, I forgot you're not French," said Aya. "He's the king who united all the Frankish tribes. He also converted to Christianity and commissioned a chapel at l'Auxerrois. The point is, it's the place where the French kings consolidated power. Then, in the thirteen hundreds, things changed big time. Charles the Fifth built another wall around Paris, enclosing more of the city, and Saint-Germain l'Auxerrois was built up.

"The Louvre was now inside the city, and the royal court grew, but it was too small to host the crowds, so the Bourbon family bought up properties surrounding l'Auxerrois. They constructed the Hôtel du Petit-Bourbon, whose grand hall was bigger than anything inside the Louvre."

Darwin jumped in. "Nice power grab."

"Agreed," said Aya. "And they secured it when Henri the Fourth was crowned king. But the point of my story is this." She ran a finger between the Louvre and l'Auxerrois. "Creating a tunnel would be a key step in accruing power. Think of it. Messengers, guards, and royals could secretly move between the court, the cathedral, and Petit-Bourbon."

Darwin studied the Louvre maps and then looked at the larger map, which included Île de la Cité. "That makes total sense," he said.

"But," Eyrún chimed in, "it's like the lava tube problem. Without knowing the entrances, we've got no proof."

"Ah, but I do," said Aya. "I found a series of letters between Cardinal Richelieu and Jacques Lemercier, the architect who designed the Louvre's Pavillion de l'Horloge, about preserving the crypt below Saint-Germain l'Auxerrois. In one, Richelieu instructed Lemercier to 'maintain the king's private access to the chapels.'"

Aya smiled wryly, like a prosecutor about to deliver the final damning evidence, as she pulled a paper from her folder. "I have this drawing from Claude Perrault of the colonnade plans. See this dashed line running from the Cour Carrée and l'Auxerrois?"

Darwin and Eyrún nodded.

"It's got to be a tunnel."

"Wow," said Eyrún. She took their empty dishes to the kitchen and returned with a cheese board while Darwin scanned the documents that Aya was quoting from.

"I agree with you," he said to Aya, "but let's be careful here."

"*Je sais,*" she said. "We're digging with a trowel in one hand and a text in the other."

"Meaning?" asked Eyrún, setting the board between them and refilling their water glasses.

"That we lose objectivity—because we're looking for tunnels, we see tunnels."

Taking their wine glasses and the cheese, they moved to a sitting area, where Aya spread out the map of Paris. She pointed at the Louvre's eastern colonnade.

"There's an ancient street under here and a series of basements and fallout shelters under the Louvre. The original moat was filled in as the palace extended, but any tunnel to Saint-Germain l'Auxerrois would have gone deep. Modern construction would be above it."

"What about the sewer?" asked Darwin.

"That's an unknown. I couldn't find detailed construction plans for this area."

Eyrún studied the map and added, "The geology is the same on both sides of the Seine. Limestone was deposited in the Paris Basin Lutetian period about forty-five million years ago. When ancient sea levels dropped, the softer ground got washed away. Hills with harder bedrock, like Sacre Coeur, stood above the Seine's channel. Paris is built from the pale stone beneath our feet. It was quarried mainly from the Left Bank because it was open space. They could just as easily have dug under the Right."

"Which means?"

"People have been cutting stone under Paris since Roman times. Creating tunnels would have been no problem, and the spoils could double as building material."

Aya caught on and picked up Eyrún's logic. "That would be the perfect cover. Pay miners to cut blocks but in a specific direction. Nothing on the ledger would read 'tunnel,' just 'quarried stone.'"

"Exactly," said Eyrún, tracing her way to Île Saint-Louis. "If I were tunneling from Sainte-Chapelle toward the Louvre, I'd go towards the island's tip and then under the river. But I'd want a safe place, one that would be undisturbed." She paused. "When was Pont Neuf built?"

"Erm..." Aya thought a moment and then said, "Right around sixteen hundred. I can look it up."

"No, that's close enough," said Eyrún. "So, if the Bourbons tunneled from their Hôtel du Petit-Bourbon to the Louvre, it wouldn't be a stretch to think they extended it to Sainte-Chapelle and Notre-Dame. Considering we found a passage between those two, I'd say it's plausible." She scanned the map and continued with her theory. "Then, if this tunnel building happened in the mid-fifteen hundreds, Henri Bourbon's architects would be around to influence what went under the Seine as well as over it."

"That's brilliant," said Aya.

"Still doesn't confirm it. We'd need to... Wait. What about Zac's satellites?" Eyrún looked at Darwin.

"Dunno. Maybe." He tapped out a message.

"Your friend who was with us under Notre-Dame?" Aya asked.

"Yes," said Eyrún, and then she filled Aya in on Zac's work with microsatellites and earthquake early warning detection.

Darwin moved between Eyrún and Aya and set the iPad on the table. "Hey, Zac," he said as his friend's face filled the screen.

"Hey, Aya. How've you been?" Zac asked.

"Great, Zac. And you?"

They caught up for some minutes, and then Zac shifted their conversation. "Darwin told me you found a tunnel from Notre-Dame to Saint Chapelle."

Aya briefed him on her research and explained her theory of tunnels connecting to the Louvre. Darwin texted pictures they'd taken in the Saint Chapelle tunnel. "Where are you now?" she asked Zac.

"This?" Zac glanced around at the handful of people in the dimly lit room he was in, working in the pale glow of multiple flat panel displays. "It's a high-energy physics lab at Lawrence Berkeley Labs."

They heard clacking as Zac's fingers flew over his keyboard. "I'm bringing up a sat image of Pont Neuf. Here we go." His face on the iPad got bigger as he leaned forward. "So, you're looking for a deep tunnel that would parallel Pont Neuf, and if we can scan near the quaysides, we might see it. Hmmm."

They waited, watching his eyes as they darted around his screen. Then he looked directly at them. "It's conceivable. Interesting problem to solve. I think there might be some military tech that—"

"Oh, my God. That's awesome," said Aya, jostling Eyrún and Darwin as she bounced on the cushion.

"I said 'might be,'" said Zac. "Eyrún, what if we combined anything I can do with you running a local GPR? There's open space in Place Dauphine. Aya, you could get some air cover from the archaeological crypt."

"Air cover?" asked Aya.

Eyrún snorted. "It's an Americanism for support from your superiors."

"Sure," said Aya. "I can get their support."

"Good. Give me a week," said Zac. "That way, I can arrange a few satellite passes without arousing suspicions."

They agreed to reconnect in a week. After the call ended, Aya asked, "Do you think he can find something?"

"Usually," said Darwin, "when I've heard Zac say 'military tech,' it means he has a specific thing in mind. He's got top-secret clearances in the American Department of Energy."

"Oh," said Aya.

"Yeah. I find it best not to ask," said Eyrún.

"This is perfect," said Darwin, who had grabbed his iPad after the call with Zac.

"What?" Eyrún and Aya asked simultaneously.

"There's a sewer entrance on Place du Louvre, thirty meters from Saint-Germain l'Auxerrois, marked on the cataphile's map."

"What?" Aya pulled the iPad toward her. "I didn't know about that. Must be new." She pinched the image to its highest zoom, but it blurred. "Shit." She grabbed her phone and messaged a group. Seconds later, someone replied.

Darwin and Eyrún waited while Aya chatted with her group. A couple of minutes later, she looked up and said, "It just went onto the grid last week. One of the cataphiles who works for the Paris sewer found evidence of foot traffic from a disused Louvre door toward the cathedral."

She stood. "We need to check it out."

"Now?" asked Darwin.

"I'm game," said Eyrún. "It's Saturday night. The cataflics will be busy on the Left Bank."

Aya grinned. "Let's get dirty."

34

Saint-Germain l'Auxerrois

Eyrún and Darwin changed into their caving suits and rode with Aya to her flat, where she put on her purple jumpsuit. All three carried calf-length rubber boots and thick gloves. Just under an hour after they'd decided to go, the rideshare angled left off Rue de Rivoli and stopped. They exited on Rue Perrault, where diners at the sidewalk cafe tables looked at the odd group.

When the driver departed, the three walked along the western face of Saint-Germain l'Auxerrois, now locked for the day. To their right, across a narrow park and entrance to an underground car park, the eastern colonnade of the Louvre glowed. Its columns appeared taller in the uplighting.

"There it is," said Aya, making a beeline to the sewer cover near the crosswalk. Pedestrians in twos and threes strolled between the Quai du Louvre and Rue de Rivoli.

Aya waited for a couple to pass and then said, "Eyrún, look out for cars. It's one way, so nothing should be turning from there." She pointed toward the cover. "Darwin, give me a hand."

She stuck a metal hook attached to a rock-climbing loop into the cover's middle hole and slipped a section of rope through the loop. "Now, take this end," she said, handing a length to Darwin, "and run it over your shoulder like this and around your back."

He copied her with the rope over his left shoulder and then under his right arm. Then he mirrored her squat as he took up the rope's slack.

"Ready?" she said.

"Ready."

They stood, lifting the cover free. "*Merde!*" he grunted.

"They're heavier than they look," Aya said, crab-walking a few steps with him before setting it down.

Darwin shined his light down the hole as Aya unhooked the loops and said, "Boots on. Let's go."

They stuffed their shoes in dry sacks and hung organic vapor masks around their necks.

"What about the cover?" asked Eyrún.

"Usually," said Aya, "someone stays above ground to replace it. I messaged my buddy who works in the sewer department. He said he'd swing by." She climbed down first.

Eyrún followed. When she reached the bottom, she said, "I thought it would smell worse."

"It gets flushed out regularly with rain, and the *éboueurs,* those crews in the green suits, pump water from the Seine to flush the streets."

"Ew," said Eyrún. "This goes into the Seine?"

"No," said Darwin, dropping down behind her. "It goes to the treatment plants."

Aya paused in the narrow passage, shaped like an inverted teardrop. The forearm-width bottom channel sloped outward to just over a meter at shoulder height and rounded overhead at two meters. "This way," she said, heading toward the Louvre.

Darwin brought up the rear, using a light touch on the walls to balance himself as they walked down the narrow channel. The space was more uniform than a natural cave, and its smooth brick was permanently moist. A fat pipe ran at head height along the left side, and thick black telecommunications cables were strung on the right.

The air, while damp and fetid, was breathable. Aya hung a monitor from her jumpsuit and told the others to keep their vapor masks ready. She turned right, into a broader channel that paralleled the colonnade. Darwin recalled his study of the Paris sewers and their construction. He could see the ingenuity behind the nineteenth-century design, which used street patterns to bring clean water in and send black water out. Because of this forethought, Paris had little need to tear up its streets. *But*, he thought, *it must have been hell building it.*

They reached Rue de Rivoli, where a sign mirrored the above-ground signage. Here, the main channel widened, and walkways on either side straddled a meter-wide central flow. "Stay out of that," Aya said, pointing at the brown water.

"It's flowing faster than the side channel," said Darwin.

"That's normal. It's like a river. Smaller tributaries dump in, making it bigger as it goes." Aya shined her light up and down the left wall. "It should be just along here."

"What are we looking for?" asked Eyrún.

"Here." Aya stopped at a metal door and ran her light around its edges.

"Looks like a submarine door," said Eyrún. "*Etanche?* What's that?"

"Watertight," said Aya.

"I've heard of these," said Darwin. "The Louvre bomb shelters, right?"

Aya examined the thick chain looped through the round door mechanism and a metal ring set in the sewer wall. "These look fresh." She ran a gloved finger over marks on the door where the thin slime had been scratched. She turned the handle until the chain resisted the movement and then returned it to its full-locked position.

"No one's supposed to have keys to this. My colleague says only the Louvre emergency services know about it. In case of a terrorist threat or something. And it's alarmed on the inside."

"Why was your colleague down here?" asked Darwin.

"Normal maintenance. He's on the crew that regularly clears the channel behind us."

Eyrún turned to look, and her feet sloshed. "Why is the water rising?"

Aya looked down. Water on the ledge was now covering the toe of her boot. She turned to the main channel and saw ripples with a noticeable increase in flow. "*Putain!* We forgot to check the weather.

"Oh, my God. It's coming up fast," said Eyrún, watching a tree branch bob in the stream. The water on the walkway now lapped at their ankles.

"Let's get back to the entrance." Darwin turned.

"No. It's too narrow," said Aya. "Let me think." She closed her eyes for a moment and then opened them. "This way. There's an opening into the Line One Metro tunnel near the Palais Royal station."

She took a climbing rope from her dry bag, tied a loop, clipped on a carabiner, and attached it to a ring on Eyrún's jumpsuit. "Darwin. Do the same thing another three meters down."

He grasped the rope and moved behind Eyrún as Aya went to the front. Moments later, he yelled, "Ready!" over the water's rising volume.

They slogged forward as rainwater surged around their calves. Each step felt like walking into a gale.

Aya turned back and yelled, "We need to cross at that cable!"

Eyrún looked at Darwin. Her expression suggested Aya must be nuts.

They reached the head-height cable strung between stout iron rings in the walls as the water crested their knees. Aya pointed ahead at the opposite bank, where her light picked out an arch in the wall. "That's the tunnel under the Metro. Follow my moves. You two hold fast while I cross. Just let your body hang in the water until you get to the other walkway."

Darwin threw a climbing loop over the wire, pulled it through itself, and clipped his carabiner to the loop. "Secure. Go."

Aya crossed without a problem. She fashioned a similar looped anchor and attached it to the cable, and then Eyrún moved across, followed by Darwin. He and Aya unclipped, and they forged their way along the wall.

"Almost there." As Aya pushed ahead, water streamed around her petite form.

The raging water reverberated overhead as Darwin tried not to think about the lowering ceiling.

Aya slipped into the side tunnel, followed by Eyrún. The trailing rope strained against the stone corner as Darwin closed the gap. He rounded it just as Eyrún yelled, "What's that!"

Aya flattened against the wall, but not before a large object smashed into her. She tumbled, taking Eyrún with her. Darwin braced himself, but the women's momentum was too great. As Aya was swept into the Rue de Rivoli channel, he flew into the water.

Eyrún screamed as she bobbed under the cable. Darwin got a hand on it but slipped off, and his head plunged underwater. He surfaced. "What?" he yelled at something Eyrún said. He tugged his way to her.

"Aya said there's a crossover walkway!" she shouted, spitting out water.

Darwin forced his brain to ignore what they were floating in as he reeled himself and Eyrún to Aya. The three raced side by side. "Where's this walkway?"

"About level with Tour Saint Jacques."

"How far is that?" asked Eyrún.

"Not very. There." Aya pointed. "That's Rue des Halles. We're close." She pushed up in the current. "There. There. Just grab it."

A dark shape stretched across the undulating water. They bounced sideways as the Rue des Halles tributary dumped into the Rivoli channel.

"Now!" Aya screamed.

Darwin's wrists slammed into the metal undercarriage. Blinding pain shot down his arm, but he held fast. Eyrún and Aya also got a grip. "Okay. Pull toward me. There's a doorway out on this bank."

They moved hand over hand. Darwin slipped once. He flashed on them being swept under and risked grabbing the looped carabiner. A surge pushed him upward as he hooked it on the catwalk. It held his body weight as he helped Eyrún get to the bank.

Aya pulled herself up onto the path and then the metal walk. Eyrún went next. She and Aya attached themselves to the rail and pulled the rope.

Darwin reached the side. He got his feet on the concrete walkway and moved to mount the catwalk.

Eyrún screamed.

He turned as a log took out his feet. He went down hard, and his head whacked metal.

4th Arrondissement

Voices came from a long, dark tunnel that emanated a warm light. He moved toward it, and the sounds grew louder.

"Ow!" A blinding flash turned the world red. He winced at the pain from speaking.

He blinked away the hurt as the light withdrew. Then Eyrún's face hovered over his. "Darwin. Oh, my God. You're okay."

Other voices and beeping noises came from behind him. Blue and red lights flashed off the walls. He could make out a metal cabinet—an IV tube. A woman in a yellow suit sat next to him, her face covered with a medical mask.

"Where? *Putain!* My head." He moved a hand to something blocking his vision.

"Go easy, Love," said Eyrún. "You were unconscious for a while. We're with the SAMU now." She squeezed his hand.

Darwin registered "SAMU," the Paris emergency medical services, and surmised he was in an ambulance.

The masked medic leaned toward Darwin. "What's your name?" she asked.

"Darwin Lacroix."

"Good. I'm going to ask you a series of questions, okay?"

Darwin answered them and, when the medic finished, asked, "What happened?"

"You have a laceration over your right eye and a contusion on your forehead," she said.

"We were at a costume party," said Eyrún. "We went as cavers and were on the way home when a car on Rue de Rivoli almost hit us. You hit your head on the curb."

"What? Where's—"

"Our friend? Remember? She caught a rideshare before the car ran us down."

"Erm..." Darwin's vision swam as the medic put an oxygen mask over his nose and mouth.

"Let's go," she said to the driver.

Pale early-morning light filled the hospital room window when Darwin was wheeled in after an MRI. Eyrún, who had been asleep in the bedside chair, listened to the nurse confirm that Darwin's head trauma went no further than a concussion. However, the neurologist had mandated he stay until later in the day.

When the caregivers left, he cornered Eyrún for an explanation. "What's going on? I'm not hallucinating. I hit my head in the sewer. What costume party? And why are you dressed like a doctor?"

Eyrún laughed, tugging at her blue medical scrubs. "I had to make up a story. It seemed as plausible as anything. But you did whack your head on the catwalk. Aya and I dragged you out in Saint-Jacques Square. It was pouring. We called emergency services, and I told Aya to leave as they showed up."

"Why?"

"She couldn't be caught dressed as *La Chauve Souris*. She'd lose her job and reputation. As it was, I had a hell of a time getting the police and medics to believe the story. Think of it: we're in red jumpsuits, barefoot, smelled like shit..."

Darwin's eyes widened.

"Our boots and socks got pulled off. Washed away."

He imagined the sight and laughed, but he stopped at the jolt of pain in his head. "Where're your clothes?"

"Hopefully, burned. When you went upstairs for the MRI, one of the nurses handed me the scrubs and pointed to the staff showers."

A knock on the doorframe drew their attention. They turned as Aya entered. "I heard you two got into some fun tonight," she said, winking. "I brought clean clothes." She handed Eyrún a bag along with the keys to their apartment.

An hour later, a nurse came to check on Darwin and kicked his visitors out. "Sweet dreams," said Eyrún.

"Yeah, I'll dream of secret doors in underground rivers," said Darwin.

35

The Farm

Christian awoke to a pounding on the door. It was pitch black inside the caravan. His body ached from the extra hours of digging. He rolled over. The hammering came again.

"What?" he yelled.

"There's a storm coming. We got to cover the hillside," said the farmer, now outside the window.

Christian looked at the time: 4:33. "*Putain!*" he groaned.

The farmer rapped on the glass.

"I'm coming. And I need coffee."

"I got a full thermos."

Five minutes later, Christian wrapped both hands around a cup as the farmer drove the dump truck up the hill. The headlights caught swaying tree branches. The farmer explained that the forecasted thunderstorms were due in two hours.

He stopped the truck with its lights aimed at the hill. "That will do 'til sunrise," he said, climbing out. He surveyed the site and then explained his plan. "I'll cut a trench along the top to channel water around where we think the workshop opening is. We cover that area with the tarps."

Christian shrugged. "You're the expert," he said and then watched the farmer dig. He refilled his coffee cup a third time, which mitigated the pain in his protesting joints. Yesterday, they'd worked almost fourteen hours after he'd promised the farmer extra money to do the job faster.

He thought of his call with Lionel the other day and still couldn't figure out his friend's increased sense of urgency. Lionel had pushed for the location again, but Christian had deferred. He wanted this discovery for himself. He enjoyed Lionel's company but didn't trust him.

As a compromise, Christian had used more money from the painting sales to speed up the project. Unfortunately, half that burden fell on him, as he refused to hire anyone besides the farmer.

The skip loader clanged the side of the dumper, and the farmer motioned that it was full—time for Christian to do his job. He started its engine and used the hillside cutout they'd created to turn around. The sky had grown lighter, but darkness still covered the valley.

He dumped the dirt, now twenty-seven piles, along the field's edge and headed back up. When he got there, the farmer was forming a berm. Christian parked the truck, sipped cold coffee, and reached for the thermos.

"I hit something!" yelled the farmer, dumping another load into the truck.

Christian put down the cup and thermos and followed the excavator, turning towards the hill. He went wide around its side as the farmer turned toward the hill. Dirt had slumped into the spot where the farmer had scooped last. Christian made out an object poking out of the dirt.

His heart leaped. In the dim light, it looked like a timber used to brace a tunnel. The skip loader's lights landed on it. *Putain!* Christian's blood froze.

A yellow-nosed cylinder.

"It's a bomb!" he yelled, frantically waving his arms.

But the farmer didn't see him until it was too late. The shovel had scooped dirt from below the bomb. They watched as the dark metal tipped downward, its nose no longer supported.

For seventy-nine years, the dud had lain inert and secure in the earth.

Until today.

Decades ago, another thunderstorm had caused a catastrophe in a B-17 formation, forcing planes to drop their ordnance near Struthof, triggering a landslide. But one of the AN-M64 five-hundred-pound bombs had a delayed fuse. Used to penetrate buildings before exploding, it contained a glass vial of acetone that broke when the bomb crashed through a reinforced roof. That acetone dissolved a celluloid disc holding back a spring-loaded trigger.

This bomb had struck the soft soil on a steep slope, stopping at an angle. The acetone had dripped onto the bomb's inner casing but not the trigger mechanism. It had remained safe in the earth, but over the long decades, the celluloid had weakened. As dirt shifted beneath the bomb, it rolled, crumbling the celluloid holding back the striker.

Christian spun, his legs churning.

The farmer leaped.

Neither made it.

A supersonic shock wave exploded the TNT, shredding the steel shell.

The concussive surge smashed the skip loader and truck. Trees splintered in a thirty-meter radius.

Hikers in a nearby valley cowered as the blast echoed.

Three kilometers away, in Rothau, the gendarmerie got phone calls asking about an explosion.

Later that morning, marble-sized hail drove people to shelter. Rain bucketed down for the next half-day.

By nightfall, the rain subsided, and the sky cleared. Just before midnight, a full moon crested the trees surrounding the blast zone, its silvery glow falling on the denuded hillside. The explosion had removed tons of soil, and the rain had left deep gullies in the newly exposed ground.

But the downpour had also cleaned the quarried granite blocks of the old Junkers workshop.

No one was there to see it.

PART II

Two Weeks Later

36

Île de la Cité

By lunchtime, Eyrún and Aya had crisscrossed the crushed-granite surface of Place Dauphine, where Île de la Cité narrowed to a point where the Seine rejoined into a single flow. Pont Neuf crossed this spit of land connecting the Left and Right Banks—a mixing point of Paris culture for the last half-millennium.

The day had begun unseasonably warm and humid, and both women hung their light jackets on the handle of the ground-penetrating radar unit. The GPR resembled a push mower. Its red-orange detectors hovered over the dirt, suspended by four wheels, larger at the rear. The upright handle, where their clothing hung, was topped by a tablet.

They moved back and forth with the tedium of mowing grass. An hour before, a group of school kids on a school outing had approached, and Aya had explained the GPR's basic operation. But the tablet displayed a stew of shapes and colors, none of them resembling treasure, and the kids had quickly lost interest.

"How long does it take to sort through the data?" Eyrún asked Aya when they broke for lunch. Cool shade covered their cafe table.

Aya sipped her iced tea before answering, "No more than a day for big objects, but anything like a tunnel would appear as a black space. We'd see the stones outlining the walls."

The server delivered their lunches: Caesar salad made with radicchio and roasted pear, topped with chilled prawns.

Eyrún glanced at her watch. Darwin was likely over Iceland. He'd taken off three hours earlier, bound for Seattle.

After a bite, Aya said, "This is so good." She drank some of her tea and then continued: "The data is uploading in real-time. Our local view combined with Zac's satellite data should give us a useful picture."

Zac had arranged passes by multiple satellites, each with differing technologies. His work with the US Geological Survey and Lawrence Berkeley Labs gave him access to various sources. His research concentrated on earthquake detection, aiming to develop early warning systems. While Paris was not an earthquake zone, satellites passed over the region during their orbits.

Eyrún's phone dinged. She read the message. "Good. Lupita's receiving our data."

The Agrippa Centre for Archaeology on Corsica had a world-class data science group led by Lupita Kumani. Darwin and Eyrún had recruited her based on her algorithms, which deciphered the text in Roman scrolls carbonized by the ancient Mount Vesuvius eruption. Zac had collaborated with Lupita on many ACA projects.

Twenty minutes later, the server was clearing their plates when Eyrún's phone chimed again. Lupita had a question. Eyrún called her, set the phone to speaker mode, and set it on the table.

"Hello, Eyrún," Lupita said in a warm, melodious voice.

Eyrún introduced her to Aya, and they spent a couple of minutes getting to know each other. Then Lupita asked, "Can you get underground? My satellite map shows a car park entrance on Rue de Harlay."

"Yes, I know that one," said Aya. "Why?"

"The data from the passes shows the car park, but there's a structure beneath the Rue de Harlay adjacent to the car park's western end wall. It's broken up. Maybe it happened during construction."

"We're on it," said Eyrún.

"But," said Lupita, "make sure the data card has enough space. You will not be able to upload while you are underground."

"We've got a spare with two terabytes," said Aya.

"That should be enough."

They said goodbye, paid the lunch bill, and pushed the GPR to the car park entrance. They wheeled the unit down the ramp, pausing momentarily to let their eyes adjust to the dark space before continuing.

Neither noticed the figure that slipped in behind them as they descended to the second level.

An hour later, they'd scanned most of the lowest level. An industrial combination of engine oil and mildew had replaced the pleasant autumn air topside. They'd zipped their jackets against the chill. Aya guessed they were thirty meters below the island's surface, putting them below the Seine's waterline.

"Stop!" said Aya.

Eyrún paused. They were moving along a row of cars on the eastern side of the car park below the Cour d'Appel.

"I heard a ping. What did you see?" asked Aya.

Eyrún rolled the GPR back. A greenish object resolved faintly on the screen. She rocked the GPR forward and backward. The object drifted in and out of focus in the haze of other data. It reminded her of watching the ultrasound of her kidney that she'd had done a few years back.

Aya looked at the sensitivity setting—one notch lower than the maximum—and turned it up. "How's that?"

The screen blurred, its colors kaleidoscoping.

"It's a mess," said Eyrún, and then a disturbance flowed across the screen, eddying like a jet's contrail. She stabbed her finger at it. "What's that?"

Aya yanked off the headphones as the colors whirled. "It's the

Metro." She laughed as the colors stabilized. "But that's a good indicator. Line Four is one of the deepest."

A man had approached. They noticed him but thought nothing of it as he went to a nearby car and stopped at its driver's door. But Aya tapped Eyrún's arm as the man came quickly toward them.

Eyrún fumbled in her handbag for pepper spray as both women got behind the GPR.

The man pulled out a knife. "Give me the data card."

Aya manipulated the tablet's slot and withdrew the microSD card. She held it out to the man but then flicked it under a car. As his attention turned to it, they sprinted away.

They were approaching the row's end when another figure came around its corner from the upper level. They skidded to a stop. Eyrún squeezed a shot of pepper spray, and the guy dove behind a car.

"Get them!" yelled the first man near the GPR.

Aya and Eyrún pressed against the wall below the row of cars. Aya ducked and pointed at the feet converging on them.

"They've got pepper spray," said the guy coming from the exit.

Eyrún found a metal service door one car over. Air, drawn by the garage's exhaust fans, rushed out of its lower grating. Its signage read "Service Access."

She grasped the handle. Locked. "Aya," she whispered, handing over the pepper spray, "hold them off."

Aya stood and shot bursts at each man. They backed off.

"That's not a large canister," said the exit man. He moved forward but then jumped back as Aya fired another burst. "You got maybe two left," he taunted.

Eyrún dug in her pack for a lockpick set. Darwin had shown her how to use them when they'd needed to access crypts or graveyards. She worked the door lock as Aya urged her to hurry.

"He's right. It feels empty."

"It's open," whispered Eyrún. "Get close to me. I'll pretend to keep working on it." She cursed, slamming a fist on the door in mock protest.

"Now." Eyrún pulled it open and then slammed it shut as Aya passed behind her. She locked it. "That will hold them. Let's go."

"Which way?" asked Aya.

"Shit!" Eyrún froze. She looked both ways. "Left. It's shorter."

The right-side tunnel disappeared into blackness, while the left glowed faintly. They ran along a waist-high railing, which protected them from a concrete pit resembling an unfinished swimming pool.

"It's for rain overflow," said Aya. "Traps water during downpours."

Eyrún's adrenaline hit overdrive as she pictured their last venture in the sewer. Metal banged behind them. "Shit! They're in. Let's go."

A few strides later, she looked back. Aya had lagged. Eyrún slowed. "You lead," she said, pushing Aya ahead. Eyrún's height and speed gave her an advantage.

She looked ahead over Aya's shoulder. The end wall came up fast. *Shit, shit, shit.* She looked around for a weapon, but the space had been washed clean.

Eyrún looked back again as Aya shouted, "A door!"

Seconds later, they burst into a space. Daylight poured in through an opposite opening. Eyrún blocked the door with her foot as the men pounded on the steel.

"We're under the Pont Neuf exhibit," Aya said as a half-dozen people stared.

"I can't hold them," said Eyrún.

"Help!" Aya yelled, running for the opening. "Men are after us!"

People fled. Eyrún sprinted as the door banged open. She glanced back and tripped over a pram as the men rushed her. She screamed, sprawling onto wide steps.

Three minutes later, Eyrún and Aya sat on a bench, their heart rates back to normal. The people in Square du Vert-Galant had returned to their picnics or resumed wandering in the green space at the tip of Île de la Cité. Above them, the bronze equestrian statue of Henry IV stood watch atop Pont Neuf.

The two gendarmes who had run past Eyrún to intercept her pursuers returned to the park. "They got away," said one.

"Are you okay?" the other one asked Eyrún.

"*Oui*. Thank you," she said, rubbing her right knee.

"Why were they chasing you?" asked the first cop.

Aya took charge, showing them her badge from the *Crypte Archéologique*. She explained they had been accosted in the garage and had escaped into the sewer overflow corridor.

"What is on the memory card?"

"Scanning data from below ground. We're looking for ancient grave sites," she said, bending the truth.

The gendarmes took notes for their report and escorted Aya and Eyrún back to the garage to retrieve the GPR unit. After thanking the cops, the two women pushed it back towards Notre-Dame and the crypt. Thunder boomed as the sky darkened.

"That wasn't random," said Eyrún. "Someone wants our data."

"I was thinking the same thing," said Aya. "But aside from my colleagues who lent us the GPR, no one knows what we're doing."

A fat raindrop splattered the pavement. Then another. Aya pushed the GPR faster as the drops increased. Eyrún grasped the other side of the handle, and they ran as the thundershower let loose. Ahead of them, Notre-Dame disappeared in a blur of wind-whipped water.

"It keeps chasing us," Aya said about the rain, laughing as water streamed down her face.

37

Paris

"You're late," said Vivienne as Lionel reached the cafe at a quarter past four.

"I had a problem with the police," he said, sliding into the chair beside her. She'd chosen a cafe in the fourteenth arrondissement, far from their usual hangouts. Drizzle rolled off the awning, pattering onto the pavement.

"Nothing that can get back to me, I hope."

Lionel ignored her vapid, self-centered comment and ordered a red wine from the server who had come over to switch on infrared heaters to drive away the damp chill.

"Have you found Christian, at least?"

"No," he said, sipping his wine. Then he added, "He's not answered my calls or texts. I haven't seen him at work, and his house is dark."

Vivienne gritted her teeth. "Why weren't you following him?"

"Because you had me following Darwin."

"You should have followed both," she said.

Lionel swore into his glass at her ridiculous statement.

"And what about the Louvre tunnels? Someone leaked intel. Who?"

"Wasn't me."

Lionel had stayed away from the Louvre basements after Louvre security got an anonymous tip alerting them to the watertight door access from the sewer. They'd restricted entry to all the basements. He had other ways into the subbasement but knew it was best to let things cool. Their secret had been kept for centuries, but it was becoming increasingly difficult with modern video and electronic surveillance.

The organization he and Vivienne belonged to didn't have a name. Its origin was steeped in legend. Some said it had begun as an informal network of collectors during the Age of Enlightenment when the first museums were created. Those wealthy elites had competed fiercely for the best works as art formerly concentrated in palaces moved into the public sphere at the Hermitage, Uffizi, Vatican, Prado, Rijksmuseum, British Museum, and Le Louvre.

As the Enlightenment's founders died off, professional curators emerged. Collections were shared and went on tour. Masterpieces gained fame, some by accident, like the *Mona Lisa's* shocking theft in 1911.

But behind the scenes, the organization carefully controlled the market through auction houses and clandestine collections. Museum directors and their puppet masters met in Europe's old halls of power to ensure their influence created the right balance of public benevolence and scarcity. Masterworks in visible space increased the desirability of works in the organization's control.

World War Two nearly broke the organization as the Nazis' industrial plundering disrupted centuries of cultivation. But it regrouped by inserting itself into the restitution efforts like the Monuments, Fine Arts, and Archives program.

However, by the mid-1950s, people were exhausted from decades of depression and war. Governments withdrew their support for restitution, and the organization settled back into its rhythm of buying and selling—creating artificial scarcity to accrue wealth.

Then, in the 1990s, renewed effort flowed into restitution. Laws were passed making it harder to subvert provenance. The organization had grown old and complacent and lacked coordination. It had been ripe for new leadership when Thierry Panchon, an archaeologist-turned-successful-antiquities-and-art-dealer, exerted influence.

Thierry brought new clients: oligarchs and tech billionaires with overflowing wallets and fungible morality. The organization's old leaders found themselves "retired" in favor of younger, more aggressive members. Wealth quadrupled.

But then it all went to shit. Panchon's untimely death left the organization leaderless. Vivienne, Thierry's second in charge in the Louvre cell, had inherited that cell's leadership and desperately wanted Thierry's other role as the organization's head. But so did the leads at the British Museum, the Met in New York, the Vatican Museums, and a dozen other global bastions of art and culture.

Lionel wanted nothing to do with that fight. However, he made an effort to show his allegiance to Vivienne. She could very well prevail. A question from her broke his digression.

"Where is Darwin?"

"He went to Seattle. I've been following his wife instead."

"Why?"

"She's using GPR to scan for tunnels."

"So what? She won't find anything," said Vivienne, reaching for her glass. "Besides, I've got it under control."

But Lionel noticed her hand shaking. *She's nervous.* The OCBC head and finance minister were investigating. She had moles inside each department but no longer at the top. And the arrival of an incorruptible outsider had caused a problem.

This was Vivienne's first genuine test as leader. Lionel had been offered the role but declined. He preferred operating without day-to-day responsibility and managing politics. He enjoyed the solitude of hands-on restoration and had plenty of informal contacts in the organization. *No, she wanted this. Let her deal with it.*

"I'll take care of Darwin. Focus on finding Christian," she said, having composed herself.

"Fine," he said.

"I want that painting, Lionel."

He studied her. Their cardinal rule was to avoid becoming attached to any artifact. *Greed leads to mistakes.*

As if reading his thoughts, she said, "It's not for me. A benefactor mentioned that particular work. And I know you like your holidays."

When he didn't reply, she excused herself.

Benefactor, my ass, he thought, watching her cross the street to a taxi stand. He'd noticed her starry-eyed expression. Selling the Raphael would elevate her family's sagging reputation.

Then, he pictured a suite on a cruise ship launching in three months. An escort service he used had emailed pictures promising seven luxurious days and six unforgettable nights for only €70,000. His lips curled as he considered it.

It's been done before. Not with a painting of this caliber. Still…

For the next ten minutes, he worked through likely scenarios. Then, he got up and headed to the nearest Metro.

The rain had stopped, and the sidewalks had filled with people. Tires hissed on the wet streets, and sunlight streamed through the broken clouds, casting an orange glow on the buildings.

As he reached the Metro's stairs, Lionel thought of another, more likely candidate to take over. *Perhaps it's time to visit again.*

He decided he would, but right now, he needed to break into Christian's house.

38

Seattle

Darwin rubbed the itch on his forehead where healing skin tugged at the week-old sutures. The day after the neurologist approved air travel, he was on a plane to see James Wilkerson, now 103 years old.

He studied Puget Sound from the window of an A350 as the big plane curled its way to Seattle's SeaTac Airport. The land masses below created a labyrinth of waterways. He thought of Eyrún and their boat. *We could get lost for weeks.*

The plane bucked, and he stowed his stuff as the flight attendants made a last pass through the cabin. A quarter-hour later, it touched down. He'd delayed this trip to Seattle because of his accident in the sewer, using the downtime to grade midterm papers that had piled up. The espresso machine had needed to run overtime to keep up.

Aya had asked him to get the OCBC's help after hitting dead ends trying to access the Louvre subbasement bomb shelter records. But he'd suggested holding off until they better understood who to trust. "Besides," he'd said, "we have no idea why it was accessed. It could have been a regular security test."

He messaged Eyrún on landing. A minute later, she called him.

"Hi, Love. I'm still on the plane."

"I'm with Aya at our place, and Zac is on the call."

"Hey, Zac."

"Hey. How's your head?"

The men talked briefly about Darwin's injury before Eyrún cut them off. "We were attacked today while scanning."

"What?" Adrenalin surged, blasting away Darwin's jetlag. People in the cabin looked at him.

Eyrún explained what had happened in the car park and their getaway. As Darwin traversed the jet bridge, Zac asked for descriptions of the two men: how they'd moved and what they'd said.

"We couldn't see them very well," said Aya. "They approached us in a darker section of the garage."

"And they only wanted the data card?" asked Zac.

"They didn't get it," said Aya. "I palmed it and threw a blank spare at them."

Darwin stopped in the customs hall and swept a hand through his hair. The inbound passengers snaked their way through the queue. He looked in the opposite direction, towards the plane, calculating the time for a return flight to France. Three hours. Plenty of time.

He was about to suggest it when Zac piped up: "I'm coming over."

"No need, Zac. Really," said Eyrún. "We can fend for ourselves."

"That's only part of the reason," he said. "I need a ground-level view of what the satellites are scanning."

"What about Siggy?" asked Eyrún. Her sister, Zac's partner, was in San Francisco, working on neurological implants at the University of California.

"She's in a critical phase of the project. She'll hardly know I'm gone."

Darwin resumed his place in the customs line, confident his wife would be in capable hands. Zac's street smarts as a former US Army Ranger would figure out who had followed them.

He refocused on his task—James Wilkerson. There had to be a connection. He knew it in his bones. He'd tried to describe the feeling to Eyrún, but the sensation eluded words. The best he could think of was the shimmering optical artifact that emerged as a precursor to a migraine. It appeared, and then it disappeared.

But it kept building.

He snapped back to the phone conversation as Aya talked about the GPR data. "I think it's hopeless. The scans are too full of noise. Over the last two thousand years, there's been too much digging and change."

Darwin could relate. He'd had years of false starts and dead ends searching for the lava tube entrances. A thought blossomed. "Wait!" he burst out.

The others paused.

As Darwin's idea solidified, he said, "Aya, the Roman baths under the forecourt. Where did they get their water?"

"The Notre-Dame forecourt, above the *Crypte Archéologique*?" asked Aya. "I assume it came from the Seine."

"*Merde!* Of course," said Darwin.

"Where did you think it came from?" Zac laughed. "They had an enormous river out their front door."

"Yeah, that was dumb," said Darwin, "but I was thinking about aqueducts. One of my doctoral candidates is researching how the Romans consolidated defenses on Île de la Cité against the Germanic tribes."

The conversation paused. In the background, Aya rustled through papers. "Found it!" she said after a moment. "It's a drawing of Paris made in eight hundred. More illustrative than actual, but it shows holy sites and churches. The island's east end was pasture in Roman times—a series of low islands that regularly flooded. They didn't combine them until Pont Neuf was built seven hundred years later. The only access was by boat or two wooden bridges."

"So…here, in the middle… Sorry, Zac and Darwin, I'm pointing to the current Justice Palace, where the Romans built a governor's residence after the Left Bank was sacked. Builders discovered the stone foundations when digging the Cité Metro station in 1906." She paused, tapping her finger on the paper. "Of course. Why didn't I see this before?"

"See what?" asked Eyrún.

Darwin riffed on the speculation. "What if the Romans tunneled under the Seine? They could move behind any force attacking the bridges. Centuries later, the French kings used old Roman tunnels."

"Exactly! Darwin, you're a genius."

"Oh, great." Zac laughed. "Like his ego needs more stroking."

"Not to worry," said Eyrún. "I'll keep his feet on the ground."

"Hey!" Darwin protested.

Aya kept them on target. "Zac, could you run another satellite pass along Voie Georges Pompidou, the road running along the Seine at water level?"

"On it," he said, adding, "Can you and Eyrún run the GPR along both quayside roads?"

Darwin cut in. "What about the guys who followed them?"

Aya solved that one. "I'll borrow two security people from Notre-Dame."

"Just be careful," said Darwin. "I gotta go. The customs officer is frowning at me."

39

Darwin arrived at the Orca Paradise Retirement Home, a single-story building between suburban homes. After signing the guest register, a nurse escorted him to James Wilkerson's room.

"How is he?" asked Darwin.

"Jim's a firecracker," said the nurse, her red ponytail swishing as she walked quickly down the gleaming tile corridors. "He's been with us almost a decade now. Don't let him talk you into playing cards. He's a shark."

"Duly warned," said Darwin, remembering his last thrashing by Eyrún.

"Here we are." The nurse paused and rapped on an open doorframe. "Jim? Your visitor is here."

The old man was dozing in a chair that faced a tall window overlooking a stand of pines.

"What?" said James Wilkerson, waking up. The nurse rearranged the blanket covering his legs. "Oh, right. I remember," he added after orienting himself. "Thank you, Candice. You're too good to me."

She smiled and said, "I'm down the hall on the right if you need anything."

Darwin extended a hand. "Pleased to meet you, Mr. Wilkerson. I'm Darwin Lacroix."

"It's Jim," he said, his voice warbling from prolonged use. He shook the offered hand and added, "Only my students used my last name." He sized Darwin up and down. "I read your bio—impressive discoveries and a serious scholar. I had access to the Apostolic Archive once years ago. What will we do when it's all digitized? I suppose all that paper will decay."

"I think we've got a good many years before that happens," said Darwin.

"Speak for yourself," said Jim.

"I..."

"That was a joke, son." Jim grinned. "Now, let's talk about why you're here. It's about eighty years late, but maybe you can do something. Tell me what you know so I don't waste time."

Darwin decided that full transparency was best, and he began by saying that the OCBC and interior minister had asked him to investigate thefts.

"I declined their request, but then I got a folio with your 1947 letter requesting an investigation on Karl Meyer. It also contained articles about insider thefts at the Louvre and British Museum. I'll admit to being intrigued and Googling you, but I left it at that.

"Then, within a week, the DGSE, our exterior security agency, like your CIA, delivered a file on my maternal great-grandmother's family. The Vichy government betrayed them. All killed."

"I'm sorry, son," said Jim.

"Thank you. I never knew them, and my grandfather rarely mentioned them, but—"

"It lays the horror right in your lap."

"Yes. I suppose that's one way to see it." Darwin reached into his bag and removed the photos of the Avercamp paintings and the Soutine gallery in Paris. Jim studied them.

"These are well done. If I'm not mistaken," he said, "there from the Dutch Golden period.

"Spot on," said Darwin. "Hendrick Avercamp."

"So, you agreed to look into the Louvre thefts based on this?"

"Almost," Darwin said, and then he explained the letters from the French president and the pope.

Jim's brows arched. "Friends in high places."

"I'm no longer naive enough to think of it that way. Let's say I'm a talented resource to some powerful individuals."

Jim smiled. "You're wise for a young man. You can probably understand my frustrations in forty-seven."

The late afternoon sun squeezed between the trees outside the window, casting a bright streak across Jim. He sighed at the extra warmth. Darwin imagined himself in sixty years, his career over and him no longer relevant. He shuddered at the memory of a dream in which he'd been left behind by a tour bus—alone on a desert road.

Jim's voice shook him from the daydream. "But something else happened. I also Googled, and you don't strike me as someone who does what he's told. You need to internalize a quest. Make it your own."

Darwin felt like the man had opened a window into his soul. "Have you been talking to my wife?" he asked, making light of the situation.

"No need, "said Jim. "You remind me of my younger self—full of piss and vinegar but maturing, thinking ahead."

Darwin laid his cards on the table. "These two paintings were recovered and are in MNR custody, on loan to museums in Périgueux and Clermont-Ferrand. These three"—he pointed to the wall of the Soutine gallery and another individual photo—"were recently put on auction on an underground site. The poster claims they were purchased legally in 1943 and have been stored at the Geneva Freeport ever since."

"But you think otherwise," said Jim.

"Yes." Darwin briefly explained how Minh had recognized them.

"How does that connect to my letter?"

"I dug into the post-war recovery efforts. The MFAA did excellent work recovering museum-owned pieces and those of famous collectors but did little to recover art looted from private collections. Museums grabbed the best pieces under the guise of patrimony, and the MNR holds thousands of paintings.

"They've made no effort at restitution. The Nazis turn my stomach, but nowhere near as much as the Vichy French who stripped possessions from fellow citizens—my family—and sent them away to die." Darwin sighed and calmed himself. He hadn't intended to get so worked up.

"It's okay, son. The scars run deep," said Jim. "It was chaotic after the war. Everyone claimed to be part of the Resistance. People turned on each other. Let me tell you what I found. Perhaps it connects with your search."

Darwin nodded.

"In late forty-four, I was assigned to the Louvre and began working with Rose Valand. My God, that woman is a hero. Risked her life to document the Nazi thefts. There aren't enough medals to recognize her contribution." Jim shook his head. "You know the MNR is nicknamed the Rose Valand database?"

"I do," said Darwin.

"Anyway, in June forty-five, a German named Karl Meyer arrived to help with the restitution. He was a low-level operative in the ERR—"

"The Einsatzstab Reichsleiter Rosenberg?" asked Darwin.

"Yep. One and the same. Rosenberg was a nasty piece of shit. Forgive my French," said Jim.

"Pas de problème."

"Sorry," said Jim. "I forgot you're French."

Darwin waved it off with a smile.

"Anyway, Meyer's bosses in the ERR faced death sentences, and the son of a bitch was saving his skin by repatriating what he stole. As if he'd grown a conscious after the war." Jim wagged his head. "Clever strategy. I'll give him that. Meyer said the Nazis sent him to Paris in 1938 to assess and catalog private collections. You and I know that predominantly meant Jewish collections. When France surrendered to the Nazis in 1940, Meyer was sent back, this time to plunder. In forty-three, he was transferred to Berlin to curate the looted art."

Jim raised a finger, pointing accusingly. "His showing up in post-war Paris raised my suspicions. Why not hide in Germany? He wasn't high up in the ERR. At worst, he would've got a few years' jail sentence.

"Nah." James wagged his finger. "The guy was looking for something. He was a weasel. I wouldn't trust him to hold my milk money."

Jim reached for his water glass and sipped. After clearing his throat, he continued: "Meyer was obsessed. I speak some German and learned to read a fair bit during the war. He was searching for records on Hans Frank. So, I did a little digging on my own."

"Hans Frank was as bad as they came in the Nazi party—Hitler's personal attorney before becoming governor-general of occupied Poland. The bastard segregated Jews and funneled them into the death camps. Get this. At his trial in Nuremberg, he said he was unaware of them."

"Unaware!" Jim doubled over in a coughing fit.

Darwin helped him drink more water until his coughing settled. "I'm sorry to get you worked up," he said.

"I'm fine. It still bothers me today. The Nazis were the most vile humans in all of existence. Most denied wrongdoing, defending their Aryan beliefs until the rope snapped their necks."

He drank more water and then continued: "Anyway, back to Karl Meyer. I talked with a guy in French intelligence who processed Meyer after his arrest. He said Meyer testified to moving boxcars of stolen art from Poland for Frank in early forty-five. These went to safer locations in southern Germany as they outran the Soviet army and Allied bombing.

"You must realize that living in any sizable German city in 1944 meant bombs. The Nazis wouldn't surrender, and the Allies bombed cities to the brink of extinction. It's hard to understand now, son, but war is madness." Jim paused, his eyes drifting toward his folded hands as if struck by a dark vision. After a long moment, he continued.

"The monuments recovery operation sounds organized today, but the years right after the war were a confusing mess. Some of the Nazi loot was found by happenstance. In Merker, for example. The Allies heard rumors, but if two French women hadn't mentioned seeing German soldiers carrying art toward a mine, the treasure would still be down there."

Darwin was tempted to ask questions as Jim's story meandered, but he willed himself to be patient. He shifted in his chair, giving his backside a break after having sat the better part of the last twenty-four hours.

"Meyer's testimony against Frank and clues that led to the recovery of many pieces were part of his plea deal. But I wasn't convinced he'd come clean. The intelligence service agreed with me. We suspected Meyer had hidden a cache of the loot for himself.

"My suspicions grew when, in May…" Jim paused. "I think it was May. Doesn't matter. It was in forty-six, a year after the surrender. I was working late, and this emaciated kid stopped into our office. I say kid, but he was only a few years younger than me. He said he had information about stolen art. But the guy was starving, so I took him for a hot meal.

"He was a French art student from Alsace Lorraine, and the German army conscripted him after annexing the region. Fortunately, he found himself working for the ERR in Germany and not on the Russian front. He was in Poland during the art removal and rode on the train to Hans Frank's estate, but he said one of the boxcars had been removed before it reached Tegernsee. He couldn't say where, but he mentioned it contained the most valuable pieces, including a missing masterpiece—Raphael's *Portrait of a Young Man*."

Darwin bolted upright.

"Yes, that one," said Jim. "I've heard it would bring a hundred million at auction today. I asked the kid if he had ever heard of Karl Meyer. He said yes. Meyer had shown up in Berlin to supervise the transfer. But Meyer and the Raphael never arrived with the train at Frank's estate."

Darwin's brain swirled, trying to connect the pieces. "Okay, let me get this straight. A boxcar goes missing, as does Meyer. He knew *Portrait of a Young Man* was in that boxcar and stole it for himself."

Jim nodded. "You got it, son."

"But the trail must be long dead," said Darwin, frowning.

"Not quite. Hear me out," said Jim. "Before my discharge in forty-seven, Meyer traveled to Strasbourg three times. I followed him once. He was looking for two guys named Heinrich and Johann. I bribed it out of a bar owner one night. I think Meyer was double-crossed. There's no way he could've stolen an entire boxcar by himself.

"When I got back to Paris, I requested access to Meyer's intelligence file but was told it had been classified. It was bullshit. I know because I saw Meyer's file on the Louvre director's desk a week later. He casually closed it, but not before I read the name."

"Why would the director want it?" asked Darwin.

"I had my suspicions, and it's why they discharged me early. I think an inside group at the Louvre was keeping pieces for themselves. To prove my theory, I followed two of them late one night into a subbasement but lost them. It was like they disappeared behind a wall. A short while later, they reemerged—carrying a Dega painting, *Five Dancing Women*. I'm certain of it. The Nazis seized it in nineteen-forty, and no one's seen it since."

Darwin considered Jim's accusation. Not cataloging or displaying the Degas was outside protocol but not evidence of insider theft by itself. He didn't doubt Jim had seen the painting. He'd seen photos of the post-war Louvre and rooms with paintings by the hundreds leaning against walls.

"I know what you're thinking," Jim said.

Darwin blinked, snapping out of his thoughts.

"How does that Degas connect to the missing Raphael? To be honest, I don't know. Maybe there's a link to Meyer's file. Why else would they classify it?"

"Dunno," said Darwin. He caught Jim checking his watch and added, "I don't want to hold you up from dinner. I have one more question. If you were in my place, what would you do?"

"I would take a close look at Hans Frank's diaries. They're kept at the National Archives in DC. There might be files they haven't digitized yet. I have a couple more thoughts. Why don't you join me for dinner? It's also poker night." Jim smiled.

Darwin agreed and walked with Jim to the dining room. The pizza was decent, and he got a fourth slice while listening to Jim's ideas. Later, he had a blast losing a hundred dollars to Jim and his friends.

At 9 p.m., he collapsed onto his hotel bed and was asleep in minutes.

40

Île Saint-Louis

The next morning, Eyrún and Aya ran the GPR over the Île de la Cité quayside road. A brisk wind whipped around the buildings, chasing yesterday's storms eastward. By one o'clock, they'd finished the island side and broke for lunch at Le Louis Philippe on the right bank. The server raised her eyebrows at the contraption beside their outdoor table but said nothing as she took their orders.

Eyrún tucked into her salad the moment it arrived. A half-dozen bites later, she watched Aya chasing her lettuce around the plate and asked, "What are you thinking?"

"Huh?" Aya looked up. "Oh, erm, I was thinking of this afternoon. We have to scan both roads on this side. The Voie Georges Pompidou at river level and Quai de Gesvres. That's hours of work."

"I'll help."

"I know, but…" Aya looked at the pedestrians along the quai. "I can't stop thinking about the subbasement tunnel. I mean, this"—she swept a hand toward the river—"is looking for a needle in a haystack. It's boring."

"I couldn't agree more," said Eyrún.

"We should be scanning l'Auxerrois. If we can't find a tunnel under the cathedral, there's no point in looking for one here."

Eyrún grinned. "Let's do it."

"Really?" Aya's eyes widened.

When Eyrún nodded, Aya attacked her salad, talking between bites. "I think a tunnel would run from under the Louvre's drawbridge gate. It's a straight line from there to l'Auxerrois. I'm guessing it would enter at the crypt level and emerge in the cathedral."

"Where?"

"That's what we need to figure out. It underwent repairs after the Revolution. The crypt was sealed, and there are no detailed records, but I'm guessing we'll find it in one of the chapels."

"I'm game. What do we need?" asked Eyrún.

"Return the GPR. I need to get some basic tools from my flat. You go to yours. Maybe I'll take a nap since it will be a late night. Let's meet at…" Aya looked at her watch. "Six thirty at the cathedral entrance. It closes at seven, so we'll need to hide."

Back at her flat, Eyrún tried to lie down but found she had extra energy. The last two days of scanning had been a dirge march, and her hips ached. She craved action. She knew archaeology was ninety-nine percent methodical work, and she loved Paris, but it meant too much walking and public transportation.

She wanted to be racing up to their mountain house on Corsica, or flying. Breaking into a buried crypt didn't quite fill her need for speed, but it had a danger factor. Her lips curled in a devious smile as she rounded up items for an underground adventure.

41

Washington DC

Darwin reached the rideshare pickup point at Dulles Airport near the US capital. He'd left Seattle on a 6 a.m. nonstop flight. His body clock had him up at three thirty, and with no more reason to be in Seattle, he'd followed Jim's recommendation to read Hans Frank's diaries firsthand. He cat-napped on the flight, but not enough to compensate for the time-zone shakeup from Paris.

A half-hour later, he was dropped off at the US National Archives research room on Pennsylvania Avenue. A cool autumn breeze propelled leaves across the sidewalk as he exited the car. Darwin liked Washington, DC. Its classical design felt similar to Paris's. He stole a glance at the capitol building far down the block, where the afternoon sun glinted on its marble dome.

Then, he studied the imposing Greek façade of the National Archive building. If you took out the modern glass, it would be easy to imagine you were entering the Roman Senate. He messaged his contact that he'd arrived and entered the building. After complying with a security check, he headed to the research room.

"Dr. Lacroix," said a younger man who greeted him. "I'm Evan Loh. Welcome to the National Archives."

"Thanks. Nice to meet you, Evan," Darwin said, shaking hands.

"Your assistant forwarded your request. I'm fluent in German and have the diaries you requested set up in a reading room. Can I get you anything?"

"No. Thanks for offering." Darwin followed Evan, answering his questions about the Vatican's archives as they walked.

"Here we are," said Evan, unlocking a door. A wooden table with a reading lamp took up most of the space. "All the diaries are here. We've not had that record accessed for some time. What are you looking for?"

Darwin didn't answer immediately. Instead, he reached for the bottom diary in the stack and opened it. The first page began on Wednesday, 1 March 1944. He explained the situation to Evan as he flipped through the pages. "During the war's closing months, Frank fled Poland for his native Bavaria. We know he shipped the art he'd stolen during his governorship of Poland to his estate in Tegernesse. Most were recovered and restituted to their original owners. I'm investigating an allegation that part of the shipment was stolen in transit."

He paused when he reached the last entry on 31 May 1945. Then he set the volume aside and opened the volume for January 1944, when Frank left Poland. "I need to know about Hans Frank's journey from Poland to Tegernesse."

"Where did you learn this?"

"From a former Monuments Man."

Evan waited for Darwin to say more. After a pregnant pause, he asked, "Okay. How can I help?"

Over the next hour and a half, Evan skimmed the journal and read sections relating to the move. With the Soviet army bearing down on Poland, Hans Frank had sent six boxcars of household goods and art to Tegernsee. He and his family had flown via the Luftwaffe.

"Does it say who traveled with the train?" asked Darwin.

"Erm, I haven't seen any names beyond Andreas Grimm, the *stabschef*, or chief of staff."

Evan went through a few dozen pages before finding another reference to the train. "Here." He put a finger on the text and read, "We arrived on 27 February 1945, three weeks late. The engineers and conductor who took over the train in Munich listed five box cars."

He skimmed ahead and then flipped back to look for notes on the switch from six to five. "The inbound crew said nothing about a missing boxcar. Maybe someone got it wrong in Poland?"

"Probably not," said Darwin. "These are Germans. Precision is in their DNA. I'd wager someone was bribed to overlook the boxcar."

He asked Evan to review the last diary recording Hans Frank's time in Tegernsee, but it contained uneventful meetings Frank had conducted until his capture by Allied troops in May 1945. "That's all there is," said Evan, "and the archive is closing for the day. We could explore other resources tomorrow."

Merde. Darwin leaned back in his chair and swept a hand through his hair. He couldn't think of any other sources. "No. I think I've hit a dead end."

He thanked Evan, who left to return the journals to the stacks. Darwin said he could find his own way out and, minutes later, stepped back onto Pennsylvania Avenue. The wind had died down, and shadows stretched across the pavement.

He walked toward the Capitol while thinking about what to do next. Hans Frank was a meticulous administrator who kept a detailed diary throughout his professional life. *Wait!* He stopped in his tracks. He remembered an article about Frank's last days where the man had tried to absolve himself of his heinous crimes. The author attributed the quotes to a personal diary Frank had written while awaiting execution.

Where is that diary? He pictured Jim sitting in Seattle, watching his pine trees, and tapped his number. It rang nine times before Jim answered, "Hello?"

"Hi, Jim. It's Darwin."

"Darwin. How are you, son? Are you still in Seattle? We've got another poker game tonight."

"No. I'm in DC." Darwin laughed. "I didn't bring enough cash to survive another game."

"DC? You get around, son."

Darwin explained his search for Hans Frank's diaries and the missing boxcars. "But there's nothing after his arrest in Tegernsee."

The connection was silent for so long that Darwin thought it had dropped. "You still there, Jim?" he asked.

"Yes, I'm here. I was thinking. Goes slower these days. If what you said is correct, I'd bet anything personal Frank wrote before his death would be turned over to his family. It's a long shot."

As Jim talked, Darwin searched for Hans Frank's family. One son was still alive—in Munich. His heart skipped a beat as he ordered a ride to Dulles Airport. Like most metropolitan areas, DC was a hotspot for transportation, and two minutes later, he was sitting in the backseat of a new-model car, wrapping up his conversation.

Darwin thrummed like a retriever sensing its prey. He booked a seat on a Lufthansa flight, leaving in just under three hours. He loved it when things worked out. *Well,* another part of his brain chimed in, *except for not knowing exactly what I'm looking for.*

He smiled. *But that's the best part of the hunt—figuring it out.*

Leaning back as the car nudged through the American capital, he messaged Eyrún:

> How are you? I found another lead. On way to Munich. Land 10 your time.

By the time his flight was airborne, she still hadn't replied.

42

1st Arrondissement

Eyrún and Aya entered the Saint-Germain l'Auxerrois just after 6:30 p.m. and wandered the cathedral, taking pictures like any other tourist. They planned to hide somewhere inside after the 7 p.m. closing and then access the tombs. At this hour, there were only three other individuals inside: a couple near the front and an elderly woman praying at the Virgin Mary chapel.

The western sun shined through the tall stained-glass windows in the transept, casting a multi-hued glow onto the vaults. Brass candelabra seemed to float, suspended on long, dark cables, and the choir had an airy feel from the warm reflections off the Lutecian limestone.

"It's bright," said Eyrún. "Doesn't feel as closed in as other cathedrals."

"It's due to restoration and cleaning. Notre-Dame will be like this when reopened," said Aya. "I can't wait to see it."

"Me neither," said Eyrún.

The praying woman walked past them, her hard-soled shoes drumming on the floor. Eyrún went to the chapel. Its elaborately carved altar was covered in gold leaf. Large stands beside the altar overflowed with floral bouquets, with smaller arrangements atop the cloth-covered slab.

"I doubt it would be this one," said Aya. "Too frequently used."

They made a quick circuit of the other likely chapels before locating a dark alcove in the Chapel of Saint Landry. His statue stood atop a broad pedestal. They squeezed behind it and sat on the floor, their backs to the pedestal. Eyrún showed Aya the time, 6:54, and then said, "Put your phone on silent."

A half-hour later, they emerged. They'd heard the footsteps of someone checking the chapel and seen a light flash around in a cursory look, but silence had followed. They split up, each examining the likely chapels where a secret exit from a tunnel might appear. Aya started in Saint Landry's chapel while Eyrún walked to the Chapel of the Tomb.

She stepped over the protective railing to the decayed stone, covered with black splotches. It was a forgotten corner compared to the vibrant cleanliness of the choir. *Maybe it's left this way on purpose?*

The Catholic ornamentation felt overdone. She had not been a churchgoer in her native Iceland other than for weddings or memorials. Darwin had explained the symbology as they'd toured churches across Europe and the Middle East. Her favorite was the chapel at Saint Catherine's Monastery in Sinai.

She crouched to study the stone effigy of Christ stretched out below the altar. At a close range, she could distinguish its stony composition, but from a distance, under the dim lighting, it convincingly imitated a human corpse.

She stood. The sixteenth-century origins fit their timeline, but the altar itself looked too fragile to contain a secret panel, so she concentrated on its platform. Four broad slabs made up the top layer. The one nearest Jesus's head had been cracked and patched.

A moveable panel? Maybe? Her heart rate increased as she knelt and examined the slab's edges. Dirt filled the seams between the slabs. She grasped a corner of the front slab. It would be heavy, but if it was manipulated as a cover, she should get movement. Nothing. She tried the other side and got the same immovable resistance.

"Must be mortared in place," said Aya.

Eyrún jumped.

42

"Sorry. Didn't mean to sneak up on you. The Landry chapel is the same."

They walked around the ambulatory to the last chapel. An intricately carved wooden retable stood above a deep brown altar. Masses of figures enacted the Christian stories in the carved panels. "Glad I don't have to dust that," said Aya. "You take that side."

Eyrún shined her light on each section as she tested the wood for sliding panels or mechanisms that moved when pressed, but after fifteen minutes, they'd found nothing. She glanced at her watch: almost nine. "Try your black light," Aya whispered from the left.

Eyrún took the ultraviolet light from her pocket and worked her way over to the altar. She moved around the right corner. Dust reflected in corners where cleaners couldn't reach. She moved to the floor. Bright specks jumped out.

She picked up the largest, about the size of the tip of her pinkie. Its edges were sharp. She shined the UV light on the floor, looking for the chip's source, but the old stone showed no signs of fractures. "I think I found something."

Aya was behind her in a heartbeat. Eyrún held out the chip. Aya produced a jeweler's loop and studied it. "It's marble." She let Eyrún look.

"You're right, and one side's polished. What are you doing?"

Aya was pulling at the side panels of the wooden altar. "Looking for an opening."

Eyrún squatted beside her. "I don't think a king would want to squeeze through there. He'd want a more natural entrance, not be seen crawling from a hole. They'd want to, erm…"

Aya finished the thought: "Step out of a magic wardrobe, like Narnia."

"Exactly," said Eyrún, walking into the nave and studying the darkened space. The street lights cast a pale glow through the stained glass. Near the transept stood a confessional with two curtained stalls on either side of the priest's box. *It's big enough.* She hurried over.

"What are you thinking?" asked Aya.

"Testing a hunch," Eyrún said as she opened the door. A closer examination showed that the whole thing was a moveable box similar to an armoire. She stepped out, her hands on her hips, and looked around, imagining other cathedrals she'd been in. Opening a tomb in the Cathédrale Saint-Nazaire et Saint-Celse in Béziers came to mind and triggered a question. "Aya, is there a crypt?"

"Yes, but it was sealed after the Revolution." Aya opened a document on her phone that she'd scanned at the Bibliothèque National. After a moment, she added, "Access would be from the apse behind the main altar."

They went to the altar, each going to a different side. Eyrún shined her black light over the floor and platform behind the altar, where she and Aya converged. "This slab is newer. See the pattern in the limestone? It differs from the slabs on each side."

"You're right," said Aya, comparing them. The tiny, ancient calcified creatures in the side stones had a wholly different pattern. She set down her pack and removed a forearm-length pry bar.

"What are you doing?" asked Eyrún.

"Hoping I don't crack it. That would be harder to explain when we ask for forgiveness later."

Aya used a rubber-headed mallet to pound the pry bar into the gap between the slab and the raised step. She worked methodically along the front edge and then wedged it deeper on a second pass.

She pressed down on the bar. The slab didn't budge.

"Too heavy?" asked Eyrún.

"I don't think so. Here." Aya motioned for Eyrún to stand close. "Hold me up while I stand on it."

Aya put her hands on Eyrún's shoulders while Eyrún grasped Aya's waist. "Okay?" Eyrún nodded.

Aya shifted her weight up and down, testing the pry bar. "I think it moved. Next time I raise up, push down on my hips. Ready? Now."

The slab groaned and rose a few millimeters.

"Again," said Aya.

"It's working," said Eyrún, "but let's move along the step, or it will fracture."

As Aya moved the pry bar, Eyrún knelt and shoved the butt of her light into the left side gap to keep it from sinking back down. Working

42

this way, they soon had the slab's edge raised, and they propped it up on either side with hymnals borrowed from a nearby table.

Eyrún lay on her belly and shined her light in the gap. "It drops down." She slid an arm into the gap and reached down. "There's a step. At least, I think it's a step. It goes in about as far as a step and then drops off again."

"Let's get this thing up," said Aya. "Time for all your work in the gym to pay off."

Each grabbed the slab, putting one foot at altar level and the other on the main floor. Eyrún adjusted her balance against the awkward position. "Okay. Go."

The mortar between the slabs ground against the limestone, reverberating in the half-domed apse. When they got past forty-five degrees, the slab moved more easily. "What do we do with it?" asked Aya.

"Lean it against the altar," said Eyrún.

They did and, dusting off their hands, looked into the hole. Ladder-steep steps receded into blackness. "Let's go." Aya worked her way down, her hands on the wall to brace herself against the decline.

Eyrún followed, and she stopped behind Aya in a crypt no wider than a small hotel room. Tombs lined the walls. The air was root-cellar cold and had the dank odor of long decay. "Is any royalty buried here?" she asked, running her light along the tombstones.

"No. They're in Saint-Denis," said Aya. "These would be bishops and clergy who served in the cathedral."

Eyrún followed Aya to the crypt's far side. She looked back once at the stairway opening and shuddered at the thought of the slab closing them in. As she turned back, Aya announced, "I bet this is it."

A carved tomb filled the far wall. Saints and other holy figures moved in a procession across its front. The top marble slab was simple and uncarved and relatively easy to slide open.

"Bingo!" Aya's face split in a smile as she shined her light down another stairway. This one went deep.

42

"How many did you count?" asked Eyrún when Aya reached the bottom.

"Sixty-three."

"Me, too." Eyrún studied the arched tunnel. "Looks the same construction method as the Sainte-Chapelle tunnel." She ran her light overhead, following the arched blocks.

"Let's go." Aya squeezed around Eyrún.

Eyrún visualized the surface above as she followed Aya. She calculated that the crypt's rear wall was level with the transept. The steps bent to the right below the tomb, and she figured they hit the bottom near the cathedral's entrance. From there, it was a straight line to the Louvre.

After walking the length of a football pitch, they reached a wooden door. Aya ran a hand over the dark oak, its original luster now hazy and rough from centuries of dampness. Molding framed the doorway, fitted snugly against the stone. Her shoulders slumped when she found no handle. "Don't tell me this is a one-way door."

Eyrún ran her fingers along the molding. "No. That wouldn't make sense." She closed her eyes, letting her concentration flow into her fingertips. There. They touched something about knee height on the left side. She worked the spot until she found a section that slid on an invisible track. *Clever.*

"What did you find?" asked Aya.

"The latch," said Eyrún, putting a finger in the loop of the iron pull rod. It held fast. She maneuvered herself into a better position and then yanked hard. A soft chunk sounded, amplified by wood. The door pivoted slightly.

"*Mon Dieu,*" said Aya in equal parts reverence and expectation.

Eyrún smiled and stepped back as Aya bounced on her toes. Aya put a hand on the door.

"What are you waiting for?" asked Eyrún.

"It's, erm, I've thought about this moment for years. Once I open it, my dream will end." She took a breath and held it as she closed her eyes. Then she opened them and pulled. The door groaned. Dryer air poured from the opening as they stepped into another corridor.

"Oh, my God," said Eyrún.

43

Louvre Subbasement

Aya's light shone down a long tunnel that was unremarkable except for the canvas draped over objects leaning against both side walls. Eyrún knelt and lifted the fabric. "Paintings!"

Vibrant colors flowed across the first one. Black lines, some angular, others curved, added form and pattern. "It's beautiful," she said, flipping the frame around. "Kandinsky, I think."

Eyrún stood, and Aya held her light on the backing. A sticker bearing the gallery name listed the artist, Wassily Kandinsky, and a large number was written in blue pencil on the wood. A black stamp jumped out like a rude stain: an eagle holding a wreathed swastika.

"This is plundered, but I need someone more expert to interpret the provenance," said Aya. "How many more are in here?"

"Hundreds," said Eyrún, setting down the Kandinsky.

"What are they doing here?" asked Aya, staring down the long rows.

The tunnel ran in both directions from the door to the cathedral, although it looked shorter to the right. Aya said she would survey the longer direction. Eyrún agreed and moved away. The floor had been finished with Lutetian limestone pavers, similar to the wall but more polished, especially in the center, where people had walked. She snapped photos of the surrounding stone and then lifted the canvas off one stack of paintings. These were landscapes, not her favorites, but very high quality. She photographed the fronts and backs of four before replacing them and moving on.

A few steps farther, she realized this shorter section ended in a hard left turn. As she got close, a light switched on. She froze, her heart hammering. When she glanced back, Aya's light was a faint, faraway glow. *Shit!* No way she could get to her and out before whoever was coming found them. She listened, straining to hear footsteps. A minute went by. Eyrún controlled her breathing and flashed her light at Aya, figuring that if she moved toward her, they'd both be closer to the door.

The light went out, and Eyrún moved. It switched on. She sucked in a breath, but it went out again as she waited.

"What is it?"

"Jesus!" Eyrún jumped. She turned to find Aya, who'd walked up behind her.

"I saw you flashing."

Eyrún pointed to the light, which was on again, and explained what she'd observed.

"Maybe it's on a motion detector," said Aya.

"That's what I think. Wait." Eyrún grabbed Aya's arm. "I have a better idea."

Aya let Eyrún pass, and near the corner, Eyrún got down on her hands and knees and then tapped her phone's camera. From the floor below the paintings, she extended her phone into the space. A light shone from the ceiling about five meters away. Eyrún pinched the zoom and looked again.

The wash of light blurred the phone screen until its optics adjusted. Just below the light, a small black object came into focus. It had a red dot. *Shit!* Eyrún pulled her phone back and scooted back to Aya. "It's a video camera."

They retreated, scanning the walls in their section, but found nothing. "Did it see you?" asked Aya.

43

"My hand and phone, but that's enough to alert someone to a break-in."

"We need to get out!" Aya stopped at the door as Eyrún bent down. "What are you doing?"

"Photos are one thing, but this..." She paused, holding up the Kandinsky. "Is irrefutable evidence."

They closed the door behind them and pushed the latch rod into place. "One more thing. Hold this." Eyrún gave Aya the painting and then studied the door frame.

"Let's go."

Eyrún ignored the warning as she looked from the latch to the opposite frame and then broke off a section of molding. She wedged it between the top of the rod and part of the door and pounded it tighter. "There. That should hold them or slow them down."

They hurried back to the crypt stairs and replaced the tomb's lid. Aya handed Eyrún the painting, wiped away their handprints, and then tossed some fine dirt in the air. It settled on the marble, giving it an undisturbed appearance. Replacing the altar slab required more effort. When they reached the green glowing *sortie*, a sign warned that an alarm would sound when it was opened.

"Well, there's nothing for it," said Eyrún, tucking the painting under one arm. "Ready?"

Aya nodded.

Eyrún pushed through the door.

Three blocks later, Aya gasped, "I have to slow down."

Eyrún led the way back to her flat along the river to avoid public transportation and cameras. About halfway there, she said, "We have to report this."

"I agree, but not yet," said Aya. "We need to investigate more on our own. I figured we were in the subbasement. The section with the camera must be near an entry point inside the Louvre."

They turned onto Pont Louis-Philippe toward Ile Saint-Louis. It was after 2 a.m. when they got to Eyrún's flat, and Aya graciously accepted the invitation to sleep in the spare bedroom. But not before they leaned the Kandinsky against a wall and stared at its mesmerizing patterns.

44

École du Louvre

"How did they get in?" asked Vivienne, storming around her desk when Lionel entered her office the next morning.

"I don't know."

"Show me the video." She grabbed Lionel's phone and watched the hand come into view and then withdraw five seconds later. "That's it?"

"What more do you want to see? Someone was in there last night." Lionel waited for Vivienne to act. No one had breached the subbasement tunnel since before the Second World War. There had been tense weeks after the ancient Louvre foundation was discovered in the 1980s, but the organization had seized control.

Lionel's predecessors had installed doors and restricted access to the deep tunnels, and when Lionel had been trusted enough by the organization, he'd taken over as protector of the subbasement vault. He'd once asked his mentor about the old door in the last section subbasement and been told it led to a disused tunnel to the nearby Saint-Germain l'Auxerrois, but its access from the cathedral had been sealed in the eighteenth century.

44

Lionel took his phone back from Vivienne. "You need to report this."

"We can handle it. No need to bother the others. Find out who they are and how they got in."

"You expect me to determine their identity from a hand in a video?"

"Use DNA," she said.

He laughed.

"They must have touched something down there. Figure it out. You're a technician. I have to go." Vivienne dismissed him with a wave of her hand and walked away.

And there it is, he thought—her arrogance, her disdain for him and anyone with knowledge. She treated them like prized objects when it suited her or shoved them aside like annoying machines she didn't understand.

He'd overlooked her appointment two years ago, but now he saw her incompetence as dangerous. The laws and courts had become increasingly difficult to navigate, and restitution had gained momentum. Worse, some of their clients had given in or died off, leaving collections to heirs willing to sell ill-gotten treasures.

He pictured the canvas-covered loot in the hidden tunnel. He'd feared this day and looked at the photo again, shaking his head at Vivienne's DNA comment. *Idiot.*

Lionel zoomed in on the hand holding the phone case—a red and white Nordic cross atop an azure background. He gasped. *I've seen this.*

His heart beat faster as he clicked a screenshot and pasted it into a search engine. The result came back: the flag of Iceland. He knew he'd seen it recently but couldn't remember where.

45

Île Saint-Louis

Eyrún tossed and turned, her sleep interrupted by visions of the tunnel. She'd heard Darwin talk about the looting and the underhanded methods used by museums to keep artwork, but hearing about it and holding the evidence in your hands was night and day.

Morning light glowed in their bedroom, reflecting off the mirrored glass in buildings across the river, which gave them the rare opportunity of having both morning and evening sun. She slid out of bed and did light yoga to activate muscles that were still sore from last night's crouching and lifting heavy stones. A hot shower soothed the rest of her aches. After dressing, she padded into the kitchen, switched on the kettle, and selected her favorite tea—a French blue from a shop in Le Marais.

Minutes later, she removed the tea bag from her cup and walked onto the patio deck. The air carried a crisp edge, a harbinger of autumn embracing the city. Below, the serene Seine resembled a lake. A barge plied the downstream current, aiming between the islands—its engine rumbled like a slumbering dragon.

45

The door slid open behind her, and Aya stepped out, holding a teacup.

"Oh, good. You found it," said Eyrún.

"Yes, thanks. I need it," Aya said. "I couldn't sleep any longer."

"Me neither."

They stood in silence, sipping their tea as Paris awoke. Diagonally to their right, the scaffolding on Notre-Dame stretched to the heavens. The spire section glowed tangerine as the sunlight descended gradually toward the nearly completed roof.

"It's beautiful," said Aya. "I rarely stop to just look at it. The last few years of restoration have been a blur."

Eyrún knew the bittersweet moments of completing a large project. On one hand, you couldn't wait for it to be done. On the other hand, you wondered what would come next after so much of your life had been consumed by the singular effort.

"What time should we go?" she asked, shifting into action mode.

"I say a little before nine. Too early, and security will question why we're there. Can we go by my flat for a change of clothes?"

"Sure," said Eyrún. "I'll get breakfast going. What do you like?"

Louvre

At 8:49, the two women entered the Louvre staff entrance in the Cour Carrée. Aya showed her badge and said she had a meeting in the restoration department. Eyrún signed in as a guest.

As Aya suspected, a few employees were at work. They went to a nearby breakroom to get a cup of tea while they assessed the situation. Then they headed downstairs to the basement. Officially, the Louvre maps showed two lower levels, with the lowest at the glass pyramid's inverted base. From there, visitors traveled up escalators to the main exhibits.

Like a famous theme park, the Louvre had service tunnels to move supplies and people, making the public think that food and trinkets appeared by magic.

45

Unlike the elegant halls above, the first basement level was stark and functional. The bright lighting was as welcoming as that of a hospital corridor. They reached the restoration department and pushed in a set of double doors. The overhead lights were muted inside the broad space. Workstations filled the room, appearing like a science lab. A task light shone on one table where a conservator cleaned a gold gilt frame.

"*Bonjour*, Gaston," said Aya.

"*Bonjour*, Aya," said the wizened man, peering over his magnifying glasses. "Pardon me if I don't get up." His gloved hands held a brush and cotton swab.

"*Je comprends*."

"What brings you here today?" he asked, focused on the frame.

Aya leaned in close, watching Gaston work. "You have a beautiful touch," she said after a long moment.

"Pfft. Hardly, but flattery will get you everywhere, my dear."

She stood. "We came to see Christian. Have you seen him?"

"Not for a couple of weeks. Went on holiday, I heard."

Aya thanked him and moved to Christian's desk, where she wrote him a note. "This backs up our story of a meeting," she said to Eyrún.

"Who's Christian?"

"An acquaintance. We've consulted on projects over the years."

As they left the department, they found that more employees had arrived, making it easier for them to blend in. Near the end of the hallway, they approached a door requiring card key access.

"Look natural, like we belong," said Aya. "There's a camera behind us."

She tapped a card key to the access panel, and the lock snapped open. She pulled the handle, and they entered a room with a jumble of sculptures, some covered, some crated. A row of paintings leaned against a wood-framed statue—elegant, but only the torso remained.

"Storage," said Aya. "These pieces are scheduled for restoration or deaccession." She crossed the room to another door and opened it with the same key. "Now it gets interesting," she added, stepping onto the upper landing of a cement stairwell and pocketing the card.

45

Eyrún caught Gaston's picture as Aya palmed the card. "You stole his badge. I didn't see it." Behind her, the door thumped closed.

"A handy skill left over from childhood. My family was poor, and pickpocketing put food on the table," Aya said as she trotted down the steps. "Don't worry. I'll give it back. Gaston will probably laugh about it."

"Where are we?"

"In the first basement, heading to the service tunnels below us."

Eyrún followed Aya through a quick series of corridors. She couldn't determine their age but figured it was a mixture of projects during the last five hundred years. Pipes ran overhead, fixed to the ceiling. Two of these were PVC, and another channel held wiring. Lighting snapped on as they moved.

She followed Aya into a dark room. They used their phone lights to navigate the ample space. Its cracked walls had been plastered smooth. Scattered lumber suggested a remodel, but Eyrún noticed thick dust covering everything, including the floor. "What is this place?"

"An expansion for the foundation exhibit," said Aya. "It looks just like I saw it five years ago." She stopped at a door on the room's opposite side and put an ear to it. Light from the gap underneath fanned across the floor. "Good. It's not dark, but no one's in it yet. Hopefully, this works." Taking a key from her pocket, she unlocked the door and pulled.

Silence.

"That's a good omen," said Aya, waving the badge toward the security camera, letting whoever was watching know that she was an employee. They moved across the finished exhibit and around the Louvre's original tower, the keep where the royals had hunkered down during sieges.

They followed a hallway into a larger room. "I wanted to see this again for perspective," said Aya, pointing ahead at a giant wall made of stout limestone blocks. Its rounded sections were the base of ramparts overlooking the gate. She paused at a vertical section standing in front of the rampart foundations.

"This is the original eastern wall," she said, walking between the three structures. The drawbridge came down and rested atop the stubby wall. "We're standing in the moat that cut into the Seine."

She pointed away from the drawbridge support. "l'Auxerrois cathedral is less than a hundred meters that way.

"So, how do we get down there?" asked Eyrún, studying the formidable masonry surrounding them and the concrete ceiling colored to match the Lutecian stone.

"From inside the keep," said Aya. "We need to go down a level."

Eyrún followed Aya as they walked around the corner of the old fort. Aya explained they were passing under the center of the current Cour Carrée. They cut through to the Sully Crypt, inside the ancient Louvre's outer wall. Here, stubby Doric columns held up the weighty castle above.

"Here we are," said Aya, reaching the steel gate. Beyond its bars, a rock wall was illuminated from overhead. Various-sized stones were mortared together. The limestone was the same as the old keep's finished blocks, but they had been left rough, appearing more like an eroded riverbank than a wall.

The brass plaque beside the gate stated that it was a fragment of the wall commissioned by Philippe Auguste in the twelfth century.

Aya produced another key, this one metal, and inserted it into the gate. Once they were inside, she relocked it. She ran her fingers over the thousand-year-old defensive wall, explaining as she went, "I heard rumors about a door. My colleague who told me about the tunnel we found under Notre-Dame said there was hushed-up talk when the foundations behind us were rediscovered in the eighties. INRAP and the Louvre tightly controlled access."

"How do you hear about it?" asked Eyrún.

"I'm patient. Small pieces of information add up over time. A drunken INRAP archaeologist suggested there was more under the Louvre. We were talking about *Star Wars* and teleporting when he said the Bourbon kings could move undetected but then clammed up. I think he was sober enough to realize when to shut up, but he'd already let the cat out of the bag."

They descended the stairs and stopped in a dark corridor. Aya flicked on her light, and the two continued until they reached a modern steel door, on which was stenciled:

Extreme Danger
Do Not Enter
Unsafe Area

"That looks like an invitation if I ever saw one," said Aya, grinning at the sign.

Lionel sat in the employee cafeteria, having breakfast after his early meeting with Vivienne. While eating, he studied the photos of Christian's house he'd taken yesterday. He'd spent the afternoon with a cop buddy trying to gain entry, but a nosy neighbor had insisted on seeing a warrant. They went around to the back to look in the patio door, but the neighbor called the cops, so they left.

What are you hiding, Christian?

His friend's grandfather, Louis Roche, had worked at the Louvre for decades. Last week, Lionel had asked a human resources colleague to look up Roche's employment history, but nothing stood out. No one still alive in the Organization had known him.

He stared at a photo of Christian's kitchen, zooming into a gleaming counter. What he wanted to see was behind the door leading to the basement.

His finger swiped to the next photo—the subbasement security camera's still shot of the phone with an Icelandic flag case. *Of course!*

Lionel scrolled back to a set of pictures he had taken five days ago —Darwin and his wife at a cafe. He'd snapped a burst from across the street before moving away. Eyrún sat with elbows on the table, one hand holding her phone. He zoomed in on the case. Its Icelandic flag pattern was visible between her fingers.

"Putain!" He tapped back to the security shot. Slender fingers with identical dark blue nail polish held the same case.

It's her! How did she get in? The answer swiftly followed—the cathedral. They'd been scanning for tunnels under Pont Neuf when he and a colleague had chased them. *They must have also scanned l'Auxerrois.*

He checked the time: half nine. The cathedral was open. *There's got to be a tunnel from the crypt to the subbasement door. How else could they get in?*

He carried his tray to the clean-up area and checked Christian's desk one more time before heading to the cathedral.

Louvre Subbasement

Eyrún, examined the deadbolt key slot. The brass was dark from age. Then she scanned the doorframe and surrounding stone for an alarm but found none. "How has this remained secret? The exhibit gate isn't the best concealment."

"I can't say for sure," said Aya, "but it's been forty years since the foundations were dug up. Most probably take the warning at face value, if they come here at all."

"And most art historians are not cataphiles," said Eyrún, referring to Aya's urban underground explorer friends.

"True." Aya's eyebrows set, and she peered closely at the keyhole. "Someone has used this recently. The bronze is scratched."

Eyrún looked again. "Want to bet the watertight sewer door and this one being opened are related."

"Not a wager I'll make."

Eyrún set to work on the deadbolt with her picks. Two minutes later, she wrung out her hands before opening the door and revealing a circular room. Its ceiling had the same concrete as the exhibit, but there was no floor.

"*Mon Dieu,*" said Aya, looking at stone steps spiraling down into darkness.

46

Munich

Darwin landed at 9:41 a.m. in Munich. His phone chimed with incoming messages and he went to Eyrún's reply to his message sent from DC.

> Eyrún: Aren't you the world traveler? All good here. Aya and I went into the cathedral last night. On way to Louvre this morning. See photos in Proton.

Merde. Darwin's stomach clenched at missing out. He tapped her number and got her voicemail. Then he opened the Proton-encrypted email app and turned sideways in his business class pod. Other passengers pulled bags from the overhead bins while he gawked at the images from beneath Saint-Germain l'Auxerrois.

He sucked in a breath while zooming in on the photos of canvas-covered paintings.

"Is everything okay, sir?" asked the flight attendant. The cabin had emptied.

46

"Fine, fine," said Darwin, pocketing his phone. He grabbed his case, disembarked, and headed for border control.

Eyrún and Aya, he speculated, had discovered an entrance to an uncharted tunnel beneath the Louvre. He tapped out a message while walking to scan his passport:

> Amazing photos. Got your vmail. I landed in Munich. Prolly take the train home later today. Text when you can.

He sent it with a heart emoji, then looked up the address for Hans Frank's son.

47

Louvre

Lionel stopped at Christian's desk in the restoration department. Papers were scattered in no particular organization, but a small note lay atop the pile, and he picked it up.

Bonjour Christian,

I stopped by, but alas, Gaston says you're on holiday.

Miss you. Call me when you return.

Bisou,

Aya

He looked under the papers scattered across the desk, searching for clues that might tell him where Christian had gone. As he opened a drawer, Gaston said, "He won't like you looking through his stuff, even if you are friends."

"I'm worried about him," said Gaston, deflecting the comment. "He should be back by now. Did he say where he was going?"

"Why do you care?"

Lionel ground his teeth. *Asshole.* Gaston was an irascible workaholic with few friends and would probably die at his desk. Lionel decided to try a different approach. Waving Aya's note, he asked, "When did the woman leave this for Christian?"

The older man didn't look up but said, "This morning. About a half-hour ago."

"What did she want?"

"How the hell should I know?

"Just curious," said Lionel. "I'm supposed to meet a curator from the British Museum. Maybe it was her." His made-up story sounded weak even to himself.

Gaston removed his magnifying glasses, pushed back from his workstation, and stood. He rolled his head to relieve the tension from leaning over his restoration. "It was Aya Raiss from the *Crypte Archéologique*. I don't know the other one—taller, dark hair." He patted his lab coat pockets. "Where's my badge?"

Putain! It's them.

Gaston rooted around in his desk. "It was here. Clipped to my coat," he said, talking to himself. "Where is it?"

Lionel knew. Aya had lifted it. He sprinted from the lab. *They're looking for the tunnel.*

He exited the employees-only area near the Denon entrance and crossed the marble hall beneath the pyramid. The museum had opened for the day. A human river descended the curved escalator and flowed up the stairs into the main galleries. He took the steps up the Sully entrance two at a time, shouldering past wide-eyed tourists.

He flashed his badge at a security guard and continued jogging to the Sully Crypt. Once there, he looked around, ensuring no one was watching him, and then keyed open the gate. He locked it behind him and then headed down the dark stairs while keeping a hand on the wall for balance.

Ahead, a faint light framed an open doorway. *Putain!* His heart hammered. He moved closer and then froze again. *Voices?*

Yes, someone was talking. He tiptoed to the door. He needed to be sure. It could be Vivienne showing off the hidden gallery. She knew it was forbidden, but he'd already decided that her ambition was larger than her brain.

47

Subbasement

Eyrún's scalp tingled as she put a foot down on the first step. "Do you think it's safe?"

"Sure," said Aya, taking the lead. "It's still here after a thousand years. I doubt we'll bring it down."

Twenty-two steps later, they hit bottom and came to a door identical to the one they'd encountered in the tunnel from Saint-Germain l'Auxerrois.

"Oh, my God," Eyrún said in a hushed voice. She determined that it opened with the exact hidden mechanism. "Ready?"

Aya nodded, and the door groaned as Eyrún pulled it.

As soon as it moved, a light burst around the gap. It switched off a minute later.

"Must be the camera," whispered Aya.

"Only one way to know for sure," said Eyrún, opening the door. The light turned on. She squatted and peered up at the ceiling on the other side. A security camera pointed away from them, down the corridor. Eyrún snapped pictures, and they retreated into the spiral stairwell to study them.

"That's it. You took your photos from there." Aya pointed to the corner.

Eyrún smiled. "You did it, Aya. You proved the Bourbons used tunnels."

From the top of the spiral steps, the metal door slammed shut, booming through the stairwell.

47

Lionel's heart hammered as he leaned on the locked door. He needed something to jam it. He pulled some coins from his pocket and wedged two between the door and frame at the top and two more at the bottom.

Too loose. He looked at the rocks in the rough wall and began pulling at them. A smaller one budged. He kicked at it until it clattered to the floor. He grabbed it and pounded both sets of coins until the rock split. But not before fists beat on the door's other side.

"Let us out!"

Lionel went back up to the gate from the Sully Crypt and listened. The banging and screaming were inaudible. He slipped out and locked the gate behind him.

Once back in his office, he massaged his temples while contemplating the massive problem.

"Stop, Aya," said Eyrún, grasping her friend's arm. "No one can hear us."

Aya kicked the door in frustration. "They jammed the lock," she said, rubbing her sore fists and looking around. "Find something to ram it."

"There's nothing here. Let's try opening the door to the cathedral tunnel." Eyrún retreated down the spiral steps to the open wooden door. The security camera light winked on. "That goes," she said, swatting it hard and cracking its mount.

The camera spun and dangled from its cable. Aya ripped it free and hurled it at the wall, causing plastic bits to explode.

"That felt good," she said in the darkness while brushing off her hands.

Eyrún switched on her phone light, casting a bright halo. She checked for a signal, but as expected, this far underground, there were no bars.

They moved slowly between the paintings. At the bend where Eyrún had taken the photo the previous night, she paused, and both women glanced back at the door to the Louvre. Their light barely illu-

47

minated it. "It looks farther in the picture," said Eyrún. "That's what, fifteen meters?"

"Yeah, about that," said Aya.

Eyrún continued to the wooden door to l'Auxerrois. She pocketed her phone and tried to pull the iron ring as Aya held her light. It didn't move, caught against the piece of wood she'd wedged into the door's opposite mechanism.

"Shit! Why did I do that?"

"To keep someone on this side from following us," said Aya.

"Made sense then, but..." Eyrún let her forehead rest against the door. She ran a hand over the spot. "Maybe I can knock it loose."

She stood and pulled the ring while pounding on different spots. Aya stopped her this time. "It's not working. We need another way."

Eyrún sighed. She looked down the longer end of the tunnel that Aya had explored last night and began walking. Her soft-soled trainers made the barest of sounds in the deathly silence. The subbasement could just as well have been a crypt, the paintings entombed like forgotten souls. She thought of skeletons and shivered.

Oh, God. What if we can't get out?

She froze.

Stop, she admonished. *It's been less than an hour.* She moved forward, and a few steps later, her underground survival training kicked in. She'd been trapped before. *Worse than this.* She shuddered at the memory of a tunnel collapse in Sinai and then shook it off.

Assess the situation.

Work the options.

We have air. We know the main ways out.

She'd mentally tallied their problems as she reached the tunnel's end and turned back. Light was key. The phone batteries would run out. "Aya," she called, "switch off your phone's cellular, wifi, and Bluetooth. Conserve the battery."

Eyrún changed her phone's settings as she tried to suppress their most critical problem.

Water.

She'd experienced dehydration and knew the average human could survive three to five days without water, but body and brain function diminished after one day. She swallowed, telling herself she wasn't thirsty—*not yet*.

They had another factor in their favor. *Both of us are experienced cavers. We need to make the next twenty-four hours count.*

"Aya, let's work out our options, beginning with who knows we might be down here."

48

San Francisco

Zac was up with the sun, gathering his data before an afternoon flight to Paris. Siggy had slept at the hospital, as her neural implant project had reached a critical phase. He took the first ferry across the bay to Oakland and got a rideshare to the Lawrence Berkeley Lab in the East Bay hills.

The early morning promised heat as autumn drove the fog far offshore. He loved this time of year. The tourist season slowed as the school year started, and summer's relaxed vibe lingered.

Once, in his lab, he examined the overnight satellite passes that he'd widened to include Saint-Germain l'Auxerrois. In Corsica, Lupita had fed the data to an algorithm that included ancient Paris street and sewer maps, geological surveys, and stratigraphy from the quarries under the city.

"That's interesting," Zac said aloud, looking at several fictitious maps. He messaged Lupita with WhatsApp. Its end-to-end encryption would keep their conversation safe.

Zac: excellent work on the maps

48

Lupita: Thank you. I like the second one best.

He tapped the phone symbol above their chat, and she answered a few moments later.

"Hello, Zac."

"Hi, Lupita. How are you today?"

They talked about the goings-on in Ajaccio, and Lupita mentioned her parents were visiting from Kenya. They laughed about the joys of house guests before shifting topics.

"How did you create the maps?" asked Zac.

"I used ChatGPT to frame the questions and learn how the AI responded. Then, I used ArcGIS to blend actual satellite data and AI output before putting the ultimate question to Wallace."

Zac knew the ArcGIS software from the Environmental Systems Research Institute in Southern California but had not heard of Wallace. "What's that?"

"It is an AI project in Nairobi led by Grace Musoke."

"Her!" said Zac, recalling Stanford University listing her as one of the world's leading scientists.

"Yes. We went to uni together."

"Are you working with her?"

"You cannot tell anyone," said Lupita.

"I won't say a word. I'm envious, and Darwin will laugh at the name." Zac knew Wallace was a key collaborator on natural selection.

"I suggested it to honor his generosity. He and Eyrún are angel investors," she said and then explained that asking the AI to reverse engineer a tunnel system had led to unhelpful results.

"So, I changed the parameters and told the AI to think like a sixteenth-century Parisian and design and build a tunnel using Renaissance technologies. Wallace created the second map, as you see."

"This is amazing, Lupita. I…" Zac paused, studying the map. "It's fantastic. How can I thank you?"

"We are looking for another angel investor."

Zac laughed out loud. "I'm in. You need friendly angels. Don't let the vulture capitalists in."

"I will tell Grace."

48

They said their goodbyes, and Zac used the lab's secure networks to download Lupita's data. After making multiple backups, he encrypted them and copied them onto a flash drive.

Then he focused on his other task, tracking the seller of the Avercamp paintings that Darwin bought. Using the Department of Energy's forensic tools, he traced the seller's IP address through a labyrinth of dark web servers. He let the traceroute run while he got a cup of tea.

An hour later, after being sidetracked by a junior researcher's request, Zac returned to his office. He read the list of two IP addresses and entered them into an Internet directory lookup.

"Holy shit!" He rocked back in his chair, studying both results.

`École du Louvre, Paris, France`

He checked the time, gathered what he needed, and requested a car to San Francisco Airport.

49

Munich

Darwin sat in a cafe across from the Viktualienmarkt, watching the locals shop for dinner ingredients from the various stalls. Tourists milled about the shops, sampling Bavarian delicacies. He looked down at the last bite of his Auszogne. The yeasty, sweet taste lingered in his mouth, but his belly protested the sugary gut bomb.

He got another coffee while contemplating his next move. The quaint ceramic cup covered in old German lettering made a pleasing thump as it hit the wooden table. He enjoyed the tactile aesthetics of natural materials. He sighed after a sip of the potent brew and returned his attention to the notes he'd taken this morning.

Hans Frank's son was out of the country, but Darwin had found his editor, who'd pointed him to a library that held Frank's personal documents. At last, Darwin sensed he'd reached the end of the trail. For the last three days, Jim Wilkerson's voice had repeated in his mind like a broken record: "If we can identify the people working for Frank, that might help us trace the stolen works."

He'd found a private diary, but it had been slow going, so he'd skimmed it, looking for the name Meyer. Eventually, he'd discovered

49

an entry that had been made just two weeks before Frank went to the gallows.

Darwin had snapped pictures of the pages, and now, sitting in the cafe, he checked his translation of the page he'd transcribed in the library:

Karl Meyer visited me today, looking for Johann and Heinrich. He asked if I knew where they could be. He lied to me about the reason. I had long suspected the bastards had stolen from me and said I wouldn't tell him anything unless he told me why he wanted to know.

He confessed to stealing a rail car en route to my estate. He said they were hiding the contents in an abandoned Junkers engine repair workshop. After the war, they intended to sell the art.
He claims he and Dieter got separated from Johann and Heinrich in a skirmish with the Allies. Dieter was killed, and he lost track of Johann and Heinrich.

Meyer thought he could win my cooperation by saying he would share proceeds from selling the Rafael. I despised that painting of some arrogant Italian, but its worth was significant.

The poor bastard. Only Johann and Heinrich knew the location of the workshop. They cut him out of his own deal. He left like a dog with its tail between his legs. I had no sympathy. The little shit got what he deserved.

Darwin did not doubt the translation—Hans Frank had Raphael's *Portrait of a Young Man*. His diary matched what Jim Wilkerson had heard. Meyer was looking for Heinrich and Johann. But there had to be hundreds of men with those names and dozens of Junkers workshops.

Still, he paused. *"Workshop" is odd. Why not "factory"?*

He checked his phone for a message from Eyrún. *Where is she?* He called and got voicemail again.

His watch buzzed. Time to catch the train to Paris. He ordered a taxi and then looked at the Auszogne. With a shrug, he shoved it in his mouth. *Never know when I'll be in Bavaria again,* he thought while licking the sugar off his fingers.

Louvre Subbasement

Eyrún and Aya sat on the spiral steps. They'd searched the tunnel, each taking a half, and now they were inventorying their options. Eyrún had a full water bottle in her pack, but the half-liter would not sustain them long. She also had a protein bar, but they could go days without food. Still, it was some comfort.

"There's no way we can use the drain at the far end. It's tiny," said Aya, eyeing the protein bar. "What about the vent you found?"

"It's large enough for a human and takes a sharp turn upward," said Eyrún, zooming into a photo she'd taken after extending her arm inside. "It looks like it goes up at least one level. But the question is, where are we? The Sully Crypt is the first basement. The stairs beyond the gate took us down another level to the door that opened into the tower and the spiral steps down here. This would be the third level down. Officially, the Louvre has only two."

"Which level goes into the sewer? Where we found the chained door?"

"The subbasement, the second level," said Aya, standing. "Let's look at your vent."

Eyrún led her to the tunnel's end wall nearest the tower stairs and pointed to the exposed body-width rectangle. Three thin stones mortared in place created a grate.

Aya leaned forward. "Looks like either a drain or an air vent. But partly closed to keep anyone from using it."

"That's what I'm thinking. We need to get these out," said Eyrún, tapping the blocks with her shoe. "Find something hard but not too heavy."

They searched but found nothing other than a slightly loose step in the spiral staircase. They took turns getting it free. At one point, Aya got frustrated with their progress and pounded on the steel door with a rock while Eyrún continued working on the step.

"It's loose!" Eyrún yelled.

Aya tossed the rock and joined Eyrún, sitting on a step next to the free block, wiping sweat from her forehead with a sleeve.

"Here. Drink some." Eyrún handed Aya a water bottle.

Aya took a sip and gave it back.

"You need to drink more."

"It's all we've got."

"Yes, and we have to stay hydrated. Water loss will affect our performance. We need to keep going while we can."

"Whoever locked us in won't leave us until we die. They can't," said Aya.

"Let's dwell on that later. Come on."

The step was too large to wield as a hammer, so they lifted it together and tossed it, cleaving it in three pieces. Eyrún carried the largest piece to the vent and began pounding it against the vertical blocks.

Their water was nearly gone two hours later, but the vent was opened. Eyrún's mouth was sticky from lack of moisture. Thankfully, it was cold in the tunnel, which helped reduce their body's need to sweat.

She pulled a canvas section off the paintings and used it to sweep away the grit before spreading it over the rough edge of the vent. She lay on her back, scooched in the hole, and aimed her phone light up the shaft.

"See anything?" asked Aya.

"It ends about three meters up, but I see a dark space, like—ow."

"What?"

Eyrún twisted herself around and backed out of the hole, then winced as her finger pulled at her right eye. "I got something in it. Hurts like hell."

"Stop rubbing it. Let me see," said Aya.

Eyrún sat against the wall and looked up as instructed. Aya held her light close as she spread Eyrún's eyelid. "You've got a small bit of stone in it. I'm going to wash it out."

"We don't have enough water," Eyrún protested.

"A few drops won't matter. Now, sit still."

The cold water ran down Eyrún's neck as she used all her concentration to stay still. One more splash trickled down. "There. It's out." Aya backed away.

Eyrún blinked. "Still hurts."

"Probably scratched your eye. How's your vision?"

"Fine. I can see."

"Rest here with your eye closed. I'm smaller. I'll go up there."

Eyrún lay flat on the floor to conserve energy and let her eye heal. She drifted into a lucid dream. In it, Darwin ran around their flat, calling her name. She stayed quiet in their hall closet. He called again.

"Eyrún." A hand gently rocked her shoulder. "Eyrún, are you okay?" asked Aya.

"Erm...yeah. I must have dozed." Eyrún sat up, working her tongue around her dry mouth.

"There's a turn that stops against a wall. It's stone, but it feels thinner. Not like these," Aya said, rapping the tunnel wall with the fleshy part of her fist. "I think we might knock it out. I'm going to take a rock up there. What I really need is a hammer."

"What about the iron rod from the door?" asked Eyrún.

"We couldn't get it out."

"No. The one here." Eyrún stood, and within minutes, they'd broken the rod free.

Aya hefted the half-meter bar of iron. "Feels like the tool my father used to change the tire on our car. How's your eye?" she asked as they moved back to the vent.

"It burns, but it's manageable. Can I help?"

"Not really," said Aya, and then she wriggled into the vent and disappeared up the shaft.

Eyrún switched off her light to conserve power. The sudden blackness threw off her balance, and she leaned on the wall. Aya scuffed her way up the shaft, occasionally grunting. She grew quiet, and then the unmistakable sound of metal on stone piped out of the opening. When Aya paused, Eyrún yelled, "Is it working?"

"I think so."

Aya hammered again, pausing every ten or so strikes to rest. Ten minutes later, she called for a break and backed out.

"Let me try," said Eyrún.

"It'll be tight for you.

"I've been in worse."

"Okay, coming down."

Seconds later, Aya's phone clattered from the shaft, followed by a nauseating crunch.

Aya shrieked, and Eyrún fumbled to find her light.

50

Paris

Darwin arrived at *Gare de L'Est* a little after 9 p.m. He hopped on the Metro to the Pont Marie stop and crossed the bridge to his apartment on Ile Saint-Louis. He needed to stretch his legs after the nearly six-hour train journey from Munich. He paused mid-span to look at the full moon—its light shimmered on the Seine. His grandfather Emelio had ingrained the habit in him of pausing to take in everyday aesthetics. "Human inspiration stems from our surroundings. Our creations mimic nature. Remember, discovery comes from seeing. You cannot see when running from place to place."

After watching a barge push its load toward the faraway harbor at Le Havre, Darwin continued, telling himself there was nothing to worry about.

"Eyrún?" Their apartment was dark except for moonlight shining through the patio windows. He dropped his bag and wandered through the rooms. "Hey, Love. I'm home."

The guest room had been slept in. He figured by Aya. Farther down the hall, he stopped in their bedroom. "Eyrún?"

Darwin switched on the lights, sat on the bed, and checked his phone. She'd sent her last message at 8:44 while he was breakfasting on the plane. He opened the Find My app. Under Eyrún's picture, it listed "No location found."

Suppressing a twinge in his gut, he messaged Aya. No reply. *Where are they? Maybe…*

He called Eyrún's sister, Siggy, in San Francisco.

"Hi, Darwin."

"Hey, Siggy. Have you heard from Eyrún today?"

"No. Why?"

"I, erm—"

"Darwin? Is something wrong?"

He explained the situation and added, "I know there has to be a logical reason. It's just…" He paused. "She's not normally like this."

"I'm sure you're right," said Siggy. "Look, you two are always getting into something. You said yourself that she's with Aya. They probably went into another tunnel. I have to prep for surgery. Check in with Zac. His plane should be taking off about now."

"Okay."

"Darwin. Chill. I'm sure there's a good explanation."

He sighed heavily. "Thanks. You're probably right."

They ended the call, and he messaged Zac, hoping his friend had connected to inflight Wi-Fi.

Did Eyrún text you today?

Zac: no why?

Darwin: She's not at our apartment. Her last text was this morning from the Louvre. Her location's not showing up in Find My app.

Zac: what was she doing at the louvre?

Darwin tapped out why and then paced the apartment, waiting for a reply.

Zac: there's got to be a rational explanation.

Darwin: I know, but

50

He sent the unfinished message and circled the dining table before opening the sliding door and stepping onto the balcony. The moon had crested Notre-Dame, and its scaffolding glinted like tinsel on a Christmas tree. He tried a technique to slow his pounding heart—a quick double inhale followed by a long exhale. *It's not working.*

He jumped as his phone emitted a loud Wookie sound—Zac's tone.

> go easy on yourself, bro. you know she's safe. there's a reason for this. she'll turn up by the time i land at 10:15.

Darwin: Thanks

His stomach growled, reminding him that dinner on the train had been more of a snack. He rummaged through the refrigerator and reheated a coq au vin they'd made the night before he left for Seattle. He briefly considered a glass of wine but decided he needed his full faculties in case… *Stop it,* he admonished.

Like Zac said, there's a good reason.

51

Subbasement

Eyrún breathed hard, fighting back nausea. Aya's left ankle was bent at a horrific angle. Blood pumped out where bone poked through. *Oh, God.* Eyrún sucked in a breath.

"How bad is it?" Aya panted.

"It's bad."

Aya cried. "It hurts. I feel like I'm going to pass out."

"Breathe, Aya. Deep breaths. In and out. Push up with your right leg," said Eyrún, breathing with her.

A moment later, Aya said she felt better, and Eyrún continued. "That's good. Can you pull yourself up?"

"I…yeah. I got finger holds between the blocks."

"Can you hold that position for a few minutes? I'm going to splint and wrap your ankle. Not a lot—just enough to support it."

"Okay. Hurry."

Eyrún spun and surveyed the available materials: painting and canvas. Working fast, she got a knife from her pack and slit the canvas into strips. Then she moved back to the vent.

51

"Aya, I'll try not to move it much, but I'm wrapping canvas strips around your ankle. How are you holding up?"

"Feeling a little lightheaded. Am I bleeding? My foot feels warm."

"Some, but not a lot. Here's goes." Eyrún wove the canvas in a figure eight over the top of Aya's foot, around her ankle bone, over her foot arch, and under her foot. On the third pass, she tightened the wrap and tied a knot with a long section of canvas she'd left from the first pass. Aya hissed as Eyrún finished the knot.

"Okay, Aya. Here's how we'll do this. Stand on your right foot. Get strong handholds around head height. Then pull yourself up. I'll get both your ankles and guide them out of the vent while you lower yourself onto your knees."

"Yeah. I can do that."

"Tell me when you're ready."

A long minute passed, and Eyrún was about to say something when Aya said, "Ready."

Eyrún saw Aya's right foot lift, and then she put a hand on each of Aya's shins and pulled them out as her friend's body lowered. Aya panted through her teeth.

"You're doing great," said Eyrún. "Almost there."

They rested while Aya's pain subsided. Then Eyrún carefully held Aya's left leg steady as she worked her way out of the vent. Once sitting up, Eyrún gave Aya the last of the water and used a small piece of canvas to fan her.

"Oh, God. It's bad," said Aya, looking at the bloody canvas.

Eyrún pulled more canvases off the paintings and formed them into padding and pillows for Aya. Then she grabbed the painting with what she thought was the ugliest frame and forced it off the canvas.

"What are you doing?"

The wooden frame cracked apart as Eyrún drove one corner into the floor and yanked its four sides apart. "Making a splint."

Eyrún put the longest parts of the frame alongside Aya's leg. She had re-wrapped the ankle earlier, and she bound the ends together below Aya's knee. The wooden pieces extended beyond Aya's ankle. Here, Eyrún fashioned bits of canvas to stabilize the fragile bones and add some traction to relieve pressure on the bones.

51

"Thanks, Eyrún," said Aya, her voice small as shock set in.

Eyrún arranged a pillow from rolled canvases and then used some as blankets. While Eyrún was sweating profusely from the exertion, the cool basement would lower Aya's temperature too much.

She sat next to Aya to rest, placing her hand on hers. "We'll get you out of here. Your ankle will heal perfectly."

"Thank you. I'm tired. Is it okay if I sleep?"

"Yes. It's only with a concussion that we keep you awake. But before you do, can I break through if I go up there?"

"I think so. Yeah, you could do it."

A few minutes later, Aya was asleep, and Eyrún caught herself drifting. *No. I can't.* She stood and walked off her grogginess. Then she checked Aya, who was cool to the touch. Her pulse was fifty-four, and Eyrún couldn't remember if that was bad or just normal for sleep.

It was nearly eleven. It was too long to wait and hope that whoever had locked them in might catch a kind streak and let them out. Darwin was due back, but even with the photos he'd sent yesterday, he might not have figured out where they were.

She maneuvered her way into the vent. Pressing her arms against the walls, she used her legs to push upward until she reached the turn. The block Aya had been hammering was about a body-length distance away. She navigated her way over the bend and shimmied to the wall. Then she shined her light over the stone and saw a fine crack in its upper-right corner.

That's hopeful. She set the phone beside her, grasped the iron rod Aya had left, and drove it into the stone. A dozen strikes later, a chunk fell away, and light streamed in. "Hello? Is anyone out there?"

She held her phone light to the hole, but the reflections were too great. She turned it off and looked without the light. A warm glow filled a wide space, but it was dim.

It's somewhere in the museum. She read the time on her phone: 10:57. Her neck muscles cramped from the awkward position, and she rested her head on the hard stone. Then she got an idea. After backing out of the horizontal shaft, she maneuvered herself feet first toward the hole in the wall.

More cramping. "Ahhhh," she moaned, wincing as her left foot seized. Her calf and hamstring spasmed. She locked her leg straight, pressing her shoe against the sidewall, and forced a stretch. A nauseous wave hit her as she breathed hard.

She needed water but pushed the thought down, and her muscles calmed. Then she heard a noise and lay still.

"Eyrún?"

"Aya? Is that you?"

"Yes. Are you hurt? What's going on?"

"Oh, my God. I'm so happy to hear your voice. How do you feel?"

"Cold. Tired. My ankle hurts," said Aya.

"I'm getting us out. I broke a hole in the wall. There's a room on the other side. I'm okay. Just got a cramp."

Grunting, Eyrún pushed backward on her belly until her feet hit the wall. She pulled her knees up, flipped on her back, and tested her leg movement. "Here goes!" she yelled to Aya and then slammed both shoes against the wall.

Pain shot from her ankles up to her knees, like she'd jumped onto concrete. She rubbed her left knee until the pain abated, gritted her teeth, and kicked again.

On the seventh kick, she saw stars. On the eighth, her legs shot into free space. Chunks of the wall flew out and clattered on the opposite side. Immediately, alarms blared, and a red light flashed from the opening.

"I'm through!" she yelled down the hole. "We got out, Aya."

But Eyrún heard no reply over the whooping siren as she rolled onto her side and crawled out. Her feet found the floor about knee height down, and her head cleared the hole when she stood. The loudest alarm came from the top of a wide marble hallway.

"Mon Dieu," she said, laughing with the emotional release. The scene was at once beautiful and comical.

Winged Victory stood in all her glory, her torso throbbing like a disco dancer in the red light.

Footsteps stormed from behind. She spun to face three armed guards.

"Arrêt! Sur le plancher! Maintenant!"

51

She held her palms outward, placing them on the floor as they commanded, and lay down.

52

Île Saint-Louis

Darwin gripped the railing on his patio. His unfocused gaze drifted over the City of Lights, and a heaviness filled him. *It's the fatigue,* he reasoned, thinking of the whirlwind travel to America and Germany.

He messaged Zac once more.

Going to sleep. Catch you in the morning.

Zac: me too, we're going off grid soon. i'll catch your messages over iceland if i'm awake

Darwin tossed and turned on the empty bed. The room felt colder without Eyrún. Normally, his ever-busy brain compensated by telling him she was traveling, but tonight, she was—*missing!* His eyes snapped open again, and his heart punched at his chest wall.

Moonlight glowed harshly through the window. He fumbled for the bedside controller and closed the blackout shades. Sometime later, in the cave-black room, he fell asleep.

52

École du Louvre

Darwin reached Vivienne's office at half-eight, planning to catch her when she arrived. He'd bolted awake before sunrise, remembering their last conversation: "You'll figure it out from the photos."

Before sunrise, he printed them and spread them out next to the maps of the Louvre that Aya had left in the sitting area. Caffeine helped him compensate for sleep loss, but by his third triple-shot cappuccino, his stomach protested, and his thoughts bordered on jittery.

However, he'd worked out that two days ago, Eyrún and Aya had found a tunnel from l'Auxerrois into the Louvre subbasement and discovered paintings. He checked the timestamp of Eyrún's last message—just before ten yesterday morning:

Eyrún: We're heading for the subbasement

He figured she meant the Louvre subbasement to look for the entrance to the tunnel with the paintings. *Why isn't her location showing?* He knew being underground blocked the signals. *But there's no reason to still be in the subbasement. Unless…*

All manner of reasons scrolled through his head. He pushed them aside as he messaged Zac with what he'd learned and put in the link to Eyrún's photos.

Forty-five minutes later, he was showered, dressed, and at the Louvre when Zac's tone sounded. He parked his bike and read the message while running upstairs.

Zac: crazy photos. wouldn't have believed it without seeing it. what do you need?

Darwin answered him while approaching Vivienne's office.

Can you track Eyrún's last known location?

52

Zac: sure, do you still have her google password?

Darwin logged into his secure password vault and sent Zac what he needed. He and Eyrún shared access to each other's vaults to protect their business. They'd set this up when his phone and iPad were taken the year before by thieves intent on accessing his intellectual property.

Zac: got it. i'll ask lupita to run this. i land in 2 hours. meet at your flat?

Darwin: Yes

While pocketing his phone, the aroma of freshly brewed coffee tickled his palate, and he was about to head towards the breakroom when Vivienne walked out of the lift.

"Darwin, you're here early," she said, dropping her phone into her Channel purse and unlocking the door.

"I need your help on a question."

"Will this take long? I have a call in ten minutes."

"No."

"How was your trip to Seattle?" she asked, setting her purse on the desk.

"It was—"

Vivienne's phone erupted in a marimba tone, and she grabbed it. "I have to take this. Shouldn't be more than a minute." She answered it and moved to the far window.

Darwin turned to her shelves, his eyes moving over the many photos of Vivienne and various officials and dignitaries. In the background, he caught snippets of Vivienne's conversation: "I see... When was this..."

He froze on a photo of Vivienne, about twenty years younger, standing with another woman about her age and an older man. *Putain!* He knew them: Thierry Panchon and Jasmin Kahn, two nefarious antiquities dealers. He squinted, studying the photo. It looked like they were at a conference. They wore name tags, and the names of a famous auction house and elite brands were stenciled on the photo's backdrop.

Darwin's vision tunneled. He was about to ask for Vivienne's help to find Eyrún. *But if she knows those two…* He considered the possibilities. Thierry was dead, and Jasmin was in prison. *But what if she's in league with them?* He knew some people had slipped through Europol's net when they'd brought down Panchon's antiquities cartel. He was so engrossed in speculation that he didn't hear Vivienne's approach.

"That was years ago."

He jumped.

"I was so young," she said, unconsciously rubbing an age spot on her hand. "Do you know them?"

"I was trying to figure out where it was taken. I… You still look great, by the way," he said, his face growing warm.

She laughed. "You're cute, Darwin."

He grinned wanly and then refocused. In past years, he'd been unhorsed by such comments—attractive women who politely put him in the "little boy" camp. He'd long since moved on, but the subtle insults still triggered him.

"What was your question?" she asked, glancing at her watch.

"Oh, it's erm… One of my Ph.D. candidates is having trouble accessing an archive in the Louvre," he said, throwing out the first thing that came to mind. "I wondered if you could intervene."

"Simple enough. Email me the request. I'll get my assistant to route the approval."

Her phone rang again. "That's the meeting I mentioned. Please close the door on your way out."

He did, cringing as she answered the call with a politician's verve.

53

Louvre

Darwin bypassed the tourist queue by showing his École du Louvre credentials and entered the Sully wing basement. The museum would open in a quarter-hour, and Zac's flight landed an hour after that. While walking around the massive walls of the Louvre's foundation exhibit, Darwin let himself drift back a thousand years, a technique he used on digs. He imagined the inhabitants—soldiers and servants—at this level of the Louvre castle.

Darwin stood in the former courtyard, now covered in the exhibit's hardwood, and pictured the walls of the immense round keep rising six stories above the modern ceiling, topped by a turret roof. The main palace formed a square around the courtyard, each corner defended by a high tower with more towers along the midpoints.

However, the royals and their court would not linger here. They entered the eastern wing by the drawbridge gate and spent all their time in the Louvre's many rooms. However, despite its size, the Louvre wasn't large enough to house the courtiers. They stayed across the moat at Hôtel du Petit-Bourbon, next to the cathedral.

Darwin reached the far side of the exhibit with the wall section on which the drawbridge rested. If Eyrún had guessed right, a tunnel would run below the gate. He came back to the keep tower while scanning the walls for doors that would give him access to a level below.

Tourists flowed in, their voices giving life to the space. He returned to the tower's massive foundation. *Think. Think.* Rubbing his temples to relieve a budding headache, he stopped at an exhibit map and continued into the Salle Saint Louis basement below. The iconic clock wing faced the glass pyramid, but it retained its chunky medieval fortress appearance.

Inside the Sully Crypt, Darwin found an iron gate that closed off a tunnel disappearing into darkness. He casually approached it and glanced around before stepping over a shin-high cable to keep visitors away from the exhibits. He leaned against the grating and shined his phone light, but the blackness swallowed the modest beam. He grasped the bar closest to the keyhole and tested it. Locked.

Footsteps approached, and Darwin looked up at a museum guard. "Sir, you can't be in there."

Darwin recrossed the wire and held up his École du Louvre badge. "I'm researching something for one of my classes. Do you know who has the key for the lock?"

"No, sir. I've never heard of anyone going in there. It's a dead end as far as I know."

Darwin nodded, but he was sure the tunnel aimed straight at the tower. He ran through people he knew who might know about it. Aya topped his list. He smiled. Then he frowned. *If they went in here, why haven't they come out?*

"Thanks for your help," he said to the guard and then turned for the exit. Zac would be on the ground in minutes.

Île Saint-Louis

Two hours later, Zac buzzed the flat's entrance, and Darwin raced downstairs. "We need to break into the Louvre," he exclaimed as Zac entered the lobby.

53

"I'm glad to see you, too," said Zac, grasping Darwin in a bear hug. "How about a coffee as we work out the plan?"

"*Desole,*" said Darwin. "It's just... I think I know where they are." As they rode up in the lift, he told Zac about his morning trip to the Louvre. "And there's something else."

Zac's eyebrows arched.

"I think my boss knows Jasmin Kahn."

"What?" Zac looked askance at Darwin. "Back up. How so? And why might that matter in this case?"

Once in the flat, Darwin made coffee as he explained going to Vivienne's office for help in locating Eyrún. "But while she took a call, I saw a photo of her with Thierry and Jasmin. Maybe twenty years ago. She confirmed knowing them, but nothing more."

Zac sipped his coffee. "Ah, hit's the spot." They moved to the balcony. "But just being in a photo doesn't mean your boss is working with them."

"No, not just the photo. I got back here an hour ago and dug into Vivienne's past. The de Poitiers were an influential family in the ancient regime, but they found themselves on the wrong side of history in the war and lost their fortune. Her father was accused of dealing in spoliated art.

"He was convicted of selling pieces with false provenance and died in prison, having served six months of a three-year sentence. He never revealed his sources. A posthumous expose suggested he had found a large cache of paintings hidden in a Paris basement."

"When was this?" asked Zac.

Darwin's gaze darted over the Paris skyline. "Erm...March of ninety-three. Vivienne would have been a young teen. Here's where the correlation comes in. She got her baccalauréat in 1997, the same year and school as Jasmin. Remember, she'd been adopted by the Panchon family when her mother was killed in Beirut."

"Like I care about her sad story. She screwed me over," said Zac, tipping back the last of his cup. "But so what? Thierry's dead. She's in jail. Vivienne is the head of the École du Louvre. What's the connection?"

Darwin massaged his forehead. "I was getting to it."

53

"Sorry, bro. Just hearing her name pisses me off. It's been a long night. For both of us. C'mon, let's get to finding Eyrún."

"Agree," Darwin said, sighing heavily. "Here's the connection. After uni, Vivienne and Jasmin worked at Christie's in London and Paris. Then Vivienne was a board member of Jasmin's antiquities trading company."

"But it sounds like Vivienne's gone clean."

"Or hiding in plain sight. What if she's connected to the paintings in that tunnel?"

"Put that aside for the moment," said Zac, looking at his watch. "Lupita should be ready."

Darwin followed Zac inside and put the cup in the sink before joining him at the kitchen bar top for a Zoom call with Lupita at the ACA in Corsica.

"Hey, Lupita," said Zac.

"Hi," said Darwin, waving.

"Hello, Zac. Hello, Darwin," said Lupita. "Still no word from Eyrún?"

"No."

"I am sorry. But do not worry. She is strong. There must be a good reason for her disappearance."

"Thanks, Lupita," said Darwin.

She jumped into what she'd found. "I am sharing a map of Paris overlaid with Eyrún's phone data for the last thirty-six hours. She traveled from your flat along Rue du Rivoli to the cathedral. She returned home at two-forty-three. Then, at 8:37 this morning, she went to an address in the tenth arrondissement before heading to the Louvre."

"Aya's flat," Darwin interjected.

"Good," said Zac. "That means they're together."

Lupita continued, showing them movements on the map. "She entered the museum from the Cour Carrée and moved into the wing facing the Seine. But we lose the position here. If what you say is correct, then she went into the basement near this point at 9:23. It has not registered its location since."

"Unfortunately, it doesn't tell us much more than we knew a few minutes ago," said Zac.

53

"I am sorry. It is the best I can do," said Lupita.

"No, no, Lupita. This is great," said Zac.

Darwin paced the kitchen, but he stopped as an idea hit him. He jumped back in front of the iPad camera. "Lupita, go over Eyrún's movements yesterday in the cathedral again."

Lupita backtracked to l'Auxerrois, and they watched a dot representing Eyrún move from the front door to a side chapel, then to the transept, and then to the altar.

"There," said Darwin. "How long did she stay at the altar?"

"Oh, my. I should have seen this before," Lupita said. "The GPS did not move for almost three hours."

"She went underground," said Zac.

"Exactly," said Darwin, looking at Zac and then back to the camera. "Lupita, how precise is the GPS data?"

"Inside the cathedral, it is no more than ten meters."

"Good enough. Zac, we need to go. That's our way in. Thanks, Lupita."

"You are welcome," Lupita said. "And please let me know when you find her."

"We will. Thanks again."

Zac ended the Zoom as Darwin ran to the closet and pulled out headlamps.

Minutes later, they got bikes from a rental stand and pedaled to the cathedral.

54

Saint-Germain l'Auxerrois

When they entered the cathedral, Mass was ending. They moved up the right aisle while the attendees formed a queue at the confessional. As the priest's assistants put away the chalice and other accouterments from the service, Darwin and Zac pretended to be tourists examining a side chapel.

Once the altar had been cleared, Darwin kept watch while Zac ducked down and studied the floor.

"Psst," said Zac.

Darwin looked across the choir once more and then walked to Zac, who pointed at the center slab behind the altar. "It's been moved. Look at the flaked edges. Someone swept, but this looks recent. I can lift this. The mortar's already been cracked."

Darwin ran a finger along the bright white marble edge where the top of the stone was dingy with use. "Someone will hear it move."

"We need a diversion. I'll—"

"No. I got this. You lift," Darwin beelined to an exit door. He pulled the fire extinguisher from the wall, moved it to the pulpit, and pulled

54

its pin. Squeezing the handle, he jammed it in a nearby chair leg to keep it open. Then he yelled, "Fire!" and sprinted toward the altar.

Zac yanked up the slab—the grating of stone on stone was another noise in the chaos. "Go!" Zac cried and then followed Darwin down. "Where now?" he asked, coming up on Darwin's heels.

"Eyrún mentioned a tomb," said Darwin, scanning the dark space with his light. A brighter light snapped on. He turned, and Zac handed him a headlamp. "Better idea." He adjusted the elastic strap around his head. "That one." He nodded toward the back wall. "Eyrún sent its picture."

Moments later, Zac swiveled open its lid, and Darwin bounded down the steps.

"I'm guessing we're passing under the cathedral's front doors, going toward the Louvre," said Zac.

They reached the far wooden door in seconds. Darwin pounded on it. "Eyrún! Are you in there?" He crouched and yanked out the piece of wood blocking the rod.

"Hold it." Zac stopped him and opened the door just far enough to yell, "Eyrún! Aya!"

He paused for a reply, but Darwin couldn't contain himself. "Eyrún! Love! Are you in there?"

Zac opened the door fully, waited a few heartbeats, and then went in low. He stood when they found no one. They walked to the right-angle turn and, after peering around, entered the shorter section.

"That's interesting," said Zac, pointing to the smashed surveillance camera.

"They were in here," said Darwin.

"Somebody was," said Zac.

"It was Eyrún," Darwin said, holding an empty water bottle. He sniffed the plastic. "Her perfume is on it. Where is she?"

Zac led the way up the spiral stairs inside the tower and froze. Crime scene tape crisscrossed the open door frame. He about-faced but collided with Darwin as two cops ran in from the Louvre side.

"Stop!" yelled the closest one.

55

Île de la Cité

At ten the next morning, someone finally granted Eyrún a phone call. Her body ached from climbing up the stone ventilation shaft, compounded by sleeping on the jail's hard bench. She had water and food, but she was worried sick about Aya.

When the Louvre guards had handcuffed her the night before, she'd pleaded for Aya's emergency care. Two guards had gone to the Sully Crypt, and she'd heard the calls over the radio explaining the jammed door. She'd begged them to open it and finally relaxed a half hour later when she saw Aya strapped to a stretcher and wearing an oxygen mask, with a medic holding an IV drip bag.

Darwin's number continued ringing as she stared into the pale corridor. The jail officer looked at her watch.

Come on. Answer.

After three more rings, Eyrún ended the call and tapped the number for her *avocat*. The assistant answered and told Eyrún that Astrid was in court and she would forward the message. Eyrún returned to her cell. Once again, her pleas to protect the art in the tunnel had fallen on deaf ears. The cops cared nothing about her story.

She and Aya were thieves—caught breaking into the world's most famous museum.

Where are you, Darwin? She leaned against the cold cement wall. Whoever knew about the paintings had had hours to move them.

Darwin sat five cells over, waiting for the head of the OCBC, Fleur Legrand, when he heard a familiar voice. He banged on his cell door and yelled through its narrow slot. "Astrid!" He smacked his palm on the door. "Astrid!"

"Darwin? What are you doing here?"

"I was arrested looking for Eyrún."

"What? Hold on?"

He listened as she walked down the hall and demanded to speak to the superintendent. She returned several minutes later and told him to be patient while she got Eyrún released.

"What? Eyrún's here?"

"You didn't know? She's been held since last night."

"*Putain!* How did she get here? I've been trying to find her."

"I don't know. Give me some time to get her out. The detective is getting us into an interview room."

Darwin paced his cell as "some time" turned into what felt like an hour. He paused on one turn. *At least she's safe.*

Fortunately, his wait wasn't much longer. Two guards escorted him to an interview room, uncuffed him, and opened the door. Eyrún sat in a metal chair. He rushed in and embraced her almost before she could stand. "I was so worried. What happened—"

"Eyrún, don't say anything," said Astrid. Then she turned to the guards and detective inspector in the room. "I need some time with my clients before you interview them. Now!" she added when they were slow to move.

Darwin whispered something to Astrid, who relayed it to the inspector. "And please bring my other client, Zac Johnson."

While they waited for Zac, Astrid phoned her assistant to check on Aya at the hospital. When Zac was seated, she explained the situation.

55

"The police have not charged you yet. Le Louvre is under the jurisdiction of the OCBC. Darwin, I understand Fleur Legrand and her team are on their way here. Eyrún, please explain what happened in as much detail as you remember."

Eyrún described Aya's theory of tunnels between royal palaces and chapels, their discovery of the Sainte-Chapelle tunnel, and the GPR scans. Then, she recounted their finding a tunnel under Saint-Germain l'Auxerrois cathedral and a cache of paintings below Le Louvre.

"At least we calculated it was below the Louvre. We turned back because there was a video camera. We—"

"What about being chased when you were scanning under Pont Neuf?" Darwin cut in.

"Oh, right," said Eyrún, and then she gave Astrid details of the two men.

Astrid made a note, double-underscoring it before saying, "There should be a police record of this. Did you make a report?"

"Erm, yes. They took notes, but I don't know what they did afterward. No one has contacted me."

"That shouldn't matter. Now, what happened from yesterday morning up to your arrest? And quickly because the OCBC will be here soon."

Eyrún gave her all the details, including Aya stealing her colleague's pass and her picking the locks before being jammed in.

Astrid reviewed her notes. "Why did you destroy the camera?

"I don't know. I was angry. Someone locked us in. Maybe they were trying to kill us."

Darwin put a hand on Eyrún's and tenderly squeezed.

Zac spoke up for the first time. "My money's on the men who chased Eyrún on Pont Neuf."

"That my be," Astrid said, "but let's hear what the police say. Stick to the story exactly as you told it." Her phone rang. "It's my assistant." She answered it, listened a long moment, and then asked, "Has anyone from the police interviewed her? Good. Tell them you are her attorney's representative. I'll be there as soon as I can."

Astrid disconnected and set her phone down. "Aya's fine. She

55

underwent surgery early this morning, and the doctors expect her to make a full recovery.

Eyrún slumped in her chair and leaned into Darwin's embrace. Zac squeezed her shoulder. Astrid knocked on the door to let the guards know they were ready.

The guards brought extra chairs into the interview room to accommodate the crowd. On one side sat Eyrún, Darwin, Zac, and Astrid. Opposite them were Fleur Legrand, two of her detectives from the OCBC, the Paris police detective inspector, and the director of the Louvre Museum.

The detective inspector started the voice recorder and then said, "Your clients broke into Le Louvre in very unusual circumstances. We plan to interview the other woman..." He looked at his notes, "Aya Raiss, as soon as we are allowed. She just came out of surgery, so her testimony would be inadmissible."

"We have two separate but, by all appearances, related break-ins. The first was by Ms. Stefansdottír and Ms. Raiss, and the second was by Monsieurs Johnson and Lacroix. Please explain what you were doing."

Astrid jumped in. "My clients acknowledge entering Saint-Germain l'Auxerrois, but they did not break in."

"They stayed illegally after the cathedral closed for the day."

"Is that a crime? Perhaps they needed sanctuary?" Astrid posited.

"Erm..." The detective fell back in his chair, his eyes darting from one face to another as if he were searching for a response.

Darwin bit his tongue to keep from smiling as Astrid seized the moment. "My clients discovered another unprecedented French treasure: a tunnel used by the Bourbon kings to move between palaces. My clients' methods may be, shall we say, unorthodox, but let's talk about what else they found." She paused and looked at each person opposite her and behind the one-way mirror.

"A newly discovered tunnel leading to an unknown Louvre

subbasement. But wait, that's not true. It can't be unknown because it was full of paintings—each one with a Nazi inventory number.

"My clients continued their search the next day, this time from inside Le Louvre, and they found an undocumented, locked door—again inside Le Louvre—leading into the subbasement tunnel full of Nazi plunder. Now, I have to ask, why would recovered art be stored in a secret Louvre subbasement? Surely not to avoid restitution to its rightful owners."

Astrid leaned forward slightly, her gaze locking onto the Louvre director's eyes. He shrugged and looked away, and Astrid looked at Fleur, not losing a beat. "Then, before my clients could properly report this, someone—that is, someone who knew about the secret locked door—sealed them in the subbasement.

She sat up and said, "I hope it was to buy time and not to murder them." She let the gravity of her last comment sink in before continuing.

"There is a crime here. Someone is actively covering up the theft of hundreds of millions of euros worth of paintings. But you're looking at the wrong people. You should be thanking my clients, not wasting our time sitting here."

Before the detective inspector could respond, Fleur asked the museum director, "Who could have known about this?"

The man shrugged and turned his palms up. "*Je ne sais pas.* My predecessor said nothing about a door, and my assistant says it's not in any of the museum plans."

"What about the basement curator?" asked Fleur. Before the man could answer, she said to the OCBC detectives, "I need you to interview everyone who's been employed since the pyramid went up."

The Louvre director said, "Please, I need all of your officers to be discrete. No photos on social media. This is embarrassing. The Louvre has been accused of holding back repatriation for years. This would be devastating. Please, I beg you."

"We're forgetting about something," said Darwin, and all heads turned his way. "There are over three hundred paintings unguarded. Whoever locked Eyrún and Aya in knows their loot is at risk."

One of the OCBC agents spoke up. "We've sealed access to the tunnel and have closed the crypt and foundation until the site is fully secured."

"What about the destroyed video camera?" said Zac.

"My people are on it," said the agent. "So far, we've determined it drew power from an ethernet cable. We're working on the IP addresses."

"Since we agree my clients committed no crime, can you please release them?"

The detective inspector agreed, but on the condition that they remain in Paris until further notice.

As they collected their belongings, Eyrún checked her phone. "Shit," she muttered under her breath. She didn't want to announce anything out loud in the station, so she messaged Darwin:

Check your calendar. Our dinner with the president and his wife is tonight.

Darwin looked up at her and then back down to his phone. Sure enough, the long-planned dinner at the president's Paris residence was tonight. He glanced at the time, 15:23, and messaged:

We can cancel it. You were up all night.

Eyrún: I'm okay. It's casual. I just need a shower and new clothes.

56

1st Arrondissement

The ink-blue DS 7 Crossback Elysee hybrid drove silently along the Seine toward the *Palais de l'Élysée.* Darwin ran a hand over the soft basalt black leather armrest and smiled at Eyrún, who was chatting with the driver about the car's performance. He chuckled and looked out his window. She loved her race-modified Macan, kept in Corsica, and regularly found excuses to take her electric Taycan outside the city, but she always had an eye for new toys.

Once they turned onto Pont Alexandre III, their driver showed off a little by rocketing past the Grand Palais before crossing Avenue des Champs-Élysées. The streets became park-like as they drove to the Élysée Palace's main entrance on Rue du Faubourg Saint-Honoré.

The Tricolore fluttered in the breeze high above a massive arched gate that split the administrative façade, architecturally similar to the Louvre's eastern colonnade. Armed security checked the vehicle and Eyrún's and Darwin's identity cards. The driver rolled up to the main entrance, and a smartly dressed woman opened Eyrún's door.

"Bonjour, bienvenue Palais de l'Élysée."

56

Eyrún thanked their driver and then stepped out of the car. *"Bonjour, merci."*

"My name is Hélène. The president and his wife will meet us in the garden in a few minutes. He is attending to a last-minute issue. Would you like a small palace tour to absorb the time?"

"*Oui*, that would be great," said Darwin.

Hélène guided them through a series of rooms on the ground floor. Darwin paused in the Cleopatra Salon to study a wall-sized painting of Mark Antony, smitten by Cleopatra's meticulously orchestrated arrival in Tarsus. He laughed.

"What's so funny?" asked Eyrún.

"The painter captured it perfectly. Appian wrote that Antony lost his head to her like a young man."

"You mean like you when we first met?"

"I did not." Darwin flashed back to their first meeting near Vik, Iceland. The late morning breeze fluttered her dark brown hair as she approached from the other side of the dig. Her glacier-blue eyes bore into him as they shook hands. Her beauty, confidence, and control swept him off his feet, leaving him virtually running to keep up the rest of the day.

It was Eyrún's turn to laugh. "Yes, Love, you looked just like Antony."

"But you followed me through a thousand kilometers of lava tube."

"What? No, I went along to keep you out of trouble."

"And you kissed me that day you twisted your ankle."

"He has an active imagination," she said to Hélène.

Eyrún took Darwin's hand as they followed Hélène and said in a low voice, "You were so cute, the way you prepared that little picnic for us."

Darwin beamed as they toured the ground-floor salons. Eventually, they reached a private garden, where the president and his wife entered through another door.

"Darwin, it's nice to see you again," said the president. "And you, too, Eyrún. Has it been three years since we met at the ceremony for Darwin's grandfather?"

56

"Yes," said Eyrún as they kissed cheeks.

After greeting the president's wife, they settled into cushioned teak chairs as a server poured champagne. "A toast to your latest discovery in the Louvre," said the president. "I know our dinner was planned before that, but having something to celebrate is always good."

They clinked glasses, and Eyrún said, "The credit for the discovery should go to Aya Raiss, who heads the *Crypte Archéologique*. She has an uncanny sense for finding Paris's secret past."

"How is she?" asked the president's wife. "Her injury sounds terrible."

"She's in good spirits," said Eyrún. "The doctors put three titanium pins in her ankle and expect her to regain full range of motion. Of course, it will take weeks to heal, but she's a fighter."

The president raised his glass at Eyrún's comment. "I'll make it a point to meet her on my next inspection at the Notre-Dame restoration. But tell me more about the paintings you found. Hélène tells me these are marked with Nazi inventory numbers, and no one at Le Louvre claims to know about them or the tunnel."

"And how did you find them?" his wife asked.

Eyrún described their theory of the royals using tunnels to move between palaces and how she and Aya had scanned using the GPR. "Ultimately, we made a educated guess based on prior discoveries."

The president laughed. "One of your detractors described your methods as 'smash and grab.'"

"We prefer calling it 'calculated risk and forgiveness on discovery,'" said Darwin.

"I like that," said the president's wife.

The conversation drifted to the ACA's work in Corsica and their projects. Eyrún advocated for more state support in helping former colonies preserve their cultural heritage. An hour later, they moved indoors for dinner, beginning with a sunchoke carpaccio with pistachio, kumquat, and black garlic. The earthy first course was paired with a Corsican Vermentino. Darwin complemented the selection, and the president credited the chef and sommelier, who were told the Lacroixs were from Corsica.

56

The main course brought Darwin fully back to his homeland: civet de sanglier, wild boar marinated overnight in red wine and maquis, garnished with sautéed mushrooms and bacon. A rich Chateauneuf du Pape, Darwin's favorite, rounded out the meal. The aromas reminded him of his grandmother's kitchen in Ajaccio and the tall tales from his grandfather.

During dinner, Darwin and the president were absorbed in the Lacroix family history and its relationship with the Bonapartes. The president confessed his interest in Corsica, as a proposal for greater Corsican independence had reached his office. Darwin summarized what he knew of the Genoese legacy: "Like continental France, we are a confluence of cultures, but our Mediterranean location means we are as Italian as we are African or Middle Eastern."

As cheese plates were served, Darwin brought the conversation back to the Louvre discovery. "You had asked me to look into the missing art. Honestly, I had no intention of doing it. But then I saw the file on my family."

"I am truly sorry for what France did to them. It is shameful."

"Thank you," said Darwin, composing himself. "I didn't know what had happened. My grandfather said little other than that they were killed. I..." His hand trembled as a white-hot fury built up. He thought he'd compartmentalized the horror and put it on a memory shelf, which was best left undisturbed, like a hornet's nest. He closed his eyes and inhaled deeply, fighting the urge to strike out.

Eyrún came to his rescue. "Darwin's grandfather is a private man and shielded the family from the awful truth. It was a shock to all of us." After a moment, to shift the conversation, she said, "Regarding the Louvre, I think there is more."

"Go on," said the president, spearing a slice of hard cheese.

"What Aya and I found in the basement was a fluke. Darwin has data showing illegal art trafficking from computer addresses inside the Louvre."

"Did you share this with Fleur?"

"Not yet," said Darwin, smiling at Eyrún for deftly rescuing him from the awkward moment. "Too many people surrounded Fleur. As you and His Holiness suggested in your letters, I sense a deeper conspiracy exists."

"How so?" asked the president.

Darwin explained what he'd found to this point, including the illegal online sale of art belonging to the Louvre. The president listened intently before asking, "How can I help?"

Without hesitation, Darwin said, "I need a file on a German recruited for post-war restoration. It should have been declassified, but for whatever reason, it has not." He wrote Karl Meyer's details on a slip of paper.

The president read it. "Work with Hélène. She'll keep me informed."

"Agreed," said Darwin. Their conversation widened, and a half-hour later, the evening ended.

When they left the palace, Darwin saw the president speak with Hélène and hand her the paper with Meyer's data. The drive home was muted as Darwin wondered what Meyer's file might show.

Île Saint-Louis

At their flat, Eyrún said, "You two certainly hit it off."

"Yeah, we did," said Darwin, kicking off his shoes. "He asked me about Corsica and my family's relationship with the Bonapartes. You also seemed to get along with his wife."

"Well enough. At one point, I asked her about Vivienne," Eyrún said, pausing while taking off an earring to look at Darwin in the mirror. "She said she didn't trust her."

"Interesting."

"Uh-huh. When I probed, she confided that Vivienne appears beautiful on the outside—the epitome of a modern French woman—but she's compensating for an unsavory past. She wouldn't say more but suggested we look into the company she keeps."

"Hmm," he mumbled, rinsing his mouth after brushing his teeth. "I'm thrashed. Let's talk about this tomorrow."

56

Darwin dried his hands and looked up, but Eyrún had already climbed into bed. He sighed. She'd had a far worse couple of days escaping from the Louvre and sleeping rough in a jail cell. He switched off the lights and was asleep in minutes.

57

Île Saint-Louis

Darwin awoke at the shower's hiss and rolled over. Eyrún's side of the bed was empty but still warm. He sat up and opened the drapes. Across the city, sunlight had just kissed the Eiffel Tower's observation deck. He watched the light creep downward before heading into the bathroom.

He cleared a circle on the mirror and assessed his five-day beard. He lathered up and was mostly done shaving when the shower turned off. Moments later, he put away the razor and looked at Eyrún, enveloped in a steam cloud. "Good morning, Love. Did you sleep well?"

"Like the dead. I feel so much better. You?"

"Yeah, well enough," he said as she opened the glass door. As the shower fog flowed around her, she looked like a mermaid emerging from the mist.

He moved toward her, and she gently brushed him aside. "I have meetings all morning."

"But Cleopatra, I've traveled all the way from Rome," he said, sticking out his lower lip in mock disappointment.

57

She combed her wet hair and smiled at him in the mirror. "A queen has her duties, Marc Antony, but she has a long afternoon break. Perhaps she could grant an audience?"

Darwin turned on the shower and stuck his head under the spray. As thoughts of the afternoon arose, he lowered the water temperature.

An hour later, Darwin brewed another triple-shot cappuccino and returned to his iPad. The cool shower had revived his pursuit of Karl Meyer. He had no idea when the president could shake the file loose from whoever had restricted it, but the question that had perplexed him in Munich now glowed like a neon sign: *Junkers Workshop. Why workshop and not factory?*

A workshop implied a garage-sized space where someone tinkered. Perhaps larger, but not an aircraft factory—a place with high ceilings that built bombers.

Darwin tapped a biography on Hugo Junkers. Hugo had started Junkers Aircraft and Motor Works in 1895, and like many aviation pioneers, the company had transitioned its product line to flying machines that captured everyone's imagination. Junkers garnered fame for its all-metal airplanes following WW1. In the 1920s, the Americans and Russians incorporated the corrugated duralumin airframe into their planes.

In the heady days of early aviation, Junkers proved himself a genius by designing a prototype that could carry passengers across the Atlantic in a mere eight to ten hours—half a century ahead of reality. But the company entered financial straits during the Great Depression and was acquired by Robert Bosch. Hugo still ran the operations but became increasingly at loggerheads with the National Socialist Party, and the Nazis ousted him in 1934.

Darwin's brain buzzed from the second cappuccino as he delved deeper in his pursuit of a needle in a haystack. The Junkers factory in Dessau had nearly been erased from the map in March 1945 as Allied bombers struck chemical factories and aircraft manufacturing plants.

57

Miraculously, it survived the war, and Dessau became part of the Soviet-dominated Eastern Bloc as the German Democratic Republic withdrew into itself.

Junkers resumed manufacturing in both East and West Germany. In East Germany, it merged into a consortium with Messerschmitt, and in West Germany, it shifted toward spacecraft design. When the wall came down, the Junkers company's assets ended up in Deutsche Aerospace. Darwin laughed out loud.

"What's so funny?" Zac asked as he walked into the kitchen.

Darwin explained his search, finishing with the reason for his outburst. "It's all part of the Airbus Group."

"Technology lives on, bro." Zac filled the kettle and switched it on. "Where does Eyrún keep the tea?

Darwin pointed to a drawer and set about making breakfast.

"So, it's a dead end," said Zac, pouring water into his cup. "I doubt the Airbus archives will have anything."

"Prolly not, but..." Darwin focused on the eggs, flipping them carefully.

Zac waited as Darwin stared into the pan. "But what?" he asked.

"Huh? Oh, I was thinking about the Deutsches Technik Museum in Berlin. There's a research section."

Zac buttered the slice of sourdough bread he'd toasted and cut into his eggs. They ate in silence, with Darwin clearing his plate before Zac got to his second egg.

Darwin rinsed the plate in the sink. "You don't suppose—"

"There might be a useful clue in the Berlin museum?"

"It's a long shot."

"True, but the Germans like their history, and I haven't had a good sausage since I was stationed in Ramstein," said Zac, wiping his hands and grabbing his phone.

Darwin took Zac's plate and washed it. As he put it on the dish drainer, Zac said, "All set. I booked tickets for us from Orly in two hours."

57

3rd Arrondissement

Eyrún entered the hospital soon after her morning meetings had finished and found Aya's room on the fourth floor. Five visitors crowded around her bed, laughing. Flowers and helium-filled balloons surrounded her. A traction device elevated Aya's leg, and one of her friends had tied a balloon to its cable.

"Eyrún!" Aya exclaimed and then introduced her as the "friend who saved my life."

The friends whooped, shook Eyrún's hand, and patted her on the back. Aya explained that they were part of her cataphile group. "The ones who come out in the daylight," she said to laughter.

A nurse entered and announced that only two visitors were allowed. The group protested but left to go back to their various jobs. When the chaos died, Eyrún sat in the bedside chair while the nurse took Aya's vitals. As the nurse massaged Aya's bruised and purple toes, she asked about the sensation. Pins stuck through each side of the bandages around Aya's ankle and lower leg.

"I feel your touch," Aya said. "It hurts a little when you bend them."

"That's good."

When the nurse left, Aya took Eyrún's hand. "I'm so glad you came. If it wasn't for you..." Her voice broke in a flood of tears. "I'm sorry," she said with a sniff. "I didn't mean to get so emotional."

Eyrún grabbed a tissue and handed one to Aya before dabbing her own eyes. "I'm happy we got you out in time," she said, glancing at the soft cast.

"Me, too. The doctor said you did an amazing job on the splint. You saved my ankle." Aya blew her nose. "How did they get me out? I don't remember."

Eyrún explained how she'd broken through the wall and begged the police to go to Sully Crypt. "The paramedics took a stretcher into the tunnel and carried you up. I insisted on seeing you get into the ambulance before being taken away."

"Can you believe they handcuffed me to the bed frame?" Aya held up a hand. "Like I was going anywhere. Idiots. What happened to you?"

Eyrún went over Darwin's and Zac's arrest and Astrid's verbal jousting at the police station.

"I would have loved to have been there," said Aya. "See the flics told off. Bastards. Your lawyer's assistant visited me and got the handcuffs removed. Why aren't they with you today?"

Eyrún told her about their trip to Berlin, and they sat silently for a time. As she studied the traction mechanism, she asked, "How long do you stay in that?"

"About ten days, but the surgeon said it depends on healing. Then I get a boot and maybe go to the toilet myself."

A radiology technician entered to take an x-ray of Aya's ankle, and Eyrún waited outside until he finished. When she returned, Aya went straight to the question that had been troubling them both: "Do they know who locked us in?"

"No," said Eyrún. "They're reviewing the museum's security videos, but I'm not hopeful. I'm guessing whoever did it is skilled enough to avoid detection."

"What about the paintings? You mentioned the OCBC. Do we trust them?"

Eyrún thought for a moment. Darwin had mentioned insider corruption, and she'd overheard him telling the president he wasn't sure who to trust. As much as she liked to think that the art crimes unit was completely above board, she had to admit uncertainty. "I don't know," she said.

"I don't like it. What if they get moved to some warehouse? You know, like that scene in *Raiders of the Lost Ark*," said Aya. "I wish there was a way we could tag with those Apple things."

"AirTags?"

"Yeah, those."

"I think they'd be easy to spot," said Eyrún. "And we'd need hundreds of them."

"Do the police have any idea what they're guarding? And what if they're corrupt?"

The more questions Aya asked, the more Eyrún's attention drifted to the Louvre and what could be going on. If insiders had hidden the paintings, they would know they'd been found.

"Eyrún, what's wrong?" asked Aya.

"You're right. I need to get on this. Sorry to cut our visit short."

"I'm not going anywhere. Text me, please."

"I will," said Eyrún, rushing out the door.

58

Gorgona, Italy

Lionel took a morning flight from Charles de Gaulle Airport to Livorno, Italy, where he boarded a ferry to Gorgona island. Forty minutes later, the boat lagged in a trough between swells in the Ligurian Sea before surfing down the face of the next. He eased into the Mediterranean vibe as the warmth and humidity chased away the Paris chill.

Ahead, hills sprang from a natural harbor. Terracotta-roofed stucco buildings crowded a small beach, becoming more prominent as they marched up the hillsides. But this was not a tourist destination. After the ancient monastery was abandoned in the fifteenth century, the island became an anchovy fishing village before the Italian state acquired it to use as a penal colony.

The lump of land sequestered minimum security prisoners who would not risk their lives swimming the nineteen nautical miles to the mainland. Instead of cell blocks, the inmates were contained by water and, in exchange, given the freedom to move about and work the agricultural plots and vineyards.

58

The ferry anchored in the harbor, and all passengers were transferred to a police boat. Lionel passed through the security process quickly. The guards had been paid not to ask questions.

Fifteen minutes later, he approached a woman working in the island's vineyard. It was harvest time, and she clipped the pale golden grapes, dropping each bunch in a bucket. His shadow covered her hands.

"I'm doing it right," said the woman. "What do you want?"

"Paintings," said Lionel.

The woman stood, almost equaling his height. A broad hat shaded her face and neck, but her skin had bronzed from working outdoors. She wore no make-up and had gathered her coal-black hair in a ponytail. For a moment, her almond-shaped eyes squinted, concealing their amber color. Then her generous eyebrows relaxed, and she smiled.

"Lionel. Well, you're the last person I expected to see today," Jasmin Khan said in a throaty voice.

"Nice to see you, too," he said, pushing down the hurt he felt.

"No, no. I didn't mean it that way. Come here." They kissed each other's cheeks, and she grasped his shoulders. Her grip conveyed strength from working on a farm. "This is full. Help me carry it back."

He grabbed one side of the plastic bucket, and they walked between the vines to a waiting trailer. Lionel studied her tanned and toned arms. Her long, slender fingers were unpolished, trimmed short, and sticky with grape juice—not the pampered, manicured look she meticulously maintained before her arrest and during her trial.

Lionel was furious when he learned Jasmin had killed his mentor, Thierry Panchon. He knew Thierry could be a controlling bastard and had been blown away to learn Jasmin was Thierry's daughter, not his wife. She was the product of a love triangle that had ended in violence when Thierry had killed Jasmin's mother—the bullet meant for the other lover.

Jasmin and Thierry had posed as married antiquities dealers, catering to the uber-wealthy while amassing their own fortune. But when Jasmin learned of her mother's murder, she lost it and emptied a handgun into Thierry's chest. The sentencing judge was swayed by the psychologist's report that Jasmin was unstable at the time of the shooting, battered by years of manipulation. She was sentenced to ten years and had that commuted to minimum security on Gorgona after a gifted attorney argued that she felt remorse.

Lionel thought that Jasmin's acting was so complete that she could have a film career. Everyone thought of her as the victimized daughter. He looked at the gold cross dancing between her breasts—another part of her false contrition. He knew she only cared about two things: money and power. Lionel liked money. Power? He preferred working in its shadows.

"It's Vivienne, isn't it?" asked Jasmin.

"Yes."

They dumped the bucket in the trailer. Fruit flies swarmed the free meal. Lionel waved them off.

"It's lunchtime. Join me. We can sit over there." She pointed to a flat rock on a grassy slope overlooking the sea.

He updated her on the missing Raphael and the break-in at the Louvre as they ate cheese on torn pieces of rustic bread. They washed it down with white wine from an unlabeled bottle. Lionel nodded in approval.

"Contact Klaus at the Geneva Freeport. He'll get the others. We knew this day was coming," Jasmin said. She stared at the shimmering ocean a long time before saying, "Show me the photo."

Lionel brought it up and leaned close to her, shading it against the bright sun. Her musky perspiration enveloped him, and he felt her warm breath on his hands.

"It looks like Iceland," she said, sitting up. "What's the name of the guy you said Vivienne hired over your friend?"

"Darwin Lacroix."

"*Putain!*" She shot to her feet and paced around the rock.

"You know him?"

"That son of a bitch and his Icelandic wife are why I'm here."

Lionel made a face, and she explained her version of events—how Darwin and Eyrún had entrapped her.

She grabbed the wine bottle and chugged from it. Lionel finished his lunch as she stood nearby, lost in some private space. A quarter-hour later, she returned and sat beside him on the rock. "When do you leave?"

"On the afternoon ferry," he said.

"Then, let's not waste time," she said, pulling off her top and motioning him onto the grass. "I have needs, and the opportunities here are few."

59

Louvre

Eyrún dashed from the Metro doors as soon as they opened, nearly tripping over a pram. "*Desole*," she said over her shoulder as she ran to the Louvre's underground entrance and then to Sully Crypt.

She slowed down in the midday crowd, not wanting to bowl over museum-goers, and reached the basement exhibit a minute later. Fewer people milled about, and she zeroed in on a gendarme and guard standing by the iron gate leading to the tunnel.

As she approached them, a man arrived from the opposite direction. Something about him was familiar. She'd seen him recently. She froze. *He's one of the men who chased us.*

Eyrún slipped behind a column. Her heart raced as his face swirled in her memory. It had been dark in the garage, but when they'd burst into daylight in Square du Vert-Galant beneath Pont Neuf, she'd caught a decent look at him before the police had chased him away.

She blended in with a passing tour group and stole a look at the gate. *It's him.* He was the same height and build, and his wild, dark hair was unmistakable. He was showing a badge to the cop. *He's an employee!*

59

Eyrún flattened herself against a wall. *It all makes sense*—or at least it seemed to. *He would have access to the video camera in the tunnel. Why has he been following us? And how?* She closed her eyes, searching her memory.

Shit! Her blood ran cold as she felt around in her purse for an AirTag, glancing up every few seconds to keep an eye on him. She found nothing, even pressing against the seams. *Maybe he put something on Aya?* She'd have to search Aya's things later.

Eyrún saw the guard look at his watch and then speak to the man. *He's asking about a shift change.* She took a deep breath to calm herself. *Stop. Don't assume. Work the problem.*

The man turned to leave. Snapping pictures of his profile, Eyrún watched him cross the room and badge into a staff-only door. Then, she moved through the exhibit until she reached the guard and cop. She paused and craned her neck, peering into the dark space beyond the gate. Then she said, "I heard there was a break-in."

"No comment, madame," said the cop.

"Was that the exhibit curator who just left?"

The cop remained impassive, but the museum guard nodded.

Eyrún stared into the blackness and shuddered at the memory of being locked in. Slowly, she moved to another part of the exhibit. Once back in the main entry hall near the inverted pyramid, she glanced up the long steps to Winged Victory. Today, the statue stood in the natural light as if nothing had happened. Halfway up, a section of marble was under repair.

She exited via the spiral escalator and hurried under the Horloge Pavilion, across Cour Carrée, and through the colonnade on her way to Saint-Germain l'Auxerrois. Walking toward the altar, she saw the police tape cordoning off the apse. A gendarme sat nearby, and her face glowed palely from scrolling on her phone. Eyrún glided past, pretending to study the stained glass windows.

Eyrún paused in a chapel and scrolled through the photos she'd taken in the Louvre. The wild-haired guy's face was perfectly visible in one in which he walked under a spotlight.

Who are you? She zoomed in on his face. He hadn't shaved in days, and his visible eye was a deep brown with a dark circle beneath it, like he hadn't slept.

Eyrún thought about sending the photo to the OCBC, but Aya's question of trust kept popping up. Instead, she sent it to Darwin and asked his opinion. Then she left, but she couldn't shake the feeling of dread. It had been easy for her and Aya to break into the cathedral. But if they could do it, so could anyone else.

60

Berlin

Their rideshare dropped Darwin and Zac at the Deutsches Technik Museum at quarter past one. The multistory steel and glass façade stood out among the red-brick former factories surrounding it.

"That's cool," said Zac, his head arching upward as he stared at a DC-3 suspended above the building. It gleamed like new. The plane's US Air Force emblem reminded them of its role in the Berlin Airlift.

They entered and paid admission. Darwin stumbled over his German while asking about the research department, and the docent explained the directions in perfect English. They moved through the exhibit, where planes, from the earliest models to modern ones, filled every available space. Stairs and metal catwalks gave people access to all corners of the exhibits.

Just before the stairs to the third floor, Darwin stopped a wrecked Junkers Ju 87, better known as a Stuka dive bomber. The engine had been ripped away from it, and the fuselage was pocked with holes where the metal had corroded. The inverted gull wings conveyed aggression, and a button on the nearby plaque, when pressed, played the wailing siren that had terrorized the Stuka's victims. He shuddered at the modern angel of death before mounting the steps.

Three levels up, Zac paused on the landing. "You don't see that every day."

"Nice," said Darwin. A bright yellow biplane bearing Swiss insignia hung vertically. The non-military craft shook off his dark thoughts.

The went right, following the docent's directions, and entered a reading room. The conversational noise of the main hall dropped off as the library door closed, and Darwin approached a robust woman with curly gray hair sitting at the reference desk, absorbed in a book.

"*Guten tag,*" he said.

She looked up. "*Guten tag. Kann ich dir helfen?*"

Darwin roughly understood that she'd asked if she could help. "Do you speak English?"

"A little."

Zac took over. "*Ich spreche Deutsch.*" He explained that they were looking for locations of the Junkers company's workshops. As he and the woman conversed, Darwin looked around the library, where the afternoon sun streamed through high windows and across rows of tall bookshelves.

A minute later, the woman directed them to a series of thick binders. When she retreated, Zac explained that they contained records of the Junkers factories in both East and West Germany.

"Can you read it?" asked Darwin.

"Yes," said Zac, pulling a binder from the shelf. "I studied German in high school, found I liked it, and continued it at West Point," he added while carrying it to a table.

"I never knew."

"You never asked. I liaised with the German Army and their intelligence unit."

Darwin knew not to probe into his friend's military experience. Zac had combined his physical abilities with his prodigious technical aptitude to become a US Army Ranger. His doctorates and work at Lawrence Berkeley Laboratories kept him at the cutting edge of high-energy physics research. He also maintained intelligence contacts in the US Department of Energy.

Zac scanned through the volume and then pulled down another. "There's a convoluted trail of the intellectual property as the company's assets changed hands after the war."

"Anything I can do?" asked Darwin.

"I'd love a coffee."

"On it."

Ten minutes later, he returned with two cups. After handing them on to Zac, he wandered over to the librarian to pursue a thought. He soon found out that her earlier comment about speaking English a little meant she was being modest.

"Would there be records from the Junkers company in other locations?" he asked.

"There is an archive at the Airbus facility in Hamburg," she said. "I have heard some is digitized."

He frowned, imagining sifting through data for hours. "Do you know a historian with a deeper knowledge of the Junkers company's operations during the war?"

Her fingers rested gently on her mouth as she stared across the library. A long moment later, she answered, "A man has come here over the years to study their records. He's a retired aircraft engineer who worked in the GDR."

Darwin's heart leaped at the news. "Where can we find him?"

"He lives in Dessau. I heard he volunteers at the Technikmuseum Hugo Junkers."

Darwin thanked her and wandered back to Zac. "Find anything?"

"Lots of things, but nothing about workshops."

"We need to go to Dessau. The librarian said we should talk to an amateur historian and former aircraft engineer at the local Junkers museum."

61

Dessau

Zac rented a car, and once outside Berlin's city limits, accelerated to 145 kilometers per hour—brisk but not breathtaking compared to Darwin's white-knuckle passenger experiences while riding with Eyrún. An hour later, he slowed on the autobahn for the exit to Dessau.

The next ten kilometers through central Dessau and sleepy residential neighborhoods were tedious. As they neared Kühnauer Strasse and the museum, Darwin's phone chimed.

> Eyrún: This is the guy who chased us. He is at the basement exhibit.

"*Merde!*" Darwin zoomed in on the face.

"What is it?" asked Zac.

Darwin explained, and Zac glanced at the photo. Then his gaze darted back at the road as they reached a gate on the left bearing a modest sign with a picture of an old single-engine aircraft. Darwin messaged Eyrún as they turned onto the drive:

Where are you now?

Eyrún: Office. In meeting.

They rolled up to the museum, where a twin-engine craft, similar to a DC-3, rested next to four aging Russian jets. Zac parked on the decaying tarmac surrounding the converted factory. Grass framed the concrete squares poured ninety years ago, a reminder that nature took back what humans failed to maintain. Only two other cars were in the car park.

"Show me again," said Zac, taking Darwin's phone.

"Eyrún wants us to identify him if we can."

"Not much to go on. Is she sure it's the same guy? What's the connection?

Another message from Eyrún popped up:

Forgot to tell you. He showed a badge to the cop at the exhibit.

"He's a cop?" Zac asked. "But that doesn't make sense. Why would he chase her and Aya?"

"Especially if he ran from the other cops," said Darwin, furrowing his brows. "Unless...he's a Louvre employee." He took back the phone and asked Eyrún:

Did the badge look like a wallet or just a card?

Eyrún: A card.

Darwin: Like an employee badge?

Eyrún: Yes. Like the badge keys we have at the ACA. OMG, do you think he's an employee?

Darwin: Dunno, I'll check.

He tapped into his email app as Zac stopped him. "Wait. Eyrún's right. If we don't know who to trust, don't send the photo. Go to the HR department tomorrow."

Darwin's phone chimed again.

Eyrún: We also need to put AirTags on all the paintings

Darwin: That's over 300

Eyrún: I'll ask my assistant to get them.

"Let's go," said Zac, getting out of the car.

Darwin did, and as he explained Eyrún's idea to Zac, they admired the planes resting on the tarmac.

"It's a good idea," said Zac, "but they're large. I mean, they'll be easily spotted. I might have a smaller source."

He tapped out a message on his phone as Darwin wandered across the old airfield. The grass had grown through the squares, and years of weathering had eaten away at its surface. Dust covered the fading paint of the old war birds, resting like old soldiers—proud but obsolete, their stories dissolving into the vastness of history.

The museum's inside collection, while mainly aircraft, also featured cars and what looked like a shipping container house—another of the Junkers company's many projects. Zac laughed. "Look at this," he said, reading the description. "A modular system for low-cost housing. It includes interior sliding panels and plans for air conditioning and solar power. This was 1931, and we think we're so smart."

They explored the beautifully restored Ju-25, a tri-engine passenger craft, and the single-wing Ju-1 built in 1915 using duralumin. "Damn. German technology was so good."

Darwin walked over to a man tinkering at a workbench. "*Guten tag.*"

"*Guten tag,*" the man said. He finished tightening a vise and then looked up. "Welcome to the museum. Do you have any questions?"

"I'm an archaeologist from France researching Junkers. We just came from Technikmuseum in Berlin. The librarian there said your museum may have records that could help me."

61

"We have some. Can you be more specific?" the man asked as he cleaned his hands on a shop towel.

Zac wandered over and introduced himself in German. The two men spoke for a couple of minutes. Darwin understood enough to catch that Zac was explaining his posting at Ramstein. The man laughed at something Zac said, which put him at ease, and Zac switched to English. "This is my friend and colleague Darwin Lacroix from the École du Louvre in Paris. I'm Zac Johnson."

The man shook his hand and then Darwin's. "I'm Helmut Otto." He looked at his watch. "Would you like a beer?"

They followed Otto to a sitting area outside the container house, where he produced glasses from behind a bar and poured them beers from a tap. "We conduct fundraisers here, and it's one of the perks of the job. I'm retired."

Otto invited them to sit and told them his history. "I worked in East German aerospace until Deutsche Aerospace absorbed our operation. Those were heady days. We finally got access to the computers in the West—no more counterfeit Russian crap."

He took a long pull from his glass. "Ah... Anyway, I was shifted to working for Airbus as the A300 became a success. My last aircraft was early work on the A380. She's still my favorite."

Zac asked which part Otto worked on, and he replied that it was the transponder system. Darwin listened intently as the two geeked out after Zac mentioned his research with microsatellites.

During a pause, Darwin asked, "How did you get involved with the museum?"

"Let's say it was a labor of love," Otto said, surveying his surroundings. "My father was friends with Hugo. They grew up together. On a street just over there, about half a kilometer away." He pointed toward the main entrance.

"They were born in the same year, and my dad joined the company just after Hugo founded it. They made boilers before Hugo caught the flying bug. Unfortunately, the Nazis kicked Hugo out, but my father stayed on. He was deemed a critical worker in the aircraft factory, which was good for me. Most of my friend's fathers were killed.

"We barely survived ourselves. The bombing destroyed eighty-five

61

percent of Dessau. The city was left in ruin, but not a single bomb hit this factory. It was a terrible time after the war."

"I'm sorry to hear," said Darwin.

"Thank you."

An awkward silence followed. Darwin broke it by asking, "We're looking for workshops where Junkers repairs were done during the war. Would the museum have records of its facilities?"

"That is becoming a popular topic. Are you chasing rumors of stolen Nazi gold?"

"No," said Zac. "But now that you mention it..."

Otto snorted, failing to catch Zac's attempt at humor. Darwin redirected. "We're not treasure hunters. I'm researching missing artworks looted by the Nazis. I've come across a scrap suggesting an abandoned Junkers workshop was used as storage."

"How do I know you are who you say you are?" asked Otto, suddenly suspicious.

Darwin took his École du Louvre ID out of his wallet, and Zac showed Otto his Department of Energy security clearance card.

"Okay. My apologies. I had to ask. Someone else was here from the Louvre."

"What?" Darwin nearly sprang from his chair.

"Two months ago, a Frenchman was here. Christian, erm, I can't recall his last name. Anyway, he wanted to know about Junkers workshops. It took a while to find it, but we had a list of all the repair shops." Otto stood. "Would you like to see it?"

62

Île Saint-Louis

The following morning felt like déjà vu as Darwin listened to Eyrún in the shower. He and Zac had gotten back to the flat at midnight after a delayed flight through Munich. Nothing flew non-stop to Paris from Berlin, and Eyrún had been fast asleep when he'd arrived.

He stood and stretched before opening the drapes. A breeze smudged the Seine's surface, and a group jogged along the quay. He went to the en suite bathroom, where Eyrún asked, "What time did you get in?"

"Midnight."

"Did you find what you wanted?"

"Sort of," he said groggily.

"Well, tell me about it over breakfast. I have a call with a museum director in Indonesia in a half-hour."

Darwin studied his face in the mirror. He was moving slowly, each decision taking longer than usual, and chalked it up to fatigue. Twenty minutes later, dressed and shaved, he walked into the kitchen just as the flat's call button buzzed. "Okay, okay." *Who the hell is here this early?*

He opened the app to see a video of Hélène, the presidential GSPR agent. "*Bonjour,* Hélène," he said.

"I have something for you." She waved a large manila envelope.

"I'll buzz you up. I'm making coffee."

"No time. Please come down." She nodded to a black SUV parked behind her.

Darwin zipped down the stairs, as the elevator was on the bottom floor. The exertion got his blood flowing. He met Hélène and the president by the quayside wall.

"*Bonjour,*" said Darwin, surprise in his voice at seeing the president.

"*Bonjour*. I envy your view," said the president, gesturing toward Notre-Dame.

An elderly woman walking her small dog stopped and put a hand to her mouth. The president greeted her and chatted for a few moments before he turned back to Darwin. "I looked into the current situation at the Louvre. The OCBC, DGSI, and National Police are investigating with Louvre security, but as you mentioned, any insiders would have infiltrated these agencies.

"I've assigned Hélène to work with you. I trust her with my life literally every day. She has the file you requested. She also has access to other agents. Start by finding out who loses most from the discovery of that subbasement artwork."

"Agreed," said Darwin.

"Good. Hélène is with me today. She'll contact you tomorrow. Report progress through her. *Bonne chance.*"

They shook hands, and Darwin watched on the sidewalk as the black SUV pulled away and crossed Pont Tournelle. He looked up to his apartment's balcony and waved at Zac, who was peering down. Then he carried the folio upstairs.

"Hanging out with the president before coffee. You a secret agent in training?" asked Zac.

"Pfft. Doubt it." Darwin laid the envelope on the counter and turned the dial on the coffee grinder. When the noise abated, he related his downstairs encounter to Zac as he spooned the last of the foam into his cup. He savored the brew and set it down. Then he began reading a typewritten page summarizing the dossier's contents, dated 17 June 1947.

"What's it say?" asked Zac. He was fluent in conversational French but read more slowly.

"Mostly what we know already." Darwin skimmed ahead. "Karl Meyer attended Reichuniversität Strassburg and was a professor there when the war started. He was absorbed into the ERR and worked in the Jeu de Paume in the early years of occupied France.

"Putain," Darwin said in a low voice.

"What?"

"The French security services changed Meyer's identity. He became Louis Roche and was given a curator job at the Louvre. No wonder James didn't like him."

Darwin's phone buzzed with a WhatsApp message from Hélène.

> I traced Meyer/Roche after 1947. He married in 1955 and bought a house at 19 Rue Vide. His grandson Christian works as a restorer in the Louvre.

"Hold on," said Zac. "Christian at the Louvre? It's got to be the guy Otto mentioned."

"What about Christian?" asked Eyrún, who had wandered in to make tea.

"We got an address for Roche," said Zac. "He died in 2007 and left the house to his daughter."

Eyrún coughed, choking on some tea that went down the wrong way. Darwin looked concerned, but she set down the cup and waved him off. "Back up. Who is this?"

Zac summarized their findings up to that point. "Looks like Christian Roche is Louis Roche's, aka Karl Meyer's, grandson. His mother never married or kept the Roche name."

"And he works at the Louvre?" asked Eyrún.

Darwin nodded.

"Then he's Aya's friend. She left a note on his desk two days ago

62

when we were in the restoration department. His colleague said he was on leave."

"Holy shit," said Zac.

Eyrún squeezed in beside them and looked over the files. After a few minutes, she asked, "How is it all connected? Or is it?"

"It's got to be," said Zac, turning to Darwin. "I mean, the president and pope asked you to look into fraud. Eyrún and Aya are being followed and find a tunnel full of looted art. A former MPAA guy accuses Karl Meyer of underhanded dealing, and the French give him a new identity."

"When did all this start?" asked Zac.

Eyrún looked at Darwin. "I don't know. When you got the file on your family?"

"Maybe." Darwin closed his eyes to think and then blurted, "No. It was when Mihn found my family's paintings for sale. It… Wait." He grabbed his iPad, navigated to the property tax collection website, and entered the address for Roche's house.

"It changed ownership to Christian three months ago," he said, pointing to the webpage.

Zac and Eyrún leaned in. The Paris property record showed the change of ownership from Louis Roche's daughter to Christian.

"He must have found something in the house," said Eyrún.

They looked at each other and grabbed their coats off the rack.

63

6th Arrondissement

Lionel sat in a cafe, trying to figure out the extent of the breach. He couldn't get close, as the police were watching both Saint-Germain l'Auxerrois and the Sully Crypt in the Louvre around the clock. For the last day, he'd ignored Vivienne's many messages asking what the police knew. They'd grown desperate. Her last pleaded:

They can't tie this to me.

True, he thought, *but my fingerprints and DNA are on the door and camera.* He'd installed a new higher-resolution camera two months ago.

So far, nothing had happened, but the art crimes unit had been all over the site. *What are they waiting for?* He guessed the Louvre had muzzled the media.

He'd heard from his sources that Eyrún and the other woman had escaped through an air vent and set off alarms. He tried picturing the subbasement tunnel section with the ancient vent and decided it must have been hidden behind the paintings. He'd not touched them other than to lift the canvas to look. His predecessors had consolidated them from various locations after the discovery of the Louvre foundations in the 1980s.

Three years ago, the organization had begun selling them again at his recommendation, but at ten a year, it would take decades to clear the tunnel. *Now it's all at risk, and so am I.*

Last night, he'd slept fitfully, working out scenarios to move the art. He'd devised a plan involving OCBC and the police they'd recruited, but moving the art through the Louvre would be impossible. Too many cameras. The cathedral side was the better option, but he'd never been through that tunnel.

I should tell Jasmin. He flashed on their sunbaked tryst, which triggered a tingling in his belly. He lingered on the pleasurable moment and then focused on the current problem. *She can't do anything from there. No. It's on me.*

He pictured Vivienne in her designer dresses, panicking as her world was about to collapse. She'd pull in the people she trusted and abandon the rest. The trouble was Lionel didn't know which group he was in. The longer he thought about it, recalling the disdainful way she'd spoken to him, the more he sensed he was outside her circle of trust.

Putain!

He'd sat on the fence, supporting both Vivienne and Jasmin, knowing a winner would emerge in time. But Jasmin's words came back to him. She'd be paroled in a year, maybe sooner. If London, Berlin, and New York aligned with her, as he suspected, he'd be a fool to stick with Vivienne.

Easy choice.

He thought ahead like a chess master, anticipating Vivienne's next move. Right now, she and the Louvre museum director were in check —but she was smart.

Lionel ran through scenarios. Vivienne had a gift for drawing attention to herself or, when it suited her needs, putting the spotlight on someone else.

Bitch'll sell me out. Paint me as the fall guy.

63

He shuddered, envisioning her throwing him under the bus at a press conference.

Christian's missing. She'll say we took the money and ran.

Lionel finished his beer and watched pedestrians as his next move resolved itself.

Of course. Same as before.

He'd used Vivienne's computer to sell pieces looted from the Louvre's collections and Christian's inherited paintings. The digital forensics would lead straight to her. The bank account might be troublesome—a dummy corporation—but Lionel's predecessor had set it up before he'd died. Nothing was in Lionel's name, and he'd transferred the money out into a series of numbered accounts.

He also had photos of the paintings in the tunnel. He'd list a large number for sale from her computer, enough to draw attention, and then evacuate the lot through the cathedral. His lips curled.

Yes, the perfect move. Checkmate! And a get-out-of-jail present for Jasmin.

64

10th Arrondissement

A half-hour later, Darwin, Eyrún, and Zac exited the Metro at Goncourt and walked to Rue Vide. Aside from shops on the busy corner at Avenue Parmentier, the street was empty on the mid-morning weekday. The block was residential, with a line of two-story homes wedged among taller multi-unit buildings.

When they reached number nineteen, Darwin knocked and then stepped back between Eyrún and Zac to await an answer.

"Try again," said Eyrún after a long minute.

Darwin did as Zac peered into the windows, straining to see anything through the closed blinds.

"*Bonjour*. Looking for someone?" asked a man who walked up with a small girl wearing a pack and riding a scooter.

"*Bonjour*," said Darwin. "We're looking for Christian Roche. Does he live here?"

The man motioned for them to wait as he unlocked the house next door and sent the girl in. "Show Maman your drawings. I'll be in shortly." He turned back to them and asked, "Who wants to know?"

Darwin explained that he worked for the École du Louvre and

showed the man his employee badge. The man studied it and then asked, "Are you Christian's colleagues? His gaze lingered on Zac, who, despite his friendly smile, cut an imposing figure.

Eyrún stepped in. "My husband is. This is our friend Zac, who's visiting from America. My colleague Aya Raiss at the *Crypte Archéologique* was working with Christian on a project for Notre-Dame. We visited his office on Wednesday but learned no one had seen him for weeks, so we decided to stop by Christian's house on our way to Gare de l'Est." She quickly added, "We're going to the Reims Cathedral today.

"Where is your friend Aya?"

"She broke her ankle. She was going to show us Notre-Dame but can't now. I can call her if you'd like."

The man waved her off. "No, no," he said, looking at the door of number nineteen. "He's not here. I haven't seen him for a month."

"Is that like him?" asked Eyrún.

"I don't know. We only talked a little. I showed him our basement once. He mentioned remodeling after finding an unused space."

"Unused?" asked Darwin.

"He said it was his grandfather's study, full of old war documents. Hadn't been touched for years. We invited him for dinner, but he's away every weekend on an archaeological research project."

Darwin snorted. "I get on digs like that."

"Did he say where?" asked Zac.

The man crossed his arms and looked away.

"We understand," said Eyrún, smiling. "We'll come back another day."

As they turned to go, the man asked, "Is Christian in trouble?"

"Not that we know of," said Eyrún. "Why do you ask?"

The neighbor looked around and said, "I'm sorry for being overly cautious, but a guy claiming to be a friend was here last week. He brought a cop with him, but when I contacted the local station, they said they had no officer by that name."

A door closed behind them, and they looked up. The man's wife approached and asked if anything was wrong. He explained the situation to her.

64

Darwin pursued a hunch. "We think Christian made a discovery and someone is after him."

"Show them," the man said to his wife.

She swiped to a photo on her phone, and they crowded around as she explained, "This one is the cop. The other one—"

"Oh my, God! It's the guy I saw in the Louvre!" said Eyrún.

65

École du Louvre

Lionel closed and relocked Vivienne's office door, keeping his face low to avoid being seen by the security cameras. Some time ago, he'd cloned Vivienne's electronic card key to access the administration wing and enter her office. While Vivianne was people-savvy, she considered technology and security beneath her.

Months ago, Lionel had heard one of the IT guys complain about security gaps, especially the cavalier attitude of most museum administration. He'd also listen to him bemoan the budget cuts and the fact that the IT department only kept twenty-four hours of video.

He shrugged. It made his job easier. As far as Louvre personnel knew, Vivienne had returned after-hours to her office, logged on, and left again forty minutes later. By the time anyone reviewed the video, evidence of a figure in a hoodie would be overwritten.

He pocketed the card key and, once outside the building, stripped off his disposable gloves and dropped them in the nearest bin. He left the USB fob with photos of the paintings in another bin a block away.

Then he checked the auction site from his phone, confirming the paintings were live. While the seller's name was an alias, with a hidden email, any competent digital forensics person would track the IP address to Vivienne's computer.

Let her explain that. He snorted.

66

Louvre

Darwin hit a wall of privacy excuses at the Louvre's human resources office. "Could you at least tell me if he's an employee?" he asked.

The human resources manager, an older man whose desk looked like he used a ruler to arrange its objects, slowly swiped through the photos on Darwin's phone. "You suspect he's an employee because he showed a badge to the police officer guarding the exhibit? I cannot tell what kind of badge it is. Maybe he is also police."

"It's possible," Darwin admitted.

"Why do you want to find him? Shouldn't this be a matter for the police?"

Darwin took in a slow breath and tried to keep his voice friendly. "I asked. They have no record of an officer who looks like this," he said, telling himself it wasn't a lie, that Christian's neighbor had called the local department.

The man handed back the phone. "I cannot verify anything. It would violate our privacy policy. I am sure you can understand, Mr. Lacroix."

66

Darwin sighed heavily to signal his frustration. He left and messaged Eyrún as he walked toward the employee cafeteria.

Nothing from HR. Heading to the restoration lab.

Eyrún: Okay. Aya texted her colleague, the one she stole the card key from, but she didn't get a reply.

Great, thought Darwin, imagining his upcoming conversation with the man. Eyrún had already described him as a cranky recluse. Freshly brewed coffee tugged at his nostrils as he drew level with the cafeteria door. Only three people queued at the cashier, a woman who looked like she'd run the till since the eighties.

He entered, filled a cup, and then queued to pay. When it was his turn, no one had gotten in line behind him.

"*Un euro,*" she said.

Darwin fished into his pocket.

"You can pay with your badge," she said.

"Oh, I didn't know. I'm from the school." He held it over the scanner. It beeped, and he asked, "You must know everyone here. Have you ever seen this man?" He showed her the picture Eyrún had taken.

She studied it for a long moment. Then she looked at Darwin, frowning a little as if debating whether to answer his question. "I have seen him, but I don't know his name."

Darwin thanked her and carried his coffee to the restoration offices, where his luck was no better, as Aya's colleague had gone on holiday. He looked around at workstations where conservators worked on various art and was mustering the courage to ask the person at the closest desk to look at the photo when his phone chimed.

Hélène: Vivienne's been arrested.

Île de la Cité

66

An hour later, Darwin met Hélène at the Préfecture de Police, where she led him to a small office. A monitor showed Vivienne sitting in a gray interview room, poised in a navy blue pantsuit, legs crossed, manicured fingers resting on one knee. Her Channel purse and phone rested atop the table.

"We're waiting for her avocat," said Hélène. "The investigators received an anonymous tip last night that Vivienne had listed looted art on the dark web."

"Anonymous?" asked Darwin, screwing his face up.

"*Oui*. I agree. It's too coincidental. The pieces for sale have been listed for less than a day."

The interview room door opened, and a woman in a gray business suit entered. "*Bonjour*, Vivienne," she said as they greeted each other. Then she turned to the camera on the ceiling. "Turn off the cameras and microphones while I talk with my client."

When the monitor in front of Darwin went black, he turned to Hélène and said, "Tell me how this happened."

"The police got the tip and passed it to the OCBC. I was alerted because of my seconding to the Louvre task force. Our technical unit traced the postings to an IP address at the Louvre, and working with their IT team, we found that the IP address belonged to Vivienne's computer. She—"

Hélène stopped as the monitor switched back on. Two detectives had barely settled in their chairs before Vivienne's avocat went on the offensive. "Has my client been arrested?"

"No. We—"

"Then why is she being held?"

"Ms. De Poitiers has been brought in for questioning about Louvre artwork for sale on an underground website." said the senior detective. He held up a hand as the avocat leaned in. "Hold on, please. At this stage, we are not charging your client."

"Not yet," said the second detective, a surly younger man who slouched in his chair.

The senior glanced at him with a furrowed brow. "Ms. De Poitiers is cooperating and requested that you be present. Three days ago, a tunnel was discovered in an unknown subbasement beneath the

Louvre. Three hundred and twelve paintings were found, each of which appears to have been looted."

"What does that have to do with my client?" asked the avocat.

"I'm getting to that," he said, reaching for a photo in the file and pushing it across the table. "This painting is in the subbasement. It was posted for sale on the website using the computer in Ms. De Poitiers's office. We'd like to know how that happened."

The avocat turned to Vivienne, who said, "I have no idea. I was at home, enjoying a glass of wine. It had been a long day."

"Can anyone verify that?" asked the detective.

"No. But my building has a video camera."

Darwin asked Hélène, "Do they think it's her?"

"No, but we're searching her home and office while she's here."

They looked back at the monitor as Vivienne's avocat asked, "What about the security video in the school's offices? They will confirm my client was not there."

"About that." The inspector leaned on the table, his eyes boring into Vivienne. "The video surveillance at the École du Louvre only covers the last twenty-four hours. The budget for longer storage was cut. Let's see..." He paused and flipped to a paper in the file. "Five months ago."

He slid it to Vivienne. "This is the change request to the video service provider."

The avocat put on glasses and read it as the detective produced more documents. "These are the emails from your client to the IT director requesting the reduction in video retention due to budget cuts."

"And you have proof of causation between this budget change and the paintings listed for sale?" the avocat asked while removing her glasses.

"No. But you have to admit it looks suspicious."

"Not to me. Unless you're suggesting that someone in the IT department who knew about the reduced video retention and the tunnel discovery might be involved?"

"We are considering all possibilities," he said.

A knock on the door caught their attention, and a uniformed officer came in and handed the senior detective a note. The detective read it and then asked Vivienne, "Is there anyone you know who might have done what your lawyer suggested?"

Vivienne whispered into her avocat's ear. The woman nodded and said to the detective, "She may. Can you tell us what's on the note?"

"Ms. De Poitiers's building camera shows her entering eight minutes before her computer was used to access the website."

"Then my client could not have done it."

Vivienne smiled. "The man you want is Lionel Mandeau. I've heard gossip that he goes on very expensive holidays."

67

Île de la Cité

The police got a photo of Lionel from the Louvre HR department within an hour. Eyrún and Zac joined Darwin at the police prefecture after he messaged that they'd had a breakthrough.

"That's him," said Eyrún, pointing to an enlarged photo. She swiped to the picture she'd taken in the Sully Crypt. "He's older now, but that's definitely him."

The detective's phone rang. "*Oui.*" He answered it and listened momentarily before asking, "She is sure?" He listened longer and then disconnected and said, "Ms. Raiss confirms he is one of the men who chased her. We'll put out a warrant for his arrest. Ms. Stefansdottír, we will need you to confirm his identity. Please make yourself available."

Eyrún agreed, and a uniformed officer escorted them outside into a blustery autumn afternoon. "We're finally getting somewhere," she said, zipping up her jacket.

Leaves swirled in the portico as they exited into a cold drizzle driven sideways by a stiff breeze.

"Are we?" Darwin asked. "I've been asking myself why someone would hide paintings in a tunnel. This can't be the work of one guy."

67

"I'm starving," said Zac, suggesting they get lunch at the Saint-Regis. "It's on the way to the flat and the perfect antidote to this lovely Paris weather."

They hurried through Place Louis Lépine, where the vibrant flowers in the open-air market starkly contrasted with the gunmetal gray clouds. Around the corner, trees lining the Notre-Dame forecourt shielded them from the rain, but the naked street alongside the cathedral churned the mist like a wind tunnel.

Darwin wished he'd brought an umbrella until a gust yanked two people's umbrellas inside out and sent another flying over the construction wall.

"Lovely," said Zac. "I suppose Mary Poppins will be along next."

The wind lessened as they crossed Pont Saint-Louis, and a few steps later, they entered the restaurant. They weren't the only people seeking refuge from the strengthening storm, but luckily, a table was open. After hanging their jackets, they squeezed into the snug space.

Eyrún shivered and, when the server arrived, ordered tea. Darwin eyed the mirror-backed bar, thinking momentarily of spiced Averna toddy to ward off the chill, but he decided he needed a clear head and settled for coffee.

As they waited for lunch, Zac picked up Darwin's assertion outside the prefecture. "Why don't you think Lionel is acting alone?"

"The time frame, mainly," said Darwin. "Think about it. Lionel was a baby when the tower foundation was discovered in 1984. My dad told me the discovery was big news in Paris, only overshadowed by the pyramid's construction.

"The archaeologists on the dig would have had access to the tunnels, but there's no documentation in either the Carnavalet Museum or Bibliothèque National."

Their hot drinks arrived, and Eyrún warmed her hands, breathing in the steam before sipping. She sighed and then picked up on Darwin's thread. "Then we're looking for a group that held the paintings in another location and moved them into the tunnel."

"Exactly," said Darwin.

"Hold on," said Zac. "You're suggesting that three hundred looted

67

paintings were hidden for forty years and then moved into this undocumented tunnel in the eighties?"

Lunch arrived, and Darwin attacked his plate, his appetite driven by the ghastly weather and two days of erratic eating. He picked up the conversation after his fifth bite. "That's exactly what I'm suggesting. Jim Wilkerson, the MPAA guy in Seattle, said it was chaos after the war, with thousands of paintings arriving in Paris. Well-known collectors got most of their stolen works back, but the smaller guys were not so fortunate—meaning they had less money to chase repatriation. In many cases, deaths and emigration complicated the ownership trail.

"By the mid-fifties, money for repatriation dried up as the world moved on from the war. And sadly, greedy museum directors kept looted pieces in their collections," he said, cutting another bite of steak.

Eyrún waved her knife for attention as she swallowed a bite. "What are they saving these paintings for?"

"Money," said Zac. "If I follow Darwin, the provenance allows them to claim the works as spoils of war or something like that."

"Close enough," said Darwin. "It's also less likely that any heirs are still alive and know the paintings once belonged to their family."

"So, we've got the why," said Eyrún, "but not the who."

"Right," said Zac. "And given the length of time that's passed since the war, it means there is a well-concealed conspiracy."

"Is Lionel Mandeau our sole link?" asked Eyrún.

"Not necessarily." Darwin drank some water before adding, "Suppose Christian Roche is connected. I don't know how yet, but it can't be a coincidence that Christian learns his grandfather is a member of the Nazi ERR and then, a tunnel is discovered."

"But he didn't find it," Eyrún protested. "We did."

Darwin realized she was right and gazed out the window where rain bucketed down. He pondered the connections when his phone rang, showing Hélène's caller ID. He answered, listened a few seconds, and then blurted out, "*Putain!* When? We're on our way."

He ended the call and then said, "They found Lionel." He pulled three €50 notes from his phone wallet and dropped them on the table as Eyrún and Zac grabbed their coats.

68

Île de la Cité

Hélène led them to a sterile, fluorescent-lit office in the police prefecture. There, a laptop displayed a map of France highlighting train routes. Darwin, winded from the jog, hung his wet jacket on a chair back. Eyrún and Zac did the same.

Hélène gripped the edge of the metal table. "Lionel's phone GPS shows it's on a TGV that left Gare Lyon at 11:42, heading to Barcelona. It should arrive at 18:27."

"How do you know it's him?" asked Zac.

"We caught him on CCTV at the station's ticket machine here." She switched windows on the laptop. "And we have another camera showing him boarding the first-class carriage here."

Darwin shot a glance at Zac. "We need to intercept it."

"I figured you might," said Hélène, taking a small notebook from her suit coat pocket. "I listed flights to Barcelona. If you—"

"No time," Eyrún cut in. "I'll fly us."

Hélène's eyebrows rose.

"She's a pilot," said Darwin.

Eyrún was already on her phone to the private terminal service at Paris-Le Bourget to ready her plane.

"What will you do when you catch him?" asked Hélène. "You're not police."

"But you are," said Darwin.

"I've got another commitment."

"I'll handle it," said Zac. They looked at him, and he added, "Don't ask me to elaborate. You won't like it."

Hélène's brow furrowed, but she let it go.

"The plane can be ready in an hour," said Eyrún. "The weather is shit, but it's clear in the south."

"I can at least arrange a police escort," said Hélène.

Roissy

Reaching the private airfield took a full hour, even with a blue flashing escort. The rain drenched the entire metropolitan area and caused flooding in a section of the RER, which sent all traffic above ground. While Paris-Le Bourget was closer to the city than Charles De Gaulle, it was on the same route.

They arrived to find that Eyrún's Avanti EVO had been towed from its hangar and fully fueled. Its wet fuselage glistened in the airport lights beneath a darkened sky. The police dropped them at the flight center office, and while Eyrún studied reports of the weather system over France, Zac and Darwin calculated the best city to land and intercept the train.

"Let's go," said Eyrún as the downpour let up. She ran across the tarmac and let down the door. Zac and Darwin followed and closed the door as the rain returned.

Darwin brought up the preflight check on his iPad and ran down the list with Eyrún. Zac sat in the cabin and spread a map of southwest France across a table between facing seats. As the first engine spooled up, he said, "Béziers is our best option. The train should be arriving in Nîmes, and the next three stops are too tight."

68

"Got it," said Eyrún and dialed in a course for Béziers. She put on her headset and talked with ground control as the plane rolled toward the runway.

Darwin watched the rain-soaked airfield from the copilot's seat. Two jets, a Dassault Falcon and an Embraer Phenom, were the only other active flights ahead of them. His heart thumped a few beats, his usual response to flying, and he reminded himself that Eyrún was qualified on instruments. She had to be, as the weather in and out of Iceland across the North Atlantic could be challenging.

Minutes later, they taxied onto the runway as the Embraer roared away. Darwin watched it rise, arcing right, and then Eyrún got the all-clear. The Avanti's engines screamed, spinning up to full power. A deep hum vibrated the craft as the scimitar blades churned the air. Rain lashed the windscreen as the wipers cleared the view.

Seconds later, the automated cockpit voice announced, "V1," and Eyrún rotated the craft skyward. The plane shot up and then bucked in the storm as it climbed through the cloud cover. Finally, at eight thousand meters, they broke through the clouds, and both pilot and copilot reached for sunglasses.

Darwin called back to Zac, "We're about forty-five minutes to Béziers."

"That'll give us a half-hour to reach the station. Should be no problem."

Eyrún studied the weather radar over the southwest and called air traffic control. "I'm seeing significant build-up north of Montpellier. Please confirm."

Darwin listened to the controller's voice over the headset: "Commercial traffic reports a massive thunderstorm on an easterly heading. It's currently twenty nautical miles north of Béziers, moving at ten kilometers per hour."

Eyrún muted the microphone. "Zac! We can't get into Béziers. What's the next option?"

"Perpignan. After that, we'd have to go to Barcelona."

Darwin adjusted the navigation to Perpignan while Eyrún talked with air traffic control. As they traveled south, the storm system blanketing Paris broke up, and at eleven thousand meters, the air was smooth. But a quarter-hour later, they saw two towering clouds directly in their path. The menacing, dark gray columns flattened like anvils.

"We need to go around that," she said and requested a route change with air traffic control.

Eyrún banked right on a heading that would take them to Madrid. "This will add time," she said and throttled up to compensate. When their airspeed reached seven hundred kilometers per hour, she grinned. Only once before had she taken the craft near its maximum. The twin eleven-hundred-horsepower Pratt and Whitney engines whined, sending a smooth vibration through the airframe.

"Are you sure?" asked Darwin, reflexively grasping a handhold above his seat.

"No problem. Maximum is 745. We're only ninety percent." She pointed at the screen, showing the power plant statistics.

Twenty-five minutes later, the plane banked left around the city of Toulouse as Darwin watched the broad metropolitan area spread out below. He blinked as sunlight flashed off the Garonne River. They leveled out for a straight shot into Perpignan. The thunderstorms loomed at ten o'clock, menacing Béziers seventy-five kilometers away.

Darwin looked out the right side into clouds swallowing the Pyrenees. Eyrún soon nosed them into a fast descent.

69

Perpignan

Darwin sprang from his seat the moment Eyrún taxied off the runway and lowered the door the moment she stopped at the private terminal. He and Zac sprinted down the steps as the props slowed, and they met the taxi they'd radioed ahead for. He checked his watch as it pulled away. "We've got eighteen minutes if it's on time."

"How long to the station?" Zac asked the driver.

"Fifteen, twenty minutes. It depends on the traffic," he said, coming to a full stop and using his blinker at an empty intersection.

Darwin sucked in through his teeth as the older man looked twice each way and rolled out with far more caution than necessary. Zac pulled out his wallet and handed the man a €50 note. "We are in a hurry."

The driver looked at the money and frowned in the rearview mirror.

Zac smiled. "If you could help us, please. We don't want you to do anything illegal, but we really do have to catch that train." He laid another three notes on the passenger seat.

The car lurched forward. Fourteen minutes later, it pulled into the

Gare TGV Perpignan. Zac paid the actual fare and thanked the driver as Darwin ran ahead to the ticket machine.

As the TGV stopped, Darwin messaged Eyrún:

Train arrived. I'll call when we find him.

Eyrún: I'll be waiting. Good luck.

Zac and Darwin boarded a second-class car and waited for the train to depart before making their way to Lionel's seat. If all went to plan, they would contain him onboard until reaching Barcelona, where Hélène would have Europol detain him. But the train had two more stops, Figueres and Girona.

As the TGV reached full speed, Zac blocked the aisle at the rear of the first-class car while Darwin walked rapidly to its front. Once there, he turned and scanned the passengers as he approached Lionel's seat.

It was empty.

Darwin paused. There was no evidence of food or a water bottle, and there were no belongings or packs on the overhead shelf.

He made eye contact with an older man in the seat directly across from number sixteen. Darwin smiled. "I'm looking for my friend Lionel."

The man shrugged. "No one has been in that seat since Paris."

"Shit," Darwin muttered and walked swiftly toward Zac. "Seat's been empty since Paris."

Zac turned, and they moved through the carriages, assessing each passenger. "Check the occupied toilets," he said to Darwin, who paused at one until a woman and child emerged.

He hurried toward Zac, scanning the faces as he went.

"Nothing?" he asked when they reached the last car.

"No."

The train slowed into the Figueres Vilafant station. "Get to the front car," said Zac. "We'll both step off the train and look for him. But get back on before we go."

Darwin moved as fast as he could, squeezing around passengers as they gathered their belongings to disembark. He was two cars from first class when they stopped. He stepped onto the platform and scanned up and down the train. Three minutes later, he re-boarded and went back to Lionel's seat as the train rolled toward Girona.

His phone rang.

"Anything?" asked Zac.

"No. I'm back at Lionel's seat."

"Be there in a minute."

Darwin pocketed the phone and sat in Lionel's chair. He sighed and closed his eyes. *Where are you?*

The train lurched as it switched back onto the high-speed track. On a whim, Darwin probed the seat-back pocket.

"Putain!"

A phone lay in the bottom. He pulled it out just as his friend arrived.

"That sneaky bastard," said Zac.

They found the conductor between carriages and asked about the passenger in seat sixteen.

"I've seen no one, but we changed crew in Nîmes," he said.

Zac exchanged a glance with Darwin. "He must have planted the phone as a ruse and gotten off before Nîmes."

"Or never left Paris," Darwin added. "But why the ruse?"

They put aside speculation for the moment as Darwin called Eyrún to explain.

"Where are you now?" she asked.

"Five minutes from Girona."

"Get off there. I'll pick you up at the Girona-Costa Brava Airport."

Girona, Spain

A half-hour later, Zac and Darwin stood on the rooftop observation deck of the private air terminal, watching the Avanti EVO descend and touch down a few hundred meters to their left. As Eyrún exited the active runway and taxied back toward them, a Ryan Air 737 took off. The airport served as a low-fare alternative to Barcelona.

Eyrún stopped her plane on the tarmac in front of the terminal. In the late afternoon, the whale tail's shadow stretched long. She met them in the terminal office. "Did you learn anything from Hélène?"

"No," said Darwin. "The phone's GPS belongs to Lionel. The cameras at Gare Lyon show him entering the train, but nothing captures him leaving."

"That was a waste of fuel," she said, looking around the bland office. Air traffic chatter droned from a squawk box on an unoccupied desk.

"What now? Back to Paris?" asked Darwin.

"I'd rather not," she said. "The weather's still bad, and I'm too tired for an instrument landing in the dark. Tomorrow's forecast is clear."

"Okay, we can take the local train to Barcelona. Have a good dinner. There's nothing around here."

Eyrún made a face.

"What?" asked Darwin. "It's only forty-five minutes away."

"I know what she's thinking," Zac said with a grin. "So is Corsica."

Minutes later, they were wheels up for the forty-five-minute hop to Ajaccio.

70

Saint-Germain l'Auxerrois

Lionel exited the passenger side of the moving van and helped set up cones, closing the street for an upper-story move. The morning chill was a bracing wake-up after riding in the heated truck.

They raised the conveyor to the fourth floor of an unoccupied apartment to make the move look authentic. Then Lionel entered the cathedral, where a bribed cop had taken over the watch an hour ago. "Is everything okay?" he asked the man.

"Oui."

"What about the priest?"

"Sleeping."

They erected a white construction tent behind the altar to conceal their activity.

Lionel calculated that he and four others would need five hours to move the paintings. If each one averaged three per trip, they'd need a hundred trips. At ten minutes per trip, each person would make twenty trips. It was doable, but they had no time to waste.

"Allez. Allez." He waved them into the crypt. The first of them

inside set up lights, and in less than twenty minutes, Lionel reached the door to the subbasement tunnel.

He studied its lock mechanism and the broken piece of wood that Eyrún had used to block it shut. He sighed heavily at the unfortunate discovery but supposed it could have happened at any time in the last forty years. Lionel opened it and waved his crew inside.

"Which ones first?" yelled a wiry woman with a lip-ring.

"Doesn't matter. Start here," he said, tossing back the canvas on the nearest paintings. Lionel scooped up three small works under his left arm and grabbed a larger one in his right hand. He looked down the tunnel toward the Louvre. His heart pounded, and he hoped his man on the museum side was in place. Then he turned and followed the others.

Eight minutes later, he stacked his paintings in the first truck and looked at his watch. "Let's go," he said, chasing the others back into l'Auxerrois. "It'll be light in five hours. We need to move."

The sky had turned pale when Lionel emerged from the cathedral on his nineteenth trip. His thighs burned from climbing the steps, and his hips ached from the walking. On the twentieth trip, he met the lip-ringed woman, empty-handed, on her way out. "The museum guards," she said, pushing past him.

The other three filed by in quick succession. Lionel asked the last one. "What happened?"

"Someone dropped paintings near the inside door. We saw a light coming down the stairs."

"Go!" Lionel sent them toward l'Auxerrois and surveyed the dark tunnel. A faint light played on a far wall. He spun and ran.

Once in the cathedral, he found the team taking down the tent. "No time. Leave it." As he hurried them out to the trucks, sunrise was imminent. He jumped into the second truck, and they pulled away, each going a different route.

Lionel lowered his window to listen for sirens and craned his neck, looking for the police. Paris still slept, but he knew better. This place would be teeming with cops soon. Hopefully, what they'd taken was enough.

71

Ajaccio, Corsica

The next day, Eyrún carried her teacup to the flybridge of her powerboat, moored toward the end of one long pier in Ajaccio. The sun bathed the sleepy harbor and all was still except near the ferry terminal, where fishing vessels unloaded their catches. Seagulls wheeled in a frenzy. Their din echoed off the bright stucco buildings.

While she loved Paris, she missed the calmness of Corsica. From her perch in the captain's chair, she stretched her legs across a side seat and gazed up at the aptly named Mount D'Oro, glowing in the morning sun. Shading her eyes with one hand, she located the ridge their mountain house sat on and wondered if they would have time to visit. Then she gazed over the harbor at the ACA, where her employees would begin their workdays in a couple of hours.

From her perch in the captain's chair, she stretched her legs across a side seat and gazed up at the aptly named Mount D'Oro, glowing in the morning sun. Shading her eyes with one hand, she located the ridge their mountain house sat on and wondered if they would have time to visit. Then she gazed over the harbor at the ACA, where her employees would begin their workdays in a couple of hours.

The movement caused the terrycloth robe to slip off her bare legs, and she reached down to adjust it. The day would be warm, but autumn had brought cooler mornings.

Footsteps followed laughter in the galley as the men padded up the flybridge stair. "Morning, Love," said Darwin, sitting on the bench across from her.

Zac sat opposite. "I hope you don't mind that I got into your tea."

"Not at all," she said. "There's lots of it, unless the Mariage brothers go out of business."

They sat in the morning stillness for a few minutes before Zac said, "I've been thinking about Christian Roche. Since we're here, I can use the computer lab at the ACA to do a little hacking."

"Sure," said Eyrún. "I was planning on checking in with everyone."

"Not before breakfast, I hope," said Darwin. "There's nothing on board."

Three hours later in the ACA, Darwin ate an apple he'd bought from a quayside market after breakfast. He studied a map he'd created with ChatGPT, an artificial intelligence tool that had burst into prominence. Minutes ago, he'd asked it to use thousands of discrete GPS locations to create a map of Christian's movements. As expected, most were in the Paris metro area.

He looked over Zac's shoulder who was sifting through Christian's phone records showing all his locations in the last six months. He compared the two as he talked through what they could see. "Christian went to Geneva Freeport on August twelfth and returned to Paris that afternoon. On the twenty-third, he went to Strasbourg. And this is weird. The GPS trail loops through the Vosges Mountains.

"Then, on September tenth, he went to Geneva again, but the time stamps show a ten-hour round trip. Did he drive? Why would he do that?" he asked, looking up.

"Maybe he was moving something larger than he could carry on the train," said Zac.

"That makes sense," said Darwin. "Can we get his credit card transactions? It might help us understand what he was doing."

"Maybe Hélène could help with that one."

Darwin checked his messages. He'd texted her yesterday when they'd found Lionel's phone on the train but had not heard back. He saw she had replied early this morning while his phone was on do-not-disturb.

Hélène: Just saw your message. Was on duty and offline. Sorry to hear about Lionel.

Darwin: No worries. It's not your fault. Can you send us Christian Roche's credit card transaction history?

Hélène: Not without a warrant. I have to operate within the law.

Darwin: Okay. Thanks.

He set the phone down. "She can't do it."

"Thought that might be the case," said Zac. "I put a bounty out for the data. Let's see what turns up."

Darwin stood and paced the conference room. "Remember Christian's neighbor mentioning a basement office and remodel?"

"Yeah."

"I think Christian found something in the basement that led him to the freeport. The timing is right. He's a creature of habits. His movements over the last year are consistent between his flat and the Louvre, with a single trip to Morrocco, probably a holiday.

"Not once did he visit his mother at home. Then, within two months of inheriting the house, he's traveling multiple times to eastern France—"

Zac's phone beeped. "Got it." He transferred it to the laptop on the table.

"That was fast," said Darwin as Zac expanded the compressed file into a folder with dozens of PDFs. "Shit. This will take hours, but..."

71

He opened another window on the laptop and typed a query into a custom AI.

"I'm asking it to link Christian's financial data to his phone records and show his movements since his inheritance."

Zac refined the query. The AI asked some questions to clarify the request before he confirmed it.

"How long will it take?" asked Darwin.

"Less than the time needed for a cup of tea," Zac said, heading toward the break room.

When they returned, the AI had detailed Christian's life more than necessary. Zac tweaked his request to remove the mundane activities and highlight significant movements and cash flow.

"That's better," said Zac. After sending the file to a printer, he spread the pages on the table.

"Nothing unusual after he inherits the house," said Darwin. "He filed a change of address with his bank when he gave up his flat." His finger traveled down the page. "He bought a train ticket to Zurich and, two weeks later, Strasbourg, where he hired a car.

"The next three weekends, he repeats the journey, and the following weekend, he takes an overnight train to Zurich, where he rents a van, visits the Geneva Freeport, and drives back to Paris. Three weeks later, €40,000 is deposited into his checking account. He must have sold something. Can we trace the money?"

"Possibly. I'll check," said Zac, tapping on his keyboard.

Darwin continued studying Christian's expenditures. "This is interesting. Three days after the deposit, he rented a caravan and drove to Struthof. The day after that, he spent €5,300 at Rothau Construction Equipment. Where's that?"

"About twenty kilometers from Struthof," said Zac. "It's the last thing he charged, and his GPS hasn't moved since. Look." He showed Darwin the GPS location on Google Maps.

Darwin stared at a red pin in the mountains west of Strasbourg. "That looks like a farm." He zoomed out.

"Stop," Zac said, touching Darwin's shoulder. "Zoom on that." He pointed to a large barren spot with a chevron pattern in the soil.

The label read: "Former concentration camp with museum."

71

"What the hell!" said Zac, adding, "I thought they were all in Germany."

A high school history lesson tumbled back into Darwin's memory. "We had this one," he said. "It was for French dissidents and spies. Wait—I know the connection. It's…" He broke off, grabbed his phone, and scrolled to a document.

"Here," he held the phone to Zac. "Struthof is on the Junkers workshop list."

"Holy shit. Christian's looking for the Raphael," said Zac. He stared at the Google Maps until he found the date stamp. "This was taken almost two years ago," he said and then sprinted from the room. "We need a live—" But his voice cut off as he rounded the corner to the computer lab.

When Darwin caught up, Zac had the open-source Intelligence database on a monitor and was stringing together a query using the precise GPS coordinates for Christian's Google Maps pin. Several satellite records came back.

"This one." Zac double-clicked on a video from midday yesterday. The image scrolled slowly eastward. A small cluster of buildings at the edge of cultivated fields moved into center view. The concentration camp was six hundred meters south but upslope from the farm.

"Can we get closer?" asked Darwin.

Zac tapped out a command, and the view closed on buildings; the image was blurry. "Hang on," he said, adjusting the zoom.

"There." Darwin pointed to a white object, and Zac paused the screen. "That's a caravan about fifty meters from a farmhouse."

"Looks like. We've no idea if it belongs to Christian." Zac zoomed out and scanned the farm. A narrow track divided two fields, followed the woods opposite the house, and then turned up the hill. Trees shrouded the dirt path until it reached a wide circle. "Christ! That's a bomb crater!" Trees lay on their sides, radiating from a central spot. One side of the bowl lay in deep shadow. He brought up some photos from an internet search to show what he meant.

"And this blast was recent. Look at the coloration. Nothing is growing. Weeds would come up in as little as two weeks. We had to do this for battlefield forensics," he said, swiveling his chair toward Darwin. "Christian found something, all right."

Darwin ran a hand through his hair, imagining the horror.

"What's up, guys?" asked Eyrún.

Darwin jumped like a firecracker had gone off.

"We found Christian," said Zac.

72

Bocagnano, Corsica

An hour later, Darwin, Zac, and Eyrún reached the mountain house. She'd borrowed her executive assistant's car for the twenty-kilometer drive. They'd split up to gather the gear they needed to explore what had happened at the farm near Struthof.

A different satellite revealed an opening framed with large granite blocks uphill from the blast crater. They scanned as close as the resolution allowed and saw what looked like a truck lying on its side, but it was too obscured in the downslope trees to be sure.

Darwin messaged Hélène that they had a last location for Christian and were going to investigate.

Eyrún drifted into the kitchen, which was as clean as the day they'd left for Paris. The initial musty smell had dissipated, replaced by the fresh pine on the breeze through the opened windows. She sighed, missing her home more than she'd anticipated. She loved their freedom to move about, but a nostalgic memory from her youth crept in of the time when she was fifteen and she, her sister, Siggy, and their parents had celebrated Christmas.

72

Darwin came upstairs from the bedroom. "What are you thinking, Love?" he asked.

"Family."

He slipped his arms around her waist and nuzzled her neck, whispering, "You mean one of our own?"

She pushed him back, her heart skipping a few beats. "Are you serious?" Her glacier-blue eyes probed his.

"Dunno. Isn't that what you were thinking?"

"No." She told him about the memory. "But it gets too quiet around here sometimes. Don't you want a family?"

"I—" He stopped as Zac bounded up the steps.

"Sorry, did I interrupt something?" Zac said, looking between them.

Eyrún turned away, and Darwin picked up the bag he'd dropped. "Nothing. Just missing home a little."

They loaded the gear and headed to the airport, where they dropped it off. While Eyrún filed a flight plan for Strasbourg, Darwin returned the car to the ACA.

73

The Farm below Struthof Camp

Eyrún, Zac, and Darwin rented a four-door Nissan pickup at the Strasbourg Airport, and Eyrún drove them west into the Vosges Mountains.

"Exit here," said Darwin, following the live map on his phone. The road undulated through the countryside, slowly rising into the mountains. Leaves had yellowed in the deepening autumn, and the ground was damp from overnight fog. Fortunately, no rain was forecast.

They drove through Barembach, the town nearest the farm. Its homes hugged the pavement where, a century ago, rush hour would have been two carts hauling goods to market. Each was an eclectic mixture of rural Alsatian heritage, and most had modern windows that sealed out drafts.

Darwin watched two elderly people talking across a fence—likely about the nice weather. He smiled. Except for the cars, it was easy to imagine the old village life. He faced forward as they passed the last homes, and the forest closed around them.

A half-kilometer later, the pavement ended, and the tires crunched

73

on gravel. A green sign indicated they'd entered Route Forestière de la Grande Basse.

"It's close," said Zac, following their progression on an app. They rolled past three homes set back from the road. "Look for a turn on the right."

The trees cast deep shadows, and Eyrún leaned forward, trying to see around the dense undergrowth. Zac lowered his window, letting in cold air that carried in the damp decay of autumn.

"This one, right?" Eyrún asked.

"Yep," said Zac.

She slowed the pickup, guiding it over a rut. The route angled sharply and reached another right turn a hundred meters farther. Then it climbed before bending left and leveling out in a small valley where fallow fields spread out to the base of the mountains.

"Over there," said Darwin, pointing to a white caravan parked under an oak.

Eyrún stopped near the camper. The sun lay full on the field, and the temperature had risen. The person who'd chosen this valley to farm must have valued its remoteness and microclimate.

Zac and Eyrún split off to examine the farmhouse while Darwin assessed the caravan. A portable table with two chairs sat a few meters from the white Fiat camper van. He leaned down so the light angled off its surface. A thin layer of dust clung to a filmy residue left behind.

He looked in the van's front window. The driver's seat had been rotated to face a table in the tiny kitchen area. A bed in the far back was rumpled. He opened the unlocked side panel door, waited a moment for the interior to air out, and then stepped inside.

A dirty pot and utensils lay in the sink, and three empty wine bottles lined the counter. He found a rental contract in Christian's name lying on the passenger seat. He left it there and slid onto the forward bench to focus on papers spread across the table.

He switched on the overhead light and was studying a hand-drawn map when the other two returned. "Find anything?" asked Zac. "There's nothing helpful in the house."

"Whoever lives there left it messy or doesn't care," said Eyrún. "The dishes in the sink have been there at least a week."

73

A gunshot roared.

Zac pushed Eyrún inside. "Get down."

She and Darwin lay on the floor as Zac slipped away. Moments later, two more shots reverberated in the valley.

"Sounds like hunters," said Eyrún. "It's too far away."

Zac returned and confirmed her suspicion. "They're within a kilometer of us but not a threat."

The caravan rocked as he stepped aboard, and Eyrún and Darwin dusted themselves off. Zac probed the sleeping area in the rear while Eyrún opened a folio box on the seat. Darwin studied the drawing on the table. "According to this, the Junkers workshop is up the mountain across the field. The Struthof camp is higher up."

"Look at this letter from Karl Meyer to Christian," said Eyrún, laying it on the table. "Start here." She put a finger on a paragraph.

... with the increasing Allied bombing, I supervised the relocation of collections away from target cities.

I thought about the end—life after the war—and how I would survive. Talking about it posed a danger, yet I found three colleagues. One of us knew of an abandoned bunker near the Natzweiler-Struthof concentration camp.

Our plan was to recover and sell the art after the war, but a fluke Allied bombing obliterated the surrounding landscape. The explosions caused a landslide and rendered the hills unrecognizable. I never heard from my colleagues again and suspect they were in the tunnel.

"That's a nasty way to go," said Zac as they read on.

I visited the Struthof camp many times to locate the tunnel, but the landscape had undergone too much alteration. In those days, GPS was unavailable, and my colleague's compass directions lacked precision. In addition, I could find no records of the bunker.

The maps in the basement document my past searches. My colleague

73

said the bunker went deep into the hillside, so the artwork must be safe. In total, we transferred the contents of three box cars from southern Bavaria.

Darwin whistled. "That's got to be worth a lot."

Eyrún flipped to a page containing a list of the box cars' contents. Some artists were familiar, but her finger stopped at:

Raphael — Portrait of a Young Man

"Do you think it's really here?" she asked.

Darwin's heart fluttered. He hadn't felt this much anticipation since entering Alexander the Great's tomb in the Siwa Oasis.

Eyrún peered out the caravan window at the house. "Where are they?"

Zac surveyed the mountain from the door. "We need to go up there."

"Agreed," said Darwin, folding the map. "There's nothing here."

74

Ravine above The Farm

After crossing the field, Eyrún stopped to examine piles of soil along its far edge. She sifted a handful while saying, "These look recent and not the same as the fields. Didn't you say Christian's credit card showed an equipment rental?"

"Yes," said Darwin.

"Then they've been moving dirt," she said, looking at ruts in the track.

They continued up the mountain, where weeds growing in the wheel ruts had been crushed. A few hundred meters farther, the soil was chewed up in what appeared to be a turnaround spot.

Darwin jerked at the sound of more gunshots.

"They're a long way off," said Zac.

The logical half of Darwin's brain knew this, but the blasts in the otherwise eerie silence made him uneasy.

Ahead, Zac rounded a bend and froze. A dumper lay on its side against the downslope trees. Jagged glass framed its windows, and its front was smashed in.

"What happened?" Darwin asked, dreading the answer and mentally resisting the satellite view of blown-down trees.

"IED or similar. Only a massive, high-explosive device could move a truck like that," said Zac, slowly scanning the area.

Eyrún picked up a chunk of pink granite. "This was broken recently," she said, surveying their surroundings. Similar-sized bits lay around them and the trees leaned unnaturally.

Zac motioned for them to stay behind him as he walked up the track.

"Wait," said Darwin.

Zac turned around.

"I don't want to find any body parts."

"Oh, God. He's right," said Eyrún.

"There won't be any," said Zac. "I've seen this kind of devastation. Ground zero is probably fifty meters ahead. The terapascal shock wave would have vaporized anything in the immediate blast radius.

"Are you sure?" asked Darwin, looking to Eyrún for moral support.

"Probably," she said. "That's the same force as a meteor strike."

Darwin shuddered, and Zac resumed walking. In twenty meters, they entered the circle of flattened trees and, in another ten, found the cab section of a backhoe. Its digging arm was missing, and only one rear wheel remained attached, though its rubber tire was shredded.

"Don't move," said Zac.

Darwin rooted himself like a tree, feeling suddenly vulnerable in the wide-open space. He turned toward the mountain, shuffling his feet in the same spot. Chunks of pink granite lay scattered around the crater. To the crater's left, a dark opening yawned, framed by massive blocks shifted in odd directions.

"Does that look like a workshop?" asked Darwin.

"More like a mine," she said.

Zac returned. "There was someone in the backhoe. And judging by the absence of recent human activity at the farm, I'll guess that both its owner and Christian were here."

"But why? I mean, booby trap a mine?" asked Eyrún.

"I think this is the obliterated landscape mentioned by Christian's grandfather," said Zac, moving cautiously to the crater's edge. He knelt, swept up a handful of soil, and let it fall between his fingers. He looked from the explosion point to the dark opening and back.

Eyrún studied the bare soil above the crater. Its edge at the forest above slumped like something had taken a bite from the mountain. She backed up to get a better view. "Zac, what do you make of that scarp?" she said, pointing to a spot about fifty meters upslope. "The trees are much larger than the ones around the bomb crater."

Zac looked at the trees and then scanned the hillside. "Huh, I think you're right," he said and slid into the pit's bottom.

"Right about what?" asked Darwin, reflexively stepping back.

Zac ignored him and began digging. A minute later, he shifted, dug around a spot, and then pulled up a twisted black shape that looked like a boot's sole. He shook off the dirt and sniffed it before climbing out of the crater.

"This needs more analysis, but it's a bomb fragment." He rotated the thick metal. One side was drab green. The other was charred black and had an acrid odor. "Judging from the paint and rust, I'd guess it's World War Two ordnance. That confirms the letter."

"Why didn't it explode?" asked Eyrún.

"Ten percent of all bombs dropped don't explode on impact." Zac thought for a moment and then added, "We need LiDAR to confirm it, but I think that scarp face was caused by a load of bombs. The hill buried the workshop, which is why Karl never found it. But I'll wager one was a dud and Christian and the farmer got seriously unlucky."

They stood in silence. Eyrún's head drooped, and Darwin put an arm around her, guessing that she might be experiencing the memory of a long-ago geological explosion that had killed her father.

"I'm okay," she whispered.

He squeezed her shoulder and let his arm drift down. Then he looked at the pink granite and wondered if the Allies were aiming for the workshop. He doubted it, as it would have been well concealed, and he'd read that bombers' accuracy had been notoriously poor. Whatever the case, there was only one way to find out. He moved toward the opening.

74

“Darwin! Stop!” said Zac.
He froze.
“There could be more.”
A chill flowed through him.

75

Junkers Workshop

They put on headlamps from their packs, and Zac led the way toward a large granite lintel lying diagonally across the opening. He stepped carefully and instructed Darwin and Eyrún to walk in his tracks. The blast had pushed in the door's left side support, partially crushing the heavy wooden door. Zac peered around it.

"What do you see?" asked Darwin.

"Mostly nothing," said Zac. "But I'm looking for..." He bent down and then backed out of the opening. "There's a tripwire just inside the door. I need to figure out where it goes. Try and defuse it."

"Zac," said Eyrún, "don't risk yourself. It's not that important. We can turn this over to the authorities."

"Let me look at it first. I've seen dozens of these things and trained on more." He removed pliers, wire cutters, and duct tape from his pack and went back inside. A few minutes later, he called them in. "It's safe."

Zac shined his light on the ankle-height wire as Darwin stepped through the opening. Then he guided Eyrún in.

"What about the bomb?" she asked.

75

"It's tucked into the wall behind these support beams."

Eyrún stared at the location where the wire disappeared into the wall. Zac said, "It's probably inert after eighty years, but it's best not to disturb it. Let's find out if anything is here. But stay right behind me."

The air got cooler as they went deeper. Darwin's ears whooshed from his nervous heart, but he calmed himself as the immediate sense of danger diminished. The forward part of the structure was office-like, with metal desks and chairs. File cabinets lined one wall, and two large chalkboards still had grids written with orders.

Darwin couldn't read much of it, but he understood "*Moteren*," numbers, and dates. He snorted. Digital tech would decay or be usable because of a format change, but a slate wall with chalk would probably last as long as the Egyptian tomb paintings.

They moved through a massive wooden door in a wall built from pink granite blocks. "Looks like a blast door," said Zac. "Holy crap. This is a hobbyist's dream. We need to tell Otto, the guy at the Junkers museum, about this place."

Aircraft engines in various stages of repair lay on workbenches, covered in dust. It looked like the workers had taken a lunch break. Unfortunately, their fascination diminished at the sight of a Nazi flag hanging vertically on one wall next to a large photo of the Führer.

They crossed another opening into a space that resembled a storeroom. Wall-sized cabinets contained engine parts and tools. Along the back wall, Eyrún found a large canvas draped over something tall. "Give me a hand," she said to Darwin. They lifted the cloth, revealing a bronze statue in the Greek style and two rows of paintings—one still in a pine crate.

A quick inventory showed fine works, but none was the Raphael. She lifted the crate and carried it to a workbench in the other room. "What do you think?" she asked.

"It's about the right size," said Darwin.

Zac found a hammer and nail puller and handed them to Eyrún. She levered out the nails, each protesting its removal, screeching like a tortured soul. When she'd removed them all, she gave the tools back to Zac, who put them on a nearby bench.

She placed her hands on the box and looked at Darwin and Zac.

"Go for it, sister," said Zac.

She lifted the lid and peered inside.

Zac's and Darwin's lights shone on the upper-right corner of a painting. Sky blue. A landscape. She sighed, her shoulders slumping. This was no portrait. Her brows knit, and she hesitated, lamenting the wasted time and lives lost.

"Come on. Don't be sneaky," said Zac.

"It's not what we thought," she said, lifting the lid and setting it down on a workbench behind her.

"Mon Dieu. C'est manifique," said Darwin, reverting to his native tongue.

"What?" Eyrún spun around and met the eyes of Raphael's young man. The artist had captured him sitting beside a window containing the landscape she'd mistaken for the entire subject. He faced the painter but was focused on someone else. The young man, perhaps in his twenties, betrayed no emotion.

His face was at once average and angelic. It was a perfect oval, with a high forehead spreading into wide, smooth cheekbones before curving inward to a narrow yet well-formed chin. Lush, dark brown hair flowed across his shoulders onto a generously cut white tunic and an ermine coat draping over his left shoulder. The brush strokes had been done so deftly that the image appeared real.

The young man's appearance conveyed a well-to-do upbringing. He possessed poise, almost indifference. Large eyebrows flowed into a long, straight nose that reminded her of a Modigliani painting.

Zac lightly ran a finger over the canvas. "I've always wanted to do that." He laughed. "My grandparents took me to the Legion of Honor in San Francisco. Everyone just stared at the paintings. I needed to touch them. Almost did, but my grandma snatched me at the last second. She told me no one was allowed."

He looked at Eyrún and Darwin. "Go ahead. Once this is returned, we'll never get the chance."

Each of them did so. Eyrún let her finger glide over the ermine coat, sensing the tiny ridges in the paint. Raphael's mastery of technique and emotion was so complete that she felt time slow.

Her hand drifted back to her side as she settled on the young man's eyes. They were so lifelike, so intently focused that she reflexively looked behind her. Of course, there was nothing but the workshop.

She returned to the painting. The same feeling grew a moment later as she observed the young man's attention was wholly elsewhere. *His lover*, she thought. His object of desire must have been standing across the studio. His gaze held her tenderly, caressing her, imagining the two intertwined. Eyrún touched the canvas again, mesmerized by the fact that a painting could convey such a deep longing. A similar famous portrait floated into her memory. *Yes,* she thought, *if the Mona Lisa had a twin—*

"Thanks. You saved me a lot of work," a voice said behind her.

Eyrún snatched her hand back and turned. All three of their headlamps converged on Lionel, pointing a gun at them.

76

Junkers Workshop

Zac crossed to the office and faced off with Lionel as Eyrún grabbed the painting and ran into the storeroom. Darwin froze, caught between protecting his wife and helping his friend. But they were trapped.

"What do you want?" he asked.

"The painting, of course," said Lionel. He called out, "Eyrún, I doubt there's an escape. Bring it to me."

"What are you going to do if we don't? Kill us?" asked Darwin, shifting to the opposite side of the room. He'd noticed Zac's subtle hand motion while Lionel's attention was on the storeroom.

"I'd rather not," said Lionel. "Messy business."

Zac stepped toward him.

"Stop!" Lionel leveled the gun at Zac's chest and said to Darwin without moving his eyes, "Your friend here has experience. If you try anything, he goes first."

Lionel settled into the doorway, where he had the advantage of open space behind him and could watch both Darwin and Zac from the widest angle.

But then he revealed his ace.

"See this wire?" Between his thumb and forefinger, Lionel held a thin line running down.

Darwin shined his light on the black line, which stopped at the horizontal booby-trap wire across the floor. Lionel pulled the line taught… Darwin's heart jumped. "Don't."

Zac stepped backward and stood by a desk, its metal inbox full of work orders.

"Good," said Lionel. "We understand each other." He looked through the office into the workshop. Dim light framed its door. "Eyrún, bring me the painting."

"I'll go get her," said Zac.

"No! Do you think I'm stupid enough to let a trained killer walk into a workshop full of potential weapons? No. She'll come out. Won't you, Eyrún?"

They waited in the silent office, lit only by the circles cast by Darwin's and Zac's headlamps. Darwin thought they could rush him if he and Zac blinded Lionel with their lights. But he quickly dismissed the idea, realizing the lights were perfect targets, and decided dialogue was the best distraction.

"Why did you wait until now to look for the painting?" he asked.

"You saw for yourself outside. Christian was my first stroke of luck, but he's dead. We've been looking for that Raphael for years."

"We? Who's we?" asked Darwin, rubbing the back of his neck.

"Vivienne, for one," Lionel said. He laughed. "Don't look so surprised, Darwin. She's our public face. We provide her alibis so she can protect us. And she, in turn, deflects the authorities."

"So, why rat her out?"

"She wanted the Raphael for herself. She thinks the money will restore her family's former glory. Vichy scum." He spat, wiped his mouth, and then continued: "She planned to sell us out. Take the money and be a national hero by exposing us. You were wise to distrust her, Darwin."

Lionel paused and peered into the darkness at the workshop's rear as if trying to figure out what Eyrún was up to.

Darwin followed his gaze.

Eyrún whispered, "Keep stalling him."

76

"Why?"

"Just do it."

Darwin refocused on Lionel. "What was your second stroke of luck?"

"What?

"You said Christian was your first? What was your second?"

Lionel snorted and shook his head. "It was you, Darwin. Literally, you and your damned curiosity. I thought Christian had found the Raphael and disappeared. The little shit.

"He said he had no money and asked me to sell the Avercamp paintings his grandfather stashed in the Geneva Freeport. When Vivienne told me you purchased them, I thought, how tragic. You bought back the very Nazi booty stolen from your family. It's almost Shakespearean."

Darwin's fists clenched, and blood pounded in his ears. He scanned the nearest desk for a weapon while Lionel's voice droned in the background.

"I am truly sorry to hear they belonged to your family," said Lionel. "What the Nazis did was horrific. But what our own people, Vivienne and her ilk, did to us is unforgivable."

Darwin breathed noisily, trying to calm himself, telling himself not to react to Lionel's provocation. He glanced toward the storeroom, wondering what Eyrún was doing.

Then, with renewed focus, he turned back. "Your parents weren't even alive at the war's end. Who are the 'we' you keep mentioning?"

"I could tell you, but then I'd have to kill you." Lionel laughed, shaking his head. "I've always wanted to say that."

"Asshole," Zac muttered.

"I won't give you the pleasure of telling you who we are. But thank you for being so damn curious. I doubt I could have found Christian's trail to the *Portrait of a Young Man.*" Lionel paused before loudly asking, "Is it as beautiful as they say, Eyrún? My patience is running out. Bring me the painting, and I'll leave you in peace."

Darwin turned to a noise behind him. Eyrún stood in the doorway to the workshop, holding up the portrait

"It is," said Lionel, mesmerized. His gun hand lowered.

Zac seized the moment, throwing a stapler as he charged.

Lionel ducked and fired.

The stapler smacked the wall.

Zac hit the floor.

Eyrún shrieked. "Zac. Oh, God, Zac." She dropped the painting and ran to her friend, who lay face down, half under a desk.

"Stay!" Lionel pointed the gun at Darwin.

"Zac?" Eyrún shook him. "Zac?" Her hand came away bloody. She screamed at Lionel, "What have you done?" while trying to revive Zac.

"Eyrún? How is he?" asked Darwin, his face pale. He grasped the desk for support.

"Zac," Eyrún wailed. Then, after a long moment, she ran to the portrait. "You bastard. It's just a fucking painting."

She scanned the desk, dashed into the workshop, and returned with a screwdriver. Then she tilted up the frame, holding it with one hand as she raised her other arm to strike the canvas.

"Eyrún! Don't!" yelled Darwin.

She paused.

"He's right, Eyrún," said Lionel. "You're holding a masterwork. I saw you looking at it. The way you smiled. It's—

"Just a painting." She raised the screwdriver.

Lionel blasted a light. Glass showered on Darwin's head.

Bits of it hit Eyrún. She jumped, reflexively dropping the screwdriver.

"Eyrún!" Lionel roared. "Bring me the goddamn painting!"

She froze like a deer in headlights.

"Now! Or I'll shoot your husband."

Darwin's head sagged. "Give it to him. Like he said, it's just…" He choked up, thinking about his best friend lying on the floor.

Eyrún carried the portrait to Lionel.

"Put it there," he said, pointing. "Against the wall. Good. Now, step back. That's far enough," he added when she'd moved two paces.

Lionel knelt to look at the painting, but in a swift movement, he produced a cutter and snipped the tripwire. He stood, holding a longer piece he'd rigged earlier.

"Eyrún, take this," he said, snatching the painting's frame and sliding into the exit.

She hesitated.

"Eyrún, no," Darwin gasped.

"Take it," said Lionel. "If I let go, you die."

She took the end.

"Careful. Don't pull it," he said, slipping out the door.

Eyrún stood like a statue while listening to Lionel's footsteps churning fast. Then nothing.

Darwin ran to Eyrún the instant Lionel had disappeared.

"What do we do?" she asked.

"I don't know. I'll see where the wire goes. Maybe I can—"

Zac grunted.

They turned as their friend tried to push himself up. Darwin ran over. "You're alive. Let me help you," he said, getting Zac in a sitting position. "We thought you were dead."

"Fortunately not," said Zac, leaning against a desk. "But Christ, my head hurts."

Darwin's face screwed up. "But—"

"It's a flesh wound. I hit the desk on the way down." Zac put a hand to his side and then looked at his bloody palm. "Another sexy scar for your sister to admire."

"Not funny, Zac!" Eyrún snapped, frozen in place holding the wire.

"No," he grunted as Darwin helped him stand. "No, it's not. Where's Lionel?"

They told Zac what he'd missed, including Eyrún holding the tripwire.

"Damn," he said, wincing as he moved toward her. Zac followed the line to where it disappeared into the wall. Then, with great care, he pulled back a panel.

77

The Farm

Lionel waited at the farmhouse. The Raphael lay covered by a blanket in the car's back seat.

Fifteen minutes had passed since he'd handed Eyrún the wire, and he began to worry they'd escaped.

He found a knife in the caravan and slashed its tires. Then he did the same to their rented Nissan. As he walked to the house to disable the farmer's pickup, an explosion from the workshop echoed across the valley.

Lionel tossed aside the knife. While walking back to his rented car, he smiled as he sent a message:

> Got painting. Problem solved by a booby trap.
> Contact the buyer.

78

Junkers Workshop

Zac could see the wire Eyrún held connected to a dead man's switch. "How long can you hold it?" he asked her.

"A while, but I'll eventually fall asleep. Can't we tie it off?

"We can. Give me a moment. I have an idea," he said, moving into the workshop. He emerged in under a minute with a spool of wire and fastened it to the end Eyrún held. "You two, get out of here. Go at least fifty meters."

"What about you?" Darwin protested.

"I'll be fine. I've done this before."

After Darwin and Eyrún had left, Zac spooled out the wire as he backed out of the exit. When he reached the end of the spool, he turned and motioned for them to lie down. He did the same and then let go.

A muffled boom splintered the broken door, tumbling pieces toward them. Fortunately, the blast energy was contained by the granite workshop wall.

Eyrún got to Zac first as he pushed up on his knees. She studied his torn, bloody shirt. He protested but allowed her to assess the injury.

"It's not deep, but it's bleeding a lot," she said, wadding up part of his shirt and compressing the gash. "You were lucky. Let me see your head."

Zac grunted as she felt the goose egg on his left temple. "Needs ice. Might be some in the farmhouse. Can you walk?"

The Farm

It took the better part of an hour to reach the farmhouse. Zac walked with his arms draped over Eyrún and Darwin for support. Fortunately, the house was unlocked, and Eyrún got ice for Zac's head and doctored the wound while Darwin looked for signs of Lionel. He'd not expected to find any and explained the slashed tires as he wandered into the kitchen.

Eyrún stood over Zac, ensuring he finished a glass of water. "I didn't lose that much blood," he protested.

"It's long gone," said Darwin, referring to the painting.

"Not exactly," said Eyrún.

They looked at her.

"I had an extra one of those GPS trackers in my pack. At first, I couldn't find it. Then I couldn't get it wedged between the canvas and frame. I was so afraid of tearing it. Then I had to register it on my phone."

Darwin didn't connect the dots until she opened the tracking app to show them. The weak cellular connection in the valley took a full minute to establish a handshake with the GPS satellite and for it to find the tracker. Then a dot appeared on the map.

Eyrún zoomed in. "There. It's on Route Fifty-Nine toward Nancy. He's probably heading for Paris."

Darwin stared at the dot and then stood and walked around the kitchen. "Something's not right," he said, running a hand through his hair. He stopped near the sink and faced them. "How did he find us here?"

At Eyrún's and Zac's blank stares, Darwin continued: "We didn't tell anyone but Hélène where we were going."

Eyrún's eyes went wide. "Shit. She wouldn't."

"Nothing else explains it," said Darwin, shaking his head.

"But how are she and Lionel connected?"

"Dunno," said Darwin. "He talked about an organization that goes back to World War Two. If there is such a group, it's got deep roots. Covering up the subbasement tunnel during the Louvre excavation means lots of people were hushed up."

"Or were involved," said Zac, wincing as he stood. "Turn off your phones," he said. When Darwin and Eyrún hesitated, he shouted, "Now!"

As they did, he pulled open the kitchen drawers until he found aluminum foil. He stretched out a long section and laid his phone on it. Then he turned, his hand out. Darwin and Eyrún gave him their phones and watched as Zac wrapped them in ten layers of foil, explaining as he went, "It's a Faraday cage. It will prevent anyone from tracking us."

He put the shiny block of phones on the kitchen table. "Hélène has the means and authority to track us. We don't know her connection to Lionel, but if they think we're dead, we need to appear dead. It's our only advantage."

Île Saint-Louis

At half one in the morning, they parked on the quayside in front of their flat. Hours earlier, they'd found an ancient Renault in the barn covered with a decade's worth of dust. After filling its tires and charging its battery enough to start, Eyrún assessed its running condition.

They found the farmer's wallet and used it for petrol in Nancy. Zac put on a trucker's hat he'd taken from the farmhouse and kept his face down while fueling. Darwin and Eyrún hid in the back seat. In a world of global surveillance, they had to assume cameras were everywhere.

Eyrún swapped with Zac before they returned to the highway, and Darwin kept him from drifting to sleep. Zac's pupils had dilated somewhat, and Eyrún was concerned about a concussion. But when they reached the flat, his eyes appeared normal. She inspected the bandages again before they headed to their bedrooms.

"What about the plane?" asked Darwin as he undressed.

"We'll get it later," said Eyrún, sliding into bed.

79

3rd Arrondissement

Mid-morning the next day, Eyrún knocked on Aya's hospital room doorframe.

"Eyrún! *Ca va?*" said Aya, wriggling upright as best she could, her leg still in traction.

"*Bien*, Aya. How are you?" They kissed cheeks and hugged.

"Miserable," said Aya. "My hair's a mess. I haven't had a proper bath. I can't move."

"I'm sorry. I brought something," said Eyrún, handing Aya a pale blue paper sack.

Aya's eyes widened as she read its label: "PDDI." She took it and peered inside the thin wrapping. "*Mon, Dieu,* Eyrún. You are my angel." She breathed in the aroma and then sighed.

The thin brown paper crunched as Aya opened it and bit into the sticky chocolate pistachio escargot from *Du Pain et des Idées* in the tenth arrondissement. Aya had taken Eyrún three years ago as they'd gotten to know each other. She compared the boulangerie to the artisans restoring Notre-Dame, each crafting wonder in a world that valued speed above all else. A few bites in, she asked, "Any leads on the paintings?"

Eyrún straightened in surprise.

"The subbasement. Didn't you hear? Two nights ago, someone took them all. I found out about it last night when the OCBC interviewed me."

Eyrún told her about chasing Lionel to Barcelona and then going to Struthof. Aya put a hand to her mouth as Eyrún explained how they'd survived the booby trap. "You can't tell anyone you've seen me," she said.

"No, no. Your secret is safe. You're sure it's Hélène?"

"It's got to be her. There's no way Lionel could have followed us to Corsica and then Strasbourg," said Eyrún.

A nurse walked in on her rounds to check Aya's vitals. Eyrún moved to the window to avoid being seen. She pressed down a feeling of being overly cautious, reminding herself that Lionel had tried to kill them. But it all made sense now.

"She's gone," said Aya.

Eyrún moved back to the bed, and Aya asked, "How did you pull it off? Geotagging all the paintings?"

"Zac got the devices from a military source. Darwin convinced the Louvre director we needed to inventory the paintings. One person held a painting while another snapped a photo. We stuck geo-trackers on during the process."

"Did it work?" asked Aya.

"I don't know. We couldn't get a signal while they were in the subbasement, and since then, we've turned off our phones. Can you look them up from yours?"

Aya downloaded the geo-tracker app and entered the data from a note Eyrún handed her. A map of Europe showed three dense clusters of red dots. "They're in Berlin…" she said, pausing while panning to the other locations. "Also Seville and Rome."

Eyrún looked and then said, "Can you snap photos of these locations and send them to me? I'll text you from a new number soon. Zac and Darwin are getting us phones."

"Sure. I'm happy to have something to do. What about the

Raphael?" asked Aya, zooming around. "You said it was going to Paris?"

"Yes."

"It's not there."

"What?"

"It's here." Aya held out her phone. "In Amboise."

Eyrún took the phone and zoomed in on a GPS pin on a house two hundred kilometers to the south. What's it doing there?"

80

Amboise

Darwin and Zac had just set up their new pay-as-you-go phones at the flat when Eyrún returned from visiting Aya.

"Someone took the paintings from the Louvre subbasement. They're showing up in Seville, Berlin, and Rome. *The Portrait of a Young Man* is in Amboise."

"What?" Darwin sat up.

Zac brought up the geotag map on his new phone. "How long has it been there?"

"No idea," she said.

They looked at each other and, without speaking, knew they needed to get there. The next thirty minutes were a mad scramble. Zac got his pistol, which he kept in a safe in their flat. "Coulda used this yesterday," he said, putting it in his pack.

Darwin pocketed cash from the safe, and they walked to the garage where Eyrún kept her Porsche Taycan. Twenty minutes later, they were heading south on Quai de Bercy. The heavy traffic on the Peripherique thinned as they turned toward Amboise.

"Something isn't right with the paintings," said Darwin. "The count is off."

"How so?" asked Zac.

"Try it yourself. Zoom in to Seville and count the pins. Then do it for Berlin and Rome."

Eyrún threaded the Porsche through slower-moving cars on the busy highway but at a sensible speed to avoid drawing attention from the police.

"I got 233," said Zac.

"Close enough. I got 236. Where are the other seventy-seven?"

"Maybe the tags fell off, or someone peeled them off."

"Or they're in another location," said Darwin, looking at their estimated arrival on the Taycan's display. He settled back and watched the vegetation blur past.

They crossed the Loire River to Amboise in a little over two hours. The late afternoon sun spotlighted the royal chateau on the bluff overlooking the valley. They followed the road downstream from the castle before turning into town to approach Rue Cardinal Georges d'Amboise from a less obvious direction.

"This looks good," said Eyrún, pulling into a car park that belonged to a building undergoing renovation. They were on a hill at the same level as the distant chateau. The street sloped downward into town past the house at number eighteen.

They decided Eyrún would be the best one to approach the house. Zac and Darwin walked with her partway and waited at a bus stop just out of view.

Cool air gathered around Eyrún as the houses grew denser. An upstairs dormer window faced her direction, so she kept her head down as she crossed the street. She continued along a fence that hid her approach. Then she slowed. The side facing Rue Cardinal Georges d'Amboise had no windows, and veins of dead ivy covered its upper level.

The house was the first one on a cul-de-sac. The one on the opposite corner had closed-up windows, its occupant clearly away. Across the street, a high wall meant few people had eyes on this location. She looked at her phone as a car approached, but it continued up the hill.

Darwin: anything?

Eyrún: At corner. All quiet. Turning up the cul-de-sac now.

Her heart beat faster as she crossed the street and then walked briskly into the cul-de-sac. Without turning her head, she focused her attention on the peripheral view of the house. Two sets of windows on the upper and lower floors, a red door, and another window pair looked onto the lane. Well-tended flower planters hung from each of the windows. Someone lived here or cared for the place.

Four houses later, she reached the end and doubled back. The corner house appeared empty, but she couldn't tell. She thought of ringing its bell but decided not to in case Lionel was there. She jumped as the door on the house next door banged shut. An older woman walked out with a trash bag.

"*Bonjour*," said Eyrún.

"*Bonjour*."

"Excuse me. I'm looking for a friend who said she was staying at an Airbnb, but this doesn't seem right. Have you seen a petite blonde woman and a man?"

"It's not an Airbnb, and I've seen no blonde woman. But the owner is a man."

"That might be her boyfriend, Lionel. When did you last see him?"

The woman's eyebrows knit as she studied Eyrún as if deciding what to share. Then she shrugged. "He arrived late last night. I was up with my grandson and saw his car."

"Thank you," said Eyrún. "I'll leave him a note and wait in town."

The woman returned to her house as Eyrún tapped out a message.

It's Lionel's. Neighbor confirmed, but she hasn't seen him. I'll look in the windows.

80

She walked to the front and peered in the first window. A cushy leopard-print sofa faced a fireplace in a small sitting room. Her gaze moved to a wide kitchen and living space where an easel stood on its far side. A throw that looked identical to another on a nearby sofa had been tossed over it. She gasped and took a photo. As she pocketed her phone, a car turned in. Through the house window reflection, she saw Lionel's face in the driver's seat. While his car rounded the building to park, Eyrún sprinted around its other corner.

"I think he saw me," she said, not breaking stride when she reached Zac and Darwin. They fell behind her. A minute later, they arrived at her car.

She panted while explaining what she'd found and showed them the photo.

"Did he see which way you went?" asked Zac.

"No, but let's go."

They piled into the Taycan, and Eyrún U-turned, heading out the way they'd come in. Five minutes later, they left the car in a public car park and walked into the town center, where they found a small hotel on Rue Nationale. Their room overlooked the busy tourist street. Eyrún turned from looking out the window. "Any—" She stopped. "Zac, you're bleeding."

He looked down at a large wet patch on his shirt. "Shit. The running." He got bandages from his pack and went into the bathroom to clean up.

"Need any help?" asked Eyrún.

"No, I got it."

81

Chateau d'Amboise

A few minutes later, Darwin and Eyrún went downstairs to a cafe they could see from their room. Zac said he'd stay inside to rest the wound and his head. As they waited for coffee and tea, Darwin walked up the block to the Bigot chocolate shop to satisfy a craving.

When their drinks arrived, Eyrún glanced at her watch and looked up the alley as her phone chimed. The painting was moving. She zoomed into the GPS dot, studying it momentarily to determine its direction. Her phone vibrated with an incoming message.

Darwin: Hélène is here. I'm following her along the street in front of the chateau.

Eyrún brought up the painting's dot and compared Darwin's phone ID to the GPS tracker. "Shit," she muttered, watching the dots converge. She messaged Darwin:

It's moving in your direction. Where are you?

She left €20 on the table, hoping it was enough, and then grabbed her coat and sprinted toward the dot's path. She zigzagged onto Rue Mirabeau, where she slowed and hid behind a large hedge. Her phone buzzed.

Darwin: She's with two well-dressed men. Can't be sure. One has a large satchel.

Eyrún: I'm two streets over from you on Rue de la Tour. Can you tell where they're going?

She slowed her breathing and waited. *There!* Her heart quickened as Lionel passed, carrying the wrapped painting under one arm. She slipped behind him as he headed toward the chateau.

Darwin: They crossed the street and are waiting by the stairs to the chateau

Eyrún used a line of parked cars for cover as she paralleled Lionel on the opposite sidewalk. The street ended at a massive round tower made from the same Lutetian limestone as the palaces in Paris. Its tall defensive windows faced all directions. Lionel stopped at its base.

Eyrún: Where are you? I'm at the pink cafe across from the tower. Lionel's looking around.

Darwin: To your left, below the chapel atop the wall

Eyrún: He's moving your way

Lionel continued along the wide walk beneath the four-story wall until he reached Hélène. They kissed cheeks, and then he shook hands with the men.

Eyrún kept to the Rue de la Tour side of the street when a hand seized 's arm.

She yelped.

Lionel turned.

81

Darwin shielded her face. "It's me," he said, pulling Eyrún into a kiss. Two lovers in a romantic spot.

"What are they doing?" she whispered through their embrace.

Looking over her shoulder, he said, "Taking the stairs."

They waited until Lionel and the others were farther up the second flight before following. Eyrún messaged Zac as they walked.

> Hope you're feeling better. Found Hélène and Lionel. Looks like they're meeting a buyer.

At the top, Darwin pulled her into a dark corner and pointed to Lionel, who'd paused to look around. When he continued, they moved from the tunnel onto the main ground of the Chateau d'Amboise. The sixteenth-century building glowed in the setting sun as Lionel entered the chapel of Saint Hubert.

"That's well-staged," Darwin mused. "They want to sell it at Leonardo Da Vinci's tomb. His *Lady with an Ermine* painting was looted with *Portrait of a Young Man*."

"Don't forget the *Mona Lisa,"* added Eyrún.

"I've always thought it overrated, but yeah, it's great drama."

Moments later, a half-dozen annoyed tourists exited the chapel. Eyrún and Darwin squeezed into the shadows cast by trees ringing a nearby statue as Hélène, brandishing her badge, shooed the last visitors away.

"Now what?" asked Eyrún when Hélène went back inside.

"We follow," said Darwin, walking from the trees.

Eyrún lingered a few steps behind as she messaged Zac again:

> Exchange taking place at Da Vinci's tomb

"Heard from Zac?" Darwin asked when she caught up.

"No. Hope he's okay. He looked pale. I shouldn't have run like that earlier."

"Not your fault, Love. He'll be okay. He's tough," said Darwin, moving a finger to his lips as they reached the chapel's entrance.

81

Darwin had noticed Zac's wobbling and grabbing the bathroom door for support, but he pushed down concern for his friend as he concentrated on the voices inside the chapel.

Lionel described how he'd discovered records from a former ERR man that had led him to a hidden workshop. His low voice reverberated off the bare stone adding to the theater. Darwin shook his head at the fabrication but had to admit it built up the sale price.

Both buyers stood beside Leonardo Da Vinci's grave and faced Lionel. Sunlight streamed through high colored-glass windows, casting the pale marble in a muted kaleidoscope. Hélène stayed behind him, her back to Darwin and Eyrún.

"Do you think she's got a gun?" whispered Eyrún.

"No doubt."

"What do we do?"

Darwin ran through different scenarios, but this was Zac's forte. He was only guessing. Ultimately, it came down to whether Hélène would shoot them. She was trained to protect, but they weren't the president.

Lionel set the covered painting against the wrought-iron railing around Da Vinci's tomb. He then took a portable easel from within the covering, extended its legs, and placed the portrait on it. As the two men stepped forward, he unveiled the portrait.

Hélène moved beside the men, blocking Lionel's view of the door.

Darwin said to Eyrún, "Call for help," and strode into the tomb.

"The Nazis looted that painting. It belongs to the Krakow Museum." He stopped in the tomb's center, visible from the door and several meters from the group.

Lionel laughed. "I should have known. I was told you have a habit of getting out of trouble."

As expected, Hélène stepped away from the men and drew her pistol. Lionel held up a hand. "Where's your friend?" he asked. "The tall one? And your wife? You weren't stupid enough to come alone, were you?"

Darwin's heart raced like a hamster on a wheel. He'd acted, but his

81

plan hadn't caught up yet. His eyes flicked to Eyrún outside the door, tapping on her phone.

Hélène caught the glance and sprinted out the door. She seized Eyrún's phone and waved her inside with the gun. Then she shattered it on the far wall. Glass and parts clattered onto the marble floor. She pushed Eyrún toward Darwin and moved back to the men.

"Let's do this," she said.

The man with the satchel handed it to Lionel, who unzipped it and held up a bundle of euros. "And the rest of it?" he asked.

The second man pointed at Darwin and Eyrún. "What about them? They've seen us."

"I'll take care of it," said Hélène, "but let's see that wire transfer."

"You're throwing away your career, Hélène," said Darwin.

The satchel man stepped forward to take the painting.

"Wait. Show me the money." Hélène waved him back with the pistol.

"Don't do this."

"Shut up, Darwin," Hélène snarled and then, to the other man, said, "Wire the money. Now."

He took his phone from his coat pocket and thumbed on it. They waited.

"How long does it take?" asked Lionel, shifting his weight from side to side.

"Not long," said the second man.

Sirens wailed in the distance.

The satchel man reached for it again.

"Not yet." Hélène stood her ground.

The sirens grew louder and seemed to multiply.

Lionel's phone chimed.

"We're not waiting," said second-man, waving at the satchel man to get the painting.

Darwin shoved them into a pillar. The portrait hit the floor with a crunch.

Hélène turned, but Eyrún drove her into the tomb railing. Both women went over.

81

Lionel grabbed the twisted frame and ran to a door in the chapel's rear.

The satchel man got up to chase.

"No!" shouted the second man. "Go." He pointed at the door and followed the satchel man out. They disappeared from view, heading toward the cemetery and away from the angry voices coming up the steps.

Darwin kicked the gun, skittering it across the marble, and ran to Eyrún, who'd gone over the railing. Hélène, dazed from slamming into the floor, pushed onto her hands and knees.

"There!" He pointed to the open door. "Lionel took the painting."

They ran through it and pulled it closed as gendarmes, their guns drawn, poured into the chapel and yelled for Hélène to lie still.

Eyrún stood on the edge of a spiral staircase. "It goes down. Turn on your light."

Darwin held his phone so they could both see while jogging down. On the next loop, they hit the bottom and peered into a long tunnel identical in construction to the one under the Louvre that ran toward Saint-Germain l'Auxerrois.

Darwin held a finger to his lips and killed his light. The darkness fell on them like a weighted blanket. As their senses adjusted, they heard a faint knocking from within a pinprick of light some distance ahead.

Eyrún put a hand on Darwin's shoulder for balance as he visualized their position, figuring the tunnel must run under the chateau. The distance seemed right. "Follow me."

A few steps later, a cracking sound bounced through the tunnel, and the light source disappeared.

"Let's go," said Darwin, switching on his light. They turned into the doorway and ran up a stone staircase. It doubled back one flight up, turning into marble steps, and ended on a landing. Alarms rang on the other side of an oak door.

They pulled it open and entered a small library. Books lined ceiling-high shelves. A red light strobed over a doorway to a wide reception area.

"Over there!" Eyrún yelled over the alarms. A figure dashed up a staircase. She pursued it. Darwin followed but, lacking her speed, only reached the steps when she was halfway.

The chateau's front doors burst open. *"Arretez!"* came shouts from below as Darwin followed Eyrún deeper into the dark chateau. The strobing lights made her move in stop-motion.

They cornered Lionel in an upper bedroom, which had been cleared of furniture and its walls stripped down to the lath. He backed away from them, holding the bent canvas.

"The police are behind us, Lionel."

He moved to an open window where scaffolding loomed outside.

Darwin and Eyrún spread out and herded Lionel toward the window. As the first police officer reached their level, Lionel ducked through it and jumped into a construction chute.

"Putain!" Darwin yelled as he dove in.

His body rolled and banged the sides of the plastic tubes. He landed in a heap three stories below. He scrambled upright before Eyrún tumbled out, sending him sprawling forward.

She landed on her feet and lunged after Lionel while Darwin limped on a banged knee.

Ahead, Lionel reached a waist-high rock wall. Eyrún yanked him back as he climbed.

Darwin cringed as the painting tumbled again.

Lionel was up, and he kicked Eyrún in the chest. She fell back but grabbed the broken painting and rolled away with it.

When Lionel saw Darwin closing the gap, he sailed over the wall.

Darwin reached Eyrún as she struggled to her feet. "I'm okay." She coughed. "Just got the wind—" She coughed again. "Get him."

Darwin scrambled after Lionel into the cemetery. Cypress trees lined the graveyard along the chateau's rear wall. Less than a hundred meters away, the back gate lay open.

When he reached it, Lionel was gone. Darwin hung onto the iron gate, panting as he stared into the empty countryside.

Lights flashed behind him. *"Arretez! Maintenant!"*

Darwin raised his arms and faced the onrushing gendarmes.

DENOUEMENT

Amboise

"We're sorry," Eyrún said to their lawyer. Across from her, Darwin, his mouth full of food, shrugged his apology. Morning sunshine streamed across their cafe table in Amboise.

"It's okay," said Astrid. "I don't have a court appearance until this afternoon. But if you keep going at this rate, I should put you on a retainer." She smiled, sipped her coffee, and added, "What would you have done if Zac hadn't got your message?"

"I don't know," said Eyrún.

Earlier, Zac had explained how he'd got Eyrún's text and figured the fastest way to intervene was to call 112 and report gunshots.

"Who has the painting?" asked Astrid.

"The local police, but Fleur Legrand, head of the OCBC, is on her way. I'm sure the art crimes unit will take it."

"What about Hélène?" asked Darwin.

"That's something we may never know," said Astrid. "It falls into a national security black hole because of her relationship with the president."

"*Merde,*" he said, setting down his fork and pausing as the cafe owner asked if they needed anything else. When she moved away, Darwin leaned forward. "So, she got away?"

"I think it's best you let go," said Astrid. "This is one for the National Police."

After breakfast, they headed back to Paris. Partway into the journey, Darwin looked at Eyrún in the driver's seat. She seemed happy behind the wheel.

What makes me happy? He faced forward, watching the other vehicles heading towards Paris. A memory of digging in Corsica came to mind. He'd been about nine, and his father had shown him how to use a trowel and brush to examine a site. He remembered spending hours scraping around his grandfather's house in Ajaccio and the mountain house. Once, he found carved shells near a picnic area, and his grandfather explained how Neolithic people living on Corsica had used the small rings to make jewelry.

Darwin smiled at that innocent memory and thought of more recent explorations that had brought the same joy: searching for a lava tube in Iceland, discovering an disused tomb in the Siwa Oasis, and finding proto-Aramaic letters carved in stone in Sinai.

But the memories weren't all peaceful. Each involved an adversary who'd sought to steal the discovery for themselves. Then, as he watched highway lines scrolled beneath them, a newer, more nuanced view of his happiness took shape: he wasn't just driven by discovery but by making what he found available for all to see, not just the privileged few.

He sat straighter. Whatever Lionel's game was, they'd thwarted him.

Evil desires had kept Raphael's masterpiece hidden for decades. Now they'd brought it back to the world.

Louvre

Five days later, Zac returned to California, and that afternoon, the Louvre Director invited Darwin and Eyrún to see Raphael's *Portrait of a Young Man*. Fortunately, the damage was slight, and the repaired painting stood beneath a spotlight on an easel in the restoration workroom's center.

"It's beautiful," said Eyrún, studying it from a short distance. She moved her head from side to side, letting the light play over the canvas.

"I heard you're planning a special showing for the Polish ambassador before sending it back to Krakow," said Darwin.

"Yes," said the director. "But there's a complication. That's why I invited you here today."

Darwin's face screwed up.

"Let me explain," the director began. "After the incident with the subbasement, I reorganized the restoration department and brought in an outside independent auditor to oversee our processes. We are also fully cooperating with the *Musées nationaux récupération* to find the rightful owners of the paintings," he said.

"Have they been returned?" asked Darwin.

"I can't comment at this time because it's an active investigation with the OCBC and their European peers, but rest assured, something is being done," he said, returning their attention to the Raphael. "Its frame was easily straightened. The conservator conducted tests on its construction. She used fluorescence and carbon dating to confirm the materials were from the early sixteenth century."

"What's the complication?" asked Eyrún.

"Some of the paint flaked off while being reset in the frame, which allowed the conservator to do the same tests on the canvas."

Darwin's head lowered.

"I'm afraid it's true. To be sure, she sampled another section of the paint, but the fluorescence showed no earlier than the mid-eighteen-hundreds."

"So, it's a forgery," said Eyrún.

"Yes," he said, then, trying to put a positive spin on the bad news, added, "It's very, very good. We had our Italian Renaissance experts examine it. They confirmed the technique perfectly mimics Raphael and concluded the copyist must have worked from the original."

Darwin swept a hand through his hair in disbelief. He walked a wide circle before stopping before the portrait. It looked like any other he'd seen hanging in museums. Ten minutes ago, it was a Raphael masterpiece, but now it was… what? He didn't know. "I can't believe we risked our lives for this."

"What happens now?" asked Eyrún.

"We're in contact with the museum in Krakow. They may want to exhibit it with a notation that it is a forgery. I'm afraid this becomes another chapter in this painting's tragic story."

A month later, Aya's cast came off, and she got back to work at the *Crypte Archéologique*. The Louvre subbasement discovery had become public, and she officially started exploring the tunnels connecting the royal palaces.

The doctors advised against strenuous caving for six more months to allow her muscles and tendons to adapt to the titanium implants, but that didn't stop her from supervising the exploration of the tunnels. Shortly into the work, her team determined that the Louvre subbasement required significant safety retrofitting and would be a years-long project.

In early December, Eyrún met Aya for lunch. A steel-gray sky blanketed Paris, its dim light providing a perfect backdrop for the holiday decorations. Eyrún listened attentively as Aya ranted about the budget police. When she'd exhausted the subject, she switched the topic to holiday plans.

Eyrún said she and Darwin were going to San Francisco to be with her sister and Zac. The two women departed, promising to catch up in the new year.

During the semester break, Darwin and Eyrún spent time in California but took a side trip to Seattle to visit Jim Wilkerson and explain what had happened with the *Portrait of a Young Man*.

"I knew it," said Jim when he heard about the recovered file on Karl Meyer. "Those bastards. And, you say some of the organization still exists?"

"That's what the OCBC says, but we're no longer involved," said Darwin.

"Well, it's a sad business all around. What about the paintings in the subbasement?"

"They tell us there is an ongoing operation to recover them, but it's complicated," said Eyrún.

"By what?"

The nurse ran into the room. "Are you all right, Jim? Your heart monitor spiked." She checked his pulse manually and adjusted the blanket on his lap. "He shouldn't be riled up," she said to Darwin and Eyrún.

"I'm right here," said Jim. "And I'll get as riled up as I want."

When the nurse left, he said to them, "Don't let the bureaucrats bury this. Time is their friend. Never give up."

They slipped away when Jim fell asleep in his chair. Darwin liked him and wondered again what he would be like at Jim's age.

Before the new term began at the École du Louvre, Eyrún and Darwin visited the museums in Clermont-Ferrand and Périgueux, where they formally donated the paintings owned by Darwin's family. They also gifted the Avercamp paintings that Karl Meyer had stolen to the museums and made a sizable donation to the restitution fund. They felt it was the right thing to do. The paintings were lovely and would bring joy to many museum-goers.

Nanterre, France

A week after the new semester began, Fleur Legrand summoned Darwin and Eyrún to the OCBC office in the northern outskirts of Paris. It resembled a police station except for the art covering its walls and furniture. Degas's dancer sculpture stood on a bookshelf along one wall, and a canvas of Monet's water lilies covered a hallway.

"They're all forgeries," said Fleur as she led them to a conference room. "Once the convictions and sentencings are complete, the art is released from evidence. We use it for training. Some forgers are good enough to fool even the best curators."

"We know firsthand," said Eyrún.

Fleur introduced them to an older man, Jean-Claude, and a woman, Marion, about their age. They took seats at the rectangular table, and Fleur said, "We've been busy since you told us about the geotagged paintings. We've tracked them to Seville, Berlin, and Rome, but I can't say more until I have your absolute promise that nothing we say here today leaves this room."

Eyrún nodded, "Yes."

"Of course," said Darwin.

"Good. Now, the explanation goes on a bit, so bear with us," said Fleur, nodding to Jean-Claude.

He cleared his throat. "We have been tracking underhanded dealings at the Louvre going back to the war. I listened to a recording of your interview at the police station in Amboise, where you said Lionel mentioned an organization. My apologies for eavesdropping."

Darwin shrugged it off.

"We have evidence that such a group exists, but they do so in the shadow of history. Let me explain. The first public galleries were founded during the Age of Enlightenment, when individual collections were publicly displayed. Former palaces like the Hermitage in St. Petersburg, the Belvedere Palace in Vienna, and the Louvre were converted into museums.

"But these collections were curated by a closely knit community. They chose what the public saw and how it was shown. Behind the scenes, they also manipulated the supply. For example, Rembrandt only painted so many pieces. Hanging one or two in key museums increases the brand value, so to speak, which raises the prices in the private market.

"Over the centuries, the curators, dealers, freeports, and auction houses formed a cartel, with the heads of the largest museums acting as its board of directors. Are you with me so far?" asked Jean-Claude.

"Yes," said Eyrún.

"The Nazis put all this at risk with the greatest art heist in history. Fortunately, the Allies prevailed, but it was a field day for the Organization to insert itself into recovery and restitution. I joined the OCBC shortly after it was founded in 1975." He turned to Darwin. "I interviewed James Wilkerson and others. We knew of people like Karl Meyer but could not touch them. Files had been classified by the Organization and buried within the state bureaucracy."

Jean-Claude paused and looked at each of them for a long moment before saying, "We believe Thierry Panchon headed the Louvre cell."

Darwin leaned onto the table. "Why didn't you tell us?"

Fleur held a hand up. "Because we couldn't expose what we knew. We hoped his murder would trigger more activity, but it did not. So, we stayed hidden, following the few people we knew. One of them was Vivienne." She nodded to Marion, who picked up the story.

"Your discovery of the subbasement disrupted the Paris cell," said Marion. "We suspected Vivienne was involved because of her connections to the far-right party. She made significant donations, which came from finders fees selling art. We subpoenaed her taxes but never found hard evidence until now."

Eyrún leaned closer, drawn in by Marion's last statement. "What have you found?"

"Can we?" Marion looked at Fleur for confirmation.

The OCBC head checked her phone and then nodded.

Marion read a note that sounded like a press briefing: "This morning at 10 a.m., Europol conducted raids on warehouses in Berlin, Rome, and Seville. In addition, over thirty people in those cities were detained on charges of art theft. Simultaneously, the OCBC, in cooperation with the National Police in Marseilles, arrested Vivienne de Poitiers and Hélène Daguier for attempting to sell seventy-seven paintings stolen from the Louvre."

She put down the paper and beamed. "Our team has recovered all 312 paintings taken from the subbasement and is having them transferred back to the Louvre, where we will work with the MNR to return them to their rightful owners."

"Yes!" Eyrún slapped the table.

Darwin pumped his fists in triumph and smiled, remembering Jim's parting words: "Never give up."

EPILOGUE

Rome

During the École du Louvre spring break, Darwin and Eyrún flew to Rome for a long-overdue lunch with their friend Richard. The day dawned clear. Overnight showers had left the streets slick, but the forecast called for sun and warmth.

They breakfasted on their patio, overlooking a courtyard with a magnificent marble fountain featuring Poseidon wrestling a sea monster. Darwin took his triple-shot cappuccino to the railing and breathed in the sweet nectar of honeysuckle climbing the wrought iron. The sound of metal on porcelain brought his attention around as Eyrún stirred her tea bag.

"Good morning, Love," he said.

Wrapped in a luxurious cotton from the towel coiled in her hair to the thick, ankle-length robe and fuzzy white slippers, Eyrún looked like a snow beast. She joined him at the railing as the sun cleared the building and cast the sea god's trident in golden light. With no agenda before noon, they'd slept in, the impossibly soft sheets holding them in their grasp.

"Good morning," she said. "It smells divine. I love Paris, but I miss the Mediterranean climate."

"Me, too."

"And I miss mornings at our mountain house and weekends on Hypatia," she said, referring to their powerboat, which took them into the hidden coves surrounding Corsica.

"We should keep the flat on Île Saint-Louis," he said, quickly adding, "For visiting."

"You've decided?"

"Yes. It was fun teaching again, but it reminded me I'm not an academic. I want to be in the field. Get my hands dirty."

A few minutes after 1 p.m. Richard arrived at a cafe on Via Nicolò III, two streets over from Saint Peter's Basilica. The big man swept in, his broad black cassock billowing like a sail.

"Eyrún!" He scooped her into open arms and smothered her in a hug. A moment later, he released her. "You are more beautiful than the day I married you, and you were angelic then."

Eyrún blushed.

"I don't know what you see in this ruffian," said Richard, scooping Darwin into an embrace.

They sat at a front window table as the owner, Fabrizio, ran over to greet them. His broom-like mustache danced as he fussed over arranging their table. Over the years, their lunches had become family affairs, with Fabrizio sometimes pulling up a chair to hear gossip from the Catholic nation next door.

The meal began with prosecco and a fava bean and English pea appetizer tossed in light extra-virgin olive oil and topped with generous pecorino romano shavings. As the courses arrived, Darwin and Eyrún recounted chasing down Raphael's *Portrait of a Young Man*.

"Do you think we'll ever find the original?" asked Richard.

"Eventually," said Darwin. "Maybe fifty or a hundred years from now. Some descendent of today's owner will put it up for public auction."

An hour and a half later, espresso and tea arrived as lunch wound down. Richard shifted the conversation. "I spoke with Max this morning. He wanted me to pass along some news."

Darwin winced while circling the tiny spoon in his cup. News from the head of Vatican security was never sunny.

"You know he stays current with anything that affects the staff in Vatican City. We have a broad intelligence network. Anyway, he says that Lionel Mandeau visited Jasmin Kahn in prison several months ago."

"They know each other?" asked Eyrún.

"Evidently," said Richard. "He mentioned talking with the art crimes agency in France—"

"Fleur Legrand?" Darwin interrupted.

"He didn't say," Richard continued, "but he confirmed Lionel and Jasmin have some connection with the Louvre. He asked me to tell you that she is being paroled this month."

"*Putain!*" Darwin dropped his spoon, and it pinged off the saucer and clattered across the table.

Gorgona, Italy

Jasmin dressed for her appointment and studied herself in the mirror. She had been allowed makeup but was careful to appear low-key. The sun had bronzed her skin from working outdoors in the vineyard. Just last month, she'd finished her degree in viticulture—a perfect cover story for the meeting.

She knocked on the warden's door two minutes early, knowing the man was punctual—not a typical Italian quality, but he was a former military officer who had served with NATO.

"Ah, Ms. Panchon," he said. "Please come in."

Livorno, Italy

An hour later, Jasmin leaned into the wind like a bowsprit, her skin tingling in the warm, salty air. The Ligurian Sea stretched before the ferry as the Italian mainland grew from a dark line on the horizon into...*Freedom*, she thought, spreading her arms wide.

She had not been off the prison island in four years and had only had limited communication with the outside world. Worse, she'd been able to see Italy from the island's highest point.

The port city of Livorno grew as the breeze whipped her jet-black hair across her shoulders. Upon boarding, she'd let out her ponytail—a first step in abandoning false contrition.

As the ferry undulated on the low swells, she reflected on the parole board's question: did she feel remorse?

She snorted. Of course, she'd lied to them about her remorse. She regretted none of her actions. Her only regret was having to suffer the indignity of prison for delivering justice.

The bastard stole my life. She relived emptying the pistol into Thierry Panchon's chest. Her lips curled as she replayed pulling the trigger, firing again and again.

Three years ago, upon her conviction, she'd recoiled at images of killing her adopted father, but she'd come to realize it wasn't from shock at having committed murder; it was realizing she'd enjoyed it—seeing the raw terror in his eyes as he'd begged for his life and her feeling of absolute power in taking it.

Jasmin knew killing him wouldn't bring back her mother, but it had released her from Thierry's dominance.

She mentally retracted her lie.

I'd do it again.

In a heartbeat.

Five hours later, her phone chimed with a message. A set of Louis Vuitton cases had been waiting in her suite along with a new iPhone, which she used to connect with her former life during an afternoon at the luxury hotel's spa. She dropped the bland slacks, blouse, and prison underwear in a bin before taking a long shower, followed by a loofa scrub and massage. She basked in the pampering of a mani-pedi. Then, the staff fussed over her appearance as her hair was properly cut and blown out.

Once back in her rooms, she sloughed off the cotton robe and admired her transformation in the bathroom's full-length mirrors. She stood erect, admiring her lean figure.

She'd lost three years of her life. *Was it worth it?* The question haunted her as she assessed her makeup in the vanity mirror.

Yes, she decided. A few years of isolation was a small price to pay for eliminating the man who had controlled her life since she was six.

She repeated the mantra she'd constructed on Gorgona.

It's all mine now.

I answer to no one but me.

She thought of the vaults in the Geneva Freeport and the untraceable accounts as she chose which outfit to wear, beginning with lingerie.

The Italian state had seized her yacht and public holdings, but they were only a fraction of what she'd squirreled away.

She stepped into teal panties and fastened the matching bra. The bespoke undergarments fit perfectly.

Yes. It was worth it.

Jasmin turned from the mirror and opened the case containing her jewelry. She reveled in the sight of her beloved gold bracelets, once again tinkling with her every move. She paused at the mirror before picking up her phone, admiring the emeralds dangling from her ears and smiling as they swayed.

Her phone chimed.

Lionel: I'm downstairs. The car is ready when you are.

Jasmin: Send the porter up for my bags. I'll be down in 5

Lionel: Done

As the doorbell rang, Jasmin slipped on a dress and eased her toes into a pair of Cesare Paciotti heels. She opened the door, directed the valet to the luggage, and walked to the lift. It opened at the lobby level, and she steeled herself for the job ahead.

Lionel stood and approached. She felt his eyes roam her body. Good. She smiled as she would to a cherished pet. "You're lovely as ever," he said as they kissed cheeks.

Their driver held open the passenger door of the Mercedes-Maybach S 680. Seconds later, they rolled away, and Lionel undid the muselet and coaxed the cork out of a champagne bottle. He filled two crystal flutes.

"To new beginnings," he said, lifting his glass.

She clinked his glass with hers and drank. "How long to Milan?" she asked.

"About three hours. Our leaders from the Met, the Vatican, and the British Museum are waiting for you. And we have a new friend from Dubai."

"What about the Louvre?"

"You are head of the Louvre cell now.

She'd known this, but she'd wanted to hear the words spoken aloud.

"Yes, I am," she said, sipping her champagne and sinking into the soft leather's embrace.

AUTHOR'S NOTE

Thank you for reading *Louvre Escape.* I hope you enjoyed Darwin's latest adventure. If you did, please write a review on Amazon or Facebook and tell a friend about the Darwin Lacroix adventure series.

Have questions, concerns, or comments? I'd love to hear from you at dave@davebartell.com

After publishing *Genesis Plague* in summer 2023, I struggled to get Darwin's next adventure organized. A few readers complained that it departed from my previous books, saying it was more medical-techno thriller and less archaeological tale. In hindsight, I agree. I am thinking of an offshoot series with Zac Johnson as the main character. What do you think?

I struggled to get words out until, once again, my development editor Annie Tucker brought me back to why I write. A Post-It above my desk guides me:

What do I want to do today?

Let the desire guide the execution.

I stepped back and looked at the Darwin Lacroix Adventure series, mapping each book's plot, theme, and character arcs. And, I reread emails from you and other readers about what they liked and did not like.

Louvre Escape brings Darwin and Eyrún back to their roots: archaeology, exploration, and adventure. Paris is an ancient city. It's hard to imagine its grandeur as a settlement two millennia ago or a Roman outpost. The Louvre, as we know it today, began as a crude fort to keep the marauding English at bay. I wanted this adventure to peel back the Hausmann facade and give a glimpse of the Louvre's evolution into the art gallery we know today.

We must stay vigilant in protecting our precious and fragile past. In a world increasingly digitized and influenced by artificial (machine programmed) intelligence, our analog history becomes a vital record of human experience.

Look for book eight to bring Darwin and Eyrún closer to archaeology and our vast unremembered past.

For those interested in the history of art, plunder, and restitution, I recommend the sources below.

Books

Geneviève Bresc-Bautier with photographs by Gérard Rondeau. *Musée du Louvre*. 2013

James Gardener. *The Louvre: The Many Lives of the World's Most Famous Museum*. 2020

Elizabeth Campbell. *Museum Worthy: Nazi Art Plunder in Postwar Western Europe*. 2023

Elizabeth Campbell Karlsgodt. *Defending National Treasures: French Art and Heritage Under Vichy*. 2011

Donald Reid. *Paris Sewers and Sewerman: Realities and Representations*. 1991

Lynn H. Nicholas. *The Rape of Europa: The Fate of Europe's Treasures in the Third Reich and the Second World War.* 1994

Robert M. Edsel. *Rescuing Da Vinci*. 2006

Robert M. Edsel. *The Monuments Men*. 2009

Wikipedia

Monuments, Fine Arts, and Archives programAllied program to help protect cultural property (1943-1946)

Amt Rosenberg (ARo, Rosenberg Office) was an official body for cultural policy and surveillance within the Nazi party, headed by Alfred Rosenberg https://en.wikipedia.org/wiki/Amt_Rosenberg

Reichsleiter Rosenberg TaskforceNazi art looting organization active in France in WWII

JunkersGerman aerospace and engineering company

National Political Institutes of EducationElite secondary schools in Nazi Germany

ACKNOWLEDGMENTS

Thanks to my friend and development editor Annie Tucker who talked me off the ledge of writer stagnation and frustration and pointed me back to the joy of storytelling.

Every book deserves a great cover, and thanks to Patrick Knowles Design, Genesis Plague has one. This is our sixth collaboration, as he did the covers on Hypatia's Diary, Templar's Bank, Tuscan Hoax, Sinai Deceit, and Corsican Gold.

And, thank you to Diane Bartell, my wife, best fan, and most important person in my life. She will soon ask, "Got anything new for me to read."

Again, THANKS, and I invite you to learn about the next Darwin Lacroix Adventure by joining my mailing list at davebartell.com.

Onward to book eight!

ABOUT THE AUTHOR

Imagine the wonder of being the first person to open King Tut's tomb. Dave Bartell loves reviving lost history, and his novels breathe "thriller" into archaeology.

As a kid, he frequently tinkered in his parent's garage. His insatiable curiosity to understand how things work led him to study biochemistry and, later, fueled a career in high technology. His what-if mindset and life experiences combine to make his fiction plausible and feel realistic.

Dave lives in Los Gatos, California; a small town tucked into the edge of Silicon Valley. He enjoys hiking in the hills behind his home, where beauty is still analog.

He hopes you enjoy his stories and invites you to share your thoughts at dave@davebartell.com. And visit davebartell.com to get a sneak peek of upcoming projects.

- amazon.com / stores / Dave-Bartell / author / B07KN8HPYP
- bookbub.com / authors / dave-bartell
- facebook.com / DaveBartellWriter
- goodreads.com / davebartell
- instagram.com / davebartell
- x.com / davebartell

Made in the USA
Las Vegas, NV
25 June 2024